Author's Note

Welcome to *Missing in Soho*, a Misty Divine Mystery!

While this book is a romp, a sparkling adventure through Misty's dark and glamorous world, it does include some violence, difficult topics and homophobic language. It doesn't shy away from some of the real-world challenges faced by our LGBTQIA+ community, but handles them with nuance and humour, in Misty Divine style. I think it's important to let you know this before we begin.

I understand some readers might find a few moments of this mystery uncomfortable to read, and trust you'll make the decision that is best for you about when you're ready to dive in.

That said, I hope you will enjoy the mystery! Now, when you're ready, let's find out together, who is 'MISSING IN SOHO'?

Missing in Soho

Missing in Soho

HOLLY STARS

MICHAEL JOSEPH

PENGUIN MICHAEL JOSEPH

UK | USA | Canada | Ireland | Australia
India | New Zealand | South Africa

Penguin Michael Joseph is part of the Penguin Random House group of companies
whose addresses can be found at global.penguinrandomhouse.com

Penguin Random House UK,
One Embassy Gardens, 8 Viaduct Gardens, London SW11 7BW

penguin.co.uk

First published 2026

001

Copyright © Holly Stars, 2026

The moral right of the author has been asserted

Set in 14/17 pt Garamond Premier Pro
Typeset by Six Red Marbles UK, Thetford, Norfolk
Printed and bound in Great Britain by Clays Ltd, Elcograf S.p.A.

The authorized representative in the EEA is Penguin Random House Ireland,
Morrison Chambers, 32 Nassau Street, Dublin D02 YH68

A CIP catalogue record for this book is available from the British Library

HARDBACK ISBN: 978-0-241-68373-6
TRADE PAPERBACK ISBN: 978-0-241-73350-9

Penguin Random House is committed to a sustainable future
for our business, our readers and our planet. This book is made from
Forest Stewardship Council® certified paper

Missing in Soho

Prologue

Friday Morning

Misty's white suit was ruined. Absolutely ruined, that was for sure and certain. The cuffs and sleeves were drenched in old-man blood.

'I can't stop it,' she said, brushing her bright pink hair out of her eyes with the back of one hand, pressing the hole in Sylvester's gushing chest with the other. 'I can't stop the bleeding.'

A tinny voice sounded through the telephone on the floor next to them. *'Keep pressure on the wound, the ambulance is on its way.'*

'Well can it hurry up!' shouted Misty. 'There's so much blood!'

It feels like water, did you know that? Blood, that is. It's not sticky or thick like you'd expect, or how it is in old horror films when it's made with strawberry sauce. It feels just like warm water when it's pouring out of someone.

It's just water, it's just water, she told herself.

Sylvester coughed a gloopy rattle and Misty's face was sprayed in a thick red mist. Then she could smell it, taste it. The unmistakable flavour of blood, from his mouth directly to hers. Make-up destroyed.

Gross.

The glossy red puddle was pooling beneath him and Misty watched as it spread all the way towards her, surrounding the phone, trickling under her knees and between her legs.

There go the white trousers, she thought.

With wide eyes and a shaky arm, Sylvester reached into his scruffy jacket pocket.

'I'm dying,' he whispered.

'No you're not,' replied Misty. 'Where's the ambulance?!'

'It's on its way. It's four minutes away.'

'I don't have . . . four minutes,' said Sylvester. He pulled his hand out of his pocket and thrust it towards her, squeezing a small black notebook and bunch of keys into her palm.

She took them and pushed her other hand hard against his bubbling wound, but it was useless, and the blood pumped out unslowed between her fingers.

'You're not dying, Sylvester, not today.'

'Listen to me, Misty . . .' His voice was fading with every syllable.

'I'm listening.'

His eyes bulged.

'The ambulance is three minutes away.'

He gasped in a soggy lungful of air and exhaled suddenly.

'You're . . . in danger. You must . . . find . . . Jeremy.'

CHAPTER 1

Thursday – Twelve Hours Earlier

Misty knew how to spot them. The looky-loos. The ones who came to a show at Lady's Bar just to get a glimpse at the drag queen who'd caught a murderer. The viral sensation, Misty Divine.

There were fewer of them now. A year had passed since the bar's previous owner and Misty's mentor, Lady Lady, had been murdered backstage, and the number of looky-loos had steadily decreased.

But there was one tonight.

'A creeper,' Plimberley had called him, the long-legged lip-syncer who was famed for her acrobatic dips and flips, 'sitting at the end of the bar.'

'I've seen him.'

Misty had spotted him right away, the creeper. He was sixty-five, easy. Maybe seventy-five. And not a Lady's Bar regular. It was unusual for older men to show up at her cabaret club by themselves, so his demographic alone made him stand out. He was also underdressed: for the venue, for the show. A slouchy pair of chinos and plain brown shoes so worn he might have run multiple marathons in them, Misty had clocked him as soon as he walked in.

You don't belong here . . . she thought, though she wasn't entirely sure she could explain why.

The shoes probably. The plain brown shoes.

Lady's Bar was one of London's hottest drag venues: a gorgeous underground auditorium accessed by a non-descript door on Old Compton Street in Soho, it had been a mainstay of the live cabaret scene for the past twenty years. When the previous host and owner, Lady Lady, died last year, Misty inherited 10% of the bar, making her one of the city's dwindling number of queer venue owners. The other 90% was owned by Mandy White, her business partner and friend. Misty had been delighted to jump from performer status to part-owner – it had raised her profile in the community, given her purpose and drive, and let her quit her toxic day job as a bored and depressed hotel accounts assistant. This was hers: this club, this stage. This was where she belonged.

The only dark spot on Lady Lady's glittering gift from beyond the grave was the bribery. Oh, how Misty hated it. Atrax, the mysterious City firm who had been trying to shut down Lady's Bar, was always lurking beneath the surface of her thoughts. Even now, as she stood onstage in front of her adoring audience, she fought to keep it at bay. She spotted Mandy across the bar, sitting with a group of patrons. Their shared secret and shame surged to the fore, the piles of cash they skimmed from the tills after closing . . .

Don't think about this now, she willed herself. *It's showtime.*

She beamed. Her teeth had been freshly whitened and she knew they were sparkling in contrast to tonight's deep red lipstick. Her corset was tight and so was her wig. The audience clapped, whistled and cheered, and Misty took the microphone to introduce the night's first act.

Plimberley was the opener, as she always was on a Thursday. She performed a limb-tastic display of gymnastic prowess while lip-syncing a track by Charli XCX. Her hair was long, down to her perfectly padded bottom, and her slinky bodysuit sparkled in the spotlight. Misty admired her from the side of the stage. Plim was young, twenty-three, and had had a tough life. Kicked out by her parents, couch-surfing, and occasionally sleeping in a clapped-out car she called Calista. But she showed up, did the job and brought the house down night after night. A real pro. An up-and-comer, Misty knew she was destined for greatness.

After Plim finished her number she took a long bow, panting and smiling and waving at the audience, enjoying her moment in the limelight. Then Misty returned to the stage.

'Let's hear it for Plimberley Walsh!' she called into the microphone, and the room went wild. Everyone was whooping, wailing, clicking fingers in the air for the young queen, except one person. Misty could see him at the back of the auditorium. *The creeper.* He sat perfectly still, a glass of whiskey next to him on the bar, watching with a straight face and crisp eyes that were visibly blue even from the stage.

Maybe he's a journalist, she thought.

Occasionally, reporters would turn up unannounced, asking Misty about last year's murder. Was he one of those?

The applause died down and Misty smiled again, batting her lashes and winking to a handsome man in the front row. She looked effortless, beautiful, and much more flirtatious than she'd ever dare to be out of drag. Part of her job was having new costumes made and tonight's was a bobby-dazzler: a lime-green strapless bodice with a taffeta train that had been bejewelled with hundreds of rhinestones. Hot-pink stilettos. White-blonde hair. Pink earrings. Perfection.

'Before our next act,' she said, as the crowd died down, 'I wanted to give you a little gift. A special treat from me to you.' On this cue, a track started playing, a relaxed, jazzy musical-theatre number that grew from a quiet beginning to a belting end. She started to sing.

Misty oozed confidence onstage and she felt powerful, like she had the audience in the palm of her hand. A song like this was an adventure, a journey from one word to another, one note to the next. Building, always building, to the big showstopping moment, a key change then a long high note. She knew before she even sang it that it would prompt a standing ovation. And it did. The whole auditorium on their feet, *except the creeper*.

It was tradition at Lady's Bar for the performers to stay after the show and have at least one drink with the audience. It was a chance to mingle, chat, receive compliments and promote the next night's cabaret. Misty had enjoyed it when she was new at the bar, but now she was an owner and hostess she loved it. It was noisy and bustling and exciting. It made her feel like a superstar.

Tonight she made a beeline for the creeper. Misty Divine

wasn't the sort to hold herself back and she didn't mind a confrontation. If this ancient looky-loo was a journalist, she wanted to talk to him immediately to put her mind at ease. As she hustled her way through the crowd, she said speedy thank-yous to gushing audience members, all delighted to tell her how great she was.

Who are you? she thought as she made her way towards him like a military missile.

As she reached him, she noticed more about his outfit, a small tear in the worn trousers and deep scuffs on the sad shoes . . . *Too old to be a journalist too,* she thought. Up close he looked quite frail, like he should have retired many years ago.

'Hello,' she said, holding out her bejewelled hand. 'I'm Misty.'

He clasped her fingers and his blue eyes shone in the lights of the bar. He looked kind, and this surprised her. He wasn't giving creeper vibes after all. *He might be just a gentle pensioner who needs a wardrobe upgrade.* She felt bad for having judged him from afar.

'I know who you are,' he replied. 'I need to talk to you.'

'Oh?' Misty leaned across the bar and waved to Jan, the bearded barman. He nodded and started preparing her a gin and tonic in a crystal glass. 'How can I help?'

'It's a bit complicated,' said the old man. 'Is-is there somewhere quieter we could go?' She heard the jitter in his voice like he was nervous or on edge and guessed he was out of his comfort zone in Lady's Bar. It's true the room was rowdy, still buzzing with guests, and drag kings and queens circulating like royalty.

'Not right now, I'm afraid,' said Misty. She could have taken him to the office but she didn't want to. She didn't know anything about this guy. 'Why don't you give me the headlines here?'

'OK,' he said, taking a sip of whiskey and a look around. 'I'm a private investigator. I've been hired by the family of a missing man to try and find him. I need to ask you a few questions.'

A missing man? A private investigator?

'What does this have to do with me?'

'That's what's complicated,' said the investigator, glancing behind him and scanning the crowd. 'That's what I want to talk to you about somewhere more . . . private.'

Misty felt a hand on her shoulder.

'Oi!' shouted Plimberley above the hubbub. 'What's going on here then?'

She raised an eyebrow, asking without words if Misty needed rescuing, whether she should pull her away from the old man.

'We're fine, Plim,' said Misty. 'I'll come find you in a sec.'

The old man stood up from his bar stool.

'I'll come back another time,' he said.

'What's the name of this missing man?' asked Misty. 'Do I know him?'

It wasn't every day she was visited by a private detective and she was intrigued. There was a flutter in her stomach; the same nervous thrill she'd felt a year ago when she started trying to work out who murdered Lady Lady.

'You're clearly busy. I'll come back tomorrow morning, if that's OK,' he said. 'I'll explain everything then.'

8

The old man pulled a business card out of his trouser pocket. It was dog-eared and tatty, like he'd been carrying the same one for a long time. He handed it to Misty and then took a step towards her, standing uncomfortably close. He leaned in and spoke hot breath into her ear. 'Don't tell anyone I was here, and if I don't make it back to see you, contact my assistant, Divya. Don't trust anybody else.'

Woah. This was a lot. It seemed ridiculous, like something out of a movie: a private detective showing up, whispering whiskey breath, telling her not to trust anybody. She almost laughed.

'OK,' she smiled. 'I won't tell anyone you were here.'

Suddenly the old man was serious, his eyes as icy as the cubes in Misty's gin. Her arms went cold.

Atrax, she thought. Stress frothed up. Her hands were clammy, her forehead beginning to sweat. This was panic, the start of pure unadulterated *panique*.

'Is this about . . .' She stopped herself before she said any more. Nobody knew about the Atrax situation apart from Mandy, and nobody should.

'You're in trouble, Misty,' he said, and her breath hitched. 'But I can help. I'll come back at ten tomorrow.'

He finished his whiskey in one big gulp and walked away, abandoning her at the bar.

'What are you talking about?' she called after him. 'What do you mean I'm in trouble?'

Panique.

She started to follow him but a gay couple in their twenties stepped directly in front of her. 'Oh my God,' one of them said, 'can I just say how amazing you were tonight?'

'Hold on,' she said, trying to edge around them, now desperate to speak to the detective and wishing she'd let him talk to her in the office.

He was swallowed up by the crowd, his shoddy brown shoes disappearing into a sea of dazzling heels and designer trainers. Misty started after him, pushing past the gays and rushing into throngs of audience members.

She couldn't see him.

She stopped, looking all around her, trying to spot the detective, but she couldn't. She'd lost him in her own club.

Turning the tatty business card over in her hand, she looked at the small black writing.

Sylvester Green – Private Investigator
25 Great Windmill Street, Soho, London

CHAPTER 2

Misty de-dragged alone, which was usual since taking over from Lady Lady, as the hosting job included her own private dressing room. Of course she'd redecorated it, recarpeted it and tried to push thoughts of Lady Lady's murder out of her brain. This was where she'd been killed after all, right here on the plush pink carpet.

A year ago, on a beautiful summer's evening, Misty's drag mother had hosted her final show. She'd been nervous, Misty remembered, distracted, and when she retreated to her dressing room she'd been poisoned with a chocolate left by a killer. Misty had found Lady Lady foaming at the mouth, a huge vein threaded under the skin of her pristinely painted forehead. The flashbacks came less often these days, but they did come. And perhaps this hint of danger, the appearance of Sylvester Green, had brought it all rushing back.

She sat at the dressing table to begin the de-dragging. Her intrigue levels were high but she was also worried. A private detective, here in her club, asking her questions.

Why am I 'in trouble'? Why shouldn't I trust anybody? It was gasp-inducingly dramatic and horribly unexpected and she didn't even know anybody who'd gone missing. That was the kind of thing she'd remember.

She started the process by taking off her eyelashes, then drenched a make-up wipe in micellar water to tackle the rest. Slowly, as today's perfect drag fantasy was washed away, she became Joe. Plain old Joe Brown. A thirty-five-year-old with mousy hair and a face that felt very bare compared to Misty's.

Joe tidied the make-up station and smartened the room, arranging their brushes in a perfect row on the counter and hanging up the taffeta costume. Within a few minutes it was ready for tomorrow. *Tomorrow.*

Sylvester Green is coming at 10 a.m. Joe looked at their watch: already almost midnight. They would have just enough time to get home, sleep, and be back here in the morning to find out what was going on.

When Joe arrived at the little flat they shared with their boy-friend, Miles, they found him still awake, sitting on the sofa waiting for them.

'Hi, love,' he said, as Joe stepped through the door.

'Hi, angel,' Joe replied, dropping their backpack on to the floor. 'Fancy a tea?'

'Ooh yes,' said Miles, 'one of those Sleepy-Time ones. It's late.'

Joe headed to the kitchen and flicked on the kettle.

'How was tonight?' Miles called from the sofa. 'Good show?'

'Great show.' The frothing stress sensation returned.

Joe knew they would need to broach the Sylvester subject carefully, if they even broached it at all. Last year, when investigating the murder of Lady Lady, Miles had been seriously hurt, and it had taken months for him to get out of hospital and recover. He still had some nerve damage that was causing weakness in his left leg, but they'd been told it wouldn't last forever. Eventually the nerve would heal and Miles would be back to how he was before, physically at least. Mentally it might be a different story. Miles was more distant, and quieter than before. Staring death in the face and winning could have a strange impact on a person, Joe thought, as they poured hot water into Miles' favourite teacup. The Sleepy-Time brew was a powerful concoction of flowers and herbs that Joe could barely face at any time of day. They made a cup of good old Yorkshire Tea for themself.

Placing the steaming cups on to the coffee table, Joe sat beside Miles and plonked a kiss on his lips.

'Tell me all about it,' he said. 'How was Plim?'

Don't tell him about Sylvester Green. Joe squashed down a Misty Divine urge to blurt out the whole story.

'She was amazing, as always,' they said. 'She did a Charli XCX number. You should have seen it. A back bend for the gods! I thought she was going to snap. You should come next week. I know she'd be thrilled to see you.'

'I'll think about it,' said Miles, but Joe knew he wouldn't come. Lady's Bar was where it had all gone down: the murder of Lady Lady, Misty's solving of the crime, Miles' poisoning . . .

'Everybody would be so pleased to see you,' said Joe, and it was true. The kings and queens would be delighted. He was extremely well-loved on the drag circuit.

A moment of silence drifted between them that Joe broke with a slurp of hot tea. Lady's Bar was a difficult topic.

'And how was your day today?' they asked, changing the subject.

'Work was fine,' said Miles. 'I'm still getting used to being back after so long away. This might sound silly . . .' He paused.

'What sounds silly?' asked Joe.

'I miss standing up at my desk. This bad leg . . . I have to sit down all day. I think I'm putting on weight.'

'I don't think you are,' said Joe. 'Even *if* you are, that doesn't matter at all. The most important thing for now is getting better.'

'I know. It's just taking longer than I'd like.'

'You'll get there.' Joe reached forward and gave Miles' hand a squeeze. 'I love you. I'm here for you through it all.'

'I love you too.'

Miles looked away, down at his teacup, and he spun it around in his fingers clearly lost in thought.

'What is it?' asked Joe. 'Is there something else?'

'Yes, but I don't know how to say it without it sounding like a criticism.'

Joe steeled themself for whatever was coming next. 'OK . . . Just go for it. Better out than in and I'm sure I can handle it.'

'I'm anxious about Lady's Bar and the bribery. Knowing it's still going on after all this time is adding to the stress of everything else.'

Joe didn't reply right away, taking a second to think instead. There wasn't much they could say to this. They knew the bar's secret survival plan would have to come to an end sooner or later and the Sylvester-induced panique had been proof of that. The dark secret behind the bright lights.

'Sorry,' said Miles, 'for bringing it up. I know you and Mandy are doing your best, but it's like we're living in the consequences of last summer and it's been playing on my mind.'

Joe couldn't deny it had been playing on their mind too because Misty and Mandy had been keeping this secret for over a year. Before she died, Lady Lady had heard the City firm, Atrax, had submitted a proposal to redevelop the Lady's Bar building and she'd set up the bribes, paying someone at the council to stop the proposal from being considered. It was an act of desperation, but she had been convinced Atrax would bankrupt the bar with legal fees if she pursued a more official route. Her secret deal was a moral and legal nightmare, one that Mandy and Misty had inherited. It was facilitated by a drag queen called Auntie Susan, a dangerous and well-connected queen who ran a dodgy pub and an even dodgier set of business operations.

'You don't have to be sorry,' said Joe. 'I hate to be causing you stress when you're still recovering. I'll talk to Mandy again tomorrow.'

'I'd really appreciate that,' said Miles. 'I know working at Lady's Bar is your dream so I don't want to cause you any problems, but I can't relax with this hanging over us. This connection to Auntie Susan is so . . . unpleasant. I think it's time to get everything above board so we can move on.'

'I'll sort it,' said Joe. 'I'll try, I promise.' They knew now that they couldn't possibly tell Miles about Sylvester tonight. If he was already this worried, depressed even, he wouldn't react well to hearing a private investigator had shown up with a mysterious line of questioning.

'*You're in trouble, Misty,*' he'd said.

Joe would never say it, but they missed old Miles. Old, fun, along-for-the-ride Miles.

'Are you in the office tomorrow?' they asked, trying to lighten the mood.

'No. Working from home but quite a lot of Teams meetings.'

'Nice to be at home at least,' said Joe, 'even if you have the dreaded Teams.'

Miles smirked and sipped his tea. 'I hate Teams!'

'Doesn't everybody?' Joe laughed.

'What are your plans?'

Meeting Sylvester Green, thought Joe. 'I have to head to the office early to catch up with some emails,' they lied. 'I'm a bit behind this week.'

'I really love you, you know,' said Miles.

'I know,' Joe smiled. 'I love you too.'

Later, once Miles had retreated to bed with drowsy eyes, Joe washed up the teacups at the sink. Their brain was buzzing with thoughts of the detective's visit in the morning. In spite of everything that had happened last year, and Miles' worries about the bribery, Joe felt a tingle of dread and excitement. There was fresh intrigue in the air.

A private investigator.

A missing person.

A sinister warning.

Though they knew they shouldn't, it was a mystery Joe already wanted to solve . . .

CHAPTER 3

Friday

Joe arrived at Lady's Bar at 8 a.m., much earlier than usual and earlier than they'd normally get out of bed. They'd had breakfast with Miles and left him to get set up for his day of home working. There was guilt on Joe's back today about lying to Miles, but all they could think was, *Who is missing? And what has it got to do with me?*

Joe let themself into the club using three chunky keys and descended the staircase from the street entrance to the auditorium. At the bottom of the stairs was a reception desk, cloakroom and a set of double doors with gold crescent handles that led into the main space. Joe pushed them open and stepped inside.

It was a wonderful feeling to be the first person to arrive at Lady's Bar, and every time they were tempted to get onstage and sing to the empty room. There had been days they'd given in to the urge, pressing play on a track and singing to nobody, but they wouldn't this morning. Sylvester was due in a couple of hours and Joe wanted to meet him as Misty. It was, after all, Misty Divine he was coming to see.

They crossed the auditorium, picking their way through

the tables and chairs until they reached the dressing-room corridor.

Sitting at their make-up station, Joe replayed Sylvester's warning. *Is this about the Auntie Susan bribery scheme?* If so, it would mean Miles was right to be concerned. Lady Lady's arrangement with Auntie Susan was a strictly guarded secret and if it was out, that would indeed spell trouble.

But Sylvester had said his visit was about a missing person. *Who, goddamnit, who? And how am I connected?* So many questions already . . . There was no harm at all, Joe thought, in having this initial chat with Sylvester and discussing it with Miles later, once they had a better understanding of what was actually going on.

They started their make-up by using a purple glue stick, applying layer after layer of adhesive to their eyebrows to flatten the hairs. Once done, it was pretty quick to sweep on foundation and powder to set everything, and start their transformation. Contouring and blush came next, then eyeshadow, highlights, lipliner, lipstick and eyelashes. It was a fiddly process, but one Joe enjoyed because becoming Misty Divine was a dream, a fantasy, a journey from shy and quiet to strong and fearless.

When the make-up was finished, Misty's face was a showstopper. Her eyebrows stretched up from the bridge of her nose to the middle of her temples and her lashes were long and fluffy like little black clouds perched on the edge of her eyelids.

Along with the dressing room itself, Misty had inherited Lady Lady's clothes rails. She'd filled them over the course of a year with dozens of new and custom-made costumes. Today

Joe plumped for a white trouser suit that had been inspired by the final spectacular dance routine of *First Wives Club*.

Joe imagined Misty emerging through the clouds of *Stars In Your Eyes* smoke.

Tonight, Matthew . . . I'm going to be . . . Goldie Hawn.

The trousers were tight at the hips and flared at the heel, and the jacket snugly fitted with a belt across the waist. It was camp yet professional and, unbeknown to Joe, about to be ruined forever. They slipped into a pair of hot-pink stilettos.

The final element was hair. Joe chose a huge pink perm that hung down to their shoulders and swept across their forehead. It was a bit of a clown wig, but with the white suit and matching shoes, *chef's kiss*. They pinned the hair to the tight head bandage they'd applied, popped on some dazzling earrings, and Misty's transformation was complete.

The tacky pink flamingo clock on the dressing-room wall told her it was 9.50, so she quickly nipped to the office to glimpse at her emails before Sylvester arrived. Misty's role at Lady's Bar was a fun one as she was responsible for booking the acts for every cabaret and hosting them, while Mandy took care of the admin. She worked at the club five nights a week and absolutely loved it. There was no better job in the world, Misty thought, than this. She loved all kinds of drag, from very grown-up stand-up comedy to the pantomimes and storytimes at the family-friendlier end of the spectrum. There was nothing in her emails, but then it was barely 10 a.m. and a lot of the drag performers Misty knew didn't pull themselves out of bed until at least 11. She headed to the auditorium to wait for Sylvester.

*

The back wall of the bar was mirrored, speckled with dots of rust as though it might have been there for hundreds of years. She noticed her reflection and paused to take it in. She looked fantastic. The pink hair and white suit were such a gorgeous combination. *Yes,* she thought, *I am everything.*

She was pouring herself a glass of orange juice when the buzzer for the main door sounded. She tapped a button on the intercom system and knew the entrance would have opened. Footsteps on the top stairs told her Sylvester had arrived. She was anxious all of a sudden.

Why am I in trouble? She popped a cardboard straw into her juice and was lifting it to her lips when there was a terrible clatter. Heavy thuds in quick succession were accompanied by grunts and groans and a pained wail. It was, without a doubt, the sound of an old man falling.

Shit.

She ran through to the reception desk at the bottom of the stairs. There, lying on his back, was Sylvester. He was covered in blood. Misty's first instinct told her the blood must have come from the investigator cutting himself somehow during his tumble. But there was so much of it – too much to have been caused by the fall.

'Ambulance,' said Sylvester with a raspy blood-filled throat. 'Stabbed.'

He pulled open his brown jacket with a shaky hand and revealed a hole in his chest about two inches wide. It was bubbling and oozing crimson, pumping out with great force. Misty pulled her phone out of her pocket and unlocked it, dialling 999 as quickly as she could. An operator answered immediately, a thin tinny voice that sounded like it was behind glass.

'*Emergency services, which service do you require?*'

'Ambulance,' Misty rushed. 'A man's been stabbed. He's bleeding.'

'*What's the address?*'

It took her a second. Her brain faltered.

'Lady's Bar,' she rushed. 'Old Compton Street, in Soho. Come quickly, there's a lot of blood.'

'*The ambulance is on its way.*'

'Thank you.'

'*Where is the injury?*'

'His chest.'

'*Is he breathing?*'

'Yes.'

'*Can you put pressure on the wound to slow the bleeding?*'

'Yes,' said Misty, without hesitating. She got quickly down on to her knees, careful to choose a spot where the blood hadn't yet pooled, instinctively protecting the white suit. She tapped the phone a couple of times to put it on loudspeaker and took a deep breath, planting both hands firmly on Sylvester's injury. It was hot and wet and blood streamed between her fingers. 'Who did this?' Misty asked him.

Sylvester's eyes rolled back in his head and he didn't answer.

'I can't stop it!' Misty shouted at the phone, 'I can't stop the bleeding.'

He coughed. A rattlesnake noise sounded deep inside his lungs and a thick cloud of deep-red droplets showered Misty's perfect face and jacket.

Gross, she thought, before silently reprimanding herself for getting the ick when the man before her was in such a terrible state. She looked down at her hands; slick and shiny and scarlet. The sleeves of the white jacket had started drinking up the blood, and the fabric felt heavy and soaked like a sopping dish sponge.

'*The ambulance is four minutes away.*'

'I don't have four minutes,' Sylvester rattled.

He reached with his left arm into his jacket pocket and pulled out a small black notebook and a big bunch of keys, pressing them into Misty's hand.

'Listen to me, Misty,' he said urgently in a wet whisper.

'I'm listening.'

'You're in danger . . . You must . . . find . . . Jeremy.'

Sylvester's eyelids flickered shut.

Crap.

'He's unconscious now!' she said to the phone, starting to panic. 'Or maybe he's dead! Is he dead? I can't tell. How do I tell? Where's the ambulance?!'

'*Can you check to see if he has a pulse?*'

She let out a slow, steady breath through pursed lips and pushed two fingers against Sylvester's crinkly neck. 'He has a pulse.'

'*That's good. The ambulance is two minutes away. Try to stay calm and keep pressure on the wound.*'

'Can it get here any faster?' she asked. 'I'm putting pressure on, but I don't think it's doing anything.'

'*It's on its way. You're doing brilliantly. What's your name?*'

'Misty. I'm Misty Divine. Or Joe Brown. I'm a drag queen.' She couldn't explain why she'd told them that.

'*Misty, do you know the name of the man who's been stabbed?*'
'Sylvester Green. He's a private investigator.'

It did take two minutes for the ambulance to arrive, and by the time it did, Misty was absolutely covered in Sylvester's blood. It had drenched her knees, her sleeves, her face. The only part of her white jacket spared the soaking was the lining of her pockets. Two paramedics rushed through the front door and Misty looked up at them at the top of the stairs.

'Quickly,' she said. 'I don't know if he's still alive. The bleeding seems to have stopped.'

The voice on the phone said she was disconnecting now the paramedics had arrived.

'Are you Misty? Joe?' one of them asked.

'Yes! Quickly!'

They bounded down the stairs two at a time, each with a green fabric bag. One of them crouched down by Sylvester and put two fingers against his neck.

'He's alive,' he said to his colleague. 'Pulse is weak, but it's there.'

'Let's get him in the ambulance.' The second paramedic reached out a hand to help Misty up and she took it, smearing blood across her palm and fingers. She watched from the reception desk, horrified, as the medics lifted Sylvester on to a stretcher and carried him up the stairs out on to the street. Misty heard sirens and car doors slamming shut.

Police.

As soon as Sylvester vanished into the morning sun, the entrance swung back open and in walked two police officers: Misty recognised them immediately as Detective Inspector

Davies and Detective Sergeant Hughes. These were the ones who had investigated Lady Lady's death last year, the detectives who arrested Misty for a murder she hadn't committed. They were based out of Charing Cross Police Station and worked major cases in Soho and the West End. Seeing DI Davies now brought back memories of how rotten he had been then. His unpressed suit and cheap shoes were only the tip of the iceberg. He had been rude and too ignorant for working cases in the LGBTQ+ community, Misty thought. On top of all that, he reeked of Lynx Africa.

She looked down and saw she was still clutching the keys and notebook. They felt hot and forbidden in her hands.

'*You're in danger, Misty . . .*'

DI Davies was already making his way down the stairs.

'Mr Brown,' he said. 'It's been a long time. You're lucky we were nearby.'

Mr Brown. Mister *Brown!*

Misty's skin started to crawl. *Lucky?* She didn't want to be in the same room as this man, never mind answer his questions. Without thinking too much about it she quickly stuffed Sylvester's treasures into her jacket pocket. She didn't want DI Davies to have them, especially if this trouble had anything to do with the Auntie Susan bribery scheme.

I'll give them the notebook eventually, she told herself. *I just want to read it first.*

'DI Davies,' she said, 'DS Hughes.' Her body was trembling.

'Morning, Misty,' said DS Hughes.

Hughes was better than Davies, friendlier. She was

sympathetic and knowledgeable about the drag and queer scene, more interested in getting things right.

'What happened here then?' asked Davies, in his usual abrupt tone. Close up, Misty could see he'd aged terribly since the last time she saw him. He looked like he'd put on ten years. His hair was greyer, peppered with white, and the bags under his eyes were dark.

She wiped her blood-soaked fingers on the already ruined jacket. 'I don't know. He just arrived and fell down the stairs. I tried to stop the bleeding, but I . . . I couldn't . . .'

She was overwhelmed and tears welled up, clouding her vision. Her hands were starting to go sticky and the stench of blood flooded her senses.

'Come on, love,' said DS Hughes as Misty burst into a sob, 'let's go get you cleaned up.'

CHAPTER 4

Thankfully, DI Davies waited in the auditorium while Misty returned to the dressing room with DS Hughes.

Tell her about the notebook, said Miles' voice in the back of Misty's mind.

No, she thought. *Not until I know what's going on here.*

Misty took off the blood-soaked jacket and dropped it gently into the dustbin so the keys she'd hidden in the pocket wouldn't make a sound. She figured that was the safest place to keep them for now. There was no saving the suit. No amount of dry-cleaning would restore it to its Elise Elliot glory. It was destined for the great landfill in the sky.

She studied herself in the mirror and saw how her face and hair were speckled red. The wig might be salvageable – it would need to be washed and re-styled, but she might get some use out of it yet.

'Would you please pass me those wipes?'

DS Hughes grabbed the packet from the counter and handed them to her.

'What happened here, Misty? Do you know him? Sylvester Green?' She had a kind and patient tone that was definitely the antidote to DI Davies' brusqueness.

Think quickly, she thought, *tell the truth but not all of it.*

'He came to see me at the show last night,' she admitted. 'He said he needed my help with something, but didn't say what, so I asked him to come back this morning. When he arrived, I heard him fall down the stairs and I found him like that at the bottom, bleeding. He said he'd been stabbed.'

That's mostly true, thought Misty, *just a few omissions.*

DS Hughes nodded like a wise old owl and then asked, 'Did he say anything? Did he tell you who attacked him?'

'No. I asked him but he didn't say. Or couldn't, I'm not sure. It happened so fast.'

Misty's eyes were drawn to the bin, where she knew the investigator's notebook was sitting in her jacket pocket. Perhaps the answers lay inside. She would read it the second Hughes and Davies were out of her hair. She scrubbed at her cheeks and forehead, wiping away blood and make-up all at once. It didn't take long for Misty's face to vanish along with her bravado. Then it was Joe looking back in the mirror, nibbling their bottom lip.

'Last night,' said Hughes, 'did Mr Green give you any idea at all what he wanted your help with?'

Tell her, said Miles' sensible whisper.

'No,' they lied. 'We didn't get chance to talk much, it was noisy and busy, and I was doing the mix and mingle.'

Joe remembered Sylvester's last words: '*You must find Jeremy.*'

Who is Jeremy? And what on earth is going on here?

DS Hughes stayed a while longer, asking more questions that Joe didn't have any interesting answers for.

Had they heard of Sylvester before? No.

Had they met Sylvester before? No.

Had Sylvester been to the club before? No.

Eventually DS Hughes left, and Joe was finally alone in the dressing room.

They stripped down to their boxer shorts and lay a towel on the floor in front of the dressing-room sink, washing every part of themself, scrubbing off the mess and watching it spiral down the plughole in pink swirls. Once clean, Joe put their day-to-day clothes back on, not yet having the energy to re-do the Misty make-up. Then they went to the bin and fished out the notebook and keys from the now-sticky white jacket.

By some miracle the notebook had remained dry in the pocket and they turned it over in their hands. It was a small bound pad with a black leather cover, held shut by an elastic band. They slipped that off and peeled the book open. Inside was sellotaped a Sylvester Green business card and Joe noticed the first half of the notebook's pages had been ripped away. Just jagged edges left. The remaining pages were blank. No writing, no detective scribbles. No clues at all.

They held the book up to the light, looking at the first of the empty pages. They noticed with a kick that there were indentations on it, as though someone had written on the previous page with a heavy hand.

They snatched up an eyeshadow brush and used it to lightly sweep across the page, leaving a blue streak on the paper. The indentations were crisp and white as if they'd been freshly written. Joe's heart raced as they read the words in front of them:

The drag queen in the photograph is called Misty Divine.

Photograph? What photograph? Clearly this is what had led Sylvester to Misty, but what did it mean?

Joe replayed Sylvester's words from the night before: *'If I don't make it back to see you, contact my assistant, Divya. Don't trust anyone else.'*

They turned back to the business card taped to the front page.

25 Great Windmill Street.

That wasn't even a ten-minute walk from Lady's Bar, just at the other end of Soho, towards Regent Street.

They picked up Sylvester's keys and took them to the sink, rinsing them until they sparkled. Thinking, so much thinking to do. The obvious reaction would be to call back DS Hughes, tell her everything, but they couldn't. If there was even a chance this was about Atrax, the future of the club could be at stake.

The next step then was surely to go to Great Windmill Street and talk to this Divya, to try to find out what had led Sylvester to her doorstep.

Who is *Jeremy?* they thought. *I need to know why I'm supposed to find him.*

There it was! That voice they'd heard after Lady Lady died, the urge to put the pieces of a puzzle together, the tingle they'd felt last night at the kitchen sink.

Miles was nearly killed last time. Stay away from it.

Joe splashed their face with cold water and patted it dry with a fluffy towel.

In spite of their reservations, they knew what they had to do.

*

It took an hour to get back into drag and as Joe painted a smattering of white freckles across their bright pink cheeks, they knew they'd made the right decision. It was definitely riskier to go as Misty. Sylvester had been attacked, and Misty would be much more visible than Joe, but they needed her. Her bold colour and hard edges made Misty the fiercest weapon in Joe's arsenal.

They dressed in a pink sequin suit and chose their favourite wig from the shelf: the big blonde Marilyn with the black streak up the front. They popped on a pair of black sequin heels and admired their own artistry. Misty Divine was back in the room: a blonde bombshell in black and rose.

The walk to Great Windmill Street was a nice one, through Old Compton Street, the beating heart of Soho, London's historic queer district. She passed cafés and bars and nodded greetings to fellow business-owners with a feeling of pride. She worked here. She owned a piece of this.

Sadly, Misty's own slice of Soho was currently a crime scene (again!) and she'd had to step around CSIs and cordoned-off bloodstains on her way out. She supposed none of the other businesses on Old Compton Street had managed two poisonings and a stabbing in the space of a year, but Lady's Bar had.

She crossed Wardour Street and turned left on to Brewer Street, making her way past a busy coffee shop where people pointed and looked at her. She waved at them, and they waved back, smiling broadly, overjoyed to see a drag queen in Soho at lunchtime.

Misty knew that Miles would be annoyed with her for

going to talk to Divya, and for agreeing to meet Sylvester in the first place, but she had no choice, surely. There were too many unanswered questions and everything had happened so fast.

Thinking of the stabbing brought back the hot-water feeling of blood pumping out under her hands and she wiped her palms quickly on her jacket.

Where was Sylvester now? Maybe he was in surgery, having his chest sewn back together. That's if he was alive at all – what if he'd died in the ambulance? It was awful. Perhaps, if Divya was at the office, she'd have an update.

The notebook and keys were weighty in Misty's handbag, like giant rocks. She was hyper-aware of them as she hurried down Brewer Street, half-expecting DI Davies to jump out and wrestle the bag right off her shoulder. She turned on to Great Windmill Street and walked until she found number 25, a black residential door next to the Duke of Argyll pub. She looked at the buzzers and saw a handwritten label, a dirty strip of masking tape that was peeling at the edges. In scrawled biro it said 'Sylvester Green'. She pushed the buzzer and a singing doorbell sounded through an intercom. Nobody answered. Divya wasn't here.

Hospital, thought Misty. *That's where she is.*

You have the keys.

Yes, but I mustn't . . .

He gave *them to you.*

She sighed, as though giving in to herself was the most difficult thing that had happened that day. She thought of Sylvester, lying on the ground, his final words before he closed his eyes: *'You must find Jeremy . . .'* She hoped he had survived.

She took the keys out of her handbag and found one that was the same colour as the lock on the front door. It was a match and slipped in smoothly.

Am I really doing this? she thought, stepping into the building's little foyer. *Am I really just going to let myself into his office like a nosy parker?*

Like a burglar.

Don't be ridiculous.

The door shut behind her with a loud click that made her jump. She was anxious and her tummy whirled with a swarm of invisible wasps. She pushed her shoulders back and stood up straight.

'I'm Misty Divine,' she said to herself under her breath, 'and I can do whatever the fuck I want.'

Ahead of her was a steep staircase with a white banister. *No lift.* She hoped the office wasn't on the top floor, not in these heels, but was relieved to find a sign that read 'Sylvester Green, Investigator' as she reached the first floor. There was a bell, and she pushed it with a pointed nail. *Ding dong.* No one answered.

She pressed her head to the door to listen but couldn't hear anything inside: no voices, no movement. It didn't seem like anyone was here.

Turning the keys over in her hands, she considered what she was about to do and what Miles would say when he found out. *What if I get caught? What if I find something terrible?* What if? What if?

It was already too late. She unlocked the office and walked in, closing the door behind her and taking a deep breath.

'Divya?' she called. 'Is anybody here?'

Silence.

Divya was not there. Nobody was.

The room was small. There was a neat and tidy reception desk on one side and a couple of chairs and magazines in a little waiting area on the other. At the back was a second door, and this one had a silver plaque that had obviously been made in the eighties. It said 'SYLVESTER GREEN'.

Sylvester's office, she deduced.

She walked straight to it and knocked, once again pressing her bewigged ear for a listen.

'Hello?' she called out. No response.

Misty pulled up the bunch of keys and found one that matched the lock. A round silver one. She slid it into the doorhandle and let herself into Sylvester's office.

CHAPTER 5

I shouldn't be doing this.

She felt it in her gut that she wasn't supposed to be here. Miles would be so cross – but that was past discussion as her choice had already been made. She'd let herself into the detective's private office, and now she was here, what was she going to do?

I'm going to look for a clue, said her investigator voice, *to find out what I'm involved in. To find out who this Jeremy is and why I have to be the one to find him.*

She stood for a second and took in the space, wondering where to begin. There was a desk and a couple of chairs where Misty guessed relatives of missing people or cheating spouses must sit and cry their hearts out to kind-eyed Sylvester before handing over their credit card details. The desk was piled high with paperwork, so that's where she'd start. If it was on the surface, it must be something he'd worked on recently.

She strode over and began flicking her way through a stack of beige cardboard folders. Each was labelled with either the name of the client, or the person he was investigating.

It was a great big file pile, but there were no Jeremys.

She turned to the filing cabinets which stood proudly against the wall by the window. The three metal units were labelled 'Active', 'Closed' and 'Unsolved' with handwritten stickers. Misty could hardly believe Sylvester was storing files like this in this day and age, on paper, in cabinets.

Beads of sweat tickled her upper lip as they emerged through the make-up: a sign of nerves and that her Botox needed refreshing. She made a mental note to book an appointment.

She pulled open the top drawer of the filing cabinet labelled 'Active'. It was arranged alphabetically, by surname. She didn't know Jeremy's surname, so she'd need to go through every single one. Four deep drawers. She sighed at the thought of it.

She wanted to get out of here already. Coming here could have been a major mistake. What if Divya was just out at lunch and came back any second? What if Sylvester had had a miraculous recovery and walked in right as she was rummaging through his drawers? Her mind raced.

She continued nevertheless, scrolling quickly through the files with her fingertips, looking at the name atop every one, racing to find a Jeremy.

Allen, Pauline
Archer, Sam
Astonbury, Jane
The files went on and on.

There were dozens of active cases. *How could he possibly be working on so many at the same time?* she wondered.

She went through the Cs and Ds and Es until finally she spotted something that caused a sharp intake of breath.

Edmunds, Jeremy

The name was scrawled on top of the file in blue ink.

Surely this was the case that had led Sylvester to Lady's Bar, to Misty. She whipped the file out of the cabinet and sat down at the desk, opening it and studying the few sheets of paper inside.

The first page was a client report, a detailed account of Sylvester's first meeting with a woman called Patricia Edmunds, which Misty read eagerly.

Client Meeting with Mrs Patricia Edmunds

03.06.2025

Missing Son

Mrs Edmunds attended my office at 10.30 a.m. on 3 June to request my assistance with locating her missing son, Jeremy Edmunds, a 29-year-old photojournalist from Chicago, currently based in North Finchley, London.

Mrs Edmunds reported that Jeremy had not made contact with his family since 16 May.

'It's not like him at all, he normally calls me at least three times a week. We live far away, you know . . .'

A photographer! From the US. Misty wasn't sure what she'd been expecting, but somehow it hadn't been an American.

There was a thorough statement from Jeremy's mother, explaining that she lived in Naperville, a suburb on the outskirts of Chicago, but had travelled to London to try to find her son. She was desperate, that much was clear through the words on the page. She hadn't heard from him for a month and he was last seen in Soho, at the Quill Club at one in the morning.

Sadly, people going missing in London was all too common, and despite a social media campaign by Jeremy's friends and family and a half-hearted attempt by the police, there was no trace of him after he left the private members' club on 17 May.

Patricia Edmunds had hired Sylvester as a last resort.

Misty flipped over the client report and looked at the second page in the file, a summary sheet on Jeremy with all his basic information: address, date of birth, a UK mobile phone number. Without a second of hesitation, she reached into her handbag and pulled out her phone, quickly snapping a photo of the page.

If I'm going to find this man, I might need this later.

She turned back in the file and took a shot of his mother's statement too.

The next document was Jeremy's most recent bank statement showing a final payment made at the Quill Club bar on 16 May, the night he vanished. *Snap, snap.*

The last document in the file was simply a photograph, and Misty's heart skipped a beat as she turned the page and saw it. It was a picture of her, of Misty Divine in full drag, unlocking the door to Lady's Bar.

She studied the picture carefully, observing all the details. Firstly, she was beautiful in it, and that was vital to acknowledge. It was a stunning photo, and one she'd love to use on her social media if it weren't tied up in an attempted-murder missing-person mystery. Secondly, she was wearing the blue hair. *An important clue because I rarely go blue.* She enjoyed the rhyme in her head as she tried to think back to when she last wore it but she couldn't recall. She remembered the outfit well: a tight navy and white dress with a peplum around the waist. She snapped another photo and got up, stuffing the file back in its place.

Let's get out of here, she thought.

As she closed the filing cabinet drawer, she heard a noise from the next room. The sound of the main office door opening and voices.

Yes, definitely voices.

A man's voice, but she couldn't make out the words.

Hide!

She looked around the room in fresh panique, desperately seeking somewhere to conceal herself.

Behind the door, she ordered herself, *stand behind the door.*

She rushed across the office towards the corner, careful not to make a single sound as she did so. Then she pressed herself firmly against the wall, hoping to God that whoever came in didn't close the door behind them and leave her exposed.

No sooner had she tucked herself away, the door swung open, trapping Misty behind it.

CHAPTER 6

'The assistant's still at the hospital,' said the man's voice.

'She'll be there for hours,' replied a second, 'but we should still be quick.'

Misty didn't recognise either of these voices, but they were low and well-spoken. They must be talking about Divya. *I was right! She's with Sylvester*, she thought smugly, pleased with herself for having guessed this earlier. *Perhaps I'm a detective after all.*

A detective trapped behind a door dressed top to toe in pink sequin.

The two men stepped into Sylvester's small and stuffy office and Misty held her breath, afraid of making the slightest move that would give her away. Her wig felt big and hot on her head, and she was damp with sweat underneath her corset and suit.

Don't move, she willed herself. *Don't move a muscle.*

The door almost touched the tip of her stunningly contoured nose and she could feel the warmth of her own breath against her skin. Her lipliner would be ruined, she knew.

'Check the cabinets,' said the first man.

She listened as one of them opened the drawers and the

other went through the stack of papers on the desk, just as Misty herself had done only minutes earlier.

'Got it,' said the second man, pulling papers out the drawer. 'Jeremy Edmunds.'

He's got Jeremy's file. That's what they came for. Just like me.

She heard the sound of a smartphone camera as one of the men took photos of the pages, just like Misty.

My photo, she thought. *They've got my photo.*

Are they police? she wondered.

Surely not. If they were police, they'd have waited for Divya, or Sylvester. They wouldn't have just let themselves in, would they?

'Shred it,' one of them said, and seconds later the sound of Sylvester's shredder whirred loudly as Jeremy's file and the photograph of Misty were split into a thousand pieces.

Definitely not police. Now she was worried. If these two men had let themselves into Sylvester's office and destroyed his file did they have something to do with the missing Jeremy? Were they responsible for Sylvester's stabbing? Whoever they were, she certainly didn't want them to find her. She steadied her breath: long, slow inhales and exhales to keep her aorta from exploding.

She listened as one of them opened the shredder and pulled out the contents. Rustling paper and plastic told her he was stuffing them into a plastic bag. Whoever they were, they were thorough.

'Let's get out of here,' said Man 1. 'The police are on the way.'

So they're not *the police!* Her instincts had not let her down. *But the police are on the way . . .*

Damn.

That meant Misty had to get out of here too. The last thing she wanted was DI Davies finding her in Sylvester Green's office with a phone full of secret documents, documents that had now been destroyed.

The men headed into the reception area with their bag of shreddings, slamming the office door shut behind them. Misty sucked in a fast lungful of oxygen.

Who were these men? And what did they want with Sylvester's file on Jeremy Edmunds?

She pressed her ear against the door, listening, waiting for the men to leave the office completely. The main entrance shut behind them and Misty knew they would now be on the stairs.

The window, she thought. *See what they look like.*

She stepped quickly to the ledge that looked out on to Great Windmill Street. Two men in suits exited the building beneath her.

That's them.

They looked clean, tidy, rich, and not what Misty had expected from a pair of office-raiders. What had she been expecting? Balaclavas in central London in the middle of the day?

Turn around, she willed them. *I want to see your faces.*

But they didn't. One of them stuffed the bag of shredded files into a bin and they continued towards Brewer Street.

To her horror, Misty's attention was drawn to directly beneath the window where two familiar faces were making their way into the building: DI Davies and DS Hughes. Misty could have vomited all over the glass but there wasn't time. There was only one place to go.

She rushed out of Sylvester's office, past Divya's desk and towards the door to the stairwell. She could hear DS Hughes humming in the foyer underneath. Quickly and silently, she snuck out on to the landing before creeping up the stairs to between the first and second floors. She tucked herself behind a wall and waited, her heart in her throat. *I can't get caught here. I just can't.*

'Well, he might pull through,' DS Hughes was saying to DI Davies as they headed up the stairs.

'He's old as time itself,' said Davies, his voice as dry as his skincare routine, 'and with an injury like that he's got no chance.'

'We'll see,' said Hughes, exasperated.

Misty held her breath as they stopped outside Sylvester's office, the one she had unlocked not fifteen minutes ago. *Is that how long I've been here? Fifteen minutes?* Maybe it was ten. It wasn't long, but it felt like a lifetime.

She dared a peek around the corner and saw DS Hughes knock loudly before Misty ducked back to her hiding place.

'There's nobody here,' said Davies gruffly. 'The assistant'll be at the hospital for hours yet.'

'Good job she gave us these then, isn't it?'

DS Hughes took out a jangly bunch of keys and turned one in the lock.

'It's already open,' she said.

Misty listened as they took out their batons, short sticks that clicked and shunted into longer sticks with which to hit criminals.

Criminals like drag queens who break into offices.

'Is anybody here?' called D I Davies into the office. There was no response. They stepped inside.

'Clear,' shouted D S Hughes from deep inside the room.

'Clear,' returned Davies.

The door slammed shut behind them.

Misty breathed a sigh of relief from her spot on the landing and took her moment, slipping off her black sequin stilettos and hopping quietly down the stairs two at a time until she passed the office.

Before she knew it she was on the ground floor in the little foyer.

I did it, she thought victoriously. *I did it!*

She touched her hand to her bag where she knew her phone was sitting, the only trace of Sylvester's shredded file she'd ever have.

She was just hours into her new investigation and it had already been fruitful. She knew now who the missing Jeremy was, and she had the details of his disappearance. She also knew, with mounting dread, that there were two mysterious men hot on her heels.

It had been quite the morning.

CHAPTER 7

By the time she got back to Lady's Bar it was almost 1 p.m. and the pavement outside the club where the stabbing had taken place was still cordoned off. Misty approached an officer standing by the police tape.

'I'm Misty Divine, one of the owners,' she said. 'I need to get into my office.'

'Nobody's allowed in or out for the time being, I'm afraid.' The police officer folded his arms and Misty just knew he was a jobsworth. She suspected he could have let her in if he wanted, because the club itself wasn't the crime scene, but he seemed so resolute there was no use trying again.

'Misty!' called a Scottish voice behind her.

Mandy. Thank God.

'Mandy,' said Misty, 'thank God.'

'What are you doing in drag already?' asked Mandy. 'And have you seen the mess on the stairs?! They won't tell me anything. Do you know what happened?'

'I was here!' said Misty.

'Let's grab a coffee or something. You can tell me all about it.'

A few minutes later, they were sitting comfortably underneath a breezy air-conditioning unit in Caffè Nero. Mandy was sweating and her dyed black fringe hung together in damp clumps. The bottoms of her thick-rimmed glasses were foggy with condensation where they pressed deep into her cheeks.

'So come on, fill me in,' she said. 'What the hell's happened at the bar?'

Misty decided to tell Mandy the whole truth. After all, they were involved in Auntie Susan's bribery scheme together. If Jeremy Edmunds was somehow connected, Mandy might well be in danger too. She had a right to know everything. That, and Misty was bursting to tell someone.

'I did the show last night,' she started, 'and this old creeper in brown shoes came in . . .'

She told Mandy about meeting Sylvester at the bar, that he had told her she shouldn't trust anybody apart from Divya, and Mandy listened with wide, curious eyes. 'Do you think it's about Auntie Susan?' she whispered. 'About the money?'

'I don't know,' replied Misty. 'But then this morning, when Sylvester arrived to see me, I heard him fall down the stairs and when I found him, he'd literally just been stabbed. It must have been right outside. He was bleeding everywhere, Mandy. It was awful. I thought he was going to die. For a moment I thought he actually *was* dead. He still might die, I suppose. Who knows? But before he lost consciousness he gave me his notebook and keys and told me I was in danger and had to find the person he's been looking for, someone called Jeremy.'

'What the balls does that mean?' asked Mandy. 'Who's Jeremy?'

'I thought the same thing, naturally, so I decided to try to find out. I've just been to Sylvester's office.'

She couldn't get the story out fast enough, eager to share her experience and get Mandy's take on the drama and intrigue.

She launched into the tale of the Great Windmill Street break-in, from letting herself into the building to hiding from the police on the stairs.

'Oh, Misty, love,' said Mandy, 'this sounds like it's going to be a right old faff.'

Misty wholeheartedly agreed.

'Check your Instagram,' said Mandy once she'd processed everything, 'for the blue hair, to see when you last wore it with the peplum dress.'

'An important clue,' rhymed Misty, 'because I rarely go blue.'

Mandy rolled her eyes with a smirk. 'Dickhead.'

Misty opened Instagram and flicked through her recent selfies. She knew she'd taken a photo in the blue wig, she remembered doing it, she just couldn't remember the date.

After a few swipes of the thumb she found it. A photo in the dressing room, a selfie in the mirror. Hair as blue as a varicose vein.

She'd posted it on 16 May. The same day that Jeremy Edmunds went to the Quill Club and never made it home. Taking her picture must have been one of the last things he did before he vanished.

'OK,' said Mandy. 'What are we going to do next?'

'I'm going to find out what we're mixed up in,' said Misty with determination. 'I need a notebook.'

*

46

They left Caffè Nero and walked together across Old Compton Street towards Foyles. If ever there was occasion for a new notebook, this was surely it.

To find out what's going on I need to do this properly, she thought, *like a real detective. And real detectives have lovely stationery.*

This probably wasn't true.

They arrived at Foyles, the enormous book heaven on Charing Cross Road, and Misty made a beeline for the stationery. There were rows and rows of notebooks of all kinds: meditation journals, food journals, diaries, calendars . . . Often, as Joe, they would spend time browsing here, assessing the thickness and quality of the paper in each book like they were a notebook connoisseur.

Today Misty already knew what she was going to buy because she'd had her eye on it for a while.

Is buying stationery an addiction? she wondered briefly as she picked up the pink glittery Paperblanks journal she'd been lusting after. It was more than £20. Expensive. But she *needed* it.

'Why you?' asked Mandy quietly as they approached the tills. 'Why was he taking photos of *you*?'

'That's what we need to work out,' said Misty.

'Sorry to interrupt,' said a skittish voice behind them.

Misty turned, faced by a woman in her thirties who was holding the hand of a small child and an armful of books.

'I just wanted to say that you look amazing. Really amazing.'

Misty smiled. She'd been so mixed up in the mystery and the notebook shopping she'd almost forgotten she was in drag. 'Thank you,' she said.

'Tell the lady she looks pretty, Amelia,' the woman said to the child.

It happened often in drag, much more than out of drag, that strangers would talk to you. Somehow, despite the intimidating height and make-up, drag removed a social boundary. It was one of the great things about it, Misty thought, so long as they had something nice to say.

Once she'd paid for the book, Misty was eager to find somewhere to sit, a quiet corner where she could concentrate and get everything written down. She needed to make a list.

'Do you think we should tell Auntie Susan?' asked Mandy. 'In case it is about the payments to the woman at the council?'

'Not yet,' said Misty. 'We need more information before we go to her.'

Misty would rather avoid another conversation with her completely. Auntie Susan had been Lady Lady's comedy partner until they fell out over her descent into criminality. In the nineties, the drag-queen double act had been widely celebrated, performing comedy sketches on national television. These days she ran the Plough, a rough pub that underpaid its performers and stank of vinegar and cigarette smoke. The pub was the centre of Auntie Susan's criminal operations and Misty had heard she was into all sorts: burglaries, phone snatching, and clearly blackmail and bribery.

Misty wished she could talk to Lady Lady about it, to ask her advice on what to do. As they walked together back towards Lady's Bar, she thought about all the things Lady Lady had missed, all the amazing performances she hadn't got to see, the life she hadn't been allowed to live. It still barely felt real that she had been murdered, or that Misty had caught the killer.

If I could find out who murdered Lady Lady, I can find Jeremy, she thought. *And if I find Jeremy, perhaps I'll work out why Sylvester said I'm in trouble. Maybe even work out who stabbed him.*

As if reading her mind, Mandy said, 'Do you think Sylvester was attacked by the men who broke into his office?' Misty could tell she was excited to talk about it more, catching the detective bug.

'Unless we're getting everything upside down, I reckon they must be. They destroyed the file in the office, and the notebook was also destroyed. As far as anyone else is concerned, there's no trace left of Sylvester Green's investigation into Jeremy Edmunds. Someone didn't want anybody looking into it.'

They arrived at the door to Lady's Bar to find that the jobsworth officer from earlier had been replaced by a new one, one who looked younger and much more approachable. She was smiling, for a start.

'Hello,' said Misty. 'We're the owners. Can we get inside yet?'

The young police officer told them that the staircase had finished being processed for forensics, and so Mandy and Misty could indeed have access to the club again. A biohazard cleaning team was apparently on its way to clean up the blood. They started down the stairs, careful to avoid the stains. Misty's new notebook was burning a hole in her handbag and she was itching to get writing. She told Mandy she needed to go through everything quietly and headed straight for her dressing room.

She sat at the make-up station and pulled out the book. Running her fingertips over the embossed cover, she wondered about Miles: what he would say when he found out she was investigating something else . . . Maybe she should call him. Maybe she should talk it through with him now before she got involved in anything deeper. She'd already been breaking and entering, and that surely wasn't something she could keep from him.

No, she thought. *This is a conversation that should be had face to face. Miles deserves that.*

Joe and Miles first met just after they finished university, thirteen years ago. Misty was not even a twinkle in her mother's eye at that stage, as Joe had had dreams of becoming a serious actor. That's what they'd studied, but it turned out Joe was a terrible actor. They'd done some university shows and had a couple of two-line parts in semi-professional productions, but they hadn't been able to get an agent, hadn't even had an audition in a year. Feeling despondent, they had started a part-time job at the bleak and dirty Empire Hotel in Bloomsbury. Joe was a receptionist at first, and one quiet evening when the hotel had barely any guests, a handsome man in a striking blue shirt appeared in the lobby.

'I'm so sorry to ask,' he said, smiling a smile that Joe would never forget, 'but could I use your loo?'

Joe's heart was already aflutter as they pointed the visitor in the direction of the toilets, and when he emerged a few moments later, Joe was almost too nervous to speak.

'Thank you sooo much,' said the handsome stranger.

'You're . . . you're welcome,' said Joe.

Talk to him! Ask him something. His name, his number, anything! But Joe was too shy. Thankfully, the visitor took the lead.

'Can I confess something silly?' he said.

'Sh– sure,' said Joe, not sure where this was going.

'I didn't actually need the loo.' He glanced coyly to the side, perhaps a sign that he was also feeling shy.

Joe laughed. 'What?! Then why . . .?'

The handsome stranger leaned against the reception desk and Joe's nostrils were treated to the scent of his perfume. Woody, earthy, but not overpowering. 'I spotted you through the window . . . I feel so awkward doing this, but I wondered if I could give you my number. My name's Miles.'

Joe grinned, thrilled that Miles had made this introduction. Miles smiled back. He had a gorgeous face: a slightly square jaw, strong cheekbones, well-maintained brows.

'Of course! I'm actually finishing my shift in a few minutes. Would you . . . fancy a drink?'

Thirteen years later. There had been jobs, promotions, celebrations, holidays, and then the poisonings, the hospitals, the viral fame of Misty catching Lady Lady's killer . . . so much had happened since that first meeting in the hotel and Miles was different now. Wasn't Joe too? Hadn't the events of last year changed them both? Thinking of Miles, opening this silly sparkly notebook felt like a moment of no return.

Misty knew once she started writing, there was no going

back. She'd be investigating a missing person and an attempted murder behind Miles' back. The guilt was a big black cloud, but she was compelled to begin.

It was a silent act in an empty dressing room, but one that had the power to change everything.

She turned to the first blank page and wrote at the top:

JEREMY EDMUNDS

She had to, and she hoped Miles would understand when she had chance to explain.

Misty decided her first task should be to write out a timeline of what she knew had happened so far, to get everything straight in her head.

16 May – daytime: Jeremy takes ten out of ten gorgeous picture of me

16 May – evening: Jeremy goes to Quill Club

17 May – early morning: Jeremy leaves Quill Club and not seen again

3 June – Jeremy's mother hires Sylvester

17 June – evening: Sylvester attends Lady's Bar

18 June – 10am: Sylvester is stabbed on Old Compton Street. The pages of his notebook are missing.

18 June – 11.30am: Two men break into Sylvester's office and destroy the Jeremy Edmunds file.

Writing it out like this didn't help her discover anything new, but it did put everything in order and she felt less frantic. It was the same way she'd felt a year ago when starting to piece together the clues of Lady Lady's murder: curious, intrigued, gripped.

Aside from those she had committed herself, Misty knew of two actual crimes so far: Sylvester's stabbing and the shredding of his file, and both were clearly connected to the disappearance of Jeremy Edmunds. With Sylvester's final words on top of that, Misty knew the primary focus of her investigation had to be finding the missing photographer.

Why did he take my picture? Why did Sylvester come to me? How are Misty Divine and Jeremy Edmunds connected?

There was a lot to do to discover the truth. Whatever was going on here, it felt complicated, and was clearly dangerous. Life-threateningly dangerous. Misty would need to be very careful indeed. And there it reappeared, the looming dark cloud of guilt telling her she really should just go home and speak to Miles . . .

Not yet.

Instead, she flipped open her laptop and turned to Google. The obvious thing to do, she thought. Tapping in Jeremy's name revealed a list of articles from a month ago, missing person's appeals from local London and Chicago newspapers. They were all accompanied by a photograph of Jeremy on a beach, smiling broadly, a gap between his front teeth.

CHICAGO PHOTOGRAPHER MISSING IN SOHO

The news reports were useless to Misty. There was barely any new information in them at all and the most recent one had been posted three weeks ago, so it looked as though the story was already dead.

People go missing so often, she thought, *it must be easy for someone like Jeremy to get lost in the news cycle.*

A short, recycled blurb about him explained that he'd been in the UK for six months, that he had no family here, and was working on freelance photojournalism projects.

Underneath the list of news articles was a link to Jeremy's own website. Misty clicked through and a page of black and white photographs of London churches opened up. She was struck by how beautiful and moving they were. The most recent piece Jeremy had published was for the BBC a few days before he vanished. It was about the evolution of Christian architecture in the capital and how it had changed through the centuries. There were stunning portraits of people, old and young, attending masses and services. The article itself was about space – how the space in which people worshipped was not as important as their faith. Their strength, Jeremy wrote, was not measured in bricks, but in their connection to God.

Jeremy's photographs detailed Romanesque, Gothic and Byzantine buildings before moving on to recent developments such as worship in entertainment venues like the Dominion Theatre. Finally, he had documented the construction of what claimed to be London's biggest American-style megachurch, due to open next year in the south of the city. One photograph showed Ginger Baker, a celebrity television evangelist from Texas, standing in front of the construction site with her hands on her hips. She looked like a comedy confection, dressed in pastels with clashing orange foundation, but it was a striking image. Ginger's cranes and shoulder pads were building a 5,000-seat venue and Misty was sure she recognised her from episodes of *Ricki Lake* in the nineties.

Could this article have anything to do with his disappearance? she wondered.

No.

It was a fascinating piece of journalism to Misty, a journey through history and time, but taking pictures of old London churches wouldn't have led to Jeremy disappearing.

So where is he?

There are three possibilities, Misty thought. The first was that he had simply left, packed up and run away without a trace, without even telling his mother, Patricia. This seemed unlikely given how upset she was in Sylvester's meeting report. The young man was clearly close with his mum and wouldn't have just abandoned her without a word. The second option was that Jeremy had been taken or kidnapped. Extreme, but somehow more likely. *Kidnapped by the men I heard in Sylvester's office? Was their destruction of his file a cover-up?* Maybe . . .

The third alternative was bleaker still. Jeremy could be dead, lying undiscovered in a ditch or under a patio. Misty glanced at his smiling picture on the laptop screen and hoped that wasn't the case.

Thinking of a dead Jeremy turned Misty to a dead Sylvester. What if he hadn't survived? What if her attempts to stem his bleeding hadn't been enough? She picked up her phone and called his office number.

I need to talk to Divya and find out how he's doing.

There was ringing on the line, but the assistant mustn't have yet returned from the hospital. A standard voicemail greeting asked Misty to leave a message and promised a quick call back, but she hung up.

She looked up from her screen to the reflection in her dressing-room mirror. In spite of the day's commotion, the blonde wig with the black streak didn't have a hair out of place. As she admired the exceptional job she'd done on her quick make-up, she realised where she needed to begin. She had to start where Jeremy's trail ended.

Misty decided to strut to the Quill Club.

CHAPTER 8

The Quill was only around the corner from Lady's Bar, not even a five-minute stomp away on Dean Street. Misty checked the time as she arrived outside. The afternoon was flying by, but she still had a couple of hours before the evening's show.

This club, like Lady's Bar, was a Soho mainstay, a social club for members of the entertainment industry. It was quite expensive to join, Misty thought, and you needed referrals. She'd only been inside once, as a guest of Caesar Theday, the Italian drag king. They had smoked cigarettes on the roof terrace until they both felt sick, a vice in which Misty rarely indulged.

The outside was painted black, with a discreet gold plaque announcing the club's name. Green bushes dangled in silver hanging baskets on either side of the entrance and Misty felt jealous that Lady's Bar didn't have a nicer facade.

Buy hanging baskets, she told herself. *Not today, probably.*

She pushed open the doors and stepped into the fancy reception area.

This is where Jeremy was, she thought with a detective buzz. *But where did he go next?*

Runaway, kidnapped or dead in a ditch. Perhaps now she'd find out which.

There were two women sitting behind the high oak reception desk, both of them in their twenties, both wearing bright floral summer prints. They cooed like high-end pigeons when Misty approached, gasping over her outfit and her hair. Her drag had disarmed them already and they didn't even know it.

'You're Misty Divine, right?' said one of them, standing up. 'From Lady's Bar?'

'Yes!' said Misty, beaming, holding out her hand for a shake. 'Lovely to meet you.'

'I was wondering when we might see you in here,' said Bethany. According to the name badge on her chest she was the club's membership manager.

'I've been meaning to come for ages,' said Misty. 'Feels like I'm still settling in over there!'

Bethany nodded with a sympathetic face. 'Of course, of course.' Then, changing tack completely, 'Are you here for a membership?' She hopefully pulled an application form out of a drawer underneath the desk.

'Yes,' Misty lied. 'I should have joined years ago.'

Bethany handed Misty the form and a pen, and Misty set to work filling it in, knowing that this particular thread of the investigation was about to cost her a pretty penny. At least she wouldn't need the referrals; being the owner of Lady's Bar definitely came with its perks. *And surely I can expense a club membership? That's tax deductible, right?* She'd check with Mandy.

She quickly scribbled down all her details.

'Bethany,' she said, handing back the completed form, 'could I ask you a favour?'

'Sure!' said the membership manager, taking the application and placing it on her desk, ecstatic to have made a sale.

'I've got a family friend who's gone missing and his mum's a bit worried. She asked me if I'd stop by because this was the last place he was seen.'

Bethany's face turned serious. 'Is this about the American photographer, Jeremy?'

'Yes, Jeremy Edmunds. Was he a member here?'

The manager looked worried, like she didn't know what she was and wasn't allowed to say next. 'I'm not sure I can . . .'

'Please, Bethany, for his *mum*. She's all alone in Chicago with nobody to help her here with the search. She's ever so worried and wanted me to ask about for her. The police have been terrible by all accounts.' The lies rolled off her tongue.

Bethany moved away from her colleague, past the computers to outside the cloakroom, signalling for Misty to follow. Then she spoke quietly, hesitating. 'Jeremy is a member. He joined when he first moved here. We all really like him cos he's so chatty, but you're not the first person to come asking about him. There was an old man here yesterday who's stopped by a couple of times in the last week, and this morning, two men in suits. Seems everyone's looking for Jeremy . . .'

Misty's scalp prickled. She was pleased with herself for coming, realising she was following the same trail as Sylvester, an actual detective, but the men from the office were a step ahead of her and she didn't like that at all.

There was a revelation in all this. If the suits were

searching for Jeremy at the Quill too, it wiped out one of Misty's day-one theories. They hadn't kidnapped him.

They don't know where he is either.

'Oh yes, that's Sylvester,' said Misty with a smile, trying to keep things light. 'He's been helping too. He's a dear.'

'I didn't take to those other two though,' said Bethany, conspiracy in her voice.

'The ones in suits?' asked Misty. 'Did they say who they were?'

'No, they didn't. They said they were looking into Jeremy's disappearance, but there was something off about them. They seemed . . . scary.'

'What did you tell them?'

'Nothing they didn't already know: that Jeremy was here on the night he disappeared but that we don't know anything else.' She looked down, scratched her nose and tucked a loose strand of hair behind her ear. Misty knew instantly. *She's lying.*

'But . . . you *do* know something else? Something you didn't tell the men in the suits?'

'Yes,' said Bethany, her voice like a whisper, 'but I'm not supposed to say.'

Misty could already see Bethany was going to tell her everything she knew. Another detective instinct? She was getting better at this. She just needed to push a tiny bit harder.

'You can tell me, if you want, for his mum. It would mean the world to her, and of course *I* won't tell anybody. We just really need some help.'

Bethany sighed and leaned forward. 'There was some

CCTV footage of him inside the club. He was with someone else. We gave it to the police at the time. I didn't want to tell the others who came asking but . . . if it's for his mum . . .'

Misty's heart skipped a beat. This was information that hadn't been in any of the news reports, and it put her a step ahead of Sylvester and ahead of the suits. The thrill in her chest was real and pounding.

'Do you have a copy?' she asked. 'Of the footage?'

Bethany took a moment, glancing over her shoulder at her colleague, and then nodded. 'Your email is on here, right?' pointing to the application form.

'Yes,' said Misty.

The manager moved back to her computer and clicked and tapped a few times, typing in the address. 'Sent. You should have it now, but it didn't come from me.' Misty's phone dinged in her bag.

'Understood.'

'Now, for your membership. I've done you a *really* special discount.'

She slid a sheet of paper across the counter top. Misty's eyes watered behind her lashes. That was the price *including* the 'really special discount'? She would definitely need to expense it.

CHAPTER 9

Misty stepped into the late afternoon sunshine swelling with pride. She had a lead! And evidence in her inbox! She'd been investigating this thing for half a day and she already had more than Sylvester. Jeremy had been with someone at the Quill.

But who?

She supposed that the police already knew, and maybe they'd followed it up, maybe they hadn't. She knew for damn sure that she was going t—

'Pervert!'

'Freakshow!'

Snapped instantly out of her mystery, out of her success at the Quill, she looked up and saw two young men dressed in summer shirts, laughing and snarling at her.

'Go fuck yourselves,' she replied, sticking her middle finger up at them, to jeers and gestures in return.

Misty was so furious she could hear her heartbeat drumming in her ears. The men carried on laughing and moved on, walking away towards Soho Square. She took a deep breath. She felt a sense of dread, knowing she'd spend all day thinking about those pricks now. Whether she liked it or not, no matter what else she had to do today, they'd be in the back of her mind. And later, when she took the drag off, then Joe would be all up in that stuff, getting nice and anxious about it. She tried her best to push it to one side.

It was hard. Discussion about drag performers in the media and online had become so toxic that once the magic boundary remover was in place, people felt entitled to say all sorts of things. Sometimes it was lovely, like the woman in Foyles and her little girl, but occasionally they'd say things that hurt. This was a result of the politics, she supposed, the natural progression of how those in power had encouraged hate to creep underneath everything like mould.

She found herself sinking into thoughts of this as she walked back to Lady's Bar.

Lady Lady would have told them to go fuck themselves too, she thought.

No she wouldn't. She'd have had something far wittier to say.

'Pervert', she thought. *Imagine just seeing a stranger and calling them that because of what they're wearing. Imagine being so full of hatred.*

Misty wanted to rush back after them and smash them to the ground in some sort of epic martial arts display on Dean Street. But she wouldn't. She couldn't.

She imagined all the ways it could have played out differently and, despite having just been called a freakshow in the street, she felt lucky there hadn't been violence. Imagine being called those things for no reason and coming away feeling 'lucky'.

She burst into the office in full stride.

'I need a cup of tea,' she said to Mandy. 'It's urgent.'

'What's happened?' asked Mandy, switching on the kettle. 'Where have you been?'

'Some bastards just called me a bunch of slurs in the street! In Soho, can you believe it? I swear to Christ it's getting worse.'

'It definitely is,' nodded Mandy. 'I'm so sorry that happened, my love.'

'Thanks. It's fine, I'm fine. I'll brush it off and I've got bigger stuff to worry about today. It's just annoying. It's knocked me off kilter.'

'Tell me then, where have you been?' said Mandy in an attempt to guide Misty back on track. 'I thought you were in your dressing room making notes about this Jeremy. I didn't even know you'd gone out.'

'I was,' said Misty, feeling herself edge towards where she'd been before, her anger subsiding, 'but then I decided I should try to retrace Jeremy's footsteps and go back to the scene of the crime.'

Mandy placed a steaming tea down in front of Misty and she took a sip, scalding the tip of her tongue.

'Damn!' she said.

'Too hot?' asked Mandy.

'Too hot.'

'So where did you go? Back to the scene of which crime? Seems like we're involved in multiple these days. Again!'

'To the Quill Club, where Jeremy was last seen.'

'Did they make you buy a membership?' laughed Mandy. Misty didn't respond, the credit card receipt on fire in her handbag. 'No, seriously. You didn't buy a membership? OK, moneybags!'

'I had to . . . to build some trust. To try and find out what's going on,' said Misty. 'They gave me a discount! And it is a legitimate business expense.'

Mandy roared with laughter. Even her laugh had a Glaswegian accent. 'A legitimate business expense?! Ha! I'd like to see you get that one past the accountant.'

'Anyway, it *was* money well spent because I've got info even Sylvester couldn't get. I charmed them.'

'Ooh, what?'

'First of all, those two guys in suits have been doing the same as me all day. Turns out they went to the Quill this morning, asking about Jeremy.'

'Did you find out who they are?'

'Not yet, but I found out Jeremy wasn't alone on the night he disappeared. I've got CCTV footage. Footage the suits didn't get, or Sylvester.'

'How did you wangle that?' asked Mandy. 'Do I even want to know?'

'I might have bent the truth just a bit.' She thought of the fibs she'd told about being friends with Jeremy's poor worried mum. More guilt to upload to the big black cloud.

'I don't need to know!' said Mandy, covering her ears. She swept the fringe out of her eyes to give herself a clear view. 'Come on then, let's watch it!'

Misty fumbled through her handbag, pulling out the phone and opening the mail app. There, like a pot of gold at the end of a rainbow, was the email from Bethany with a link to download a video file. She tapped on it and footage opened. It showed Jeremy Edmunds arriving at the club at 19:27 and signing in at the front desk. He was carrying three camera bags, all strapped across his chest in thick black stripes.

Then the perspective cut, from the camera in the lobby to a camera in the bar. It was bustling but Misty was able to make out Jeremy ordering a drink before sitting alone at a table by the far wall.

'Can you fast forward it or something, Misty love?' said Mandy, as impatient as Misty was to get to the moment that Jeremy was joined by someone else.

She skipped ahead in the video. Jeremy sat by himself at that table for four hours.

He didn't check his phone, didn't go to the bathroom, didn't order another drink. He sat still, cool as a cucumber, for four entire hours. Eventually, at 23:35, something interesting happened. A new man arrived. He too was carrying cameras. He was shorter than Jeremy, maybe 5'9", and wore glasses and a tank top, but not in a cool way. He was a bona fide nerd. Misty didn't come across them too often in her line of work and always enjoyed it when she did.

A nerdy photographer friend, deduced Misty, like a genius.

Jeremy and the geek had what looked to be a fairly animated conversation for the next hour and a half before, just after 1 a.m., the newcomer picked up his cameras and left. Jeremy sat with his head in his hands for a moment before heading to the door.

The CCTV footage switched perspectives to show him leaving the club, facing the camera above the door on his way out.

Does he look worried? thought Misty. *Or am I imagining things?*

Where is he going?!

The video ended as the doors closed behind him.

'Well that doesn't tell you much,' said Mandy.

'No . . . although at least we know what his friend looked like now. Maybe we can find him on social media.'

'Slow down, Misty . . . just slow down a minute.'

'Why?'

Mandy tucked a strand of black bob behind her ear and looked up at Misty with a serious stare. 'I think we're getting caught up in the drama of it all. Maybe we need to take it a bit easier, you know.'

Misty was offended, possibly even a little hurt. 'What do you mean?'

Her business partner shuffled from side to side on the spot. 'It's good, really good, that we're going to work all this out, but what about the club? Our reputation is going to be rock bottom once news of the stabbing gets out. That, on top of what happened last year, and if we add your breaking and entering to the mix . . . I know we're trying our best to save Lady's Bar, but if you get caught for all this, it could ruin everything.'

Rebellion thrust itself to the surface and Misty's fiery side burst through. 'We can't ignore this, Mandy. A man was stabbed on our doorstep. There's a missing man being hunted by the suits, and if the trouble Sylvester was warning us about is to do with the bribery, everything will be ruined anyway. We need to get ahead of it. We have to know why Sylvester came to warn me and what happened to Jeremy.'

'OK, OK. I get it, I do. I just think we need to be really careful.' Mandy ruffled her fringe with a frustrated hand.

'Have you tried the assistant again? Sylvester said she was who you should talk to, didn't he?'

'He did,' said Misty. 'Divya . . .' She whipped Sylvester's notebook and her mobile out of her bag and called the number again.

It rang. Three times, four times. Mandy sighed.

There was a beep on the line and a woman's voice spoke in a light Indian accent. The voicemail greeting had been updated from earlier, re-recorded by Divya.

'You've reached the office of Investigator Sylvester Green. Unfortunately, due to an emergency situation, the office will be closed until Monday morning. Please leave a message and I'll get back to you as soon as I can.'

'Damn,' Misty said, hanging up. 'She won't be available until Monday and I don't have another way to contact her.'

'Then I guess we have to wait till then,' said Mandy.

'What do you think we should do now? Social media?'

'I don't know, Misty love.' Mandy seemed tired of it all now, exhausted by Misty's persistent curiosity. 'Honestly, I might have to leave you to it. I've got a stack of supplier invoices to get through. We have a club to run, remember? I'm probably no use to you on social media anyway. You're the great detective.'

Misty laughed, the tense moment broken. 'Great detective?'

'You know, always getting into detectivey scrapes. It's like working with a drag queen Sherlock Holmes.'

Disheartened by Mandy's caution but determined to press ahead, Misty settled in her dressing room where she turned her attention back to the CCTV footage. She felt sure there was something in it she should have noticed, some detail or clue she had overlooked. She watched it again, narrating the video out loud to herself under her breath.

'Jeremy arrives at the club and signs in . . . he orders a gin and tonic at the bar and pays for it with his card . . . he sits in the corner and waits for his friend . . . he waits . . . he waits . . . the friend arrives . . . the friend leaves . . . Jeremy leaves.'

It seemed totally innocent, except for the unreasonable amount of waiting Jeremy had done. Just two friends having a drink. Misty hovered her finger over the screen, about to close down the video. And that's when she noticed what she'd been overlooking the first time around.

The camera bags. Only two camera bags.

She scrolled back to the start of the video and watched Jeremy arrive. He was definitely wearing *three* cameras. She skipped through the video again, this time watching only the bag straps. He was wearing all three when he ordered his gin. When he reached the table he put all three cameras down on the floor underneath it, and that's where they stayed for four hours.

When the nerdy friend arrived, Misty counted that he too was wearing three cameras. He placed them down under the table. But later, as the friend got up to leave, he picked up one, two, three . . . FOUR. Four cameras.

He took one of Jeremy's cameras . . . or Jeremy gave it to him.

Was this something the police would have noticed? Probably, if they were paying close attention, but it didn't seem they'd been particularly interested in Jeremy's disappearance. *At the very least they'll have questioned the friend though, right?*

Misty sent a quick email back to Bethany, thanking her for the video and asking, in the most sickly sweet way, if she might be able to share the name of Jeremy's friend from the guest pass system. For his mum, of course.

Bethany replied instantly with the name: John Smith.

For God's sake.

CHAPTER 10

It was going to be a nightmare to find any information at all on Jeremy's companion with a name like John Smith. There must be ten gazillion John Smiths in the UK alone and even more in America. Google would be useless this time. Misty was irritated.

Maybe John Smith wasn't even his real name. It was definitely the kind of name a mysterious criminal might use to avoid detection. She stared at his bespectacled face on the screen and whispered under her breath, 'Who are you, John Smith?'

The no-brainer place to search was Jeremy's social networks, to see if he was connected online to the mystery man who took the camera.

Checking the flamingo clock, she saw it was nearly 6 p.m.; time she should be doing final preparations for the Lady's Bar show. But she couldn't resist – she was on a roll. She opened Facebook. Thankfully, Jeremy Edmunds was not quite as popular a name as John Smith, so she found his profile quickly. Annoyingly, it was locked down with tight privacy settings and she could see a profile picture and a cover photo, but that was it. No friends list, no posts, nothing else was visible. She clicked the 'add friend' button just in case.

From Facebook she went to Instagram but, again, a private profile with no information. This was so frustrating.

Her third attempt brought forth something more useful: LinkedIn.

It seemed Jeremy was a prolific LinkedInner. He had over 4,000 followers there for his photojournalism work. Misty clicked on his profile. The last update had been posted a week before he vanished: the BBC article on London architecture.

She scrolled down and scanned through his career history, seeing that he'd started work as a photo desk assistant at the *Chicago Sun-Times* before moving to the *Huffington Post* and then finally on to working as a freelancer. He'd studied at DePaul University in Chicago, a school Misty had never heard of.

Close to home. Interesting.

In the UK, students tend to move away from their hometowns when they go to university, thirsty for a first drink of freedom at the tender age of eighteen. Perhaps Jeremy had wanted to stay near Patricia, or maybe the culture was different. If she found him, if he was still alive, it was something she might ask.

Underneath his professional experience was a list of glowing references from previous employers and publishers who had all—

'Pervert!' 'Freakshow!'

And there it came back to her. Suddenly, and as intensely as she knew it would. The words from the men on the street. Her body boiled with anger as the thought of it returned and she pushed it away by squeezing her eyes closed.

I saw a stabbed man this morning, and those pricks are what I'm getting upset about?

She tried to return her focus to LinkedIn, to Jeremy Edmunds' professional profile, but between the echoing insults and the approaching show-time, it was no use. Her focus was lost and she wasn't really sure what she was doing any more.

Her phone dinged the little ding it made for a message from Miles.

> *Hey Joe. Decided to be brave and come to the show tonight! Think I need to get out the flat for a bit. Leaving in a min so I'll be there at about 6.30. Will you reserve me a seat at the bar?*

Shit. Miles was coming to the club. He was definitely going to find out what had happened this morning then, the stabbing. People would be talking about it, about the entrance having been a crime scene mere hours before.

She was going to have to fess up.

He answered the phone right away and Misty stuttered. In fact she didn't feel like Misty at all because, although she was in drag, this conversation was for Joe to have. Joe and Miles.

'H-hey, Miles, how are you?'

'I'm looking forward to your show tonight, that's how I am! I need to get out of the house – think I've been working from home too much and it's probably time I finally faced Lady's Bar again. How are you? How's your day been? Did you catch up on your email backlog?'

Misty's gut gurgled with nausea as she was reminded of

the lie she'd told him this morning. Her secret meeting with Sylvester, the blood, the ambulance, the office break-in . . .

'Well, actually, Miles, that's why I was calling. I have something I need to tell you before you come to the club tonight.'

'What? What is it?' He sounded uneasy, as though he knew just from the tone of Misty's voice that she was about to make a difficult confession.

'I didn't want to tell you yesterday because I wasn't sure it was important, but at last night's show a private investigator turned up. He said . . .'

'What did he say, Joe?'

'He said I'm in trouble and he needed to explain something. He said I couldn't trust anyone but him and his assistant.'

Silence down the line.

'Miles? Are you still there?'

'I'm here . . . I'm just thinking. What's the trouble?' Miles was serious now and obviously concerned. 'Oh God, this is about the bribery isn't it? Atrax?'

'I don't know. He said he'd come back to speak to me this morning, to go through everything. I didn't tell you because I didn't want you to worry.'

'So the emails you had to do? That was a lie?'

'A white lie,' said Misty. A vein throbbed in her neck. 'I wanted to know what it was about before I told you. You've got a lot going on already and I didn't want to stress you out.'

'No, no, no,' said Miles. 'Don't put this on me. You told me a lie because you *chose* to tell me a lie, Joe. Don't tell me it was for my own good.'

'I'm really sorry. I didn't know what else to do.'

Miles sighed. Actually, it was more of a huff.

'So, did you meet him this morning? The investigator? What did he tell you about this trouble?'

'Well,' started Misty, 'he came to the club, but when he got here, he fell down the stairs. I went to try and help him, but he'd been stabbed outside before he arrived. I had to call an ambulance. There was blood everywhere. The club's been closed off for a lot of the day.'

'Stabbed?!'

'Yeah, in the chest.'

Her fingers went cold, wet with the memory of Sylvester's injury. Her stomach turned.

'Is he OK? Are *you* OK? Oh my God.'

'I'm fine, Miles. It happened on the street and he's in the hospital now. He was in a pretty bad way.' Misty was roasting hot in the pink sequins. This was a horrible conversation to be having.

'Jesus, Joe. What time?' asked Miles.

'What?'

'What time did this happen?'

'Around ten a.m.,' said Misty.

'Eight hours ago. *Eight* hours ago! A man was stabbed at your bar eight hours ago and you didn't think to call me, to text me, to tell me anything about what had happened? Were you expecting I just wouldn't find out?'

'I don't know . . .' said Misty. 'I didn't want to worry you.'

'Well, I'm worried now, Joe. Really fucking worried.'

Miles was rightly upset. Misty knew he'd be even more upset when he found out the rest: the notebook, the suits shredding Sylvester's paperwork, the photo of Misty in Jeremy's file. She had to tell him. She couldn't not tell him.

'There's more,' she said. She started at the beginning, from Sylvester falling down the stairs, and that his last words to Misty were that she must find Jeremy.

'Please don't tell me, Joe, that you're actually going to try and find this Jeremy?'

Misty didn't know what to say. How to tell Miles, who had nearly died in the last investigation, that she'd started another.

'Actually . . . I already kind of did,' said Misty. 'Started anyway, to look for Jeremy.' She took a deep breath and filled him in on the rest with complete candour.

'Oh no,' groaned Miles. 'How do you manage it, Joe? You're just a normal, quiet human most of the time and then twice in a year you're running round Soho like Agatha Raisin! Poisonings, stabbings, mysterious warnings from private detectives . . . these aren't things that happen to regular people every day.'

'But you see I was right to do it, Miles,' she insisted, 'because something's going on here, isn't it? Those men in suits, they're definitely not police. So, who are they? Who stabbed Sylvester? Why do they want to cover up his search for Jeremy? And where *is* Jeremy? Don't you see, Miles? I need to know why I'm involved in this.'

Miles tutted and the subsequent pause was huge, like an avalanche of silent boulders running between them.

'Miles, say something.'

'I'm really disappointed, Joe, that you'd do this again after what I've been through this year.'

She felt like crying, like she'd betrayed the person she loved the most.

'I'm sorry,' she said, 'but I think I *have* to do this. I need to know why I was in Sylvester's file. Not just for me, but for us, for our life together. If it is about the Atrax bribery and the deal with Auntie Susan, we need to know so we can sort it all out. And if it's not related to that, what was Sylvester warning me about?'

Silent boulders.

'Are you still coming to the show tonight?'

'I don't know,' said Miles. 'I'll think about it.'

He sounded depressed and Joe's shame rose up like a mouthful of sick. 'I'm really sorry, Miles.'

'I might see you in a bit,' said Miles. 'I have to go.'

He hung up.

He hung up without saying goodbye.

Without saying 'I love you.'

Miles was really upset.

CHAPTER 11

Just before doors opened at 6.30 p.m., Misty popped a small brass reserved sign in front of one of the stools at the bar, just in case Miles did decide to show. She didn't think he would. The chances of it were next to zero. He was angry with her and she could completely understand why. But even with a mystery to solve and her relationship in trouble, the show must go on. She had to be the smiling, singing face of Lady's Bar no matter what else was happening.

She hurried through a fast warm-up, ran over her introductory jokes and songs, and greeted the kings and queens who were performing alongside her tonight. They were busily getting ready in the dressing rooms while Misty was out front, doing her final checks, directing the front-of-house staff to tweak flower arrangements and polish glasses.

The place looked stunning. The walls were draped in heavy red velvet with gold tassels and the tables were so clean they shone like mirrors. This week's flowers were crisp red tulips and bright green ferns. It felt like luxury in Lady's Bar, it always had.

Mandy burst out of the kitchen doors into the auditorium. 'It's time to let the bastards in,' she said.

*

For tonight's show Misty had slipped into a floor-length, figure-hugging, awe-inducing silver gown. It had a split up the thigh that reached Misty's waist and her long, elegant legs were glossy and tanned in three pairs of thick dance tights.

She'd changed her hair too, to a dark green swirly up-do that was big and unwieldy on her head. The wig was pinned to within an inch of its life and her brain ached from the tight strip of bandage that held it to her skull. The pain was irrelevant. Delectability was the goal.

She was focused. She needed to get through tonight's show as flawlessly as possible, so she could get home and talk to Miles.

And look at LinkedIn.

As the guests made their way in, Misty played an impeccable hostess, greeting everybody with a light handshake like Princess Diana. She showed patrons to tables and posed for photographs with eager drag fans.

Despite the early excitement, there was a darker feeling in the room tonight. Misty spotted audience members pointing at the bottom of the staircase, where Sylvester had landed. Word was out. The stabbing was clearly the talk of the evening.

People had dressed up smartly and Misty was overjoyed to see three trepidatious young queens on what looked like their first night out in drag. They must have been eighteen or nineteen, barely old enough to get in the place. As she approached, she saw them nudging each other and pointing excitedly. They were about to talk to Misty Divine!

'Hello, my lovelies!' said Misty 'I *had* to come over and tell you how stunning you all look.'

The baby queens giggled and thanked her, and one of them stood up.

'Misty, I hope you don't mind me saying, but I am such a big fan. I've watched all your YouTube videos. I'm so excited to meet you.'

'Me too!'

'And me!'

One of them grasped Misty's forearm with scratchy press-on nails and leaned in, asking, 'Is it true though, that someone was stabbed here today?'

She replied with confidence, knowing that the hostess must never let her guests feel worried. 'There was a little incident here this morning, but it's nothing you need to be concerned about.' She flung her arms out wide in a movement that felt forced and too much. 'We're all ready for a fabulous show at Lady's Bar!'

There was a cheer from the table behind, from a group who had been eavesdropping. The young queens looked relieved.

'Can we have a selfie?' asked one, already unlocking her phone.

'Of course!' beamed Misty. 'I love having selfies with beautiful queens.'

The other two youngsters got up from the table and Misty called over a waiter to take the pictures. It took a couple of minutes because everyone wanted a photo on their own phone. *Of course.* There were edits that needed doing, curly laces that needed smoothing away.

'And can you please bring a bottle of prosecco for this table? On the house.'

The queens gushed at the prospect of complimentary fizz from Misty Divine and she thanked them all for coming and told them to enjoy the show.

She hoped she had been encouraging to them, and that she'd put their minds at ease about Sylvester. She remembered how much guts it took to get into drag for the first time, and how brave she had felt just for leaving the house. For Misty, those young queens were a highlight on what had otherwise been a fraught and stressful day.

She took to the microphone and the room fell silent. You could have heard a pin drop and the Lady's Bar regulars knew they were in for a treat: Misty's opening number. Usually she performed a big belter to welcome the crowd – a Celine Dion or an Adele, something like that. But tonight, she'd gone rogue. She was doing pop. The eighties classic 'Especially For You' by Kylie and Jason, though she had no Jason, so had planned an arrangement that worked for her on her own.

She knew as she sang that it was faultless. In her mind there had never been a better live rendition of 'Especially For You', not since Kylie and Jason themselves sang it together, and when she finished the crowd went wild. There was cheering and the clacking of fans. Misty saw the three baby queens stand up in a mini ovation at the back of the room and from there her eyes were drawn to the bar, to the empty stool with the little brass reserved sign. Miles hadn't come.

She introduced the first act of the night, the drag king

Caesar Theday. He was slick and sleek and wiry, and just looking at his chiselled abs made Misty want to do a hundred crunches. He danced a wild and outrageously sexy rodeo to a mix of Steps' '5, 6, 7, 8', and while she should have been enjoying the performance, all she could think about was Sylvester, about his blood pumping out of his chest on to her hands and the taste of it on her lips and teeth. *Please don't be dead*, she willed.

After the show Misty did the usual mix and mingle with the crowd, chatting to as many guests as possible before they disappeared off into the Soho night. This evening, thankfully, there were no creepers, no private detectives, no weird and mysterious messages.

Once the guests had gone and Misty had profusely thanked the bar staff, the security team and the other kings and queens, she retreated to her dressing room. Apart from her brief blood-washing reprieve with DS Hughes, she'd been in drag since 9 a.m. this morning. It was now 11.30 p.m. Fourteen and a half hours in drag. Her skin was desperate to be splashed with cold water.

She sat down, took off her lashes and unpinned the green wig.

There, looking back in the mirror, exhausted from a day full of stress, investigating and tough conversations, was plain old Joe Brown.

CHAPTER 12

Saturday

Joe got home just after midnight and found Miles hadn't waited up like he normally would. He'd gone to bed alone in a clear statement he was pissed off.

Can you really blame him? Joe thought as they popped two slices of bread into the toaster.

Have I been selfish? they wondered.

Freakshow.

Go fuck yourselves.

The Dean Street lads flashed through their mind and they tightened their eyes again to force the memory away. Their laughing, jeering faces faded out of view.

The more Joe thought about it, the more they didn't think they'd really been *that* unreasonable to Miles. Sure, they shouldn't have lied about going to meet Sylvester, that much was definitely true, but they'd apologised for that on the phone. And they'd do the same again in the morning.

To Miles it was life-threatening peril for Joe to take this path because it had been exactly that last time, but surely it was normal to want to know why a private detective had shown up, half-dead, telling them they were in danger.

Wouldn't anybody in my position be trying to find Jeremy now? To Joe at least, there wasn't any other option but to investigate.

They slept badly to begin with, waking up every half an hour thinking about the men in suits, until eventually they drifted into a deep sleep at about 4 a.m. When they finally opened their eyes at 7 a.m., Miles was gone.

Joe staggered into the kitchen, body still sore from the fourteen hours in heels and lashes. They made themself a pot of coffee and spotted a hand-written note on a Post-it on the kitchen table.

Gone to Mum and Dad's.

No *love you*, no kiss at the end, no invitation for Joe to join him.

Was this Miles' way of storming out, without even a conversation? How could it have come to this? Not showing up to Lady's Bar was one thing, but *leaving*? That was a much bigger reaction than Joe had expected. They pulled their phone off the charger to text him. It took a while and a few sips of strong coffee to know what to write.

Miles, I'm so sorry I lied and upset you. I didn't mean to and I feel awful. Let me know when you'd like to talk. I love you so much. Joe x

They put the phone down on the table and glanced at the pink glittery notebook with misgiving. In the thirteen years since Miles happily wandered into the Empire Hotel they'd hardly argued at all, not seriously. Of course there were disputes over cleaning or lateness or misunderstanding each other, but never had either of them left like this.

I should stop, they thought. *Stop this investigating now before it goes any further.*

Joe got up from the table, distancing themself from the phone and the notebook. They knew what they wanted to do now, but weren't sure they should. They wanted to open LinkedIn and return to their search for John Smith but it felt sullied, the whole investigation, by Miles' terrible reaction.

Instead they moved to the living room, lay on the sofa and flicked on the television, depressed by the Post-it. Skipping to YouTube with the remote control, they quickly found an old episode of *Airline* and pressed play, basking in the glorious sound of easyJet employee Jane Boulton telling off a passenger who was late for check-in.

They let the airport argument wash over them, not really paying attention, the screen becoming a haze of orange uniforms and angry faces. They picked at their cuticles, scraping off nail glue from last night's press-ons, and thought about Miles. This was moping, they knew, self-pity, the start of a gloom that could last all day.

You're languishing, they told themself.

On-screen, a woman who had missed her flight was making her way to the customer services desk, but Joe couldn't focus on the crying passenger, or even on Jane.

'*You're in danger, Misty,*' echoed Sylvester's voice over and over and over again.

Joe stood bolt upright in the middle of the living-room rug.

Miles and Mandy might not want Joe poking around in

this Jeremy business, both for very good reasons, but Joe had very good reasons too: Sylvester, on death's door. A photograph of Misty in the missing man's file. Her Goldie Hawn suit, gone forever.

'Jane Boulton wouldn't be sitting on her arse with her life in danger,' Joe said out loud to nobody at all. 'Miles and Mandy aren't here.'

They weren't the ones who'd had the mysterious warning. They weren't the ones who'd kneeled in sodden trousers as Sylvester's blood poured out of his chest.

Joe switched off the television and returned to the notebook. The languish was over.

Joe poured a fresh coffee to boost their energy for looking through Jeremy Edmunds' LinkedIn profile. They would handle Miles and Mandy later, whenever that might be.

Thankfully, Jeremy's list of connections had public visibility so Joe was able to see every name on it. All 4,393 of them. They typed 'John Smith' into a search bar at the top and took a sharp inhalation as only one popped up. There he was. There was no doubt about it: this was the man Jeremy had met at the Quill, the one who had taken Jeremy's camera.

Joe clicked on to the profile with haste, reading eagerly.

John Smith
Freelance photojournalist

This is it! This is him. And it wasn't a fake name!
'Gotcha.'
John had had a similar career to Jeremy, working as a

freelancer after a few years with major publications. The main difference was that Jeremy was from Chicago and John was from Newcastle. *Professional contacts?* Joe wondered. *Friends?*

I should message him.

Message him?!

That's what Misty would do.

Joe knew if they had been in drag they would have already sent the message. They'd have done it immediately. Misty had a decision-making superpower, or an impulse-control problem.

A click through to John's website led to a short menu of social media profiles. Joe selected Instagram, where the photography was undeniably beautiful. It featured gorgeous portraits of people, with paragraphs of their life stories in the captions underneath. A pink ring around his profile picture told Joe that John had recently posted an Instagram Story. They tapped it.

A poster for a drag brunch flashed on to the screen, one of the big party brunches that took place in a fancy restaurant in Shoreditch every Saturday.

'Can't wait for this!' John had captioned on top of the poster, and he'd tagged some friends.

When is it? thought Joe, their eyes scrambling for the date and time.

It's today! Today!

So, just like that, they'd gone from languishing on the sofa, to having a time and place where John Smith was actually going to be, in person. Today.

An interesting development.

Jeremy had taken a picture of Misty, a drag queen, and his

friend with the camera was heading to a drag brunch. Two drag connections . . . A coincidence or a clue?

Their eyes turned guiltily to the Post-it from Miles. He'd be so mad if he knew what Joe was planning, but there really was no other choice. What else were they supposed to do?

Joe got ready for the day slowly, over an hour, taking a long leisurely shower and then shaving their face at the bathroom sink.

The missing camera had felt like a real lead, suspicious and almost imperceptible in the CCTV footage. Joe was proud of themself for having spotted it. Going to the drag brunch to confront John Smith was the best approach, they thought. With Misty on home turf, it would be an easier interrogation.

Interrogation? You're not a detective, Joe.

No, but there were questions Mr Smith had to answer. Who was he to Jeremy? Why did he take the camera? What did he know about where Jeremy could be now? Was John Smith himself responsible for the disappearance?

This would be Misty's first confrontation with an actual suspect since she caught Lady Lady's killer last year. Joe's belly churned at the thought, nerves that getting into drag would surely banish.

Mandy didn't like it, Miles didn't like it, but Misty needed to know.

Where is Jeremy Edmunds?

Runaway, kidnapped, dead in a ditch.

CHAPTER 13

Misty arrived at the Showstopper Diner just after 11 a.m. She hadn't booked a ticket but knew the owner, a woman called Mariska Bee, would find her a seat to watch the performances and give her a glass of bubbly to boot.

There was strong community among the queer venue owners, a feeling of camaraderie and mutual support, and since Misty had inherited 10% of Lady's Bar, the other owners had embraced her with open arms.

Welcoming as Mariska was, the Showstopper Diner was truly a riot of a place. An enormous American-style diner on Shoreditch High Street, it was where crowds of excited drag fans and hens in 'bride to be' sashes whooped at incredible performances and joyously guzzled bottomless mimosas. A quick glance around told Misty that today's audience was 50% hen party, 40% daytime revellers and 10% tourists who had no idea they were coming to a drag show.

Drag brunches were big business and, as Misty took her seat in the diner, she wondered whether anybody had ever calculated the value of the drag brunch industry. Internationally, and if you included all the cash tips, it must be hundreds of millions.

Misty had dressed up for the occasion in a yellow silk

dress she'd had designed to look like Kate Hudson in *How to Lose a Guy in 10 Days*. If she couldn't be Goldie any more, she'd be her daughter. Her hair was a soft blonde bob with golden orange roots – hideous, but gorgeous in the way only a drag queen can pull off.

Watching the guests file in and excitedly flap to find their tables, Misty was reminded what an adventure it was to experience drag for the first time. To see mind-blowing dancers and singers and comedians who had their own creative universes: make-up, costuming, hair . . . every detail was planned out for *you*, the audience member. She suspected some of the audience might take it for granted, that there'd be the odd hen slurring her words and grabbing performers' padded bums with sticky mimosa fingers by the end of the brunch, but for others, this would be a life-changing day. An eye-opening experience. The discovery of a new world where genders and talents merged and intertwined to create magic onstage. She caught herself feeling the pre-show excitement and had to remind herself she wasn't there to have fun.

The other thing to note about the Showstopper Diner was that the smell of egg was strong. Plate after plate of American breakfasts were served, and poached eggs sitting atop English muffins, doused in Hollandaise sauce. Misty wasn't hungry and her corset was too tight to add an English muffin into the mix, but seeing the eggs made her miss Miles. He was a wonderful cook . . .

She boxed off the Miles situation in her mind and imagined locking it away with a key and padlock. She had to concentrate on her plan: find and interrogate John Smith.

*

The first performer to take to the stage was a queen called Cherry Kiss. Misty had watched her before and knew the crowd were in for a wild ride. Cherry was one of those queens who could fling herself across a table in a high-sprung backflip one minute and have you sobbing into your eggs benedict to an emotional ballad the next.

Her opening number was 'Gold' by Spandau Ballet. Twenty hens sang along, waving arms and dildos in the air to the horror of a German family who watched open-mouthed like they thought they'd booked a quiet meal at the Ivy.

Misty kept half an eye on the performance but scanned the room for men in tank tops and glasses. The place was rammed and she estimated there were at least three hundred brunchers.

Cherry flung herself on to the floor in one of the liveliest moves Misty had ever witnessed. People stood up to get a better view as her legs split and spun and twirled in the air. A woman screamed with excitement so great Misty genuinely worried she might make herself faint.

Over the top of Cherry's upside-down feet, Misty spotted a table of gays at the other end of the venue. Four of them, faced to watch Cherry, flutes of bubbly in hand. Her heart skipped a beat as she realised one of them was John Smith.

It's him!

There was no doubt about it.

He wore the same tortoise-shell glasses as in his LinkedIn profile picture and was holding a camera, snapping photos of Cherry from the sidelines. In real life he looked a little older than Misty had expected. She knew from his online profile that he was twenty-nine, but he could have been forty. His chin was smattered with stubble that was grey beyond his years.

She felt the tingle in her tummy, the excitement of reaching the next step of her investigation. She'd found a witness.

Or a suspect.

The brunch was long and Misty was impatient for it to be over so she could talk to John and put her interrogation plan into action.

A woman on the table next to her leaned over in between numbers.

'Are you doing a turn or what?' she asked. Misty got a blast of the woman's breath directly up her nostrils. Hollandaise and mimosa. *Gross.*

'Not today.' She smiled politely, trying her best not to engage.

'Ha!' laughed the woman in a rotted choke. 'So why are you dressed like *that*?' And then, in a swipe that Misty could barely believe, the drunk egg-breathed hen reached forward with both hands and squeezed Misty's padded bosoms. 'What have you got *these* on for?' she slurred.

Misty was enraged but tried not to let it show. 'Don't touch me,' she said. Cool, crisp, don't-mess-with-me vibes.

The hen leaned back, chastened, rejoining her group and whispering to her neighbour. Misty checked her dress, hoping the drunk hadn't smeared poached egg into the yellow silk, but thankfully her fingers had been clean.

She turned her attention back to John Smith, and watched as he snapped photos of non-binary drag artist The

Australian, who was performing a hilarious and passionate love song in a suit covered in pink hearts. She thought about the CCTV footage, about John leaving the club with Jeremy's camera. Had Jeremy handed it over or had John stolen it? Did the police know? Was there something on that camera that Jeremy had wanted to hide, or expose? Perhaps John himself would be able to tell her. Whatever had happened in the Quill that night, Misty was sure this camera business was connected to Jeremy's vanishing.

By the end of the brunch Misty had quaffed three mimosas and was a little tipsy. Still in control, but boosted by the extra confidence a bit of alcohol provided.

She stayed in her seat by the door as the parties headed out on to Shoreditch High Street having been fed, watered and entertained for over two hours. She waited for the table of gays to reach the exit and then got up slowly, ducking behind a group of tourists and following John out on to the pavement.

She watched from the doorway as he said goodbye to his friends, air kissing and hugging them one at a time.

Hurry up, she thought.

Now she had a choice to make: she could either confront him here in the street or she could follow him in the hope of catching him somewhere quieter. In the best-case scenario he was heading home.

Yes, she thought, *following him is the best option.* She would have to maintain quite a distance because the yellow dress and blonde bob were certainly not discreet, perhaps a bad choice. This might be a challenge, especially after the drink.

She waited as he separated from his friends and walked past her, turning on to the long and narrow Redchurch Street. Now she was excited.

The top end of Redchurch Street looked like a million others, a tree-less line of terraces that was once working-class accommodation and was now home to luxury design brands and gorgeous boutiques. She kept a block's distance behind John as he walked ahead of her.

On the opposite pavement a group of teenagers passed by. Misty put her head down and braced herself for it.

'*Freakshow.*' Yesterday's insults rang fresh in her head.

But the teenagers passed by without so much as a second glance at Misty and she sighed a breath of relief.

John walked all the way to the top of Redchurch Street, to where it met Brick Lane and disappeared out of view. Misty raced ahead, wobbling on her heels on the uneven pavement.

Don't lose him. Don't lose him now.

She turned on to Brick Lane just in time to see her tank-topped witness, *or suspect,* entering a coffee shop. She peered through the café window and watched him at the counter as he ordered a drink. He looked geeky, awkward, not the type you'd expect to steal a camera or kidnap a photographer in the middle of the night, but Misty knew appearances weren't everything. Lady Lady's killer had been the most unsuspecting of all.

The shop was quiet, almost empty in fact.

This is the perfect place to pounce.

She watched as John collected his coffee and took a seat

at the back of the café. He tugged his camera out of his bag and started looking through it, pressing buttons and studying the little screen, no doubt reviewing his pictures of Cherry Kiss and The Australian.

Now, Misty. Now's your chance.

CHAPTER 14

'John Smith?'

He looked up and his mouth fell open. Misty towered over him and channelled the movie star vibes of her Kate Hudson dress.

'Erm . . . yes.' He smiled. 'You're a-a . . .'

'Drag queen?' finished Misty with a grin.

'Yes,' he laughed, nervously. 'How do you . . . how do you know my name?'

'In this country, there's about a one in three chance any man could have your name,' she winked.

'Touché,' he smiled.

She pulled up a chair and sat down opposite him. 'You don't mind if I sit with you a minute, do you?' She'd already sat, leaving him no choice.

'No, of course. But . . . do I know you?'

'You don't,' said Misty. 'I'm a friend of Jeremy Edmunds' mother, Patricia. She asked me to talk to you.' She recycled this lie with such ease it was almost scary. The 'for his mum' line had worked so well on Bethany at the Quill Club it was definitely worth trying again.

'About the night Jeremy disappeared?' asked John. She

could tell he was already tense as his shoulders hunched and eyebrows furrowed.

'Yes. You were the last person to see him.'

'I know,' said John, rubbing his eyes with his thumb and index finger in a big eye-pinch. He put his camera down on the table. 'Oh, it's just terrible.'

Misty thought back to her notebook, to the interrogation plan she'd cooked up in the shower.

She told the story she'd prepared. 'Patricia asked me to help follow up on some things. She's worried the police haven't done a thorough job.'

'They haven't,' snorted John. 'They've done hardly anything that I can see.'

'You don't mind if I ask you a few questions? For *Patricia*?'

'Of course,' he said. 'I'm happy to help however I can.'

She sensed this wasn't true. His body language told her his desire to speak to her had vanished the moment she mentioned the missing photographer.

'Thank you,' said Misty with what she hoped was a kind voice. 'How long have you known Jeremy?'

'Not long,' said John, chewing the side of his tongue. 'Since he came to London six months ago. We met at a networking event and went on a date. That didn't go anywhere but we stayed friendly.'

'Would you say you were close?'

'Not really,' said John, and he turned his paper coffee cup in circles on the table between them. 'Until the night at the Quill, I hadn't seen him for a few weeks.'

'So how did you end up meeting that night? Did Jeremy reach out to you or vice versa?'

John's fingers twitched against the cup. 'It was Jeremy's idea. He didn't know many people here and I got the impression he was lonely and needed to talk.'

'OK . . .' Misty replied. 'And what happened at the Quill? What did you talk about?'

John shifted in his seat, and Misty knew: *Here comes some bullshit.*

'Nothing. Everything. It was just a general catch-up.' He shrugged and widened his eyes in a display of innocence Misty didn't believe. She pressed ahead with her questions, wondering how long John would tolerate her impromptu interview.

'Did Jeremy seem depressed? Worried? Was there anything in particular that stood out as unusual?'

'No, nothing,' said John, blinking a few too many times. He was a terrible liar.

Misty had planned for this. She knew from her many years of watching *Criminal Minds* that revealing a piece of evidence at exactly the right moment was a powerful persuasion technique.

'Did he tell you anything? Or *give* you anything?'

A layer of sweat appeared almost instantly on John's forehead. '*Give* me something? No, why would he . . .' His eyes brimmed with tears.

Misty reached her hand forward and placed it on his – a kind but direct approach. 'John, I know you left the club with Jeremy's camera.'

'His . . . camera . . .' stuttered John. 'I don't know what you're . . . talking about.'

Misty sighed in a performance even DI Davies would have admired. 'John, there's no use lying to me about it. I've seen the CCTV footage. I can show it to you.' She pulled her phone out of her bag and unlocked the homescreen. 'It shows you arriving with three cameras and leaving with four. Jeremy arrived with three and left with two. I need to know, are the police aware that you have Jeremy's camera?'

John's shoulders sank and to Misty it was a sign of admission, almost relief. He shook his head and whispered, 'No.'

'OK, John,' said Misty, 'this is really important, for Jeremy's *mum*. She's far away, on the other side of the world, and she's worried out of her mind.'

'I know . . . I'm sorry . . .' His eyes were wet and sparkling.

'John,' she soothed, 'there's no use crying about it.' She hadn't expected that her first interrogation would get teary-eyed but she kept her cool. 'I need to know about the camera.'

'Jeremy told me not to tell anyone.' He looked eaten up by it and it reminded Misty of a year ago, when she'd first confronted Mandy about the bribery scheme with Auntie Susan. Mandy had looked this way then: consumed, and desperate to tell the truth to someone.

'Yes, but this is for *Patricia*. Her son's been missing for a month. If you know something, it's time for you to tell me. I can help.'

John let out a gasp that was half stress, half exhaustion. He glanced around the empty coffee shop, suddenly self-conscious about his crying.

'How do I know you're really a friend of Patricia's?' he asked. 'How do you even know her?'

'She came to Lady's Bar when she was in London last

month looking for Jeremy. We hit it off and I offered to help,' Misty replied with confidence. Then, holding out her phone, 'Call her if you want.'

Please don't call her, she willed.

John studied the phone in her hand for a second as though he was actually considering taking it. Then he let go. The tension in his body released and he shook out his hands like a dog shrugging off a rainstorm.

'Did you steal that camera, John?'

'No!' he protested, scanning the surrounding tables to make sure nobody was listening. 'Jeremy *gave* me the camera.'

'Why?'

'He asked me to keep it safe for him. He was worried. He said he was in danger. He said I mustn't trust anybody. He begged me not to tell anyone and said to only hand over the camera if he was found dead. I asked him, *"Why? Who would want you dead?"* I pleaded with him but he wouldn't tell me.'

Jeremy was worried his life was in danger?!

The man in front of her seemed genuinely distraught.

'I'm a quiet person, you know?' he whispered. 'I've never been involved in anything like this. I barely knew him!'

'It's OK, John. It's time we found out what was going on. We need to know he's safe, right?'

John agreed, nodding. 'I should have told the police, shouldn't I? I should have told them everything.'

'I don't know,' said Misty. 'Jeremy must have been pretty convincing and it's too late to think about that now. Didn't the police ask you about the cameras after they watched the CCTV footage?'

'I don't think they can have watched it at all,' said John.

'I keep expecting them to show up at any minute with a search warrant, kicking my door through. I've hardly slept.'

He was probably right. If the police had seen what Misty had spotted in the CCTV footage, they might have had grounds for a warrant to search John's home for the camera. It would have kickstarted a real investigation. There would have been updates, news stories. But instead, John had said nothing like Jeremy wanted, and so nothing had happened. The police's half-hearted efforts to look into the disappearance meant they hadn't paid enough attention to the video from the Quill, but Misty had.

'John,' she said, as seriously as she could, 'I need to know what's on that camera.'

'I'll show you.'

She was confident now, having seen John crying and sorrowful, that he was an innocent in all this. She believed his story. He'd been caught up in it as accidentally as Misty herself had and as they left the café together, she knew that John Smith was no longer her suspect, but he was leading her to her next clue.

John explained that he lived close by, a few blocks away on Turin Street. It was a fifteen-minute walk, he said. 'Are you up to it in those heels?'

Misty assured him that she was. She'd done the London Pride Parade in a pair of stilettos taller than the ones she was wearing today. She could manage a short walk.

As they strolled, Misty tried to get John to open up, asking him questions about his date with Jeremy and how they'd met. John talked freely, explaining that they'd attended a mixer for young photography professionals and gone for dinner a few weeks later. By the time they got to Turin Street they were like two old friends sharing a stroll.

John opened the entrance to a block of flats with a black key fob.

'I'm on the second floor,' he said, heading to the staircase.

'Is there a lift?' asked Misty, thinking of the heels. Streets were one thing, stairs quite another.

John's apartment was clean and tidy. Immaculate in fact. There was evidence of his geekery all over the living room as a collection of special edition *Star Trek Voyager* DVD box sets took pride of place on the mantlepiece. Artwork on the walls appeared to be Dungeons and Dragons related.

'Do you want a cup of tea?' he asked.

'No, thank you,' said Misty.

'I'll just get the camera then,' said John, and he scurried into another room.

Misty supposed she should have been more cautious about coming here, into this stranger's home, but she trusted her gut and it was telling her this man was not a villain. No, she didn't think John Smith was a danger at all.

He returned carrying a black bag and unzipped it, sliding out an expensive-looking digital camera. He pushed a couple of buttons and the screen came to life.

'There are three photos on here,' he said.

'Have you looked at them?' Misty asked.

'I don't want to,' said John. 'I'm a portrait photographer, I tell life stories. I don't want any trouble. This whole thing has scared me out my wits. Whatever's on here, whatever this is, you can keep it. I hope you find him, I really do, but I just want out of the whole thing.'

He handed Misty the camera. She couldn't believe it.

'Did Jeremy tell you what he was working on next?' she asked on her way to the door.

'I asked but he wouldn't say. Listen, Misty, you won't tell the police, will you? That I was keeping secrets from them.'

'I won't,' said Misty. 'You can trust me. All I want is to find Jeremy.'

CHAPTER 15

She stood proudly on Turin Street like she'd struck gold. Not only did John Smith still have the camera, but he had given it to her.

Given it to her!

She swung the long strap over her wig and head so it hung across her chest and then took out her phone to call an Uber.

There was still nothing from Miles. She wanted to tell him: about the camera, the interrogation, everything. She missed him already. She wanted to share this with him to find out what he thought and have his help like she'd had once before.

Maybe he'll have a change of heart while he's at his mum and dad's, she hoped.

But what were the three photos on the camera? Whatever they were, Misty knew they were the next stage in her quest to solve Jeremy's disappearance – an insurance policy left by the missing man himself in case he turned up dead. She could scarcely wait to take a peek.

She clambered into the back of the Uber.

'For Joe,' she said.

'Yep,' replied the driver, looking her up and down over his shoulder. 'Nice dress.'

'Thanks.'

She looked at her watch. It was already after 4 p.m. Finding and talking to John had taken her all day, but it had paid off. She had something. *Evidence.*

What was it they called it on TV? An exhibit?

Her first exhibit.

She pulled the camera out of the bag. It was heavy and complicated like it cost a lot of money. She spun it in her hands, checking the casing, then switched it on, tapping the menu button to reveal the three files.

She opened the first one.

It was a photograph of a man who looked familiar to Misty but she couldn't place him. He was skinny and bald, exiting a set of rotating glass doors with wire-framed glasses perched on his nose. His tie was plump and perfectly knotted. He was obviously rich.

The subjects of the second photograph were the men in suits Misty had seen at Sylvester's office, only this time she could see their faces clearly. She revelled in the knowledge that they had tried, and failed, to get the Quill Club CCTV footage for themselves. In this photo they were outside the same set of rotating doors as the wealthy man in the first photograph.

And then the third picture. One that Misty had already seen. A photograph of herself, unlocking Lady's Bar, wearing the blue hair.

My God, she thought, *I'm a knockout.*

But why? Why did he have this picture of me?

A glance at the driver's phone on the dashboard told her they had twenty-five minutes until they reached Soho. Traffic to Central London was bad at this hour but it would give her time to make some new notes. She whipped her pink investigation notebook out of her handbag.

The first thing she did was check the times and dates of the photographs so she could add them to her timeline. She clicked through the camera menus to find the data: the photos of the unknown men were taken *before* the one of Misty.

Who are they? she wondered. If she could identify these people, she'd be able to join the dots, to deduce the connection between the three images.

She clicked back to the first, of the man in the perfect tie and wire-rimmed glasses.

Why do I know you?

The longer she stared at his face, the more she was certain she'd seen it before. Only briefly maybe. Perhaps even only once.

Yes, I've seen this man before.

Misty arrived at Lady's Bar and raced straight to the office. Even though Mandy had been hesitant about continuing the investigation, she wanted to fill her in on the latest revelations. It was only right she was up-to-speed and besides, Misty needed someone to talk to.

'Mandy,' she said as she barged in, 'I've got evidence!'

'What now?' asked Mandy, standing up from her desk, her mouth stuffed full with a Tunnock's caramel wafer.

'Jeremy Edmunds' camera.'

Mandy sighed mightily.

'You're crazy, Misty,' said Mandy, shaking her head. 'You could have been killed! You know that, right? John Smith could have been a psychopathic psycho.'

'Yes, but he wasn't was he? And I got something big.'

'OK, I admit,' said Mandy, 'you got something big, but I don't like any of this.'

'Neither do I,' Misty said, in a half-snap. 'But I like the idea of stabbed detectives on our staircase even less. What about you?'

Mandy's shoulders dropped. 'Go on then, show me these photos.'

She switched on the camera and the screen flickered on to the man in the glasses.

Mandy jumped up off the floor. Literally. With both feet.

'Fuck me!' she shouted, a little shower of caramel wafer crumbs escaping her mouth. 'I know who that is.' Her accent had got so thick it was almost impossible to understand. 'I know who that motherfucker is. Mind my Spanish, Misty.'

She rushed back to her computer and quickly typed on her keyboard, pulling up something on the internet. It was an article about Atrax Misty had read a year ago, when she'd first discovered the secret bribery, written by a journalist called Jessica Gethyn.

Founded by two German entrepreneurs in 2016, Atrax are notoriously secretive about their affairs but are believed to provide consultancy services and representation for investors, as well as private security and, rumour has it, private military.

At the top of the article was a photo of the wealthy-looking man and the caption read: *Stefan Weber, CEO*.

'Shit,' said Misty. 'Excuse my German.'

'*Scheiße* indeed,' said Mandy.

CHAPTER 16

Misty knew there was scant information available about Atrax online and Jessica Gethyn herself had shown up at Lady Lady's funeral last year urging Misty to steer clear.

She thought back to how Jessica had cheerlessly approached her, her face covered with a black veil. *'Stay away from Atrax – it's dangerous,'* she'd said.

A shiver ran up Misty's spine.

'Does this mean we need to tell Auntie Susan?' she asked Mandy. The very thought of it set her on edge. Auntie Susan was terrifying: a drag queen in her sixties with flame-red hair and a chihuahua who sat on her knee like Mr Bigglesworth. 'If Jeremy Edmunds was running around taking pictures of me, and taking pictures of Atrax, then surely we were right to suspect this is all connected to our ... situation.'

'We probably should,' replied Mandy with caution in her voice, 'but not now. We need to think about it carefully and not rush into anything. Maybe it's time to speak to Mr McDermott.'

Misty loved speaking to Mr McDermott, their handsome solicitor with the impressive chest and silky voice, but she didn't think going to him now was a good idea.

'OK,' she said, placating her partner, 'let's sleep on it.'

'Anyway,' Mandy rushed, 'we've got a show starting in a couple of hours and you might have done your face, but you're not rehearsed or warmed up. And I *know* you're not hosting in that wig.'

'Harsh,' said Misty. 'I like this wig!'

'Then you're the only one,' laughed Mandy, raising an eyebrow at the blonde bob with orange roots.

Damn. Misty had been so caught up in solving the mystery she had barely thought about tonight's show. She knew what she was singing, that was planned out weeks in advance, as were her costumes. It shouldn't take her too long to get ready.

'OK,' said Misty, 'we can talk about it tomorrow. I can see Auntie Susan by myself if you don't want to.'

Mandy slurped a mouthful of tea and swilled it around her cheeks, cleansing her teeth of caramel. 'So Jeremy Edmunds knows about the arrangement with the council? That's what this all means.'

'I'd guess so . . .' said Misty.

'And who are the men in suits? Are they Atrax too?' Mandy ruffled her thick fringe anxiously.

'Probably,' said Misty, 'but we shouldn't assume . . . we need to find out for sure.'

'This all makes me sick.'

For this evening's cabaret Misty was dazzling. Her dress was strapless and red, covered in a million black crystals that made up a giant rose down her left side. The bustline was trimmed with elegant black feathers that she'd matched with a blonde beehive wig with curls at the temples and a fluffy fringe, Bet Lynch style.

She took to the stage in the empty auditorium and asked Jackson the technician to press play on her first track. She'd done some YouTube warm-up videos in her dressing room but wanted to run through her songs one last time.

The room came to life around her as she sang, cleaners, servers and security guards working busily to get the venue ready for opening.

She rehearsed a short stand-up set she had prepared for after the interval and was confident her jokes would land. Comedy wasn't her forte, and she wasn't in the mood for it, but she was a natural host so she knew she could make it work.

What if the men in suits aren't *Atrax?* she thought as she hit the big note.

Then who are they?

She glimpsed at the stool she had reserved for Miles last night and wondered what he'd done today. Had he gone to the office or worked from home? Had he taken a sick day? Had he told his parents that Misty/Joe was once again embroiled in something dangerous? She also wondered, for the first time, whether Miles might not come back.

What if he's left me? asked Joe's voice, sadly.

Don't think about this now.

Tonight was a competition show, Lady Lady's Star Search. It had been running at Lady's Bar for over ten years and was one of the scene's staple contests. Misty herself had once been a contestant, but that felt like an age ago. Twice a year, twelve up-and-coming drag performers would prepare acts based on a theme. Each week, one act was eliminated until finally there was a winner. It was a pretty standard format, but the crowds loved it. Week after week the auditorium was rammed with regulars, reviewers and influencers, cheering on their favourite acts and, importantly for Misty and Mandy's bottom line, drinking a lot from the bar.

Misty loved hosting the Star Search. It was amazing to see how the acts progressed over the months, both in terms of their confidence and creativity. As the weeks went on the costumes and mixes got more complex as acts tried their best to wow Misty's carefully selected guest judges.

She finished her rehearsal and headed backstage to wish the competitors good luck and talk through the running order. Crossing the auditorium in her black and red outfit she felt regal. This was possibly the most beautiful she had ever looked, though she thought that every time.

While she busied herself on the way, adjusting a couple of vases to make sure they were perfectly set, she couldn't stop thinking about Stefan Weber and Atrax. She hated the thought that their scheme with Auntie Susan was exposed, that somebody else might know their secret. This was scarier and closer to home than she'd have liked. Sylvester had dragged it right to her doorstep and Miles had been right all along.

She decided she would go to see Auntie Susan on her own tomorrow. Mandy wanted to take things slowly, to think about every move before they made it, but Misty didn't think there was time. She was in a race against the suits.

She was already dreading it. Auntie Susan's pub, the

Plough, was a rotten place: all boarded-up windows and peeling paintwork, and the red-wigged criminal ringleader would be mad when she found out about Jeremy. Secrecy was the name of Auntie Susan's game.

Misty stepped into the dressing-room corridor and her thoughts were instantly transported by the hubbub of drag performers getting ready. It was one of her favourite sounds because there was always so much laughter. Tonight was no exception.

This evening's guest judges were a London drag power couple, king and queen extraordinaire, Martin and Martina Maximillion, famed for sharp suits and dozens of wig changes. Misty greeted them with a speedy hello and left them to get ready in peace while she went to visit the Star Search contestants across the hall.

It was nearly the end of the competition; tonight was the semi-final. Three contestants remained and they were performing two numbers each on this week's theme: The Life and Works of Meryl Streep. Misty laughed as she entered the dressing room. In front of her stood two drag queens, dressed as the nun from *Doubt* and Miranda Priestly. Next to them was a very tall king who was clearly the witch from *Into the Woods*.

'Wow,' said Misty, 'if Meryl shows up she'll be impressed.'

'Oh my God, Misty,' said the Miranda Priestly, a queen called Camp Knickers, 'we heard about the stabbing here yesterday. Are you OK?'

'I'm fine, I'm fine. You know me.'

They nodded.

'Well, if you need anything, you must let us know,' said the drag king, Ben Eleven. Out of drag, Ben worked as a nurse in the NHS and Misty knew his offer to help was genuine.

'Thanks Ben. Will do,' she said. 'So, are we all ready for the semi-final?! It's so exciting.' The less they talked about Sylvester, the better.

The competitors chatted all at once about how thrilling and nail-biting it was to reach this round of the contest, and Misty was starting to catch the pre-show buzz. To get up in front of a crowd and perform an act you've designed from scratch was to put your whole creative soul on show.

She wished everyone luck and returned to the auditorium, ready to welcome tonight's patrons.

She knew already that in spite of everything happening with Jeremy and Sylvester, and Atrax and Miles, it was going to be a fabulous show.

CHAPTER 17

Joe got home to find the flat empty. Camp Knickers had been eliminated from the Star Search after lip-syncing the cerulean-blue speech from *The Devil Wears Prada*, a performance the London drag scene had seen many times before. Joe felt sorry for her, understanding how disappointing elimination felt when you'd poured in your heart and soul. The remaining contestants now only had six days to prepare their final acts as the grand finale always took place on a Friday to get those bumper bar sales.

Aside from empathizing with Camp's misery and thinking about cocktail sales, Joe had other things to worry about. The flat was cold and quiet, despite the June heat and the summer revellers outside. Miles hadn't returned, which meant he was spending the night at his parents' place and Joe was spending the night alone.

They stood in the lifeless kitchen wondering if they should send something to Miles. A goodnight message, an 'I love you,' an apology . . .

You've apologised enough.

Are you sure?

They opened WhatsApp and stared at the blank screen

for a moment, debating what to write, whether to write anything at all. Eventually, they chose to say nothing.

Joe ate a plate of Pop-Tarts at the kitchen table and got out their investigation notebook. As well as visiting Auntie Susan, there was a new move Misty could make: contacting journalist Jessica Gethyn.

Her funeral warning had been crystal clear, but she was the only person Joe knew who might have more information about Atrax. It was already almost midnight, too late to reach out now. *I'll do it in the morning.*

They also needed to speak with Divya, Sylvester's assistant, but that would have to wait until she was back in the office on Monday. There were questions only she could answer, like if the photos on the camera were Jeremy's secret insurance policy, how did Sylvester get the one of Misty?

There was so much to do, and so much to think about.

Flicking through the pages of notes, they knew they were procrastinating, putting off going to bed on their own, but it was time for sleep and they couldn't avoid it any longer: a night without Miles.

CHAPTER 18

Sunday

Joe tossed and turned all night in their empty bed. They kept stirring with a busy head, their dreams a jumble of Miles, Jane Boulton and Auntie Susan's chihuahua. By the time they got up at 8 a.m., they felt like they'd barely slept at all.

They poured a coffee, feeling conflicted. On one hand, there was the guilt. They'd definitely done something wrong by going behind Miles' back and lying to him about Sylvester. But on the other hand, wasn't Miles overreacting? Running to his parents instead of staying to talk it through . . . As much as they loved him, and they did, very much, they couldn't help but feel a little annoyed. If it was the other way around, if a detective had shown up at Miles' office saying he was in danger, there's no way he would have ignored it.

Joe wouldn't be the one to break the silence between them. It was best to let Miles cool off in his own time.

The first thing to do after breakfast was get into drag because Misty was going to go and see Auntie Susan as soon as the Plough opened. Mandy wouldn't be happy about her doing this without her, but Joe couldn't wait any longer. Their relationship was on the line, as well as their business. There was also no way on earth they were sending Joe to meet Auntie Susan. She'd eat Joe Brown alive! Misty had survived an Auntie Susan stand-off once before and knew that in drag she was stronger and less likely to get trampled by the fierce redhead.

Last night Joe had chosen the perfect outfit for Misty's second meeting with the scariest queen in London: a scarlet satin jumpsuit with a gold statement belt, to be worn with a bright white high ponytail. Bold, powerful, and in Auntie Susan's colour palette.

It took an hour and a half to do the make-up, carving deep red eyeshadow with crisp white lines. By 10 a.m. anxious Joe had been stashed away, and Misty Divine stood in the kitchen, radiant in the summer sun.

She arrived at the Plough just after eleven with butterflies in her stomach. The pub was as rough as it had ever been with its peeling exterior and boarded-up windows. A sad and dirty rainbow flag hanging limply above the door was the only sign to the outside world this was a queer venue. Since Misty had last visited, the 'O' of the pub's name plate had been stolen or fallen off so the front of the pub was emblazoned with 'THE PL UGH'.

Ugh indeed, thought Misty.

She headed to the front door and pushed it open, bracing herself for the smell she'd encountered last time. Her nostrils were not disappointed as she inhaled a pungent waft of vinegar and stale cigarette smoke. It was clear that after-hours, Auntie Susan didn't care about the smoking ban and 'cleaned' her venue with the cheapest possible products. A far cry from the fresh flowers and gentle air freshener that kept Lady's Bar scented to perfection.

The Pl ugh was divided into two halves, a front room with a bar and pool tables, and a dingy performance space out the back, accessed by swinging saloon doors. Both had sticky wooden floors that needed sanding and revarnishing. There were already customers here and a group of older men turned from the pool tables to stare at Misty, morning pints in hand. One of them wolf-whistled. Misty loved the older gays, especially those who appreciated drag, so she gave them a wink and said, 'Hello, fellas.'

She strode to the saloon doors and heard someone behind the bar shout, 'You can't go back there!'

'Yes I can!' replied Misty. Nothing would stop her now.

The performance room at the Pl ugh was a jail cell of a place, a square box with bare breezeblock walls and a makeshift stage at one end. Misty knew there were regularly fights here, objects thrown at performers, hecklers . . . It was a pub with a wild and rowdy crowd, and she presumed most acts who performed here only did so once.

To the left-hand side of the performance room was a door that had the word 'Office' written on it in black marker pen, and she knew what lay beyond. A dragon. Misty was a medieval knight, about to open the beast's lair. Hinges creaked like a scream as she pushed through the door and she was immediately confronted by a young lad in a tight white T-shirt standing guard.

'What do you want?' he said.

'I'm here to see Auntie Susan. Tell her it's Misty Divine.'

He muttered under his breath and disappeared into Auntie Susan's office, returning just seconds later.

'She'll see you,' he grumbled.

'I knew she would,' said Misty.

Into the lair she stepped.

In brash contrast to the rest of the Pl ugh, Auntie Susan's office was elaborately and luxuriously decorated. The carpet was soft and clean, there was a white marble desk and a green velvet dog bed where the little chihuahua glared at Misty with sharp and beady eyes. Auntie Susan stood up behind the desk.

She was of course wearing her signature red hair, with the tight white minidress and red shoes she was known for. She'd been wearing variations of the same outfit for thirty years. The room smelled strongly of tobacco smoke and Misty noticed a cigarette burning in an ashtray on the desk.

'Misty Divine, to what do I owe the pleasure?' Her tone was dripping with sickly sweet sarcasm.

'Auntie Susan,' said Misty, returning the smarmy attitude and smiling in spite of rising discomfort, 'it's wonderful to see you.'

'Don't push it.' The smile dropped. 'What do you want?'

'Something's happened,' said Misty, heading straight to the point.

'I've heard. A private investigator stabbed in your club. People talk about such things, Misty.'

Auntie Susan sat back down and gestured to a chair opposite, encouraging Misty to do the same. 'I suppose if you're here without an appointment on a Sunday morning, dressed like Anneka Rice, you must have something important to tell me. Come on. Out with it.'

Misty's pulse throbbed in her neck with every beat of her heart. She sat down and tried not to show how intimidated she felt. 'It's about Atrax,' she said, 'the stabbing. We need to talk.'

Ugly as it was, honesty was the best policy with Auntie Susan. Misty was going to tell her the full story, starting with Sylvester visiting the club, and finishing with the discovery of Stefan Weber's photograph on Jeremy's camera. Auntie Susan may have information that could help, and even if she didn't, she needed to know the details. Like her or loathe her (and she mostly loathed her), the criminal queen before her was a vital part of Lady's Bar's survival. After all, it was possibly only Auntie Susan's bribery scheme that stood in the way of the bar being redeveloped by Atrax. If their scheme was about to be exposed by Jeremy Edmunds' photographs, Auntie Susan needed to know.

When Misty finished her tale, Auntie Susan plucked a fresh cigarette out of a tin and lit it, sending a plume of silver smoke into the space between them.

'Well, well . . .' she said, sucking a second puff, 'looks like you've shat the bed, Challenge Anneka.'

'What? I've done no such . . .'

'My side's clean, Misty. I'm tight as a duck's arse. So if there's been a leak from somewhere, it's you or Mandy with the runs. You've told someone, you must have.'

Misty held up her hands. 'Listen, I'm not here to make accusations about who may or may not have "shat the bed", which is a disgusting analogy by the way. I'm here because we need to find Jeremy to ask him what he knows and who *he* might have told. And because I thought you should know so we can be . . . extra careful.'

'Tsk,' tutted Auntie Susan. 'You've a nerve, telling me to be "extra careful", showing up here dressed like that in broad daylight.'

'You know what I mean.'

Auntie Susan clicked her fingers and the chihuahua came running from its bed, its little teeth bared in Misty's direction. She plucked it up off the floor and stroked it in her lap.

'What's he called?' asked Misty.

'Keanu.'

'Lovely.'

'What do you want, Misty? What are you hoping I can do for you?'

Keanu growled.

'I need help finding Jeremy Edmunds so we can work out how much trouble we're in. I wondered whether you might have a contact who could get me his phone records, his WhatsApps, location data or anything.'

Auntie Susan nodded. 'What's his phone number? I'll see what I can do.'

'And I wondered,' asked Misty, 'whether your contacts might have a better idea than me of where to start trying to identify the men in the suits.'

There was a severity in Auntie Susan's eye that told Misty she was pushing it. 'You're asking a lot, Misty Divine, but I can ask around quietly if you email me the photograph.'

'Thank you.'

She got up to leave, hoping her business here was done.

'Your partner doesn't know you're here, does she?' Auntie Susan asked with a smirk on her face.

'What?'

How does she know everything?

'You know, Mandy White, the squat and Scottish Soho power-lifter. This isn't the first time we've had a meeting without her.'

'What difference does that make?' asked Misty, realising she sounded like a petulant child.

'Seems like you're outperforming that ten percent you own,' tutted Auntie Susan, 'but I'm not surprised. Mandy didn't have the nerve when Lady Lady was knocking on my door and now you're here again, doing all the Lady's Bar dirty work for just a fraction of the profits. When will Mandy White pluck up the courage to earn her keep, I wonder? Or will she always let a drag queen shoulder the weight?'

Misty's defensiveness surfaced rapidly as Auntie Susan struck a nerve she hadn't even known was there. Misty had never thought about it this way, that Mandy was letting her bear the bar's burdens. 'That doesn't matter,' she snapped, trying not to show she'd been affected, 'but thank you for your help.' She turned on her sparkling heel and headed for the door, flicking her long white ponytail over her shoulder.

'Where do you think you're going, young lady?' asked Auntie Susan. 'Sit your perky arse back down. Our negotiation is not yet concluded.'

Uh oh . . . thought Misty, dread rising. *You don't make a deal with the devil and get away without paying.* She wanted something in return. She always did.

'I've been thinking,' she continued, lighting a fresh cigarette, 'about your Star Search competition. It's the final on Friday, isn't it?'

'It is . . .'

Where is she going with this?

'I thought it might be nice,' said Auntie Susan, 'if the organisers were to, for once, invite me to be a judge on the panel. I *am* one of the biggest bookers in the city, after all. Feels like I've been overlooked for a long time in that regard.'

'Oh, I see,' said Misty, horrified at the thought.

'If I were to be asked nicely, I'm sure the *illegal* information you've requested would be significantly easier to find. And of course, wouldn't it be nice for me to finally see Mandy White face to face? She'd love that, wouldn't she?'

'Of course.' Misty feigned a big plastic smile. 'Auntie Susan, we'd be honoured to have you on our judging panel.'

There was no way out of it.

CHAPTER 19

Misty got home in the early afternoon, having promised to keep Auntie Susan updated on her investigation into Jeremy Edmunds and vice versa. To her shock, when she stepped through the door, she found Miles standing in the living room. He had a jacket on like he was about to go out and there was a suitcase in the hall.

'Joe,' he said.

'Miles. I – I – erm . . .'

'What are you doing in drag? It's your day off.'

Shit.

'I had a meeting,' said Misty. 'I wasn't expecting to see you. You haven't texted.'

'In drag?'

'What?'

'You had a meeting in the red jumpsuit? On a Sunday?'

'Yes. What's this?' She pointed at the suitcase.

Miles sighed. 'I need some time away, Joe.' He sat on the sofa and put his head in his hands before looking back up steely-eyed. 'I need time away from you. From this, Misty, the bar, all of it. I just need a break.'

'OK . . .'

This wasn't a conversation for Misty to be having. This was a conversation for Joe.

'I think we should talk about it. Will you give me ten minutes to get changed and we can talk properly?'

Miles looked at his watch as though he had a schedule Misty didn't know about. 'Fine,' he said. 'I'll wait.'

Joe had never de-dragged so quickly and when they emerged from the bedroom in a pair of regular jeans and white shirt, they knew their eyes were still streaked with eyeliner that they hadn't fully removed. Talking to Miles was the priority.

Joe sat down opposite him.

'Do you want a cup of tea or anything?' they asked.

'No, thank you,' said Miles.

There was an uncomfortable pause and the suitcase by the door was enormous and imposing.

'I don't have much more to say,' said Miles.

Joe took a deep breath, trying to get back into the right headspace. The shift from Auntie Susan to Miles was a lot to process.

Start with an apology.

'I'm sorry that I lied. I feel like I'm in an impossible situation. Sylvester said I was in trouble and it turns out I might be.'

'Where were you today, Joe?' asked Miles. His voice was cold, hard, as though he wasn't even slightly interested in Misty's latest mystery.

Joe decided the best course of action was to tell the truth, just like they had with Auntie Susan, to explain what was going on even though Miles wouldn't like it. *No more lies.*

'I went to see Auntie Susan,' they admitted, embarrassed, and maybe a little ashamed.

Miles shook his head slowly like his entire body was brimming with disappointment. 'I knew it.'

'I had to, Miles,' said Joe. 'Everything's happened so fast, but please trust me when I tell you, everything I'm doing is to keep us safe.'

'That's not true,' said Miles. 'You're not doing this to keep us safe. You're doing it because it's exciting to you, this investigating thing you've got going on. This is what happened last time – you, wanting to play detective no matter the cost! But you're not a detective, Joe. When me and you went poking our noses all over London last year trying to find out who killed Lady Lady, we weren't detectives then either. I nearly died, Joe, just moments away from it, and I'm still sick. I can't *walk* properly! So don't you dare tell me any of this is for me. Don't you dare.'

Joe looked at their own feet. They felt the weight of responsibility for Miles' injuries and depression and knew deep down he was speaking the truth. Last year's investigation did indeed lead to his poisoning and it had been fuelled by Misty's thrill of the mystery, as well as her quest for justice for Lady Lady. But as Joe recalled, Miles had been a willing partner in those escapades, happy to play Watson to Misty's Sherlock as they hunted the killer together.

Now, wasn't Joe in the same situation again? Caught up in a danger that could only be resolved by pursuing Sylvester's case and finding Jeremy Edmunds?

'Miles,' they pleaded, 'this photographer took my picture and disappeared the same day, and nobody, not even the police, is looking for him. What if he's been kidnapped and needs rescuing? What if he's dead and I'm next? I don't know how you can't see it or what else you want me to say.'

'Yes, you do,' said Miles. 'You just don't want to say it.'

'Listen . . .' But before Joe could continue, they were interrupted by the doorbell.

Ding dong.

They both turned to look and Miles shrugged. Who would be calling unannounced on a Sunday afternoon? A sales call, a religious recruiter or bad news. And Joe didn't want any. They got up from the couch and opened the door.

They were taken aback to see a man they recognised. He was wiry, with muscly arms under a black Lonsdale T-shirt with yellow trim. He wore a tight pair of jeans and burgundy Doc Marten boots and on his cheek was a line of little scars, all in a row, like he'd been stabbed in the face with a fork. It was Auntie Susan's courier. When they first met him a year ago, Joe had named him Baseball Cap on account of his headgear.

'Delivery for Misty Divine,' said Baseball Cap, handing Joe a large brown envelope.

'Thank you,' they said, tucking it under their arm. The courier hurried away, down the walkway and steps to the street.

A delivery from Auntie Susan already . . . The phone records? The location data?

Joe closed the door and returned to the living room with a sinking feeling. Miles was bound to ask what was in the envelope and then they would have to open it in front of him and confess to another dodgy deal with Auntie Susan. *Christ, what a mess.*

'What's that?' asked Miles, just as Joe had predicted.

'I don't know,' they said. 'I haven't opened it.'

'Don't be smart.'

'I wasn't . . . never mind.'

'Open it then.'

Joe turned the envelope over in their hands. There was nothing on the outside, no note or writing or anything. 'You're going to be cross. When I open this, you're going to be annoyed with me.'

Miles rolled his eyes. 'I'm already annoyed with you, Joe.'

Joe tucked their thumb under the seal of the envelope and ripped it open. They pulled out a few sheets of paper with a Post-it note on top. It read: *More to follow. See you on Friday. AS x*

Auntie Susan, the Star Search's new grand finale judge. God . . . what had Misty got herself into?

'So, what is it?' asked Miles.

Joe flicked through the sheets of paper. 'It's phone records,' they said. 'For Jeremy Edmunds.'

'Phone records?' Miles was aghast. 'How did you get his . . .? This is Auntie Susan, isn't it?'

'Yes,' Joe admitted.

'And there's no way this is legal, is there?' asked Miles. 'I know this isn't the kind of information you can just download from Google.'

'No,' said Joe quietly. 'Probably not legal, but I need them if I'm going to find him. You said you wanted the bribery stopped. No more danger. For us to live a normal life again, that's what you said. Finding Jeremy is the only way I know how to do that.'

'I can't be here.' Miles waved his hands like the conversation was over and got up, walking to the hall. 'I'm going back to Mum and Dad's. Why don't you call me when you come to your senses?'

'Miles . . . don't.'

But it was too little, too late. Miles took his suitcase and slammed the door behind him, leaving Joe alone.

CHAPTER 20

Monday

As Joe sank their teeth into the first toasted pastry of the week, they looked at the jars of muesli ingredients that Miles kept on the kitchen side: glass urns of oats, dried fruits, seeds and nuts. They felt a pang of anxiety deep in their chest. Miles had gone. Left. Moved out for God knows how long. It had been a restless, lonely night.

'You've really fucked things up this time,' they muttered to themself quietly.

Joe expected that from an outsider's perspective, siding with Miles would be the obvious thing to do: to give up the investigation into Jeremy Edmunds, to stay away from Atrax and Auntie Susan . . . but they couldn't. They *wouldn't*. Not until they'd found the missing photographer. Miles would forgive them eventually, Joe thought.

Or will he?

Maybe this was it – the end. The end of the great romance that had started with a chance sighting through a hotel window. Joe didn't know what they'd do without Miles. He was everything. Joe's entire life.

They looked at Auntie Susan's envelope on the kitchen table.

The only way to get Miles back is to get us out of this once and for all. To clean up the mess. And the only way to do that is to keep going.

Last night, after Miles had left, Joe had been too upset to look at the phone records, but today, if there was any hope of saving their relationship, they needed to.

A wave of anguish crashed like a tsunami as they reopened the envelope and turned their attention to the sheets of paper inside. It was an itemised statement from O2, Jeremy's phone provider.

How did Auntie Susan get this so quickly?

It was best not to know.

They channelled all their energy into the task at hand. Of course, phone records wouldn't give them everything. Jeremy would have made calls and sent messages on WhatsApp, Zoom, FaceTime and a gazillion other internet-based communication apps that were triple-encrypted, but if he had used his actual phone plan, there might be something useful here.

The statement was a list of dates, times and call durations with accompanying phone numbers. Joe flicked through, noting it dated back six months, to when Jeremy had first moved to London and set up the account. Auntie Susan had been thorough.

The last number he'd called was on the afternoon before he vanished and the call had lasted three minutes.

Joe quickly typed the number into Google and found an immediate result: John Smith, the nerdy photographer. His contact details were listed on his website. Not much learned there, then. This call must have been when they arranged to meet at the Quill to hand over the camera.

Joe scanned the rest of the list. Most of the calls were to a US number. They cross-checked it with Sylvester's Patricia Edmunds meeting report. From what Joe could see, Jeremy called his mother every other day. They thought about how worried she must be, how stressed their own mother would be if they disappeared without a trace in a foreign country.

I'm trying, Patricia, they thought. *I'm doing my best to find him, even if no one else is.*

There weren't many other contacts in the records. A few 0845 numbers were included that Joe was able to quickly identify as telephone banking services.

Damn.

There was one more that popped up, a British mobile number Jeremy had called three times in the days before his disappearance. Joe searched for it but found nothing.

They wondered whether a real detective would have access to a database of phone numbers. Would Sylvester or DI Davies have been able to work out who this mystery number belonged to in a flash?

It was starting to feel as though the extent of Joe's investigative prowess lay with typing things into search engines. *There must be a better way.* Joe wrote the unknown number down in their pink investigation notebook with a double exclamation point. *Who was Jeremy calling?* There was only one person connected to a real detective Joe had access to: Sylvester Green's assistant, Divya. And according to her voicemail, she was due back in the office this morning.

It's time to finally meet Divya.

*

Joe arrived at Great Windmill Street just after 10.30 a.m. They'd bought a revolting green smoothie on the way, thinking that vitamins were probably now overdue following their two-day Pop-Tart marathon. They managed to finish half of it before the straw became clogged with a piece of spinach, which Joe saw as a sign from the heavens, promptly binning the rest in silent celebration.

Tucked into their satchel was the pink notebook, Jeremy's phone records and a USB stick with copies of the photographs from Jeremy's camera. Sylvester had said they should trust Divya, so they'd brought everything they'd discovered so far.

With Miles out of the picture and Mandy hesitant to investigate, Joe could certainly do with somebody to talk to, preferably someone less scary than Auntie Susan. They hoped that's what they'd find in Divya.

They pressed the buzzer next to the sticky tape that read 'Sylvester Green' and waited. A woman's voice answered. 'Sylvester Green's office.'

'Hello,' said Joe, 'my name's Joe Brown. I'm one of the owners of Lady's Bar on Old Compton Street. My other name is—'

'Misty Divine,' said Divya. 'I've been expecting you. Please, come up.'

Here we go, thought Joe as the door clicked open, reminiscing on the breaking and entering they'd done here just a few days before.

Divya was waiting on the first-floor landing. She was younger than Joe had expected, in her late twenties, and beautifully dressed in a smart suit with pointed shoes that Misty Divine herself would have envied. Her hair was long and glossy and hung over her shoulders down to her chest.

'Should I call you Misty, or Joe?' she asked straight away. 'And what are your pronouns? Best to know from the off isn't it? I'm she/her.'

Joe was taken aback. It wasn't often that people asked this when they first met, but Joe felt pleased Divya had. It made them feel at home with her, at ease.

'Call me Joe, and out of drag I'm a they/them,' they smiled. 'When I'm in drag, it's Misty, she/her.'

'Understood.' Divya nodded, holding out her arm for a handshake. 'It's nice to meet you, Joe, though I'm saddened it's under such dark circumstances.'

'How is Sylvester?' asked Joe.

'Come inside, come inside,' said Divya, ushering Joe into the little waiting area. Their memory flashed up images of rifling through the filing cabinets, of the men in suits destroying Jeremy's file. 'Would you like some tea? I have fresh mint.'

'That would be lovely.'

Divya set about boiling a kettle that stood on a fridge in the corner of the reception area. She moved as though she weighed nothing at all, gliding through the office, plucking leaves from a plant growing on her desk and dropping them into a glass teapot. This was the kind of healthy beverage Joe would aspire to make but never bother. Furthermore, there was no sunlight in the Lady's Bar basement office and a potted mint would be dead within minutes.

'Sylvester is in a very serious condition,' said Divya, 'and he still hasn't woken up. I've been with him since Friday.'

'I'm sorry to hear that,' said Joe. They thought of the white suit, the blood. *You must . . . find . . . Jeremy.* 'Have the doctors said . . . do they know if he's . . .?'

'They say he'll pull through but it will be a long road.' She was difficult to read, as though she was hiding her emotions very well, but Joe was immensely relieved to hear Sylvester would survive.

She placed the teapot and two cups on the coffee table and sat on a leather armchair opposite Joe.

'We'll let it steep,' she said.

'He came to see me,' said Joe. 'Sylvester. The night before he was stabbed and then again on Friday morning. It was me who called the ambulance. I did everything I could to stop the bleeding.'

Divya placed her hand on Joe's. 'You probably saved his life,' she said kindly. 'If you hadn't been there he'd have certainly died.'

'He said I should talk to you if anything happened to him. Do you know what he was investigating? Jeremy Edmunds?' Joe asked.

'I do,' said Divya. 'That's why I've been expecting you. I also know you searched his office here on Friday, let's get that out in the open now.'

Caught.

Joe was shocked, guilty, but unsurprised. They supposed now it would have been foolish to think they could break into a detective's office without anybody knowing. Their cheeks flushed red.

Divya smiled. 'There are cameras of course, in the pot plants.' She stood up and walked to the fridge, taking out a punnet of strawberries. 'I watched your close call with those men when I arrived this morning. You were smart, to hide behind the door like you did.'

'I'm sorry,' said Joe. 'I know I shouldn't have . . .'

'He gave you the keys, right?' asked Divya.

Joe nodded.

'Then I think you probably did exactly what he wanted you to do.'

'Can you explain what's going on?' asked Joe as Divya rejoined them at the table. 'I need to know, why was my picture in Jeremy's file? Why did Sylvester say I'm in danger?'

'I don't know details,' she said, holding up her hands, 'but I know a few headlines.'

'Tell me,' said Joe. 'Please tell me what you know.'

They sipped hot mint as Divya told Joe how Sylvester had accepted the case when Jeremy Edmunds' mother, Patricia, showed up at the office. She'd made her way from Chicago to London to try finding her son herself, appalled at the lack of interest from the police and press, and champing at the bit to spread the word about Jeremy's disappearance. She'd arrived with armfuls of posters and flyers, but had no luck. Before she returned to the States, she hired Sylvester to continue the search – she chose him because he was the closest private investigator's office to the Quill.

Divya explained that Patricia and Sylvester had had a long consultation in private in Sylvester's office. Cameras were always off for client meetings, so she didn't know what they might have discussed beyond what was described in Sylvester's meeting report.

'When Sylvester arrived at Lady's Bar on Friday, injured, all the pages of his notebook were missing. Torn out.'

'Hmm . . . that's not like him,' said Divya seriously. 'There's no way he'd have done that himself. He's always very specific about how he keeps his notebooks. Meticulous about them. He never removes a page in case the book needs submitting as evidence at a later date.'

'I think it was those men in suits,' said Joe, leaning in, 'the ones who searched the office. I think they're behind the stabbing and the notebook. They destroyed the file and thought by destroying Sylvester's notebook too they'd get rid of all trace of the investigation.'

'But who are they?' asked Divya, balancing her chin in her fingertips.

'I don't know but I think Jeremy does, if he's still alive. I found something . . .'

They told Divya about the Quill CCTV footage, meeting John Smith, the photos on the camera, and she listened with sincere intrigue.

'One thing I haven't worked out is, if the photos on the camera were Jeremy's insurance policy, how did Sylvester get the one of me? How was it in his file?'

'Ah,' said Divya. 'That I can tell you. On the first day of Sylvester's investigation he managed to access Jeremy's Dropbox account, with Patricia's help to guess the password. The photo of you was the only file in it from the week he disappeared. Sylvester showed it to me because he loved your blue hair.'

Who doesn't *love the blue hair?* thought Joe.

'What about the other photos? The ones of Stefan Weber and the men in suits? They weren't in the Dropbox?'

'Not that I'm aware of,' said Divya. 'I never saw them but, as I said, he doesn't tell me everything.'

She plucked the pointed green leaves from the top of a strawberry and popped the whole thing into her mouth. Joe picked one from the punnet and did the same.

'I have something else,' they said. 'Jeremy's phone records.'

'Interesting . . .' said Divya. 'Do I want to know where you sourced them?'

'Probably not,' Joe replied, thinking of Keanu's snarling tiny teeth, 'but there's a number in there, one I couldn't find on the internet. I wondered if you had a database or system where we can find out who it belongs to.'

'I don't,' said Divya. 'I'm just the assistant here, Sylvester's administrator. Anything like that, he'd do himself.'

'Damn,' said Joe. 'I was hoping you'd have a trick up your sleeve.'

''Fraid not.'

Joe had to admit they were disappointed, and they realised they'd been expecting Divya to crack the case wide open.

'We'll have to call it then,' they said, sliding the O2 statement out of their satchel.

'Call it?' echoed Divya. 'Now?' She looked unsettled at the thought but also a smidge excited, hankering to help for Sylvester.

'No time like the present,' said Joe.

She reached out and took the papers, 'You're right! One thing I have learned from Sylvester is that sometimes the most obvious solution is best. I'll make the call.' Switching to her desk, she tapped the mystery number into her phone and pushed a button that put it on loudspeaker.

It rang, just once, and then went straight to voicemail.

'Hello, you've reached Jessica Gethyn. I can't answer the phone right now, but leave me a message and I'll get you back.'

Joe could hardly believe it.

Divya ended the call without leaving a message.

'Jessica Gethyn,' she said. 'Know her?'

'Yes, actually,' said Joe. 'She's a journalist. She wrote Lady Lady's obituary last year and an article about Atrax, the company Stefan Weber owns.'

Divya returned to the coffee table and scratched her scalp with elegant nails. 'OK, so Jeremy took a photo of the Atrax CEO and has also been in communication with a journalist who wrote about them. That's something, right? What do you know about Atrax?'

More than I should tell you, thought Joe.

They might trust Divya with the details of the Jeremy Edmunds case, but letting her in on the deal with Auntie Susan was an impossibility. That agreement was *'tight as a duck's arse'*, as the nightmare queen herself might say. Joe couldn't reveal that to anybody.

'All I know about them,' said Joe, offering Divya half the story, 'is that they're proposing a redevelopment project for the Lady's Bar building. We don't know if it's Atrax directly or one of their clients. They're very secretive.'

Divya sighed and patted the palms of her hands together. 'Now we're joining the dots . . . Atrax is trying to take over your building. Jeremy has pictures of you, and Stefan Weber, and is in contact with Jessica Gethyn. Sylvester must have made the same connection. That's why he came to warn you.'

'Divya,' Joe replied. 'This is dangerous. The stabbing, the

break-in, the disappearance of Jeremy . . . I want to find him, to get to the bottom of it, but the truth is I'm on my own and I'm stuck.'

'I'm an administrator, Joe. I do the bills and the filing and the contracts.' She shook her head gently and her long hair spread around her shoulders. 'I can't wave a magic wand and get you any answers.'

'But will you help me?' Joe asked, thinking of how both Miles and Mandy had given up, how they'd abandoned them and warned them away from pursuing the investigation. 'Sylvester said I could trust you.'

'And you can,' said Divya. 'Trust that I want to find Jeremy and get justice for Sylvester too. I have to remind you though, Joe, I'm not an investigator . . . and neither are you.'

CHAPTER 21

They sat in silence for a while. Divya picked apart another strawberry and Joe took a slurp of mint tea that was now lukewarm and bitter.

'What should we do first?' she asked herself out loud, closing her eyes to reveal eyeliner that was exquisitely neat. She breathed steadily through her nostrils and Joe waited, watching her think.

'I can look for Jessica Gethyn's address,' she said eventually, opening her eyes, 'if you don't already have it. I know how to do that. Would that be useful?'

It would be useful, Joe thought. *Very useful.*

'Yes,' they said immediately.

I can turn up unannounced just as Jessica did at Lady Lady's funeral.

Divya went back to the desk, nudging her mouse to awaken the computer. 'Provided she hasn't moved since the last election, she might be on the electoral register and I do have access to that.'

'Really? You can find that?'

'I can,' she replied. 'It's public record.' She tapped and clicked and typed a little, and Joe waited impatiently. 'Got it! She lives near Angel station, in Islington.'

Joe jumped up as she scribbled the address on to a sheet of printer paper. 'Brilliant, Divya, this is brilliant! Let's go.'

'Go?!' she scoffed. 'What, me and you? To Jessica's house?'

'Yes! You said you want to get justice for Sylvester, and I want to find Jeremy Edmunds. We can do it together – two heads are better than one and all that.'

Divya patted her hands together again and Joe realised this was her thinking move. 'I don't know . . . I'm never out and about with Sylvester. I'm an office bod.'

'Come on,' Joe pleaded. 'All we'll do is knock on her door and ask her how she knows Jeremy Edmunds. It'll be easy.'

'I suppose it would make me feel of use to Sylvester instead of just sitting here waiting for the hospital to call. Is it against the rules though? To go questioning people if we're not actual investigators. We don't have qualifications or anything.'

Joe took this as a sharp criticism because they'd been paying little attention to any rules whatsoever. They replied, 'I'll admit I don't know the ins and outs of the investigation business, but I'm pretty sure that stabbing a detective and shredding his files is even more against the rules than us going to talk to Jessica would be. We'd just be asking a few questions. She can always tell us to piss off if she doesn't like it.'

Divya processed the idea, thinking it through carefully. 'OK,' she said eventually. 'I'll come with you.'

Once the lights were switched off and the office doors locked, they headed down the stairs to the street.

'How long have you worked for Sylvester?' Joe asked on the way.

'Gosh,' said Divya, 'getting on for ten years. Since I was nineteen. His wife was his assistant before that, but she passed away.'

'Oh dear,' said Joe, 'that's sad.'

'Yes,' said Divya. 'I don't like to speak ill of the dead and God rest her soul, but professionally she was a bit of a catastrophe. The files were in disarray and everything was done on paper. Most things still are! He was even using fax, can you believe? I've been trying to bring him into the twenty-first century but he resists. He's old school.'

They climbed into the back of a taxi and Joe gave the driver Jessica's address.

'I should tell you,' said Joe as the car set off, 'I met Jessica once before. Last year.'

'Do you know her well?' asked Divya.

'Not at all. After she wrote Lady Lady's obituary I tried to get in contact with her to see if she might know anything about her murder. She didn't reply, but she showed up at the funeral telling me to stay away from Atrax.'

'Hmm . . .' Divya pulled a hair bobble out of her pocket and tied her locks into a low ponytail, clearing the hair out of her face. 'Maybe she had a point. Poor Sylvester.'

She whipped up her phone quickly and Joe glanced at the screen to see her typing Jessica's name into the internet. Their taxi wound through the Soho streets as Divya rapidly used her thumb to scroll the search results.

'She's a finance writer. A politics writer. What's she doing writing drag queen obituaries? No offence.'

'None taken. I wondered the same myself – that's why I

reached out to her. I assumed she must have known about Atrax trying to take over the bar.'

'Yes,' said Divya, 'that would be my guess too.'

But did she also know about the bribery that was stopping them? That's what Joe needed to find out. That, and whether she knew what had happened to Jeremy Edmunds.

Jessica Gethyn lived on Colebrooke Row, a line of red-brick townhouses with grand doors and beautiful little gardens. Divya's research said Jessica shared a first-floor flat with a woman called Rachel Packet. It was a nice area to live, thought Joe as the taxi pulled up outside the house. Jessica's writing and public speaking engagements must pay her handsomely.

Joe paid the driver, then walked with Divya up a short path. They pushed the doorbell and waited.

A woman who was not Jessica answered. She was rushed, her blonde hair a mess, a bag half-on, half-off her shoulder.

'Yes?' she said, already annoyed.

'Hi,' said Joe. 'We're looking for Jessica Gethyn. Is she here?'

'She's not,' said the woman. Her skin was blotchy and her cheeks puffy, like she hadn't slept.

'We're investigators,' Joe followed up in a hurry. They sensed Divya giving them the side eye.

'We *work* for an investigator,' she clarified.

The blonde woman's irritation instantly subsided and relief seemed to pour out of her. 'Oh, thank God, you're the police. I've been trying to get hold of someone all morning.'

'No,' said Divya. 'We're definitely not the police. We're working with a private investigator, Sylvester Green.'

'Are you expecting the police?' asked Joe, curious to know why the woman was so visibly stressed.

'Well I'm bloody hoping for them!' she snapped with loose lips. 'I've been ringing them non-stop.'

'Why?' asked Divya. 'Has something happened?'

'Jessica hasn't been home since Friday. I can't reach her on the phone and nobody's heard from her. I'm at my wits' end! Isn't that why you're here?!'

Joe had come here expecting all sorts of possible outcomes: friendly chats with Jessica, being told to 'get lost' by Jessica . . . the thought of finding Jeremy Edmunds in Jessica's bed had even crossed their mind. What they hadn't expected was that Jessica would be missing too.

She's missing?! Like Jeremy?

Runaway, kidnapped, dead in a ditch?

'Can you help?' There were tears in the woman's eyes and she looked forlorn and wretched. 'If you're with an investigator, can you help?' she begged.

'I don't know,' said Joe. 'We'll try.'

'I'm Rachel,' she said, holding out her hand for introductory shakes. 'I'm Jessica's flatmate. Come in, please come in.' She turned her back to them and headed into the house.

Joe and Divya followed her inside and Joe planned a new question to write in their notebook:

Where is Jessica Gethyn?

Rachel led them up the stairs and through an aquamarine painted door on the first floor. *A jazzy blue*, Joe thought.

'Do you want a tea or coffee or something?' she asked as

146

they entered a very clean and tidy apartment. 'I think I have some juice.'

'No thank you,' said Divya and Joe shook their head. She seemed jumpy, twitching her jacket sleeves with her fingertips. A fish out of water.

'OK, come through.' Rachel walked them down a pristine hallway to the flat's living room. It was modern, with chic furniture and all the latest mod-cons. There was a potted hydrangea in the centre of the fireplace and the mantle was loaded with a set of journalism awards, each one engraved with Jessica's name.

'Nice place,' said Divya, looking around.

'Thank you,' said Rachel. 'Please, sit.' They did as she instructed and perched on the edge of a yellow sofa that was neatly lined with Liberty print cushions. 'So you say you're private investigators?' she asked as she tucked a loose strand of hair behind her ear and leaned towards them.

'Yes,' said Joe. 'Well, kind of.'

'No,' said Divya, shooting them daggers with her eyes. 'I work for an investigator called Sylvester Green. I'm his assistant. Joe is our . . . temporary associate.'

'I've never heard of this Sylvester Green,' said Rachel. 'Does he know that Jessica hasn't been home? Is that why you're here?'

'Sylvester was attacked on Friday,' Joe told her. 'And the notes in his case files led us to an article Jessica wrote. We didn't know she was missing until just now. Is it like her to disappear like this?'

'Not like her at all,' Rachel replied. 'She always tells me

where she's going and when she's coming back, but when I got in from work on Friday she wasn't here and hasn't been home since. I can't get her on the phone, by text or email. I've tried everything. I'm worried out of my mind.'

Divya was running her fingertips backwards and forwards over an embroidered patch on one of the fancy cushions and Joe wondered if perhaps she shouldn't have come. 'You said you'd called the police,' she asked. 'Have they helped at all?'

'No,' replied Rachel, and she placed her hands on her hips. 'There are too many missing people and they said Jessica had probably just gone on holiday without telling me! I *know* that's not true. I was thinking about contacting those missing persons charities today, to see if any of them had any advice. That's why I was so glad to see you. Do you think you can help find her?'

'We'll certainly try,' said Joe.

'We can't make any promises,' added Divya. 'We're helping Sylvester because he's injured, but we don't have the resources of real investigators. We're just trying to understand what's happened and how it's all connected.'

'OK, OK. I understand. God, this is stressful.'

'Rachel,' said Joe calmly, 'what can you tell us about Jessica? Does she talk to you about her work?'

'Never. She's very secretive about that – always wants to protect the scoop, you see. She says I have to read it in the paper like everyone else. She's really good at it though. She wins prizes and trophies and all sorts.' She pointed at the shelf of awards as if to demonstrate Jessica's success. The elegant way she moved her arm reminded Joe of the models who show-cased prizes on gameshows like *The Price is Right*. 'She's been freelancing, trying new things, and it's going well but she's been . . . quieter, I suppose. I called all the publications she's worked with recently – I even called her old boss – and nobody's heard from her at all since Friday. There will be loads of other colleagues I don't have details for though. She must have dozens of contacts I don't know.'

'What about friends or family?' asked Joe. 'Does she have anyone else she might be staying with? Anyone she might have told where she was going?' This was a whole new can of worms – a second missing person connected to Atrax, connected to Misty and Lady's Bar.

'I don't think so. She doesn't have much family. Just her mum, Alice, who's in a home near Archway station. She has dementia or something. Jessica moved her there last year because she was getting confused. I even called them to see if she'd visited, but they haven't seen her since last week either.'

'And there isn't anyone else?' asked Divya. 'Friends? Romantic interests?'

Rachel sighed deeply. 'No. She dates a lot, but there's no one close. It's a new woman every week it seems. She meets them on the dating apps but hasn't had a girlfriend in years. Don't tell her I told you this, but it's mostly one-night stands. Jessica's a bit of a Casanova by all accounts. I'm probably the person who's closest to her, but even with me she's secretive. She spends most of her time working . . . and shagging. I keep telling her, you need to get out more, with actual friends, but she never listens.'

Rachel seemed flustered and it was all tumbling out, fast and furious.

'What about a photographer called Jeremy Edmunds?'

asked Joe, moving to the crux of it all. 'He's an American who's also missing. Have you ever heard her mention him?'

'Jeremy? No,' said Rachel with what seemed like absolute certainty. 'Who's he?'

'Nobody important,' said Divya, shutting Joe down before they went any further. 'He's someone else Sylvester was working with. Just a long shot.'

Rachel rocked forward and dug her fingers into her thighs.

'What can we do?' she pleaded. 'What can I do? It's terrifying – people can't just vanish without anyone caring. How is it possible that I'm the only one who cares?'

Joe reached forward and patted gently on Rachel's knee. 'We care, Rachel. That's why we're here.'

CHAPTER 22

They left Jessica's posh flat and Joe was perturbed by the latest developments. Should they have pushed more about Jeremy? Divya obviously hadn't wanted them to.

Could Jessica be with Jeremy somewhere?

Joe hoped there wasn't a secret ditch filling up with bodies. Would Misty be next? Would Mandy or, God forbid, Miles?

Divya had been cautious in there, and Joe could sense she was antsy being out of the office, about crossing the line from administrator to investigator.

Beyond the elephant-sized fact that Jessica had vanished like Jeremy, they'd learned a few things about her that helped build a picture of her in Joe's mind. Hard-working, successful, secretive. A prolific womanizer. But they hadn't learned about her work, or a connection to Jeremy, or anything that might help them find either of them.

'What do you think?' asked Divya as they exited the house on to Colebrooke Row.

'I don't think it's a coincidence that Jessica and Jeremy were both looking into Atrax and now they've both disappeared,' said Joe. 'There's something rotten happening here.'

'Agreed,' said Divya. 'Definitely not a coincidence, but

where are they? You don't think . . .' she hesitated and used her fingernail to scrape mascara out of her tear duct. 'Do you think they've been killed by whoever tried to kill Sylvester?'

'I don't know,' said Joe. 'It's possible, but I hope not.'

'I don't like it,' she replied. 'We should go to the police now. This is all very disturbing.'

Absolutely not, thought Joe. Taking this to the police would reveal the Lady's Bar secret survival plan and land everyone in hot water. They couldn't even imagine the wrath of Auntie Susan in such a situation.

'The police already have information they haven't pieced together yet,' they said, trying to soothe Divya and keep her calm. 'Rachel reported Jessica's disappearance and Patricia reported Jeremy's, but they've done nothing. We don't have the answers yet, but once we do, as soon as we know who stabbed Sylvester, or we've found Jeremy and Jessica, *then* we go to the police. We need to take them answers.'

She huffed, thumping her palms against her thighs. 'I don't like it,' she repeated.

Joe didn't either. It was a rabbit hole, this Jessica Gethyn business. A new thread of the investigation that was taking them deeper and deeper into a conspiracy worthy of a Julia Roberts adaptation.

'You don't have to do this with me,' they said. 'If you'd rather go back to the office, I can go on alone.'

'No, I want to help. I feel like I should, for Sylvester. I know he'd do it for me. But what do we do next?'

'Rachel did give us a lead,' said Joe.

'What's that?' asked Divya, and Joe wondered how she could have missed it.

'Jessica's mother, in the home near Archway. She's the only other person we've heard about.'

'What about her?'

'We should go to see her,' said Joe with enthusiasm. 'She might know where Jessica is, and Jessica might know where Jeremy is. Maybe they're even together.'

'I'm not sure,' Divya replied. She patted her palms together and squinted, deep in thought. 'It feels like we're veering off the road. The Sylvester road.'

'The Jeremy-Jessica road and the Sylvester road are one and the same,' said Joe. 'Everything's connected and, right now, Jessica's mum is the only lead we have. I think we should go to Archway.'

Divya reluctantly agreed.

A quick online search revealed three care homes near Archway station.

'Call them then,' urged Divya. She seemed impatient and Joe wondered whether she was fully on board or just wanted it to be over and done with.

They dialled the first home, but it was a strike-out as the receptionist told them there was no Alice Gethyn there. They called the second, a place called Daffodil House, and this time they had more luck.

'Jessica's asked me to stop by and visit her mum for her,' Joe said, cooking up their cover story on the spot. 'She's had to go out of town for a story and was worried Alice might be lonely without any visitors. I'm in the area this afternoon if that's any good?'

The receptionist assured them that Alice was fine but

a visit would of course be appreciated. Joe gave Divya a thumbs up.

'We're in?' she asked as they tucked away their mobile.

Joe couldn't hold back their smile, elated that it had been so easy.

'It's like working with a drag queen Sherlock Holmes,' Mandy had said.

They travelled again by taxi, determining that would be the fastest way to get to Daffodil House from their current location.

'Have you ever thought about becoming an investigator?' Joe asked. 'About doing what Sylvester does?'

'No,' she replied. 'You might have noticed, but it's not for me. I'm a computer person. I'm good with systems and data, and I like that. It makes more sense to me than people. I wouldn't like the stress.'

'You don't think eventually you'd want a promotion or anything?'

Divya tugged at her ponytail and let out a sigh. 'Honestly, Joe, I wouldn't. I like to go to work, nine to five, collect my pay check and go home. I don't want to be following cheating husbands to hotels in the middle of the night like he does. I especially don't want to be doing all *this*. My only ambition is to save up enough money to buy a little flat, have my friends and family over for dinner, and live a quiet life. It's a job for me, not a passion.' She folded her arms in a sign that this was her final word on the subject.

Her attitude was refreshing for Joe. Everyone else they knew was striving for the next thing, or at least pretending to.

Miles was always planning the next career move. The drags all wanted bigger gigs, better gigs, TV opportunities, more fame and fortune. It was unusual, Joe thought, but delightful, to meet somebody who was content where they were.

'Do you live in London?' they asked, moving the conversation along as Divya looked out the window at the London streets.

'Yes,' she said. 'North London, with my sister and her daughters. They're sixteen so it's a house of four women. It's rowdy.' She ran her fingers across her eyebrows and some of the tension in her shoulders softened. Talking about her family had comforted her. 'But I've spotted one of those shared-ownership developments and I'm saving up for a deposit. Hopefully next year I'll have my own place.'

They rode without speaking for a while and Joe noticed her tapping her foot up and down against the seat in front of her.

'Are you OK?' they said. 'Doing this? Going to see Alice Gethyn?'

Divya turned from the window to face Joe eye to eye. 'No, I'm not OK, Joe. I'm not OK with any of this. Sylvester in hospital, my workplace broken into. Taxiing all over London and questioning a crying woman . . . I didn't sign up for this.'

Joe nodded. 'Neither did I, Divya. You really don't have to come if you don't want. I can go by myself, I mean it.'

She looked away, breaking the eye contact. 'I'll come. If you'd sat at his bedside for the last three days like I have, watched his breathing and seen his sheet-white face, you'd understand. I'll come for Sylvester, but I don't have to like it.'

Joe remembered Lady Lady's contorted face on her dressing-room floor and simply replied, 'I understand.'

Divya whipped out her wallet as they pulled up outside Daffodil House, tapping a bank card against the reader.

'I'll put this on Sylvester's account,' she said. Joe was relieved, because the fare totalled £27 and the memory of the Quill membership was still fresh and sore.

They climbed out on to the pavement and Joe took in the sight of the care home. It was a miserable-looking place. The outside was pebble-dashed with small grey stones and a pitiful front garden was overgrown and needed urgent tending.

What a place to end your days, they thought, thinking briefly about where they might end up in their own old age. *Hopefully somewhere nicer than this.*

Hopefully somewhere with Miles. An LGBTQ+ retirement home in the countryside with big gardens and pet dogs, where Joe and Miles could sit by a window in matching pyjamas and watch birds hopping across the lawn . . . that's what Joe was hoping for.

Daffodil House looked as though it had been built in the 1970s and the path that ran from the pavement to the front door was crazy-paving, a large-scale concrete slab mosaic that had once been all the rage. Joe supposed it might have looked nice when it was first laid, but now there were weeds growing through all the cracks and it looked shoddy and unkempt.

'Deep breath, deep breath,' said Divya, steeling herself and clenching her fists by her sides. When she was done she turned to Joe and asked, 'Ready to go in?'

'Sure am,' said Joe, not sure if that was entirely true. 'Are you?'

'For Sylvester . . .'

They walked up the path to the front door and Joe pushed the bell. It sounded a drawn-out electronic beep, low and slow, as though the thing was running out of battery.

A thin woman with ginger hair appeared. She was dressed in a white tunic and her cheeks were glowing red like she'd been run ragged all morning long.

'Can I help you?' she asked. She seemed irritated, in the middle of something else and without the time to deal with a pair of strangers.

'We're friends of Jessica Gethyn,' said Joe with a veneer of great confidence that wasn't the truth. 'She asked us to stop in and visit Alice. I called ahead.'

The story they'd created rolled off their tongue. Joe wondered whether this was how Sylvester and other real detectives worked, with trickery and half-truths. Damn, they weren't dealing in half-truths any more. These were flat-out lies.

'Oh yes,' the care worker replied. 'My manager did mention you'd be coming. Alice is in the dining room. She's only been a tiny bit difficult today, you'll be pleased to hear.'

'Difficult?' asked Divya with caution.

'Oh, the confusion. Overall it's a good day. You'll be fine for a visit.'

'Are you sure?' asked Divya, evidently guilty that they were lying their way into an old people's home.

I should feel guilty too, thought Joe. *Miles would be appalled.*

There was no time for guilt. There were now two missing people, on top of the stabbed detective.

And one old woman who might have the answers.

The care worker swung open the door and beckoned with her free hand for them to come inside.

'The dining room is just down the hall on the left.' She pointed towards a bleak corridor with old-fashioned paintings of countryside scenes on the walls. They stepped inside.

The first thing that struck Joe was the smell: bleach. It was almost overpowering and Joe wanted to hold their breath for as long as possible so as not to breathe it in. The whole place made them feel sad inside, but at least it was clean.

'I'm on my way to fetch her lunch, but you can go ahead and I'll join you shortly,' said the care worker.

'There's no need,' said Joe. 'We'll be fine on our own.'

The ginger woman was taken aback, like it was highly unusual for her not to be wanted in the room. 'Are you sure?' she asked.

'We'll be fine,' said Divya, with a tone that made it perfectly clear the carer wasn't needed, or wanted.

'OK,' she said. 'There's a phone in the room. Call 01 if you need a member of staff, or if Alice seems distressed at all.'

'Thank you,' said Joe.

The care worker made her way through a door behind the reception desk, leaving Joe and Divya alone in the entrance, both of them looking at the corridor to the dining room.

Divya whispered, 'This feels really wrong, doesn't it?'

Joe couldn't argue with her. 'Yes,' they replied, 'but what else are we going to do? Sit in the office and wait until someone else disappears without a trace?'

'Perhaps we shouldn't do this,' she said. 'It might be better to go back after all . . .'

Sylvester's words rang through Joe's head, an echo on a loop from days before.

You're in danger, Misty. You must find Jeremy.

'We're here now. Let's just do it.'

Joe set off first and Divya followed close behind, her heels clicking loudly against the hard linoleum floor. Rooms along the way were labelled with what seemed to be the names of the residents. Joe noticed the last one before the dining room had a laminated print-out taped to it that read 'Alice G'.

They pushed open wooden doors with glass panels that led to a room set up like a café, or a B&B breakfast room. It was nice. Cosy. There was only one person in it, an old woman in a red cardigan sitting at a table near a patio window. Beyond her lay a pretty garden full of summer flowers.

Alice Gethyn. Jessica Gethyn's mother.

Joe felt instantly anxious, hot, sweaty under their blouse. This was so intrusive, to be here, to question someone's elderly, ill mother.

Her daughter's missing.

Patricia Edmunds' son is missing.

Your boyfriend's left you.

'Alice?' said Divya kindly, hiding her nerves well.

'Yes?' Alice smiled in return. Joe noticed that at least three of her front teeth were gold and she seemed placid, quiet, as peaceful as the garden she'd been watching.

'Is it OK if we talk to you for a little bit? We don't want to disturb you.'

She readjusted her position in the chair, leaning into one of the arms. 'You don't have to talk to me like I'm a baby, you know.'

'Sorry,' said Divya. 'We thought . . .'

'You thought that because I'm here I'd be drooling into a corner, well let me tell you, that might happen on the days when I'm . . . away, but there's no drool now as far as I'm aware.'

'Nope,' said Divya. 'No drool.'

'Then it must be a good day,' said Alice, winking. To Joe she seemed sharp as a tack.

'I'm Divya Manohar.'

'And I'm Joe Brown.'

'She's in trouble, isn't she?' said Alice. 'Jessica's in trouble.'

'We think so,' said Joe.

Divya and Joe sat down in the chairs opposite Alice. A small coffee table between them was stained with the rings of a thousand cups of tea.

'Do you want a cuppa?' asked Alice. 'Or squash? They won't serve anything harder, I'm afraid. I'd kill for a Cognac.'

'I'm fine, thank you,' said Joe and Divya agreed. No drinks were necessary.

'So come on, out with it,' said Alice. 'What are you here for? What's she done?'

'Jessica hasn't been home for a few days, and we wondered whether she'd talked to you about what she was working on?' said Joe, right to the point.

Divya sighed and rolled her eyes, as though Joe had asked completely the wrong thing and should have warmed into the conversation. They nodded at her to tell her *go on then, you do it*. Two amateurs, that's what it felt like.

'Joe's right,' said Divya steadily. 'Jessica hasn't been home since Friday and we don't want to worry you, please don't be worried. We're trying to find her, but we wondered if you might know where she could be.'

Alice bit her bottom lip with a golden fang.

'She was here,' she said. 'I don't know when. Maybe last week. I have my funny days, you see, when I'm not quite here, not like I used to be. But *she* was here. I don't think it was long ago. Last week perhaps . . . yes, last week.'

'And how was she?' asked Divya, leaning forward. 'Did she seem OK to you?'

'She brought biscuits,' said Alice, smiling happily. 'Shortbreads, my favourite. You know the Scottish ones in the tartan wrapper? Oh, but you're not here to talk about biscuits. About Jessica . . . Jessica. She seemed . . . fine.'

Joe caught themself tapping their foot on the worn carpet, frustrated, wishing Divya would hurry up and get some answers.

'Did she mention her work to you?' they interrupted. Divya sat back in her chair and Joe spotted a hint of a scowl.

'She's a journalist,' said Alice. 'Won trophies for it, she has.'

'Yes,' replied Joe. 'She's very talented. Do you know what she was planning to write about next?'

Alice thought for a moment, puzzling over the questions. Eventually she said, 'Financials. That's what she was working on.'

Joe groaned inside. They weren't getting anywhere here.

'Has she ever mentioned anyone called Jeremy Edmunds to you, Alice?' they asked. 'He's a photographer from the United States.'

'No, dear. Jessica's a lesbian.'

Joe laughed. 'Oh, yes, I know. I didn't mean—'

'We didn't have them in our day, you know, the lesbians.' Alice took a long, slow drink of blackcurrant squash out of a plastic cup. 'Well, we did and we didn't. Of course there *were* lesbians, but they were more discreet about it. For a time, I think. Kept it to themselves more, where I lived anyway. Then there were those ones on the news who invaded the BBC studios. Do you remember that? Ha! They weren't messing around! Good for them. When was that? Never mind, I expect you're too young to remember. Anyway, it wasn't like these days, that's what I'm saying. Lesbians all over the place now, shouting it from the rooftops. Good for them, that's what I say. Even Madonna!'

'Madonna?' asked Divya.

'The pop singer, dear. She did a lesbian kiss, didn't she, the other day. With that young girl, Britney Whassername. All over the news it's been.'

Joe knew what she was talking about, but the Madonna-Britney kiss at the MTV awards had taken place over twenty years ago, certainly not the other day.

Trying to steer the conversation back to Jessica, but now doubting they'd get anything useful, Joe said, 'So she hasn't mentioned a work friend or colleague called Jeremy?'

'Hmmm . . .' thought Alice. 'I don't think so.'

'What about a man named Sylvester?' asked Divya. 'Or a company called Atrax?'

'No, my Jessica works for herself now, sweetheart,' she said with pride. 'Striking out on her own, she is.'

Joe and Divya made eye contact, silently acknowledging that this might have been a wasted trip.

'We should find Jessica,' said Alice, suddenly almost panicked. 'Do you promise you'll find her?'

'I promise we'll do our best,' said Divya calmly.

Joe suspected it was nearing time to leave but wanted to push one more time. 'Is there anything? Anything at all that you can remember that might help us? Something unusual perhaps?'

Alice swilled her blackcurrant squash around in the bottom of her beaker, creating a small purple whirlpool. She didn't say anything.

Joe made a move to get up. Jessica's mother was confused, clearly, and the shame was taking hold. They shouldn't be here, questioning her, pretending to be Jessica's friends. But as Joe was about to stand, Alice spoke in a soft, hushed whisper.

'She made me promise not to tell anybody.'

Joe's ears pricked up. 'Tell anybody what?'

'Sshhh . . . it's a secret,' said the old woman.

'Yes,' said Divya, 'a secret. We won't tell.'

Alice fidgeted with her wrinkled fingers. 'Jessica has a place. A secret place. I didn't want to sign it – I said to her I didn't think I should be allowed to sign a contract, not with me being in here and everything, but she made me. She *made* me sign it.'

'What was it you signed?' asked Joe, trying to slot together the fragments of information she was giving them. 'A storage unit? A contract for a flat? Do you know what it was?'

'A house,' said Alice. She held her finger to pursed lips and whispered dramatically. ' "Hide it," she said. "Hide it, Mum, but don't tell anyone." It's OK to tell you though, isn't it? Because you're her friends.'

'Yes,' Divya replied kindly. 'It's all OK, just don't tell anyone else.'

Alice nodded.

'When did this happen?' asked Joe. 'When she was here last week?'

'Noooo . . . A long time ago – weeks, maybe months. It was sunny then but it's snowed since . . . When did it snow?' Her eyes drifted to the garden, to the bright flowers that bobbed in the breeze. 'Gosh, I can't remember. It was last summer – that's it!'

'Alice,' said Joe, pulling her attention back. 'Do you still have the contract? Did you hide it like Jessica told you?'

'Yes!' Alice hissed. 'The secret house, the secret . . . Sshh. Jessica might be at the secret house.'

Joe's heart was thumping, pounding behind their ribs. They were so close to something enormous that there was even a light shower of pins and needles forming across their scalp.

'Where did you hide it?' they asked.

And right then, the doors to the peaceful dining room swung open and in marched the ginger nurse they'd met when they arrived. She was carrying a plate of ham sandwiches.

'Right, Alice. It's time for lunch.'

Alice glared at Joe and raised her finger to her lips again. 'Sshh.'

CHAPTER 23

They quickly wrapped up a polite conversation with the nurse, thanking her and Alice for their time and making their way to the exit.

'Do you want me to walk you out?' the nurse asked.

'No thank you,' said Joe. 'We'll be fine.'

They waved a final goodbye to Alice and headed out into the corridor where, back on the linoleum, Divya stopped and said quietly, 'What do we do now?'

'If Jessica's bought a house there'd be records, right? On the electoral register you looked at earlier?'

'I don't know,' whispered Divya. 'Only if she's registered to vote there, which I don't think she can be if she's registered in Angel. There might be something on Land Registry if she's bought it, but if it's a rental there won't be anything at all. We might never find it.'

Damn.

Alice had given them a tantalisingly delicious clue and then they'd lost it, at exactly the wrong moment, thanks to a plate of ham sandwiches.

'Let's go back to the office,' said Divya. 'Maybe I can reach out to some of Sylvester's contacts to see how we'd go about finding whatever it is that Alice signed.'

'OK,' said Joe. They felt both pleased and disappointed at once. They now knew that Jessica had a house, *a secret house*, but there were millions of houses. Finding it could be impossible.

Divya's heels clicked as she walked around the corner, up towards the exit, and as Joe trailed behind they spotted something they'd seen earlier.

Alice G. Laminated. Stuck with tape to a plain white door.

'Divya,' they said, 'look.'

She stopped and read the sign, realising what Joe was suggesting. Alice Gethyn was a frail old woman in a care home. She wouldn't have many places to hide a secret document, but she did have a private room. And they were right outside it.

Joe reached out and put their fingers on the door handle.

'No!' Divya was outraged. 'Don't you dare.'

'There's nobody here,' said Joe, glancing up the corridor and double-checking it was completely empty. 'If you wait here and keep an eye out, I can just have a quick look inside.'

This was Misty Divine behaviour, clearly. Impulsive, reckless, spur of the moment.

'Joe, I said no.'

It was too late. Joe was going, or Misty, whoever was in charge right now. They turned the handle and the door pushed easily open. 'Two minutes, just give me two minutes. Keep watch.'

'Absolutely not! This is a really terrible . . .'

Divya's protests turned to silence as Joe slipped into the room and shut the door behind them.

Oh my God, they thought, looking around the bedroom. *She's right. This is awful. I really shouldn't be doing this. Why am I doing* this?!

It's too late now. Get searching.

The room was tiny – there was a wardrobe, a vanity desk with three drawers, a single bed and a bedside table. Across the bed lay a crocheted blanket in the orange, pink and purple that Joe recognised as colours of the lesbian pride flag. It looked home-made, though likely not by Jessica. From what Joe had learned about her so far, she didn't seem like the crocheting type.

Vanity drawers first.

They rushed the few short steps to the drawers and slid open the top one. Trinkets. Thimbles. Pencils. Crochet needles. Wool.

This was surely a moment of absolute madness. The shame descended again as Joe imagined a proud Alice crocheting her lesbian blanket to celebrate her daughter. And here they were, digging through her balls of wool.

That daughter is missing. I'm helping Alice by being here.

Drawer two: socks and pants and nothing else.

Not me rummaging through an old woman's underwear. Creep.

Drawer three: loose coins, an empty purse, a copy of *Take a Break* magazine, some of Jessica's newspaper clippings, a photograph of a younger Alice with a handsome man.

Jessica's dad? It didn't matter.

Joe's hands were starting to shake with adrenaline and their brow was dripping with sweat. They stepped sideways to the wardrobe and flung it open. Seven or eight hangers held dresses and trousers and blouses but there was nowhere for a hidden contract.

The door opened behind them and Joe jumped out of their skin.

'Hurry up!' Divya snapped.

'One more minute,' they replied, pacing towards the bedside cabinet. On the surface: a glass of water, a lamp, Martine McCutcheon's autobiography titled *Who Does She Think She Is?*

The top drawer contained just an unplugged alarm clock and the bottom drawer was empty.

Shit. It's not here. It's not here!

Joe dropped on to their hands and knees and looked under the bed. Some dust and an old Chewits wrapper scrunched into a ball.

They'd done it quickly, but they'd looked everywhere.

Get out now.

They headed back to the door, where Divya was no doubt absolutely seething on the other side, and just as they were about to exit, they took a last look around the room.

The mattress.

It was the only place they hadn't checked.

Quickly rushing back to the bed, they lurched at it, slipping their hands between the mattress and bed frame, sliding them along the length of it, frantic. And that's when they felt something. Their fingers brushed against the cold, sharp edge of thin cardboard and they snatched at whatever it was, whisking it out into the open.

Joe stood up straight and looked down at what they'd found: a green A4 wallet with a few sheets of paper inside.

They peeled back the top corner and read the top of the first page.

Foxton's Letting Agency. Rental Agreement. Alice Gethyn.

It was almost a year old, signed in the week following Lady Lady's funeral.

They'd found Jessica's secret house.

Joe emerged into the corridor, taking a quick look around to make sure nobody was coming, and found that Divya was indeed furious. Her whole face, her entire body, was tense, and her frown was so deep there were dark shadows in the middle of her forehead. As soon as Joe closed Alice's room behind them, she started marching up the corridor.

Joe ran to catch up with her, hot on her pointed heels. 'I found it,' they said, desperate to tell her what was inside the folder. 'I know where Jessica is.'

She shut Joe down immediately. 'Let's talk about this outside.'

Divya led the way through the reception area and down the crazy-paving pathway to the pavement outside Daffodil House, where she stopped and took out her phone. Joe saw she was opening the Uber app. The air smelled warm and fresh, delightful after the stench of bleach.

'Jessica's in Dartmoor,' they said, eager to tell her about the contract. They'd snapped photos of each of the pages before putting it all back in Alice's hiding place.

'I don't care,' said Divya, still looking at her phone. 'I'm going back to the office.'

'I'll come with you,' Joe replied. 'We can . . .'

She turned to face him with a jerk of the neck, brow still furrowed. 'No, you won't come with me. And *we* can do nothing else. You went too far, Joe. What you did in there, going into that woman's room, that was unacceptable.'

'Yes, I know,' they said, and they meant it, 'but we need to find Jessica, don't we? To find Jeremy and work out who stabbed Sylvester.'

Divya wasn't even listening. 'Not just unacceptable. Illegal!'

They knew she was going to be annoyed, but not like this. 'I thought you wanted—'

'Sylvester's reputation could be destroyed by this. I could lose my job. We could both be arrested. I'm out, Joe. If this is how you're planning to do things, you can do it on your own. I'm *out*.' She emphasized this last word with a forceful point of her finger.

This felt like their conversation with Miles all over again.

'Divya, please, hold on a minute.' They didn't want to lose her now – they had literally nobody else.

She looked down at her phone. 'My car is nearly here.'

'Please, let's just talk it through. I'm sorry, OK. I'm really sorry. I thought I was doing what Alice wanted. She told us about the contract. Surely this is the best way to find out who hurt Sylvester.'

Divya's voice grew so loud Joe was worried the staff inside Daffodil House might hear. 'I've realised you're not really interested in Sylvester. If you were, you wouldn't have put his business, his livelihood, his life's work on the line by searching that room and stealing that contract. *My* job on the line, my life. That's the opposite of what you do if you care about someone.'

A white Mercedes turned into the top of the street, slowly heading towards them. Divya's Uber. She reached up her arm and waved to the driver.

'Come on! You're overreacting here. I did the right thing – I found Jessica's secret house.'

The vehicle came to a stop and Divya stepped into the street. 'Then you go there, Joe. You go to Dartmoor and find Jessica and do whatever you've got to do next, but don't pretend it's for Sylvester. It isn't.' She opened the car door and climbed inside. 'What you did in there, that was for you – and I don't want anything else to do with it.'

She slammed the door shut and the car turned and made its way to the top of the street as Joe watched helplessly on. Was this really happening? How had it gone from nought to a thousand in just a few minutes?

'Fuck,' muttered Joe. They'd blown it. Again.

CHAPTER 24

Joe plonked themself down on the kerb and rubbed their eyes until they hurt. They'd messed everything up now and pushed everybody away. First Miles, then Mandy, then Divya. They'd upset everyone based on the warning of a man in shoddy shoes and torn trousers.

It was more than a warning though, wasn't it?

Jeremy and Jessica had really vanished. Misty was really in the file, with the beautiful blue hair. And it was all connected to Atrax. Lady's Bar was at risk, which meant Joe's own clean criminal record was at risk. Everything was.

But is it worth all of this? Arguments, break-ins, lies and deceit. Miles leaving. This investigating was stupid, stupid, stupid. Their chest tightened up as a rocket of anxiety smashed through it. Their breath caught in their throat.

'What was I thinking? Idiot!'

They leaned back and placed their hands firmly on the pavement, looking up to face the sun, taking a deep slow breath.

What's really important in all this?

Miles.

Whether they liked it or not, and they didn't, Miles was never going to come back as long as anything dangerous or illegal was happening. He was right of course, neither of them should have to live their lives with crime, bribery and violence hanging over them, but that was already in motion. Miles wanted them to sit still, to stand back like Mandy or opt out like Divya, but that wouldn't resolve or stop anything now. If Joe did nothing, the bribery would continue, the suits would be out there doing whatever they're doing, Sylvester would still be in hospital. Jeremy and Jessica would still be missing.

And we'd still be in the middle of all of it.

It was a runaway train and Joe/Misty was the last passenger aboard.

If Joe had any chance of winning back Miles, of returning to the life they had before, they had to keep going and return offering a clean slate. A safe one.

The only way out is through. I need to find Jessica to find Jeremy, and then get us out of the Atrax mess once and for all.

They opened their photos of Alice's hidden contract. The front page included a picture of a white cottage surrounded by trees. It had a thatched roof and a big garden. The accompanying text said it was located outside a small Dartmoor town called Moretonhampstead. This was all they had now – a secret, possible location for Jessica Gethyn. She was at the middle of it, Joe thought, like Misty was.

There's no choice, is there?

This was a lonely business.

I have to go to Dartmoor.

Joe walked from Daffodil House in the direction of Archway Station, remembering that Junction Road had a nice

173

independent coffee bar they'd been to once before. They ordered a latte and took a seat to think about the best way to get to this house in the middle of the countryside.

The internet said that Moretonhampstead was over 200 miles away and, as was all too common on British railways, the trains were delayed. A coach would take six hours, which seemed way too long, and Joe didn't have a car.

Who could drive me? They racked their brains. Mandy didn't have a car and neither did Miles, but neither of them would have wanted to help anyway. *Who else?* What working drag queen or king living in London could afford to run or even park a car? Not many. Then Joe remembered . . . there was one queen they knew who had one. She called it Calista and was the biggest gossip on the scene. She was the last person Joe would want involved in a secret investigation conspiracy, but now they couldn't think of another way.

They were going to have to call Plimberley.

Plim was finishing up at a gig but agreed enthusiastically to Joe's offer of petrol money, a service-station dinner and a hundred pounds cash.

'You'll have to wait a bit,' she'd said. 'I'm still in full face here.'

Joe ordered lunch.

At 5 p.m., stomach filled with the driest falafel salad known to humankind, Joe was waiting on the pavement outside the Mother Red Cap pub on Holloway Road. Plimberley's rusty car, Calista, pulled up with a bang. It back-fired as it braked, startling everybody on the pavement and unleashing a plume of black exhaust fumes. The exterior was covered in dents and scratches and the back windows were blocked off entirely by a duvet, pillows and what appeared to be drag costumes rolled up into tight balls.

'Oi oi!' shouted Plim from the window. 'Get in then, you slag! Road trip time!'

Out of drag Plimberley looked so very different. Without her long locks and teeny skirts, she was a fairly masculine youth. Her face was dotted with pimples and she wore a loose grey tracksuit that looked wonderfully comfortable. Her hair was brown and spiky with a fresh fade, accented with two big diamond stud earrings. Joe suspected they were not real diamonds.

They opened the front passenger door with a loud creak and jumped in. 'Thanks, Plim. And we'll have less of the slag! I'm a happily married woman,' said Joe, playing along with the banter and genuinely pleased to see her. She wasn't as serious as Divya and it was nice to be with a fellow drag. A much-needed moment of queer connection after a stressful few days.

'Dartmoor then?' asked Plim, typing the address into a phone plugged to the dashboard.

'Yes please, driver,' winked Joe.

'You're lucky I didn't have a gig tonight,' said Plim. 'I bloody love a road trip.'

'And cash,' Joe replied.

'Oh yes. Ha! Love me that cash.' She pulled into the traffic and they set off, making their way to Jessica Gethyn's countryside hideaway.

*

The GPS said it would take over four hours to drive to More-tonhampstead and Joe would need to think carefully about what to say or, more importantly, what not to say to Plimber-ley about the purpose of this mission. It didn't take her long to ask. As they exited the city and joined the motorway, she piped up, straight to the point as always.

'Come on then, Misty, what's happening in Dartmoor? Long way to go for a hook-up.'

'Definitely not a hook-up, Plim,' said Joe. 'I've got a friend there I need to see and all the trains were off.'

Joe knew it was an obvious brush-off and Plimberley was too bright and sparky. She saw through it instantly.

'Is this something to do with that old guy who got poked at the bar? Everyone's talking about that you know.'

'No,' said Joe. 'Really, it's just a friend I need to visit.'

The younger queen's face twitched like she disagreed, like she knew there was more to it.

'The old guy,' she said, picking for the details, 'they haven't said who he was in the news, but you were talking to one on Thursday, the night before. Remember, at the mix and mingle? I tried to see if you needed a rescue. That creeper at the bar in the crap shoes. It's him, isn't it?'

'I can't say,' said Joe. 'I'd tell you if I could, but I'm not allowed – the police said.' It was another lie to add to Joe's repertoire, but Plimberley couldn't be trusted with a secret. She was tits-deep in every WhatsApp group, every Reddit thread. She knew everyone and didn't hold back.

'I knew it!' She slapped the steering wheel with the palm of her hand. 'It's the same guy. So, a mysterious stranger appears at the bar on Thursday and then he shows up on

Friday morning *stabbed*. And now, a few days later, you call me out of nowhere telling me you need an urgent lift to some countryside village I've never even heard of.'

She was working it all out too quickly for Joe's liking, but perhaps they shouldn't have expected anything less. They said nothing and looked out the window.

'If I know you, Misty Divine, which I do . . . you're up to something you shouldn't be.'

'Do you mind, Plim, if I close my eyes for a bit? I've had a rough few days and could do with a bit of shut-eye.' Surely that would stop her prying.

'God that's so boring,' said Plim. 'Can I have the radio on at least?'

'Of course,' said Joe.

CHAPTER 25

Plimberley nudged Joe awake. 'Oi, Snorefest, we're nearly there.'

Joe opened their groggy eyes and looked outside. The skies were completely black, with just a sprinkling of stars and a bright moon. They were driving through a beautiful little town centre: old buildings, an ancient-looking church and a short, pretty high street of shops and cafés. 'What? What time is it?'

'It's nearly ten. We hit some roadworks. Not that you'd know – you've been dreaming and groaning the whole time!'

'I'm so sorry,' Joe said. 'I was knackered. I didn't mean to sleep for so long.' It was true, they'd only meant to close their eyes for a few minutes, just to get Plimberley off-topic, but now it seemed they'd slept through the entire journey. 'Where are we?'

'Moretonhampstead. The nearest village to your friend's house. We're about ten minutes away.'

'It looks nice here,' said Joe, admiring the cottages and old architecture.

'Does it?' asked Plimberley. 'Looks right dull to me. Not a gay bar for a hundred miles I'd reckon.'

They drove old Calista from one side of the town to the

other, entering rural lanes that felt too dark and imposing. Joe began feeling hesitant, an anxious whirling in their stomach and warm moisture on the palms of their hands.

'Are you going to tell me,' said Plimberley, 'who this friend is? And what's the plan? Are we staying the night or something? I've got a gig tomorrow.'

'Me too,' said Joe, thinking of Lady's Bar. 'We'll see how it goes with my friend and then find a hotel. There's bound to be a Travelodge somewhere.'

Tall black branches hung over the roads and Joe tried to recall the last time they'd seen so much nature – they hadn't left London for the country for years. Feeding almonds to the tame squirrels of Russell Square probably didn't count. As they got deeper into the darkness, Joe hoped they weren't on a wild goose chase and that this address from Alice would be worth the journey.

What if Jessica isn't even here? they wondered, hoping that wouldn't be the outcome.

Plimberley followed the map, and a few twists and turns carried them deeper into the rural landscape. Then she pulled up at the end of what looked like a private road.

'I think we're here,' she said, pointing at a gate with a dirt track behind it. 'The house is up there. Should we open the gate and drive up?'

'No,' said Joe, 'best that my visit is a surprise. We should find a spot to park and I'll walk.'

Plim drove until she found a grass verge. She bumped Calista up on to it and parked.

'Are you all right to wait for me here?' said Joe, feeling awkward to ask this. They didn't enjoy the idea of leaving

Plimberley twiddling her thumbs on the side of the road, but liked the thought of her meeting Jessica even less.

'No way!' said Plimberley. 'I'm coming with you! I'm not sitting in the dark in a pile of bushes while you go off on top-secret drag detective business. Anyway, I need a piss and I don't like going outside.'

'I'm not doing top-secret drag detective business,' Joe replied.

Plim smirked and snorted. 'I wasn't born yesterday, Misty, and you might need me! If you're hunting the stabber, which is what I reckon is really happening, you might need my moves, my high kicks.'

Joe paused, unsure. It was unreasonable to expect Plim to pee on the grass verge after she'd done all the driving and safety in numbers was probably smart. They hoped there would be no need for high kicks.

'OK,' they said, 'but I do need to talk to my friend in private.'

'Yeah, yeah,' said Plimberley, opening her door and getting out the car, happy to be included.

The gate was padlocked, so they climbed over it together, landing with firm feet on dry soil. Plimberley's long legs had scaled it with ease, her tracksuit glowing in the moonlight. Joe switched on the torch on their phone to light the way.

'Are you going to let me in on what's going on then?' Plimberley asked quietly. 'I'm all for doing you a favour, God knows you've looked after me enough over the years, but this is a bit weird.'

It was true; occasionally when Plim had nowhere to go, she stayed with Joe and Miles, sleeping on the sofa, drinking coffee with them in the morning. She was a presence that came in and out of their lives and their home easily. Joe stopped walking, the torch shining its beam on Plimberley's feet. They needed to tell her something, it was only fair. They took a deep breath.

'OK, Plim, you were right. This does have something to do with the stabbing at the club, but I can't tell you what exactly because it might be a little dangerous, and also a little illegal. I need us to be completely discreet about it.'

'Right . . .' said Plim. Even in the half-light of the phone Joe could see a twitch in her lips. 'Is it really a friend in there, Misty? Or is it the stabber?'

'It's not the stabber, but it's someone who might know who they are. She might not even be here. It's a bit of a long shot.'

Suddenly, Plim bounced into action, seemingly unfazed and easily satisfied. 'Come on then,' she said. 'Let's go!'

Before long a house came into view, one Joe recognised from the sunny photographs on the Foxtons rental listing. It looked different to the pictures: boxy, small, run-down.

Joe had goosebumps sprinting up their arms and thighs by the time they reached the front door. The silence of the location was so intense it was terrifying and the slightest movement seemed like a shout of 'someone's here!'

Joe stepped in front of Plimberley and steeled themself before knocking three times on the door.

They thought about the last and only time they'd seen Jessica Gethyn. '*Stay away from Atrax. And stay away from me.*' If she was here, she certainly wouldn't be pleased to see them.

A soft light appeared inside, a living room door being

opened perhaps, and footsteps padded quietly on the other side.

'Hello?' called out a woman's voice. 'Who's there?' She sounded afraid.

'Jessica? Is that you? We need to talk to you. It's Joe Brown, although you might know me as Misty Divine.'

There were some clicks and jangling as she unlocked the door, and then it opened.

They'd found her. They'd found Jessica Gethyn.

CHAPTER 26

Jessica was wearing a pair of light beige pyjamas and purple slippers. Her dark hair was pulled back into a high ponytail that was messy and lopsided – she obviously wasn't expecting visitors.

She looked the drag queens up and down, Joe in their floral blouse, Plim in her grey tracksuit.

'Well,' she said, irritated, 'that didn't last long.'

'What didn't?' asked Joe.

'My time here. I wasn't expecting anyone to find me so quickly.'

'Jessica, this is my friend, Plimberley, she works at Lady's Bar too,' said Joe, trying to explain the lanky youth they'd brought with them.

'What the hell kind of a name is Plimberley?' said Jessica.

'Plimberley Walsh,' said Plim. 'You know, like from Girls Aloud, Kimber—'

'Kimberley Walsh,' finished Jessica. She rolled her eyes. 'For God's sake.'

'Never mind that,' said Joe. 'I need to talk to you about something very important.'

'You must if you've managed to track me down and come all this way.' Jessica shuffled on the spot and craned her neck to look around them. 'Does anybody else know you're here?'

'No,' said Joe. A little fib this time – there was Divya of course.

'I guess this is about Atrax?' she said.

'It is.'

Plimberley gasped dramatically at this, as if an enormous juicy secret had been dropped. 'Oooooh, what's Atrax?'

'Never you mind,' said Joe. Then, turning to Jessica, 'She doesn't know anything – I haven't told anybody.'

Jessica pointed a finger towards Joe's face. 'I warned you about this. I told you to stay away from it.'

'Well it's too late for that now,' said Joe. 'I need your help.'

Joe hoped Jessica would invite them in, but she was still deciding.

'Listen,' said Plimberley, 'I don't want to be cheeky or nothing, but I really do need to tinkle.'

Jessica sighed, giving in and holding open the door. 'You'd better come inside.'

The interior of the bungalow felt much more spacious than the outside, or even the rental listing, would have had you believe.

'We're not a shoes-off house,' said Jessica, laughing as though she'd cracked the ultimate hilarity and Joe could quickly see why. The house was in keen need of renovation. The walls were cracked and flaking, and the floors were an old plastic that should definitely have been replaced before occupation.

Jessica led them down the hallway and pointed Plimberley

to the bathroom before walking Joe to the only open door that had a light on, a sitting room. Despite the state of disrepair, it was surprisingly cosy. There were a couple of chintzy nineties sofas, a table and a television paused on what Joe recognised as a Lindsay Lohan Christmas film.

'What's *she* doing here?' Jessica hissed about Plimberley.

'I had no way of getting here. She drove me.'

'And you haven't told her why you've come?'

'No, nothing. Is there somewhere else she can sit while we talk?'

'The kitchen.' Jessica scratched her chin. 'How did you find me?'

'I don't think you'll like it.'

'No shit,' she grimaced.

'I visited your mother this morning,' Joe admitted with great shame, trying not to think of their rifling through Alice's drawers.

Jessica's mouth dropped wide open, acknowledging this for the invasion it was. She looked like she might be just about to scream when a toilet flushed deeper in the house and Plimberley came marching in.

'Any chance of a brew or something?' said Plim, her loose dangly arms waving unnecessarily. 'I'm parched here.'

'Come with me,' said Jessica, firing an angry stare at Joe. 'I'll take you to the kitchen.'

Jessica and Plimberley headed back into the gloom of the bungalow and Joe stayed alone in the living room. They wanted to jump up and down with excitement – they'd found her! But they were also terrified, anxious about what might be to come and what secrets she might reveal.

The only way out is through, they reminded themself. If they were going to save everything, Miles and the club, they needed to do this.

Jessica returned alone with two steaming mugs. 'Coffee,' she said. 'It's late – and it's all I've got.'

'Thank you,' said Joe, taking a seat on the sofa and accepting a hot mug.

She sat opposite but Joe spoke first. 'I'm sorry, OK, for going to see your mother. I also went to your flat and met Rachel. She was out of her mind with worry and I told her I'd help to find you. I probably shouldn't have, but I needed to because of Sylvester Green. Do you know him?'

'I've heard of him, of course, and about what happened to him outside your club,' said Jessica. 'How's Mum?'

'She's fine,' said Joe. 'A little worried about you, but in good spirits.'

'Did she tell you that Madonna is a lesbian?' There was a hint of a smile about this on the edge of her mouth.

'She did,' said Joe.

'That seems to be her thing at the moment. She tells me about it every time I visit. She has these . . . I call them time slips.' She paused, fiddling with the gold chain around her neck, lost in thought momentarily. 'So tell me, what's brought you all the way to Dartmoor? I thought I was very clear at the funeral.'

'You were,' said Joe, 'but Sylvester Green showed up at Lady's Bar and told me I was in danger and that I had to find Jeremy Edmunds. Looking for Jeremy led me to you, and Atrax, and the fact you've been out of contact with everyone for a few days. I haven't worked everything out yet, but I know you and Jeremy were in contact with each other before he vanished. That's why I'm here. I have to know what's going on and you're the only person I can ask.'

Jessica looked at Joe with genuine concern in her eyes. 'I told you to stay away from this, Joe. I tried to warn you.'

'And I did,' they replied. 'I stayed away from it for almost a year. And then it landed on my doorstep in the form of a bleeding Sylvester Green. So now I'm in it, maybe as much as you are.'

'I doubt that,' said Jessica, rolling her eyes.

'Tell me then,' said Joe. 'Do you know where Jeremy is? What's your connection to him? What's his connection to Atrax?' The television flickered and an 'are you still watching?' message popped up on-screen. Jessica tapped a button on the remote control to switch it off and Lindsay Lohan's festive face vanished.

'I don't know where to start,' she replied.

'Start at the beginning. Do you know where he is?'

'That's not the beginning,' replied Jessica, swallowing a mouthful of coffee, 'but I do know what happened to Jeremy. More than you. I'll get to that.'

'So where's the beginning?' asked Joe. 'Where did this all start?'

'It started with your friend,' she said. 'It started with Lady Lady.'

CHAPTER 27

'Lady Lady?'

Jessica nodded. 'She came to see me about six months before she was murdered and told me she had information about a potential finance story. She said a big City firm was forcing the closure of independent businesses in Soho. She only knew for sure about Lady's Bar but suspected there were more.'

Sometimes, for Joe, even a mention of Lady Lady was enough to hit like a punch in the gut. And hearing Jessica say her name, hearing her reveal this new moment in Lady Lady's life, brought back visions of her lavender hair and the scent of her perfume. They tried to push it to one side.

'She told you about Atrax's proposal to the council?' asked Joe. They were surprised by this because Mandy had never mentioned it.

Mandy didn't know! they realised. *This was Lady Lady striking out on her own, trying to expose the rot before it destroyed the bar.*

'She did,' said Jessica. 'She was worried it would spell the end for Lady's Bar, that her life's work would be swallowed up by corporate greed. I'll admit, it was a little out of my wheelhouse and, if I'm totally honest, I was more interested in seeing if there was a story than I was interested in saving Lady's Bar. I'd already written a short piece about Atrax, just a write-up of a conference that the CEO Stefan Weber attended, so I agreed that I'd look into it.'

'I've read that,' said Joe. 'But why haven't you written anything about them since? Didn't you find out anything else?'

Jessica took a glug of coffee, nearing the end of her cup. 'I found out a lot, actually. More than I had anticipated and there was definitely a story to be had. But it was . . . complicated.' She sighed. 'I don't know if I should be sharing all this . . .'

'You absolutely should be sharing it! I need answers. My life, my career, my business . . . everything I have is caught up in this. What did you find, Jessica?'

Joe's eyes were growing tired from the late night and the long journey. Plimberley must be tired too, having done all the driving, and they felt bad for shutting her in the kitchen, but they had to hear the rest.

Jessica took a steady breath, thinking through where to begin. 'I'd been hoping to spread my freelance wings and move away from the finance news, and this story seemed small, no offence, but with a personal touch. I thought, what's the harm in looking into it on my own time? If Lady Lady was right and the story had legs, maybe I could use it to make a splash for myself, get more into the investigative side of things. If not, no skin off my nose. I was foolish not to have the support of a big outlet from the start. Maybe more arrogant than foolish . . .

'What happened?'

'The first thing to say is that Lady's Bar was not, and is not, the only venue in trouble because of Atrax. I recruited a research assistant, just a few hours a week, to trawl through development proposals and venue buyouts all over the country, and she discovered more. Seven venues, all LGBTQ+ venues, were in one way or another being targeted by Atrax. Two in Manchester, one in Brighton, one in Edinburgh, one in Belfast and one in Norwich. And though the Atrax involvement for some was tenuous, they were present in all the paperwork. They had filed documents, provided legal support, that kind of thing. In a few cases they'd offered cash, way above market value, to take over venues that were part of brewery chains.'

Joe tried to take this all in. It was so much bigger than Lady's Bar and they'd had no idea at all. 'Did Lady Lady know about all these other venues? Did you tell her this?'

'I did,' said Jessica. 'And that's when she confided in me about the bribery scheme she'd started. She told me her business partner was trying to get everything above board, but it was bigger than Mandy knew. It's a co-ordinated attack against the queer community – one that stretches the length and breadth of the country.'

Joe thought back to the night Lady Lady died. Misty had overheard an argument between Mandy and Lady Lady in the dressing rooms. *'We don't have any choice,'* Lady Lady had said. *'We are all out of options now.'*

Suddenly things were becoming clearer. A neater, tidier picture that explained at least some of what had happened last year. It made sense now, why Lady Lady hadn't wanted to do as Mandy was asking and go to their solicitor Mr

McDermott. There was something larger at play and it wasn't just Lady's Bar at risk.

Jessica continued, 'Shortly before Lady Lady's death, my research assistant, Pascale, was visited by a group of men at her apartment. She said they had weapons, knives, and one even a gun. They told her she needed to stop asking questions about Atrax, to stop looking into the venue takeovers. She was terrified.'

'They had a gun?!' said Joe. 'No wonder she was terrified.'

'She quit working for me, blocked me everywhere and moved back to France. Said she couldn't handle it. I was annoyed at the time, but I understood.' Jessica seemed sad and her eyelids drooped. Clearly the threats against her assistant had hit her hard. 'Then Lady Lady died and I felt stuck, sick. Pascale and Lady Lady had been my only allies and suddenly I was alone with all this information. That's why I came to the funeral to warn you to stay away from it all. I didn't want you in danger, threatened like Pascale had been.'

'What did you do after that?' asked Joe. 'Why didn't you publish anything? It's *our* community that Atrax is targeting.'

Jessica shook her head and closed her eyes. 'I know. And I did what I could. I pushed as hard as possible with all my contacts. I even took it over their heads to really senior people at all sorts of publications, burning my bridges at the *Guardian* in the process. No one wanted to hear it.'

'Why?' asked Joe, feeling outraged.

'They all said Pascale's evidence wasn't strong enough, that it was circumstantial, that in the world we live in there are corporate ventures taking over small businesses all the time. I was told it could result in legal consequences for me personally, and combined with what happened to Pascale . . . it was scary.'

'So, what? You put it to one side?' Joe's heart quickened with irritation at this.

'No. Not right away, anyway. I was worried about my career and my safety, but I tried for months! Eventually I felt like I was becoming an obsessive stereotype, so in December I locked away Pascale's research and told myself someone else would pick up the fight.' She looked directly at Joe with teary eyes. 'I'm really sorry, OK?'

Fear, Joe could understand. Fear had pushed Jessica to rent this house, had driven Pascale out of the country. But *giving up*, that had left Atrax doing whatever they wanted, unexposed and unchallenged. They looked at her now, hiding in her pyjamas in the middle of nowhere, and felt conflicted. *I shouldn't judge her*, they thought. *I should try to put myself in her shoes.*

But could she have prevented all this? Jeremy, Miles, Auntie Susan . . . could all of this have been prevented if Jessica Gethyn had been braver?

'Something's happened since then, hasn't it?' Joe asked, trying to remain as sympathetic as possible. 'Recently, with Jeremy and Sylvester. How did they end up involved?'

Jessica played with her gold chain necklace and wrapped it around her fingers, twisting and releasing it over and over again.

'Somebody had already picked up the fight, I just didn't know it – Jeremy. He'd started months before, but was looking at it from a different angle,' she said. 'I felt awful about it, Joe, honestly, about Lady Lady and Pascale and the venues being targeted. Jeremy contacted me unexpectedly and I was relieved to have someone to talk to.'

'What did he want?'

Now they were approaching the juicy centre of the mystery: Jeremy Edmunds.

Runaway, kidnapped, dead in a ditch?

'It seems my little piece about Atrax was a lightning rod, attracting people who wanted to know more about them. Lady Lady, you, and then him. He called out of the blue and said he'd been looking into something that led him to Atrax. He had evidence of a conspiracy, he said, a video of CEO Stefan Weber meeting with a client, and he didn't know what to do next. We met, and after he'd explained his situation, I told him about mine. The next day, the day he "disappeared", he took photos of you and Stefan, but when he returned home, there were men with guns on his doorstep. He panicked.' She said the word 'disappeared' with air quotation marks with her fingers.

'Why do you say it like that?' asked Joe.

'Because he didn't disappear. Not really. Not from me. I sent Jeremy here, to lie low for a while. He's been here the whole time, staying in this house. I rented it for this kind of eventuality, a back-up plan in case I needed to get out of town after what happened to Pascale.'

Joe almost jumped out of their seat. 'He's alive?! In this house? He's here now?'

'No,' said Jessica, 'not now, but he was here . . . until this morning.'

Jeremy's alive! thought Joe. *And I've found out where he's been for the last month.*

193

They didn't know the man at all, just what he looked like from gap-toothed newspaper photos smiling on a beach, but Jeremy had consumed Joe's brain for the last few days. They thought of Patricia, coming to London, handing out flyers and putting up posters. What could have been so serious that Jeremy would put his own mother in such a position?

'Where did he go?' asked Joe. 'Who is the Atrax client?' There were answers now, and so many more questions.

'I don't know where he went. I came here on Friday after I heard Sylvester had been stabbed. I'd been keeping tabs on news of Jeremy's disappearance and figured if someone had tried to kill Sylvester things were getting serious. It was only a matter of time before they connected everything to me. Seems I was right. Jeremy was furious when I got here and told him about the stabbing. He said Atrax would find us here sooner or later, that this house wasn't as safe as I'd promised it to be. He had a point. You found it, after all. I don't know for sure where he went, but I think he was heading back to London because he didn't have his passport. He said he was going to try to leave the country.'

'He left this morning?' asked Joe, reeling from the realisation they'd missed him by hours. 'How? Does he have a car?'

'A second-hand motorbike he bought for cash in Moretonhampstead, unregistered. The only problem is . . .'

'The *only* problem?' mocked Joe. They were facing a million problems: financial, legal, moral . . . *Miles*.

'He took the evidence with him,' she finished. 'The evidence that proves who's behind the venue closures.'

'Who is it?' said Joe, on tenterhooks to hear the answer to the mystery, to know the identity of the Atrax client.

'An American woman,' said Jessica. 'You might have heard of her. She's one of those famous television evangelists, reportedly a billionaire. She's building London's biggest American-style megachurch. Her name is Ginger Baker.'

They both jumped and Jessica yelped as the living-room door opened without warning. *Plimberley.*

'What's this?!' Plim exclaimed. 'There's a famous church type trying to shut down Lady's Bar?'

Oh God . . . thought Joe. *She's been eavesdropping.*

Jessica rubbed her face with frustration. 'I told you to stay in the kitchen!'

'How much did you hear?' asked Joe.

'All of it,' said Plimberley. A smug little smirk spread across her boyish face. ' "Sit in the kitchen" my arse.'

CHAPTER 28

Tuesday

'You nosy cow,' said Joe, annoyed but not entirely shocked. She was the drag scene's biggest gossip after all.

'So some American church lady's trying to shut down all the queer bars and Lady Lady was doing a scam to stop her,' said Plim, matter-of-factly. 'Well, well, well . . .'

'Shit,' said Jessica, looking to Joe.

'Don't blame me!' they protested. 'I thought she was in the kitchen.'

'Can't spend the whole time sitting in the kitchen while you two are involved in all sorts in here,' Plimberley shrugged.

Joe got up from the sofa and walked towards her. 'You can't tell anyone, Plim, no matter what. Nobody at all.'

'Who would I tell?!' she said, her face as innocent as the Virgin Mary.

'Everyone, Plim. I know you, remember.'

'Joe's right,' said Jessica. 'You really can't tell anybody about this. It's too serious. Too dangerous.'

'God . . .' groaned Plim like a cartoon of a teenager. 'I might like a gossip, but if you ask me not to tell anyone, I won't tell anyone.'

'Promise me,' said Joe.

'I promise!' she insisted. 'On my baby's life.'

'You haven't got a baby.'

'Calista,' she smirked. 'She's my precious angel.'

'Jesus, Plim,' Joe moaned.

What would Mandy say? What would Auntie Susan say? The scene's very own *National Enquirer* now had more information than either of them! Plimberley had plonked herself smack bang in the middle of everything.

'What a mess,' said Jessica, shaking her head and glancing at her watch. 'It's just gone midnight. I think we should talk more in the morning, unless you're planning on driving back tonight.'

Joe looked at Plim. They hadn't made any sleeping arrangements, and Joe didn't much fancy sharing the back seat of her 'precious angel'.

'Is there a hotel nearby?' they asked.

'You can stay here,' replied Jessica reluctantly, 'if you don't mind sleeping on the sofas. I have spare sheets and blankets.'

'That would be great, thank you,' said Joe. It was either that or top and tails with Plim on a grass verge.

'Sleepover!' clapped Plimberley, then, realising the sombre tone of the evening, 'Sorry.'

Jessica got up and walked into the hallway. Joe pointed at Plimberley to sit on the sofa and stay there before running out after the journalist.

'What is the evidence?' they asked her. 'The evidence that this Ginger Baker is behind the venue closures?'

Jessica stopped by the entrance to the bathroom, whispering so as not to share even more details with nosy Plim. 'A video. Jeremy was looking into the new megachurch and its financing. He followed Ginger to the bar at the Ritz where she met with Stefan Weber. She basically admitted to everything, her attacks on the queer venues, and Jeremy was close enough to catch it on camera. He got away, but she clocked him and the very next day there were armed men on his doorstep. That's why he handed over his photos to John, so that if he showed up dead, God forbid, there'd be a trace he was looking into Atrax.'

'Do you have it?' asked Joe. 'The video?'

'I don't. And that's why I argued with Jeremy. He said he was keeping it until I could be certain I had a way to get it out there. He took it with him when he left this morning. He has the only copy.'

Joe was shocked, worried and relieved all at once. They now knew there was evidence proving who was behind the attack on Lady's Bar and the other venues, but it was just out there, with Jeremy on his motorbike, location unknown.

'Let me go fetch the blankets,' said Jessica.

Once the lights were off and Joe and Plimberley were under their respective covers, Joe could tell from her breathing that Plim was still awake. Jessica had retreated into the depths of the bungalow, leaving them alone for the first time since they'd heard the full story. The quiet outside boomed in a way one never experienced living in London.

'Misty,' said Plimberley in a hushed voice. 'Are you awake?'

'Yes,' Joe whispered.

'Is it true? All that about the Baker lady turning our bar into a church?'

'It's not quite that, Plim. She is building a church, but we don't know what she wants with Lady's Bar, just that she's been trying to close it down. Mandy and I have been trying to stop it for the last year but didn't know it was her until tonight.'

Plim remained silent for a moment, thinking it through. 'I don't like it, Misty. Lady's Bar . . . it's the only place I really call home.'

'I don't like it either, but we're on to her now. I'll find a way to stop her.'

'Do you really think you can do it?' asked the younger queen.

'Yes,' said Joe, and they believed it. They'd come this far, hadn't they?

'I'll help, you know,' said Plimberley. 'I can help if you want. I'll do whatever and I won't gossip, I promise.'

'Thanks, Plim.'

'You know,' she said from her sofa in the darkness, 'my first ever gig was at Lady's Bar. I went there when I was seventeen to try and get booked, but Lady Lady could tell I wasn't old enough. She told me to come back and audition for her after my birthday and I couldn't believe it when she actually hired me.'

This warmed Joe's heart. Lady Lady had looked out for Plimberley just as she'd looked out for Misty and though her mentor was now long gone, perhaps they could rescue her legacy by finishing what she started.

'You can trust me, Misty. You know that, right?'

'I trust you, Plim. We'll stick together.'

'Through thick and thin, my love. Through thick and thin.'

Before long, Plimberley had fallen asleep. Her breathing was droning and regular with a soft snore. Joe reached into their jeans pocket and pulled out their phone for the first time since they'd got out the car. Turning down the screen brightness so as not to disturb Plim, they saw they had messages – from Miles. *Miles!* They sat upright, full of hope. Overjoyed. They read the messages rapidly.

> Three hours ago: *Hey Joe – sorry things aren't good between us right now. Maybe we can talk tomorrow?*
>
> Two hours ago: *Joe, I wasn't stalking, but I just saw your location in the Find My Phone app. What are you doing in Devon??*
>
> One hour ago: *I'm starting to feel worried. Are you ok? I need you to tell me what's going on. Can you text me back?*

Joe's thumbs hovered over the keypad for a moment as they decided what to say. What could they say? That they'd interrogated an elderly woman and searched her room, that they'd discovered there were men with knives and guns threatening people into hiding, that there was a megachurch evangelist trying to close down Lady's Bar? None of these were things that Miles would want to hear. Eventually they wrote a short reply.

Everything is fine, Miles. No need to worry. I'll update you when I see you next. I love you and I miss you very much. Joe x

They put their phone screen-down on the floor beside the sofa, turned away from it, and closed their eyes to go to sleep.

There wasn't much more to say for now.

CHAPTER 29

Jessica Gethyn's hideaway sofa did not provide much comfort. Joe was hot in the night, thinking over everything they'd learned and whether they'd done the right thing by holding back from telling Miles the truth.

It was a relief after days of searching to discover that Jeremy Edmunds had been safe the entire time and not dead in a ditch – that he'd been at the Dartmoor bungalow until yesterday morning. It was not a relief that the only evidence against Atrax and Ginger Baker was in the wind.

Joe picked up their phone and tapped out a message:

Hey Miles – sorry for not telling you I was going away. I'm trying to put an end to the Lady's Bar troubles and it led me here. I've found out some things that could help. Will fill you in when I see you.

A response came through immediately.

So you're still 'investigating'?

Joe's heart sank and they decided not to reply. They simply weren't having this conversation again. Miles wanted them out of the bribery scheme and now there was a way to do it. If Joe could find Jeremy, and convince him to hand over the recording of Ginger Baker, they could find a way out of this mess and save Lady's Bar and their relationship once and for all.

Plimberley started stirring at around 8 a.m. and Jessica knocked on the living-room door about the same time.

'I'm famished,' Plim announced, rubbing her stomach in a big drama.

'I don't have much in for breakfast,' said Jessica. 'I have coffee. Instant, mind.'

'Coffee would be good,' replied Plim, stretching her long arms and legs. 'And we'll get food on the way back to London, right, Misty? At the services like you promised?'

'Yes, Plim. At the services.'

'I bloody love a services.'

'Milk? Sugar?' asked Jessica, before disappearing off to the bungalow's kitchen with everybody's preferences.

'What time are we leaving?' Plimberley asked while folding up her blankets. 'I know this is all dead serious and stuff, but I've got a gig tonight and can't be late.' She was ever the professional.

'We'll leave after coffee,' said Joe. 'I have Lady's Bar this evening too.'

Aside from the show tonight at the club, Joe could feel London calling. They wanted to get back there, figure out how to locate Jeremy and get the evidence, try to work out the Miles situation, and finally explain the truth to Mandy.

Once all three of them were sitting around the small dining table at the back of the living room, Jessica said, 'I take it you're going to try to find Jeremy now then.'

'That's what led us here,' said Joe, 'what we've been doing for the last three days.'

'I feel awful,' she said sadly. 'I thought I could protect everybody – that I could protect him, with this house. I've royally fucked everything up.'

Joe didn't say it, but they kind of agreed. Hiding in the countryside watching Christmas films in the middle of June wasn't helping anyone. Plimberley stayed silent except for an occasional loud slurp of sugary coffee.

'What are you going to do?' Joe asked. 'You can't stay here. You're not safe here for much longer. If we could find you, they will too.'

'I guess I'll B&B it. You can pay for those with cash sometimes and I'll keep moving so I'm not a sitting duck. That would probably have been a better plan to begin with.' She glanced at her drink and turned the mug around on the table top. 'I'm sorry but . . . I can't come with you. I can't help any more. I'm worried, about my mother, my job, ending up like Sylvester did.'

But you started this, thought Joe, *and now you're leaving us to clean it up.*

'How can we reach you?'

She pulled an old-model iPhone out of her pocket and plonked it on her lap. 'I bought this pay-as-you-go before I left London. Let me find you the number.' She unlocked it and read the number aloud to Joe, who saved it into their own contact list.

'Does Jeremy have one too?'

'Yes, but it'll be switched off,' said Jessica, reading out the details for Joe to save.

'Is there anything else we should know?' asked Joe once phones were down.

Jessica pondered long and hard and licked her lips. 'I suppose you should bear in mind that Atrax, Stefan Weber, Ginger Baker . . . they're obscenely rich and incredibly powerful. Trying to stop them by exposing what they're doing via the press is not the way to go. Most of the traditional media outlets won't be your friends in this. Jeremy and I learned that the hard way.'

'What would you suggest we do?' asked Joe.

'If I had the answer to that, I wouldn't be hiding in this house, would I?'

'I guess not,' Joe replied. Hopefully Mandy would have an idea of what they could do with this evidence if they found it, or even Auntie Susan. 'Well, if that's everything, we should be going. We need to head back to London and it's a long drive.'

'OK,' said Jessica, standing up and collecting the mugs.

'Just one last thing,' said Joe, playing Columbo. 'Could you give us the names of the other venues who are being targeted by Atrax? Would you please email them to me?'

Jessica budged uncomfortably on the spot with her fistful of cups. 'I don't know, Joe. I've spent eighteen months working on this story and Pascale quit her job and moved countries because of it. I don't know if I should just be handing over our research. Sorry, I know it means a lot to you, but it doesn't feel right.'

'That's selfish,' said Plimberley calmly, finally joining the conversation with a hot take that Joe was delighted to hear. 'I know I'm new to all this, but given everything I've heard, that sounds right selfish.'

Joe was in wholehearted agreement. Keeping any of this information to herself was out of line now. Did she still, despite everything, think she would take credit for the story if it eventually came out?

'Selfish?' snarked Jessica. 'I've told you everything you asked, answered every question, breached all sorts of professional confidentiality agreements. It's not selfish at all. I'm thinking of you too, of your safety. Those men, they threatened Pascale with a *gun*, Misty. In London! If something happened to one of you because of me, I don't know how I'd live with myself. Not on top of Jeremy and Sylvester and everything else.'

Lady Lady came to mind, of her bringing the story to Jessica in the first place and doing everything she could to stop the redevelopment. Then Mandy and Misty, counting out cash from the bar sales to cover the weekly bribe money. They wondered about the other venues and whether they might be doing something similar, panicking about their closure.

'We're already in danger,' said Joe, suddenly more Misty Divine than Joseph Brown. 'You think your career's in the hole now, but wait until the entire queer community finds out you had information you kept to yourself, that you could have stopped all of this but chose to hold on in the hope that one day it'd still get you a headline.'

Joe was riled up, hot, and their heart was beating too fast. Their frustration with Jessica had turned into a clammy forehead and beetroot cheeks.

'Fine,' she surrendered. 'Fine! I'll give you the venues. I'll email them to you later.'

There might not be a later, thought Joe. *She could head off on her tour of British B&Bs and we might never find her again.*

'No,' said Joe. 'Now.'

Joe and Plimberley said their goodbyes to Jessica and left her in the bungalow, with her promising to stay in touch should anything new come up that they needed to know. They ambled down the long driveway together and it was an entirely different place to the gloomy track they'd walked in the dark last night. The colours were vibrant, the summer sun was blazing, and flowers and bees and butterflies danced in the wind. Of all the places Jessica could have chosen to lie low, this was certainly a nice one.

When they reunited with Calista on the grass verge, Plimberley popped open the boot and started rummaging until she found a plastic carrier bag full of cans of drink. She took two out the bag and held one up towards Joe, who looked at it with disdain.

'Jesus, Plim, what's that?'

'It's called Power Hour.' She snapped a tab open and took a long gulp, and a chemical strawberry smell drifted from it. 'It's a new energy drink, for stamina. Everyone's drinking it. Keeps you dancing all night. Or driving all day in my case.'

Joe took a can and turned it around in their hand. It had a paper label that instantly came loose, like it had been glued on with the cheapest adhesive.

'Plim . . .' they said, 'is this home-made? It doesn't even have an ingredients list. Do you know what's in it?'

Plimberley laughed. 'What's in it, my dear Misty, is me not falling asleep at the wheel.'

Joe chose not to ask any more questions but turned down the can of Power Hour, just in case.

Once in the car and on the road, Plimberley said, 'Have you ever heard of this Ginger Baker then? Is she very famous?'

'I think she was on telly in the nineties, on the chat shows. *Ricki Lake* and stuff like that. Jeremy mentioned her in an article he wrote about churches in London that I read the other day.'

'Jeremy's the missing guy with the evidence we need, right?' said Plimberley as they drove out of Moretonhampstead and back towards the motorway.

Joe nodded. 'He's the one with the video.'

'Look her up then,' Plim urged, 'on your phone. Let's see what the internet's got to say about her.'

Joe opened a browser, tapping the preacher's name into the search engine. The first result was a Wikipedia listing. Joe scanned it and read chunks aloud as Plimberley drove.

'It says she started a megachurch in Tennessee in the nineties and that by the end of the first year it had 10,000 worshippers.'

'Ten thousand! Blimey!' said Plim. 'My biggest gig was about two thousand and I thought that was massive.'

'From there,' Joe continued, 'she opened a second church, then a third. By 1998 she was a regular guest on talk shows and Christian television stations . . . She moved from Tennessee to Texas . . . She's got an online shop.' Joe laughed. 'She sells her own Bibles with customisable covers. Wow, she's sold over a million of them!'

'So she's definitely rich. Bet she's not driving a rust-bucket like my sweet Calista.'

'I'd guess not,' said Joe, scrolling further through the article. 'It says here she's appeared on magazine lists of the USA's Richest Women every year for the last ten years. And always near the top.'

'Minted,' said Plimberley. 'What a world! From a few churches.'

'It's not enough,' muttered Joe, thinking out loud.

'Sounds like enough to me: chat shows, churches, millions of Bibles. I'd be all right with all that,' nodded Plimberley, imagining the wealth.

'No . . . some churches, television bookings and customisable Bibles wouldn't put her at the top of the rich lists. Think about it, Plim – it's *billionaires* on those lists. She must have other businesses too, investments and that kind of thing.'

'A woman with her fingers in many pies!'

Plimberley was buzzing and Joe gave her a look. 'Are you all right?' they said.

'Don't mind me, Misty love. I'm wired now from the Power Hour!'

They smiled. It was wonderful to be discussing this with Plimberley. Everything else had been so gloomy: the long and arduous conversations with Miles, the legal pressure of dealing with Mandy and Auntie Susan, the disastrous team-up with Divya. Here, with Plim, was it right to say it felt like fun?

Joe turned back to the browser and searched for the most recent rich list, feeling vindicated as they read. It turned out Ginger Baker had used her megachurch money to generate incredible wealth through other channels. She'd invested in all sorts of businesses, and none of them sounded especially good for the world. Her largest source of income came through a significant stake in a fracking company. A further scroll revealed an attempt at an exposé by a blogger five years ago: Ginger's customisable Bibles were made by prisoners who earned next to nothing for their labour and delivered her huge profits. She owned the prison too. Beyond that there were investments towards the privatisation of all sorts of public services, from health insurance and medical clinics to utilities such as water and gas.

Joe relayed all of this to Plimberley who tapped her temple like she was figuring it all out. 'So she's well connected, our Ginge. To get contracts like that, I think you need to be connected: to important people, government people.'

'Maybe I should see if there's a record of her political donations,' said Joe.

'Do it, Misty! Do it!' Plimberley was the most enthusiastic investigating partner Joe had had to date and they loved her for it. 'This is all well juicy.'

Joe searched again and found a flurry of photographs. Ginger Baker, arm in arm with political figures from the US, some that Joe recognised, some they didn't.

'Yes,' said Joe, scanning a list of recent donations, 'she gives big and, it seems, to the worst politicians – the ones in it for the money and prestige. It also looks like she makes her donations in the same states where she has her biggest investments.'

'Cash for contracts,' announced Plimberley, putting on a wise newsreader voice. 'She spends money to make money, that's what it boils down to, isn't it?'

'Yes,' said Joe. 'But don't all big companies make political donations? Isn't that just how these things are?' They were thinking of how in the UK such donations were a regular part of the election cycles.

'Oh yes, it's probably not illegal,' said Plimberley. 'I reckon it's one of those things that's *nearly* illegal – like when you don't scan everything at the self-service checkout.'

'No, Plim, that's actually illegal.'

'You know what I mean.'

Legal or not, Joe wasn't happy about it. It meant Ginger Baker not only had money, she had power.

'OK,' said Joe, 'what do we know then? A chain of megachurches and television preaching makes Ginger some millions. Then she uses those millions to support decision-makers in various states, allowing her easy access to win big contracts for all sorts of stuff. Those investments multiply her wealth even more until she's one of the richest women in the country.'

'So she's a rich, rich bitch,' said Plimberley.

'But that doesn't explain what she wants with Lady's Bar and the other queer venues. It's small fry compared to everything else she's got going on.'

'And what's she doing it *here* for?' asked Plim with twisted lips like she'd eaten a mouthful of Marmite. 'Why can't she just stay over there in America? Lady's Bar is none of her business!'

Joe had been asking themself this too. 'I wonder . . . Maybe there's fresh money to be made in the UK, a new market for her. She could have maxed out her opportunities in the US and is looking for pastures new. Building the megachurch in Tennessee is how she started there, gaining followers and respectability. Perhaps she's about to do the same here. Rinse and repeat.'

Plimberley sighed and her face grew more serious. She drummed her fingertips against the steering wheel. 'Money . . .' she said quietly.

'Money.'

Plimberley steered Calista around a busy roundabout towards an exit with signs for London. She wasn't the greatest driver and cut in front of a whole lane of waiting traffic. She didn't seem to care at all despite angry arms being waved and beeps from the other vehicles.

'Shurrruppp!' she yelled out the window as she sped past them all.

'Are you OK?' Joe asked. 'You seem a bit stressed. Is it the Power Hour?'

'No, it's not that, Misty. It's this . . . this old *cow* Ginger coming for us. It feels personal, you know? And what if it's not about the money? What if it's worse than that?'

'How do you mean?'

Plim's forehead was sheeny with sweat now. 'You know what I'm saying, Misty. There's another reason she could be doing this that has nothing to do with cash.'

Joe nodded. 'That she's a homophobe, a transphobe,' they said plainly. 'She's one of those extremists who hates queer people because she thinks her Bible tells her to. So she's trying to destroy our community spaces because of that?'

Plimberley turned from the wheel to look them in the eye. 'The only thing more dangerous than money, Misty, is hatred. And what if Ginger's come here to spread hers a bit further? A real basic Betty bad guy.'

Joe didn't enjoy the thought of this one bit. 'That might make her harder to stop, Plim. If what she's doing here is some sort of religious mission, that makes her pretty scary.'

After a short pause, Plimberley spoke again. 'My dad's like that you know, Misty. He got gobbled up by the internet, the conspiracy theories and the lunatics in the comments. The hatred, it got in his brain somehow and rotted it inside out.'

'I know,' said Joe, giving Plimberley's shoulder a squeeze. 'I'm sorry, love.'

They sped down the motorway and Joe looked out the window, watching as the fields and other vehicles passed by. They thought about Lady Lady, how she'd worked her entire life to create a safe space for queer people in the heart of Soho. She'd fought for it in the end. She'd gone behind Mandy's back, and Auntie Susan's, to try and save Lady's Bar with Jessica, but she hadn't even known who she was fighting against.

Now Joe knew, and whatever Ginger Baker's motives, it was time to finish what Lady Lady had started.

CHAPTER 30

Years ago, before the poisonings and the bribery, Lady Lady had given up her television comedy career to become the owner of her very own cabaret club. Joe remembered one night after a show, Misty had gone to Lady Lady's dressing room to congratulate her on her performance and to weasel for a bit of gossip.

During the post-show mix and mingle, Lady Lady had lavished attention on one man in particular. Misty had never seen him before, and it was unlike the hostess to spend so much time with one person while she was working the crowd. Misty was curious and wanted to know who he was.

A shiny brass star on the dressing-room door said 'Lady Lady' in swirly engraved writing. She knocked gently and within seconds the door swung wide open.

Lady Lady was a full foot shorter than Misty but still imposing, holding a power and grace that could intimidate even the cockiest performer. She'd already changed out of this evening's gown and her body was draped in a purple robe with feather trim, and her face, wig and jewellery were still in place. Her hair was a beehive, the same lavender colour as always.

'Misty,' she said. 'You almost caught me in my birthday

suit!' She made a show of pulling her robe closed at the neck and Misty laughed. 'Come on in.'

Lady Lady sat elegantly behind her make-up station and started taking off her earrings. 'Don't think I don't know why you're here,' she said, a cheeky twinkle in her eye.

'Why's that?' asked Misty, feigning innocence.

She turned in her seat to look Misty full in the face. 'Do you know, I think you're the nosiest drag queen I've ever met in my life, and that's really saying something!' She winked and cackled with laughter.

'Hey!' Misty protested.

'But oh, how we love you for it, sweet Misty.'

'So you think you know why I'm here,' she said, leading into it.

Lady Lady wagged a finger. 'I *know* that I know! You're here to scrounge for scraps about the friend I was talking to after the show. And, before your thoughts descend to the gutter, Miss Divine, I can tell you that that's all he is – a friend. A very old and very dear friend.'

How did she know?!

As if reading Misty's mind, she rolled her eyes. 'You were like a meerkat out there turning your head every few seconds to look at us. You're not the most discreet person.'

Misty knew not to take this personally. She shrugged away the critique and unleashed her full nosiness. She might as well now it was out in the open. 'Go on then,' she said. 'Tell me about him. You were talking for ages.'

Lady Lady clasped her hands in her lap and her purple nails glittered. 'I knew him years ago, back when I first opened this place. He moved out of London long before you and I met, and he doesn't come back very often. His name is Steven and he means a great deal to me.'

'How so? If you don't mind me asking . . .'

Lady Lady smiled. 'You're asking anyway. But no, I don't. Steven started coming here in the early days. He was going through a divorce, from a woman of course – men couldn't marry then. They had three children together, and it was messy with money and property and such. I didn't know any of this to begin with. At first he would simply come in once or twice a week and sit at the bar nursing a Hooch or a Bacardi Breezer. We don't sell those now, but they were all the rage! I remember I tried a few times to make conversation, but he was very nervous of me, of everybody, and would run right out as quickly as he could.

'Then, one day,' she continued, 'young Mandy collared him on his way out the door and told him he should stay and have a drink with us after the show. To both of our surprise, he did, and over the following weeks he stayed more and more. One night, when Mandy wasn't working, it was just me and Steven in the bar.' Lady Lady turned back to the mirror and started unpinning her wig as she talked. 'You know how it is, Misty, how people like to dump their trauma on drag queens, telling us their deepest and darkest because they think we've been through it all. Well, it wasn't quite that, but something like it. Steven told me about his divorce, about his wife and kids, and then he told me something surprising.'

'What?' asked Misty.

'That he's gay,' said Lady Lady. 'He said he'd always known but hadn't ever told anyone before. He came out,

216

to me, in Lady's Bar! The first person he ever told. What a privilege.'

'That must have been quite a lot! For both of you.'

'Yes,' said Lady Lady as she lifted off the beehive and wig cap, revealing a shiny bald head beneath. 'Eventually he got through his divorce, got a boyfriend, shared custody of the kids, and he kept on coming here, for years after. Then he got a job in Spain and now I don't see him very often. I think because it happened in those early days, when me and Mandy were still starting out, it made me realise how important this place is. Not just for cabaret performers and drag artists, but for everybody. You don't know what anybody's going through when they step through those doors, what they might need a place like this for. Steven found himself by coming here. Accepted himself. Transformed his life so he could live his truth.'

Misty hadn't seen the club through this lens before. 'I guess I'd always just thought of queer spaces as a place for the gays and theys to hang out together and have fun,' she said.

'And they are!' grinned Lady Lady. 'They're *exactly* that. But not everybody comes in looking to party. You don't know who they are when they walk down those stairs. For some people, coming to a place like this is the first step in a life-saving journey. Steven changed the way I saw Lady's Bar. It's not just a place for cocktails and cabaret.'

'Thanks for telling me,' said Misty, emotional about what she'd heard, grateful for Lady Lady's candour and guilty for prying into such a personal story.

'You're very welcome,' she replied, reaching for a towel and a pot of coconut oil to take off her make-up. 'But you'd better go and get that drag off. I'm not keeping the doors open late because you were being a busybody. Go on, hurry up!'

Misty thanked Lady Lady again and headed back down the corridor to the queens' dressing room. The other performers were already de-dragged and packing up their costumes into suitcases and bags-for-life to carry home. And as Misty began by taking off her eyelashes, she thought about Steven and Lady Lady. Lady's Bar, and their time together in it, had changed both of their lives for the better.

This years-old conversation played itself back in Joe's mind as they neared London in Plimberley's rust bucket. They looked over at Plim. She too had found community, safety and new family at Lady's Bar. Many people had, Joe supposed, but now the club was in danger. Not just from a nameless corporation who wanted to turn it into a PizzaExpress as Lady Lady had feared, but from a wealthy and powerful individual who might be targeting them simply because of who they were.

It was mid-afternoon by the time they reached Soho. Plimberley dropped Joe off a short walk away from Old Compton Street and asked, 'What are your plans now? What can I do to help?'

Joe looked at their watch. It was already 3.30 p.m. They knew they had emails to do and admin to complete at Lady's Bar that they'd been putting off for days. 'I have to go to the club,' they said. 'I'm behind with stuff there.'

'You can trust me with this, Misty,' Plimberley said. 'I know it's too serious to tell anyone.'

'Thanks, Plim. I appreciate it.' Joe moved to get out of the car, before turning back and looking at the duvet and pillows in the back seat. 'Where are you sleeping tonight, Plim? In here?'

She nodded and shook her head at once, immediately looking like a lost little boy. 'It's not so bad, Misty. At least it's summertime. And I'm saving, I am. I'll have a deposit soon . . .'

'Stay with me tonight, will you? Miles is away, so come to mine after your gig. I can put out the sofa bed, order us a Chinese and we can watch some trash on the telly. And I'll talk to Mandy this week about getting you extra gigs. We can't have you keep doing this.'

The young lip-syncer's face spread into a smile she couldn't contain. 'I'd really like that, Misty. A lot.'

As Joe took the short walk to Lady's Bar, they felt overwhelmed by the last few days. A year ago, while investigating Lady Lady's murder, they'd only had Miles to rely on and neither of them knew anything about how to investigate a murder apart from what they'd seen on T V. This time around, Joe was going it alone. Sure, there'd been help from Plimberley, Divya, Mandy and Auntie Susan, but Joe had done something, hadn't they? Something they couldn't have done before. They'd followed the leads, collected the evidence, and now they had the full story.

CHAPTER 31

Though they usually loved getting into drag, today, after their long drive with Plimberley, Joe really didn't want to. They washed and shaved at the dressing-room sink and then sat behind the make-up station to begin the process.

Glue came first, for eyebrows. Then powder, foundation, more powder . . . blush, eyeliner . . . it took about an hour. By 5.30 p.m. the face was done and, in spite of the fatigue, Misty Divine was looking fresh and fruity.

Tonight she was wearing a 1950s-style cocktail dress. It was royal blue and hemmed with burgundy lace. Joe knew it was going with a blonde Marilyn Monroe wig and a pair of blue vintage heels that were shorter than Misty's usual stilettos. They pulled on their hip pads, held their breath as they tied themself into a corset and whipped tights up over the top. Next was a padded bra, and then the dress itself. Once fastened, they spun on the spot, watching the skirt ripple out around their legs.

Time for the Marilyn.

Joe fixed the wig with pins to hold it in place and dabbed glue to blend the lace edges. The final steps were jewellery and perfume.

Before they knew it, Joe Brown was gone and a thoroughly exhausted Misty Divine was back in action.

The doors opened at 7 p.m. and the auditorium quickly filled with all types of people excited for the cabaret that awaited them. Misty went immediately to get a drink and Jan, the beardy bear who ran the bar, greeted her with a welcoming smile. She was pleased to see him.

'How are you, Misty?' he asked. 'I heard about the stabbing. Are you OK?'

To Misty the stabbing felt like a lifetime ago. A whole entire world ago. Since then she'd been off interrogating old people and uncovering the truth about her new nemesis, Ginger Baker. It all flashed through her mind as Jan handed her a gin and tonic.

'I'm fine, thank you,' she said. 'Here's to a fabulous, drama-free night!'

She raised her glass. It was showtime, and at showtime Misty had to be focused.

As she walked away from the bar towards the stage, Jan called out, 'Have a good one, Misty!' and she turned and gave him a wink.

Misty sang her opening number to rapturous applause. She expected the applause for this one: 'Everything's Coming Up Roses', the enormous musical theatre hit that she always delivered faultlessly. Then she bowed, said a few words, and introduced the next performer of the evening.

First up was a baking-themed queen called Faddy

Crannock. Out of drag she was an actual baker, Misty knew, with a small shop that specialised in celebration cakes and elaborate doughnuts. Her non-drag name was Sarah and her Instagram feed was primarily pictures of a small dachshund she'd adopted with her partner during the COVID lockdowns. Faddy didn't perform often at Lady's Bar, but when she did, it was always a delight. Tonight was a ridiculous *Great British Bake Off* sketch and Misty found herself laughing heartily along from the side of the room. But as Faddy was wildly stirring a bowl of squirty cream onstage, Misty noticed some movement at the back of the auditorium. It distracted her from the performance and she turned her head to see what was happening.

Two men. In black suits. Of course Misty saw men in suits all the time, but suits as corporate as this were a rare sight at Lady's Bar. And given everything that was happening with Sylvester and the men in his office, this felt especially remarkable. She was tense suddenly, on edge, twitching muscles in her calves. She watched the suits take seats at a vacant table at the back of the room and quietly order drinks from a waiter who returned moments later with two bottles of beer.

She tried not to stare, glancing over and noticing that they weren't even watching the show. They were paying no attention whatsoever to Faddy's cream spectacular. Instead they seemed to be looking around the venue, studying the customers and the staff.

It's them, she thought. *It's Atrax.*

It wasn't the men from the photographs, the ones who had broken into Sylvester's office, but an instinct deep inside told her that these two suits were definitely related to the business with Ginger Baker.

Are they trying to intimidate me? she wondered. *Have they realised I'm searching for Jeremy too and are trying to scare me off?*

Whatever their reason for showing up, she didn't want them here. They were not cabaret regulars and definitely hadn't come for the show.

Faddy Crannock started her second number, a mix of songs from *Shrek: The Musical*. Misty had time, a few minutes at least, before she'd be needed to introduce the next act. She got up from her stool at the side of the stage and hurried in her blue fifties heels to the club's reception desk where Tess, the head of security, was standing.

'Hey, Tess,' she whispered so as not to disturb the show.

'Everything OK, Misty?' Tess looked worried.

'Yeah, fine. I was just wondering, the two guys at table 41, are they on the guest list? Do you have their names or emails?'

Tess glanced over at the table and then, remembering, said, 'No. They just arrived and paid cash on the door. It wasn't an advance booking, so I don't have any details at all. Why? Is there something I need to be concerned about?'

'Not now,' said Misty. 'But keep an eye on them, would you?'

She stepped away from the reception desk and took a new position at the back of the room by the bar. She was just a few metres away from the suits. Neither of them had even taken a sip of beer, and one of them was sending messages on his phone. His screen glowed white and bright.

Talk to them, said her inner don't-give-a-shit Misty. *It's your club after all.*

Yes, she thought, *I should just confront them.*

Feeling confident, cocky, and safe in her home surroundings, she made the approach. She walked right up behind them at table 41 and bent down, placing her head directly between theirs.

'Good evening,' she said quietly so as not to distract neighbouring tables from Faddy's onstage moment.

The suits didn't flinch. They didn't look at her. The one on his phone didn't even look up.

'Just popping over to check you're OK here,' she said, with a big fake smile across her face. 'I don't think I've seen you here before.'

Her stomach turned as they failed to respond again. They reminded Misty of the Buckingham Palace guards.

'Do you need another drink?' she asked.

Nothing. Silence. Ignorance.

'Very well. Enjoy your night.'

Misty turned to walk away. Faddy was coming to the end of her set and Misty was required onstage. That's when one of them spoke.

'Heard about what happened on your staircase,' he said.

Misty turned back to face him. He was cold, emotionless.

The one on his phone looked up at last, staring Misty right in the eyes. 'Wouldn't like to hear of anything like that happening again, would we?'

'No,' said the other. 'We definitely wouldn't want anything like that happening again.'

Her mind skipped back a few days to Sylvester, lying

on the stairs, blood pumping out between her fingers. Her Goldie Hawn suit, ruined. She stepped forward and put both hands down firmly in the middle of the cabaret table. 'Are you threatening me?'

'No, no,' said the first man. 'We're just here to enjoy the cabaret.'

He lifted his beer in a sort of 'cheers' and Misty walked away. Faddy had finished her performance and the rest of the room was in full applause. Threats or no threats, Misty was needed onstage.

She bustled her way through the tables and mounted the small staircase. Gracefully taking the microphone from Faddy, Misty called to the crowd, 'Let's hear it once again for Faddy Crannock!'

I've been threatened. That's all she could think. *I've been threatened in my own club!*

She decided to take control of the situation.

Nobody messes with Misty Divine on her home turf.

'Wasn't she fantastic?' Misty asked, and there was a huge cheer in response. 'Now,' she continued, smiling brightly, 'I recognise so many of your lovely faces here tonight. Jack and Andrew . . . Lesley, great to see you . . .' she pointed at a table on the front row and a couple waved back at her. 'So many regulars in this evening, but I want to take a moment to say a special welcome to two Lady's Bar first-timers.'

Am I really doing this? she wondered.

Yes, I damn well am.

She could see the suits fidgeting in their seats, uncomfortable already at what may come next.

'If you would, all of you,' Misty said to the packed venue, 'to make our new guests feel especially welcome, especially *seen*, please take a moment to turn in your seats to face them – the two gentlemen at the back of the room in the gorgeous suits. Look closely at their handsome faces everybody, and let's give them a huge round of applause!'

Everybody turned. Necks craned. People all over the auditorium strained to see the men with the undrunk beers and then they clapped, fiercely and ferociously, applauding the Lady's Bar newcomers.

As the applause rolled, Misty smiled at the two men and nodded her head towards the door. The signal was clear.

Get out.

And once everyone turned back around and Misty began introducing the next performer, she watched from the stage as the suits got up from their table and hurried out the venue.

She felt pleased with herself. Smug.

Hundreds of people in here saw you, you bastards.

She was confident they wouldn't be back.

CHAPTER 32

Wednesday

Midnight had passed by the time Joe got home. The rest of the cabaret had gone without a hitch, though Misty had been distracted by her confrontation. She was glad she'd done it. If ever she needed them, she now had hundreds of witnesses that those men were in the club.

After the show she kept the mix and mingle shorter than normal so that she could de-drag as quickly as possible. She was longing for a night in her own bed after Jessica's countryside hideaway.

Joe was surprised to find themself relieved that Miles wasn't home. Yes, Joe missed him, but they felt lighter for not having to tell him about Alice and Jessica Gethyn and the new threats at Lady's Bar.

Selfish, Joe, that's what you're being in keeping these secrets.

They opened the fridge in the kitchen and saw that there wasn't really anything to eat or drink, and Plimberley would be here soon for a second sleepover. They placed a quick delivery order and as it was confirmed, there was a knock on the door.

'How was Lady's Bar?' Plim asked as she struggled into the

little hallway with an overnight bag. Her face was clean and sparkling – her evening's drag make-up pristinely removed.

Joe filled her in on the Lady's Bar events and Plimberley listened intently. It felt like they had a friend in all this now. And not just any friend – a friend who understood the importance of the bar in a way nobody else could. After all, Lady's Bar had saved Plimberley, just as it had saved Misty and Joe.

Once the food arrived (a banquet for two with a side order of spring rolls) the conversation died down. They were both shattered. Misty put on an episode of *The Hotel Inspector* with Alex Polizzi and the queens both laughed as the posh hotelier explored a rancid bed and breakfast.

By the time the show was over, they were both too tired to be awake any longer. Joe set up Plimberley's bed in the living room while their houseguest took care of the dishes. It was lovely indeed to have another soul in the flat.

Joe said goodnight to Plim and jumped in the shower, washing quickly but making sure to scrub away any remnants of tonight's Misty face before getting into bed. The room was so much bigger without Miles in it and, even in the summer heat, his side of the bed was cold. They sent him a text – short and simple.

Night, Miles. I love you. x

Joe closed their eyes, tried to push out thoughts of Ginger Baker, and went to sleep.

CHAPTER 33

Joe was woken at 7.56 a.m. by the sound of a text message. They grabbed at their phone through sleepy eyes. It was from Plim.

Hey babe – thanks for letting me stay. I've headed out cos I had to move Calista. Let me know if I can help with you know what . . . She signed off the message with the detective emoji and a pride flag that made Joe smile.

They replied, telling her to have a good day, and then got up to start packing away her living-room bed.

As they folded up a summery blanket, the flat's front door opened and closed softly.

It's the two men from the bar last night, Joe panicked. *It's Atrax!*

Joe looked around the room for a makeshift weapon, half-asleep and too slow, but in walked Miles. They rushed forward, arms outstretched to give him a hug. Seeing him now, his beautiful face, Joe was filled with emotion.

'What are you doing here?' asked Joe.

'I do still live here,' said Miles.

The hug was light, unenthusiastic, and Miles patted Joe on the back like an old friend.

'Yes, I just wasn't expecting you to . . . I wasn't expecting to see you, that's all.'

'I'm on my way to work,' he said, 'but I needed to talk to you first.'

Had he come to break up? Was this it? The end of it all?

'Do you have time for a tea?' asked Joe, trying to sound calm and casual.

'Sure,' said Miles, sitting on the freshly tidied sofa and looking at the bedding. 'Did you have guests last night?' he asked, as Joe started to make the drinks.

'Plimberley,' they replied. 'She's been sleeping in Calista again and I didn't think you'd mind.'

'I don't,' said Miles kindly. 'I'm glad you weren't on your own.'

Joe placed the teacups on the coffee table and joined Miles in the living room.

'This feels awkward, doesn't it?' they said. 'It doesn't feel like us.'

'Yeah,' said Miles.

'How are your parents?'

'They're fine, Joe. Same as always.'

'So . . . what did you want to talk about?'

They were nervous now, worried that Miles was going to tell them he was moving out for good, that their thirteen years of happiness was finished.

'What were you doing in Dartmoor?' he asked.

Joe's stomach turned. Was this it? The moment they had to come clean about everything and tell Miles the truth about how far down the rabbit hole they'd gone?

You're doing this for *Miles*, they reminded themself. *To stop Atrax, the bribery, to get everything back to normal.*

Keep it light. Leave out the bad stuff.

'I went to visit Jessica Gethyn.'

Miles looked surprised, his eyes wide. 'The journalist? The one who came to Lady Lady's funeral?'

'Yes,' said Joe. 'I know it's difficult for you because of everything that happened last year, but I'm trying, really trying, to sort things out like you wanted.' They stayed calm, their voice low and smooth. 'The stabbing at the club last week is connected to Atrax and the bribery. What Sylvester was trying to warn me about . . . it's that.'

Miles leaned forward and covered his face with the palms of his hands. 'I knew it,' he said. 'I hate that you're doing this again, but tell me, honestly, there's a way out of this, isn't there?'

'I think so,' said Joe, 'but it's complicated.'

They talked for a while and Joe gave Miles the headlines of the story so far, leaving out Alice Gethyn and the search of her knicker drawer.

'Maybe it's time for the police, Joe, or your solicitor, Mr McDermott. He'll know what to do.'

'We can't, Miles, we just can't. We'll lose everything! And it wouldn't be just Lady's Bar who loses, but all those other venues. They'll be shut down by Ginger Baker. We mustn't let her win.'

Miles leaned back and looked up at the ceiling with exasperation. 'I can't be involved, not like before. It's too much.'

'I understand that. *I* can do it, Miles. I can sort this out, I promise.' Joe was pleading now and knew they sounded desperate.

'I hate to do this . . .' said Miles.

'Do what?'

'It's Wednesday today,' he said gravely. 'If this whole business with the bribery, the deal with Auntie Susan, if we're not out of it by Monday I'm going to go and see Mr McDermott myself. It's time to take this seriously.'

'I am! You don't know how seriously I'm taking it. You haven't seen it because *you left*, remember? You haven't been here while I've been doing everything I can to fix this on my own.'

Joe was mad now. This was another threat, an ultimatum from Miles.

'You're not serious though, Joe. You're running around the country with Plimberley, Misty Divining like this is some big adventure! This is a legal problem that requires a legal solution. It's not something two drag queens on a road trip can solve. It's our lives. Your life, my life . . . our life together.'

'Please, Miles, you don't understand.'

He placed his teacup on the coffee table. 'I do understand,' he said. 'We're in over our heads and this isn't a game. A man was stabbed, people are in hiding and you're being threatened at work. I'll give you the rest of the week to go to see Auntie Susan, tell her whatever you need to, and for you and Mandy to sort things out at the club, but after that we're going to deal with this like grown-ups, like we should have done from the start. On Monday we'll get proper legal advice so everyone can move on.'

'Please . . .' said Joe.

'I'm not going to keep doing this,' he said. 'Do what you need to do to get things in order, but on Monday we're taking this above board or else . . . well, I don't know.'

But Joe knew. The words Miles hadn't dared say out loud, the end of his sentence was going to be: *or else it's over.*

CHAPTER 34

At 11.01 a.m., one minute after opening time, Misty Divine thrust open the doors of the Plough and stepped inside like she owned the place.

She meant business and had dressed accordingly: a skin-tight faux leather catsuit and a pair of leopard-print heels. Her handbag was leopard print to match the shoes and her hair was swept back into a tight high pony. Lips were red. She was giving dominatrix vibes and it was very much intentional. The threat from Miles had lit a fire under her ass and she was on the warpath.

One of the bar staff looked up from wiping a table and was about to speak when Misty held up a finger to hush him, saying, 'I'm going to Auntie Susan's office.' There would be no discussion about it.

She strutted past the bar and the pool tables and pushed open the saloon doors to the back room. Then she took the short corridor to Auntie Susan's decadently deco-rated office. The guard outside, who looked to be about sixteen, looked up at Misty and said, 'You need to have an appointment.'

Misty didn't even slow. Didn't even look at him. 'Not this time.'

She reached Auntie Susan's door, knocked on it twice and then opened it and let herself in.

Auntie Susan was stubbing out a cigarette into a big gold ashtray on her desk as Misty strode into the office. She looked up, shocked, and long red synthetic hair fell around her face. Misty closed the door behind her.

'This can only mean one thing,' said Auntie Susan.

'And what's that?'

'A pain in my arse.'

'Maybe so,' said Misty, feeling that despite the power her outfit was giving her, this was about to be a difficult conversation. Her second in a day.

'You'd better sit,' said Auntie Susan. 'And is this a quick thing or will it warrant refreshments?'

'I think we'll both want to feel refreshed,' said Misty.

'Very well,' replied Auntie Susan, plucking up her phone from the desk. 'What's your tipple? Gin and tonic, isn't it? Bombay Sapphire if I'm not mistaken . . .'

Misty didn't like these stupid mind games that Auntie Susan so enjoyed. The way she dangled snippets and details to make it seem like she knew everything. She did it simply to intimidate, to put Misty on the back foot, but she wasn't falling for it this time.

'Yes,' she smiled. 'Bombay Sapphire and tonic would be perfect, thank you. And make it a double.'

Auntie Susan tapped the drinks order into the phone and pressed send with a little whooshing sound.

'So, Misty Divine. It's been . . . days. Whole, entire *days* since I last saw you. A year went by in a flash, as though the writer of our story had taken a break, and here you are now, twice in a week. I'm assuming you're here to talk about your missing photographer friend?'

'Yes. And Atrax,' said Misty.

'So naturally, you thought you'd dress as leopard-print Olivia Newton-John for the occasion.'

'Naturally,' said Misty.

The criminal mastermind leaned back in her chair and interlaced her fingers across her stomach. She was wearing the traditional Auntie Susan look again – the one she'd worn since her TV days with Lady Lady. A tight white Lycra minidress, red shoes and red jewellery.

'I shouldn't be involved with anything to do with Atrax,' she said. 'Our agreement from the beginning was clear: you pay your bill to me every week and I keep the bribe going to the council. I am not involved with Atrax, nor do I want to be. You don't pay me enough money for that.'

'But you are involved,' said Misty, 'whether you like it or not.'

There was a knock and the young man from the bar walked in carrying two gin and tonics with plastic straws. He placed them down on the desk.

'Thank you,' said Misty. She didn't really want a double gin at 11 a.m., but she was playing the game.

Auntie Susan shooed the youngster away with a flick of her hand and he left in a hurry. In the corner, Keanu the chihuahua stirred in his sleep.

'Tell me then,' she said.

'Firstly, I know who the client is – the one who hired Atrax to take over Lady's Bar,' said Misty. 'Her name is Ginger Baker and she's one of those anti-gay megachurch leaders in the United States. I think she's bringing her homophobic money-making schemes to the UK. She's opening a new venue in London.'

'I've heard of her,' said Auntie Susan, intrigued, and clearly wanting to know more. 'How do you think I'm involved? I'm simply a middlewoman between you and the council.'

'For how much longer?' said Misty. 'Jeremy Edmunds, the missing photographer, has evidence that Ginger Baker isn't just trying to take over Lady's Bar, but six other venues. All queer venues. He has a recording of her meeting the Atrax CEO Stefan Weber and wants to expose her, but that could reveal our little scheme, and your connection to the council. We need to find Jeremy and get the recording to see what's on it.'

Auntie Susan rolled her eyes. 'This smells very much like your own dirty diaper, Misty. You're the one with the dodgy accounts, you're the one with a club on the line. None of this is my problem.'

Misty was irritated and let it show with a performative sigh. 'It will very quickly become your problem. Your council shenanigans could be exposed, Mandy could be interrogated . . . How long do you think it will take for someone to drop your name into the mix? Then it's not just the bribery that gets looked into but everything else, whatever else you're up to here, the rest of your so-called business.'

The red-headed criminal thought it over and patted her Lycra-clad belly. 'I was right,' she sighed. 'This is a pain in my arse. *You* are a pain in my arse. Every single time.'

Misty continued. 'It's not just your illegal activity that's at risk either. If Ginger Baker is working on shutting down seven queer venues before she's even properly established here, you know she won't stop there. If she gets herself the same support and political influence in the UK as she has in the US, every queer space could be targeted. The Plough could be next.'

'The Plough will be just fine. I own it outright, every last brick.'

Misty's frustration was building. Auntie Susan just wasn't seeing the big picture, but she had to open her eyes and convince her. 'And your licence?' she said. 'You think that won't be brought into question? How long do you suppose it would take one of the world's richest women and a company like Atrax to find out about your indoor smoking, your underage staff, your underpaid performers . . . It'll be your diaper that's dirty when the bastards come digging.'

Gross, thought Misty. She felt sick with herself for throwing one of Auntie Susan's disgusting analogies back at her, but there was a time pressure now. Miles' deadline. And she needed the old queen's help.

Auntie Susan drummed her fingertips against her desk, thinking. 'OK,' she said, leaning forward and picking a cigarette from a silver tin. 'Let's say you're right. This Ginger Baker and Atrax are coming for Lady's Bar and somewhere down the line they might come for me too, one way or another. What do you expect me to do about it? What do you actually want?'

'I know you like to keep your business private,' said Misty.

'I do indeed,' replied Auntie Susan.

'So if you want to keep it that way, we're going to need to work together.'

'How so?' Auntie Susan lit the cigarette and blasted out a cloud of smoke.

'We need your resources. All of them. Use them to find Jeremy Edmunds before he leaves the country. Apparently he came back to London on an unregistered motorcycle to try and get his passport.'

'Jesus Christ, Misty. You want me to find one man, on an unregistered motorbike, in a city of nine million people? I don't know what resources you think I have, but I'm not turning water into wine over here.'

'Mandy once told me that you were running gangs,' said Misty. 'Mobile phone thieves on bikes or something. Is that true? Could they not help with searching? Can you ask some of your "employees" to watch his flat? Stake out his place in case he comes back for the passport?'

'When? When do you expect me to do this?'

'Now!' said Misty. 'We might have already missed him.'

Auntie Susan took another puff and Misty sipped her gin. It was strong, and despite not wanting it initially, she was glad for it now.

'What do I get?' said Auntie Susan. She said it greedily, like a child, and Misty was riled.

'This time,' she replied, 'this time you get nothing. I am giving you nothing more than I already have. You'll do this one because it's the right thing to do – for the venues, for Lady's Bar, for the Plough.'

Auntie Susan tsked and crossed her arms again.

'You'll do it because if you don't, we're all in a million kinds of trouble.'

What she didn't say was that Miles was planning to drop a legal bombshell on them all in the shape of Mr McDermott.

CHAPTER 35

Misty clambered into the back of a car outside the Plough, careful not to scrape her wig on the door on the way in.

'How long will it take?' she asked the driver.

'About twenty minutes,' she replied. 'I like your hair.'

'Thank you,' Misty smiled.

She popped in her AirPods and opened her phone, turning on some peaceful piano music to soothe her brain. The ultimatum from Miles, the heated and testing conversation with Auntie Susan, all of it was building up like a big stress bubble ready to burst.

Auntie Susan had agreed to everything in the end, like Misty had known she would. The old queen liked to play hardball, but when her businesses, legitimate or otherwise, were at stake, Misty knew she'd fight for them. And, she thought, there was a softer side to Auntie Susan, a side she hadn't yet seen but could sense throughout their difficult exchanges. She had been Lady Lady's best friend once, many moons ago. She couldn't be a complete villain.

She hadn't told Misty exactly what she was going to do, but she'd taken a mouthful of gin and tonic and said, 'I'll help, Misty. I'll make all the calls and I'll help.' Whether she was helping for her own survival or to support the other venues was unclear. Misty hoped it was at least a bit of both.

She closed her eyes in the back of the car and took the twenty-minute drive to clear her head. She had somebody else she needed to talk to as soon as possible: Mandy.

Misty arrived at Lady's Bar on Old Compton Street just after 1.30 p.m., let herself in, and headed down the stairs. Memories of Sylvester lying there, bleeding, rushed to the fore.

'*You must find Jeremy . . .*' he had said.

I'm trying, Sylvester, she thought. *I'm really trying.*

She found Mandy in the auditorium, working on a laptop at one of the cabaret tables by the bar.

'Fancied a change of scene,' said her co-owner with the Claudia Winkleman fringe. 'That office is doing my head in. We need to paint it or something, put some sun lamps in.'

Misty smiled. 'You do know you could work from literally anywhere you wanted for most of the day. If you can work from a laptop in here, you can work from a laptop in the park, in a sunshiney café . . . your options are endless, Mandy.'

She grinned and then looked Misty up and down. 'Oh no,' she groaned.

'What?' asked Misty.

Mandy pointed her finger from Misty's head to her toes. 'You, in full drag. In full . . . what is that? Is that a *leather* catsuit? It's June! You must be sweating like a pig's backside in that.'

'It's leatherette, actually. Vegan. It's very light.'

'Nevertheless, if you're in full dominatrix drag at lunchtime on a Wednesday afternoon, that can only mean one of two things: either you've got yourself a kinky side-hustle or there's some sort of trouble going down.'

Misty shrugged.

'Which is it?' said Mandy. 'Have you been out there telling off naughty daddies, or is one about to roll down the stairs with a knife in his chest? It could go either way with you these days.'

Misty laughed, but she didn't feel much like laughing today.

'I'm not joking!' said Mandy, though it was clear she was, just a little.

'OK,' said Misty, walking behind the bar to pour herself a lunchtime gin and tonic. If Auntie Susan could do it, so could she! 'Do you want a drink?' she asked.

'Do I need one?' replied Mandy.

'Possibly.'

'Go on then. A big brandy.'

Misty fixed two drinks and, as she was doing so, said, 'We do need to talk. Things have . . . progressed since last time we caught up about everything.'

'Did you find him? The photographer?' asked Mandy. 'The photos in his camera, are they because of our deal with Auntie Susan?'

'She's who I've just been to see. She's helping.'

Mandy looked horrified. 'You went to see Auntie Susan? Without us discussing it first?!'

Misty stayed cool, collected, business-like. 'There was no other choice. We need her help.' She placed the brandy down in front of Mandy and sat opposite.

'What did she want from us this time?'

'To be a judge at Friday's Star Search.' Misty knew this would go down badly and Mandy's entire face fell wide open.

'No!' she gasped. 'She's coming here? To Lady's Bar?!'

'She is – but it's urgent now and she's going to help us find Jeremy.'

'So you still don't know where he is? What if he's dead, Misty, did you ever think about that?'

'He's not. I almost found him – missed him by a few hours. I tracked down Jessica Gethyn to a house in Dartmoor where she'd gone into hiding. I went there on Sunday with Plimberley.'

'Dartmoor!' Mandy said it as though it was the furthest away place on Earth, the way *Coronation Street* characters talk about London. 'Plimberley?!'

'Yes,' said Misty. 'That's a long story, but what you need to know is that Jessica told us who's trying to take over Lady's Bar. The Atrax client. It's a rich American preacher woman called Ginger Baker.'

Mandy coughed as the brandy went down and then said, 'Ginger Baker . . . I recognise the name. Wait, was she on the telly a bunch of years back?'

'Yes,' said Misty. 'The church channels and the talk shows.'

'God,' said Mandy. 'I'd never have thought about her again. What does *she* want with Lady's Bar?'

'Probably just money, possibly the decimation of the queer community as we know it. But we're not alone. She hired Atrax to target us and six other queer spaces, spread all across the UK.'

'That's insane,' said Mandy. 'Why would an American TV preacher be meddling with a bunch of British queer bars?'

'We don't know yet,' said Misty. 'Could be some sort of religious thing. Or it's simply about the cash – she's got loads of horrible investments according to the internet.' Misty sipped on her second gin of the day and it tasted heavenly.

Mandy stood up, restless, pacing in front of the bar. 'Now we know who it is, we can do something. Surely we can do something to stop her! Tell the papers, post it on the Lady's Bar Instagram, something like that?' She clenched her little fists and the muscles in her thick arms bulged.

'Not yet,' said Misty, watching Mandy walk up and down. 'Jessica Gethyn tried to get a story about it published for over a year, but nobody would print it, and Lady Lady was helping her. She'd confided in her about the bribery months before she died.' She knew this might sting a little for Mandy, to learn that Lady Lady, her best friend and business partner, had gone behind her back to a journalist.

'Lady Lady was talking to the reporter about our secret Atrax business?' Mandy's mouth was agape again – the kind of face you might see in a viral video of someone discovering their partner cheating. 'The sneaky old so and so!'

Misty nodded. 'She was trying to get you all out of it. I didn't know either until we talked to Jessica.'

'There's a turn-up for the books!' Her Scottish accent was double-strength. She plonked herself down in her chair and finished the brandy in a big gulp. 'Right, tell me everything from the beginning so I fully understand what's happening.'

'I'll make us fresh drinks,' said Misty.

*

Over the next half an hour Misty explained everything, laid all the details out on the table, from Jessica hiding Jeremy, to Misty's morning with Auntie Susan.

'OK,' said Mandy, 'so if I'm getting this right, our next job is to find Jeremy Edmunds, get the evidence and see if we can use it to stop Atrax and Ginger without revealing our own shenanigans.'

'Exactly,' said Misty.

'And Auntie Susan is using her contacts to do that?'

'Correct,' said Misty.

'Bloody hell, Misty. You've pulled out all the stops this time.' Mandy looked impressed.

She didn't want to tell Mandy about Miles' threat to go legal. Not yet, not before she'd exhausted every avenue to save Lady's Bar. 'Yes,' she replied. 'It's time to put an end to this, for all of us.'

'I couldn't agree more,' said Mandy.

'There is something else,' Misty started. 'There's danger around all this and it's getting closer to home.'

'Tell me something I don't know, Misty love. A man nearly died on the stairs!'

'Last night, during the show, two latecomers arrived, paid for tickets on the door and sat at the back. In suits.'

'The ones from the photograph?' Mandy was nervous and scanned the empty auditorium as though the suits might still be there.

'Two others, but they're all connected, I'm sure of it. They threatened me, said we wouldn't want a repeat of the stabbing. It definitely sounded like a threat.'

Mandy put her hand over her mouth, shocked. 'What did you say?'

'I gave them a big Lady's Bar welcome from the stage,' Misty laughed. 'Made everyone in the room look at them. They left pretty swiftly after that.'

Mandy seemed very worried about this indeed. 'I'm calling Tess,' she said. 'I'll get her to increase the security team with agency staff until this is over.'

'Good idea,' said Misty.

While Mandy called Tess to boost security at short notice, Misty headed to her dressing room. It was getting on for 4 p.m., she'd had a few gins and was ready to take off the leatherette catsuit. Mandy was right: she was too hot, and sweating like a pig's backside, whatever that meant.

She swapped the catsuit for a night robe. A light, glamorous silk gown that flowed down to her ankles. She cinched it with a belt and sat down behind her make-up station.

She decided to text Divya. It had been a couple of days since their street-side argument. Maybe she'd calmed down a bit since then.

Divya, I'm sorry about what happened with Alice. I was wondering how Sylvester is?

There was an immediate reply.

Still in ICU. Please don't contact me again.

That was that, she supposed. Any budding friendship she might have found with the detective's assistant was clearly well and truly over.

She messaged Jessica Gethyn next, on the new number she'd given them yesterday.

> *Jessica, it's Misty. Did you get away from the Dartmoor house? Just want to know that you're safe.*
>
> Jessica replied: *Yes. I'm keeping moving. How's everything going on your end?*
>
> Misty responded: *We have help with the search for Jeremy. Atrax showed up at the bar last night, but we're all safe.*
>
> *Be careful,* said Jessica, *and keep me updated when you can.*

Misty placed down the phone and used a light foundation brush and some powder to touch up her forehead – the catsuit had caused a sweat-astrophe that needed fixing before this evening's show.

Make-up fixed, she wandered to the rail, looking at tonight's costume. It was a camp one, almost a pantomime-dame look: a big floofy, flouncy skirt with a tight top that had giant buttons fastened all over it. There was a matching wig, a towering bright blue hair pyramid with a wave of yet more buttons up one side. She didn't often go full camp, so she was looking forward to wearing it. Florentina, her costume designer, had outdone herself and the comedy look paired perfectly with the evening's theme.

It was stand-up night and Misty didn't have to do much for those, just an intro and an outro. The rest of the show was hosted by a special guest, usually a comedian who'd had a few TV appearances or huge social media success but wasn't completely mainstream yet. The Wednesday night comedy gig was thankfully the easiest of the week.

There wasn't much else she could do right now. She'd acti-vated everyone she could, set all her wheels in motion. Miles had returned with his serious face and Misty had sprung into action in response. Now it was simply a case of waiting to see whether Auntie Susan would be able to locate Jeremy. She wandered back down the corridor to the bar.

'Look what I've done!' said Mandy, clearly pleased with herself. She turned her laptop around. On the screen were stills of the suits who had shown up at the club. 'I found the bastards on the CCTV. I'll make sure the door staff all have a print-out so they know they shouldn't let the shitheads in. Excuse my Portuguese.'

'Excused,' smiled Misty. 'Great work, Mandy.'

'We've got a couple of hours till the show,' she said. 'Do you need to rehearse anything, do any tech?'

'No, nothing,' said Misty. 'It's my easy night.'

Mandy got a cheeky glint in her eye. 'Well maybe we could, you know, have a little tipple? Not a big one! Not drunk or anything . . . but it has been a tough few days, hasn't it?'

'That it has, Mandles, that it has.'

So the co-owners of Lady's Bar sat together in the auditorium to take a quiet moment as their army of employees slowly started arriving for the evening's set-up. Flowers in vases needed to be set and tabletops were to be polished. Kitchen staff prepared ingredients for bar food and Jan the barman hauled bags of ice cubes and crates of beer around.

'I need to talk to you about Plim,' said Misty.

'What about her?' asked Mandy. 'What's she done this time?'

'I don't like her sleeping in that car,' she replied. 'I know she couch-surfs most of the time, but I wondered if there's a way we can help her find something more stable. Could we offer her some extra work? Another night's residency on top of her Thursdays? Flexible bar shifts to top her up?'

Mandy agreed. 'I've offered in the past,' she said, 'but she's a stubborn one. If you can convince her to accept the help, I'm happy with whatever you decide.'

'Thanks, Mands. And I know money's tight here, especially with our Auntie Susan situation, but do you think we could advance her enough for a deposit? She says she's been saving for one, but she's not quite there yet.'

'I'll need to check the books tomorrow,' said Mandy, 'but I think we can figure something out.'

At 5.30 p.m. Head of Security Tess and around a dozen new security staff arrived. She worked diligently, showing them around the venue, giving them print-outs of the forbidden guests.

'We've got your backs,' she said to Misty and Mandy.

Before they all knew it, it was time to let the audience in. Guests in flashy, splashy outfits piled down the stairs and took their seats. Usually at the start of a show Misty felt excited, but she didn't want to do this one. The power of her drag was such that she'd used it for years to squash down anything negative in her personal life. When she became Misty, Joe simply disappeared, but the walls between the two identities were thinning. The longer the Lady's Bar troubles dragged along, the more serious the situation with Miles was getting.

'The show must go on, my love,' said Mandy, sensing Misty's worry.

'I know,' said Misty. 'I'll be fine.'

*

And she was. Despite being a few gins down, she performed her hosting duties impeccably. A brief but gorgeous intro, an interval announcement, and then a 'thank you all for coming' at the end. It was as easy as she'd hoped it would be. No men in suits arrived and nobody caused any trouble. Aside from the fact that Misty was a tiny bit tipsy, there had been nothing to worry about at all.

As she was unzipping her dame costume, Mandy knocked on her dressing-room door.

'Can I come in, Misty love?'

'Yes,' called Misty. 'Enter!'

Mandy stepped inside. 'I wanted to tell you you did a smashing job tonight, and not just because I've had six brandies. There's a lot going on right now, but you didn't let it show for a second. Really professional, Misty. Really impressive.'

Misty felt a little moved. Mandy had never come to her room to compliment her like this. 'Thanks, Mandy. I appreciate that.'

'I want you to take a taxi home. A taxi home and back in again tomorrow. No more walking home through Soho after dark – you can expense it all. The club can cover it until all this is sorted out.'

They hugged before Mandy left and Misty de-dragged alone in her room, lifting off the blue pyramid hair that she had so enjoyed wearing.

It was time to go home.

CHAPTER 36

Thursday

Joe was sleeping peacefully for once, deep in a warm and relaxing slumber. They had just turned over, lifting the summer duvet to cover their bare shoulder, and that's when Thursday started with a bang. Or a ring, to be more precise. The sound of a phone ringing split through whatever nonsense Joe was dreaming about and woke them instantly. Their mobile. Bedside table. They stretched their arm out quickly to grab it, careful to avoid knocking over a glass of water. They noticed the time first: 8.39 a.m. And then they read the name on the screen.

Auntie Susan.

Auntie Susan at this hour?!

'Hello?' they said, answering the call with a voice they knew would sound groggy.

'You'd better wake the hell up, Misty Divine, and get out of bed right now.' She was serious, not messing around. Something was happening.

Without even questioning it, Joe threw back the duvet and got out of bed. A blast of cool air hit their cosy warm body.

'What's going on?' they asked, reaching for a T-shirt.

'Jeremy Edmunds. We've found him.'

'Where he is right now?!'

'Yes, Misty,' snapped Auntie Susan. 'Are you getting dressed?'

'Yes!' Joe started struggling to get into a pair of jeans while holding their phone at the same time.

'I put one of my guys outside Jeremy's flat like you asked. He ran in and out this morning. It was quick, but definitely him. We followed him to St Pancras station, to the Eurostar entrance. My guess is he's trying to leave the country by train and managed to grab his passport. There are departures to both Brussels and Paris leaving in the next couple of hours.'

'Why didn't your guy stop him?'

'Jesus Christ, you are so ungrateful. He couldn't. He was driving and there was nowhere to park. Jeremy dumped his motorbike outside the station and we lost him at the entrance. Your flat's nearby, Misty. If you run now, you could be there in ten minutes.'

'Shit,' said Joe. *Panique.* 'It'll be rush hour. It'll be packed. How will I find him?'

'That's up to you, just get there as fast as you can. I'll see if there's anything else I can do from here.'

'OK, leaving now,' said Joe.

Auntie Susan hung up and Joe threw on a pair of trainers and a shirt, grabbed their keys off the kitchen table, stuffed their wallet into their pocket and headed out the door.

It was a fifteen-minute fast walk to St Pancras from Joe and Miles' flat. A cab or an Uber at this time of day might take even longer, so Joe decided to run. Maybe Auntie Susan was right and they could do it in ten.

Already sweating, they were halfway there, outside the British Library, when they received a message.

I've sent my driver and a few guys to help search the station but not sure if they'll make it in time.

Joe responded with a thumbs-up emoji and hurried on their way. They knew the Eurostar entrance was on Pancras Road between the two main stations: Kings Cross and St Pancras International. That's where the taxis parked – Joe had been there before on a continental trip with Miles.

Miles.

Not now!

As they approached the station from Euston Road, the pavements were getting busier. There were already too many people in their way and Joe dodged around them as quickly as they could.

I can't believe I was cosy in bed just minutes ago and now I'm on a manhunt.

Joe rounded the corner and headed straight down to the entrance opposite the taxi rank, weaving through tourists and travellers with suitcases and buggies. In between two taxis was a red motorbike sitting alone. Joe didn't know the make or model, or anything about motorbikes at all, but this one had no registration plate and wasn't in a proper parking space.

Jeremy's bike, they knew. *He's here.*

A couple of moments later they were passing through glass automatic doors into the Eurostar departure zone. Here there were screens announcing when security would open for upcoming trains and a snaked queue that was at least 100 people long, all waiting to go through.

Joe rushed to the top of the queue to check the signage. The next departure, a train to Paris, would be opening in fifteen minutes.

Where is he? Where is he?!

Joe spun on the spot, glancing by all the cafés, bookshops and luxury goods stores that filled the station, scanning the length of the queue. No Jeremy. There were so many people it might be impossible to find him.

They turned again, thinking one last spin here might be useful before heading deeper into the station. Faces, buggies and suitcases moved around them in a blur and it was on this spin that Joe spotted the suits, the originals, the OGs from Sylvester's office, heading through the glass doors into the station.

Joe's insides turned to stone. A lurching dread set in.

Oh my God.

They weren't looking at Joe, not yet anyway. They were doing what Joe had done moments earlier, checking the departures screen.

Joe ducked behind a group of French tourists, clearly returning home after a sightseeing trip to London. They were wearing fake Oxford University sweatshirts from a tourist-trap shop and their luggage was bedazzled with clips and keyrings of Union Flags and red telephone boxes.

Hiding, Joe rushed through the options. There were only two reasons the suits could be there: *they staked out Jeremy's flat like Auntie Susan did, or they're following me.*

Joe hoped it was the former, but now the pressure was on to find Jeremy and get him out of the station before the suits did.

Before both of us end up like Sylvester.

The main stretch of St Pancras International was like a high street, with shops and cafés on both sides. Joe thought the best thing to do was check each of them, to run quickly past them all and see if they could spot the missing photographer. They started with M&S: no Jeremy. Then Hatchards: no Jeremy. This was madness. He could be anywhere!

They started sprinting, glancing down at the Eurostar gates to see the suits inspecting the queue.

'Siri, call Auntie Susan,' Joe said into their headphones.

She answered instantly.

'Did you find him?' she said.

'Not yet,' said Joe, out of breath, 'but the suits are here – the Atrax or Ginger Baker suits – whoever they are. They're here looking for Jeremy too!'

They squeezed through a group of businesspeople with laptop bags and satchels as they passed the tall escalators to the upper concourse.

'Stay calm, Misty dear. My driver is nearly there,' said Auntie Susan.

Joe reached the top of the shopping area and passed the domestic train gates.

'Can you tell your driver to park somewhere very close and keep the engine running?' they said, trying to think through the beginnings of an escape plan. 'If I find Jeremy, I'll need to get us out of here as fast as I can.'

'Yes,' said Auntie Susan. 'Hold on.' There was a beep and then the line went silent as she put Joe on hold.

Joe leaped onward, past a French bakery and an over-priced card shop. No Jeremy. They didn't even dare look back to see where the suits might be. At the top of the station was a Starbucks. It was a small one – just a few tables and chairs inside with tall glass windows separating it from the hubbub of the regional departures. They ran in, looking around, checking all the customers as quickly as they could.

Joe couldn't believe their eyes. There, in a corner by the counter, unmistakable: it was Jeremy Edmunds. He was sitting in an armchair, a coffee in his hand, with an identical and empty armchair opposite him.

'You must find Jeremy,' Sylvester had said days ago.

I did it, Sylvester, thought Joe. *I finally found him!*

CHAPTER 37

Joe threw themself into the empty seat opposite Jeremy, panting, but filled with relief. The photographer looked up, tired and annoyed, as though he didn't want anyone to join him.

'Excuse m—' he started.

'Jeremy,' said Joe between gasps for air, 'we don't have much time. I'm Misty Divine, one of the owners of Lady's Bar. You photographed me, with the blue hair. Do you remember?'

How could he forget? I was gorgeous . . .

'How did you find me?' said Jeremy, reaching for his bag like he was getting ready to leave in a rush. His voice was scratched and serious.

'I can explain everything, but we have to get out of here.'

Jeremy hissed, 'I *am* getting out of here. I'm about to board a train.'

'You're not boarding anything,' said Joe, not quite sure where this new-found confidence was coming from – that was normally reserved for Misty. 'You can't. The Atrax or Ginger Baker people are here, whoever they are. They're in the station, looking for you right now. We have to leave this second.'

'How do you know about Ginger Baker?' Jeremy asked.

'Jessica,' they replied.

Joe's eyes were distracted by movement outside the café door. The suits. They weren't coming into the Starbucks, not yet anyway. They were parading the concourse outside, looking into every store and café one at a time.

'Put your head down,' said Joe, 'in your hands. They're here.'

Jeremy moved to glance over his shoulder.

'Don't look,' said Joe. 'Head down.'

'Shit,' said Jeremy quietly. 'Shit, shit, shit.' He lowered his head and placed a hand at the top of his forehead, like a baseball cap shielding his face.

'Auntie Susan?' said Joe. 'Are you still there? We need the car now.'

'I'm still here,' she said into their ear. 'You found him?'

'Yes,' said Joe. 'But quickly, the car! Our closest exit is the Pancras Road one. Is the car nearby?'

Joe could hear tapping, as if Auntie Susan was in front of her computer. 'There's a car park, just behind the station. The driver is around the corner. Take the Pancras Road exit, and turn left. Walk up a block and then into the underpass. He'll collect you there. Stay on the line until you get into the car. It's a black BMW.'

Joe looked out the window and saw the suits, walking in the opposite direction, heading towards some boutiques on the other side.

'Now!' said Joe. 'Now! Let's go.'

Joe stood up but Jeremy was hesitating, fumbling over his bag.

'Come on!' said Joe.

'Where are we going?' asked Jeremy.

'*Now, Jeremy!* There's a car waiting for us around the corner.'

The photographer grasped his bag straps tight and got up, abandoning his coffee on the table. Joe checked through the window and saw the suits, busy looking in the wrong direction.

'We're taking that exit,' said Joe, pointing at the huge glass doors on to Pancras Road, 'and then turning left to the car park.'

Jeremy nodded.

'OK,' said Joe. 'Let's run.'

Joe rushed through the Starbucks as quickly as they could, checking over their shoulder that Jeremy was right behind. From the café it was a short sprint to the Pancras Road exit and they cleared it quickly, descending a couple of short steps on to the pavement. They turned left and Jeremy caught up, running alongside Joe towards the car park.

They passed a big pub, busy with people sitting outside in the sun eating full English breakfasts and drinking coffee. Then, there on the corner was a sign for the car park, the underpass. They bounded left into it and saw a car sitting on the kerb a few metres ahead, its hazard lights flashing. A black BMW.

'This is it,' said Joe to Jeremy.

They reached the car and pulled open the passenger door.

'For Auntie Susan?' asked the driver.

'Yes,' said Joe.

'Who's Auntie Susan?' asked Jeremy.

'Just get in, I'll explain everything.'

They both clambered into the back of what seemed to be quite a fancy car. Joe recognised the driver as Baseball Cap, Auntie Susan's courier they'd dealt with before.

'Auntie Susan?' said Joe. 'Are you still there?'

'Still here, Misty. You're in the car?'

'We are.'

'We're bringing you back to the Plough,' she said.

'The Plough?'

Auntie Susan sighed down the line. 'We don't know if the suits were following you or if they'd tracked Jeremy, so you can't go home or to Lady's Bar. The Plough is your safest option.'

She was right, Joe knew. There was nowhere else to go.

'This has completely ruined my plan,' said Jeremy as they sped away from St Pancras in the direction of the Plough. 'I was supposed to be in Paris this afternoon, away from all this.'

'A lot's happened,' said Joe. 'The situation we're in now, it's inescapable. Paris or no Paris.'

Jeremy rubbed his face with his fingers and sighed. 'How did you find me? The passport? You were watching my flat.'

'Yes,' said Joe, 'and I'm guessing that's how the suits found you too.'

Jeremy grumbled, 'The police obviously weren't.'

'Doesn't look as though they've been doing very much to find you at all.'

'That's what I was banking on,' said Jeremy. 'Too many missing people, not enough time.' He paused and then, finally realising his European escape was over, smacked his thigh with the palm of his hand. 'Damnit!'

Joe didn't say anything. They could only imagine how stressful this had all been for Jeremy. Threatened, disappearing, a month hiding in Jessica's cottage . . . only to be caught by a drag queen in a coffee shop just moments before making the ultimate escape overseas.

They each looked out of their windows at the London rush hour. Joe studied the commuters everywhere, the tourists all over the place. It was a city full of people, going about normal, everyday business. And here Joe was, in the back of the car with the previously missing Jeremy Edmunds, neck-deep in trouble that was once again feeling like a life-or-death situation.

Joe glanced behind, out the rear window, looking in vain to see whether they might be being followed by the suits. They doubted it. It had felt like a pretty clean getaway from the station. Spotting Joe doing this from the driver's seat, Baseball Cap said, 'There's nobody following, Misty. I'm keeping an eye.'

'Thank you,' said Joe.

As they headed out of central London towards the east of the city, Jeremy turned to Joe. 'You said you'd spoken to Jessica. Is she OK?'

'She's in the wind,' Joe replied, 'like you. But she's OK, and we have a number for her if we need her.'

'We had an argument,' said the photographer.

'She said. But I don't think she's angry with you – just worried.'

'I guess you found the Dartmoor house?'

'I did. I went there on Sunday. The investigator, Sylvester Green, told me I needed to find you, so that's what I've been doing.'

Jeremy scratched his eyes. 'I feel awful about what happened to him. I'd never have expected my mom to hire an investigator.'

'She's worried out of her mind,' said Joe, 'but you couldn't have predicted this. The only people responsible for what happened to Sylvester are the ones who stabbed him.'

'How do I even know I can trust you?' said Jeremy. 'How can I be sure you aren't working with them, taking me straight to Ginger?'

'It's obvious I'm not,' replied Joe, in a tone they knew was dismissive. 'You photographed me outside Lady's Bar, you already know about Lady Lady and Atrax from Jessica, and I just stopped you getting grabbed by the suits. We're going to need to work together.'

'How?' asked Jeremy.

'I'm not sure yet,' said Joe. 'We'll talk it all through when we get to Auntie Susan.'

'You mentioned her before. Is she a drag queen too?'

'She's a lot more than that. You'd better brace yourself.'

'Home sweet home,' said Baseball Cap, parking the car on the pavement opposite the pub.

Joe watched as Jeremy took it in: the peeling paint, the broken signage, the boarded-up windows.

'Nice,' he said.

'You'll get used to it,' said Joe, knowing that they'd begun to.

'This is where we'll find Auntie Susan?' asked Jeremy.

'It is. You'll get used to her too.'

'Can't wait,' said the photographer, the sarcasm crystal clear.

The three walked from the car to the pub's dingy front door. Baseball Cap knocked hard against it and moments later the rattling of deadbolts and chains signalled someone unlocking the other side. It opened and there was Auntie Susan in her usual attire: white dress, red hair, full face first thing in the morning.

'In,' she said, 'inside quickly.' She stepped to one side as Baseball Cap, Jeremy and finally Joe rushed past her into the main bar area of the Plough.

As Joe stepped inside the realisation hit that they'd only ever been there as Misty, and without her glamorous armour, Joe was intimidated. It was also the first time Joe had seen the career criminal outside of her private office. In there, she looked correct, in situ, at one with her surroundings. The marble desk and gold fixtures suited her nineties drag style and gave her a grandeur that befitted her forty-something years in the business. But here in the bar, with its faded wooden floors and dirty walls, she looked very much like a tired, aging drag queen in a tired, aging pub. But then it was barely 10 a.m., hardly even getting-up time.

'Do you need me?' asked Baseball Cap to Auntie Susan.

'Not for the moment, but stay close by,' she replied.

Baseball Cap disappeared through the saloon doors towards the performance room and Auntie Susan's office.

Joe wondered what else might lie beyond those doors. There must be an upstairs, they thought, suddenly registering that they'd never thought about the Plough's upper floors.

Auntie Susan stepped up to greet Jeremy and held out her hand. He took it and they shook in what felt like a very formal greeting.

'Jeremy Edmunds,' she said. 'I was beginning to think we might not find you.'

You didn't want to look for him at all! thought Joe, saying nothing.

'That was the plan,' said Jeremy.

'They so rarely go as we intend,' Auntie Susan replied. She was being nice, sickly sweet. 'Plans, that is. Isn't that right, Misty?'

Jeremy moved away from the older drag queen's intimidating presence and paced around one of the pool tables, his backpack still hung across both shoulders.

'What am I doing here?' he asked. 'What are we all doing here?'

'Let me fix us all a drink,' said Auntie Susan, ignoring Jeremy's questions and heading behind the bar, 'and then we can talk properly.'

'It's a bit early for that isn't it?' said Joe, keen to get straight on with the talking, to discussing the evidence that Jeremy had collected.

'Pish, posh.' Auntie Susan dismissed Joe with a wave of her hand. 'It's not been an ideal start, and as I recall, you were in here merrily guzzling a morning Bombay Sapphire not long ago. Also, imagine Jeremy here had made it all the way to

Paris. Wine for *breakfast* on the continent! I think we can permit ourselves a little tipple given the circumstances. What can I get you, Jeremy?'

'I'll have a rum,' he said, rolling a cue ball across the green felt pool table and landing it in a corner pocket. 'Rum with Coke.'

Auntie Susan set about pouring the drink and looked over her shoulder at Joe. 'A gin for you, Misty? You like a double don't you.'

She was taunting, and Joe knew her well enough by now to see through it. They sat on a tall stool on the opposite side of the bar and smiled. 'A gin would be fine, thank you.'

Auntie Susan finished preparing the beverages and, once they were lined up on the bar, she encouraged Joe and Jeremy to take them.

'Let's sit over there,' she said, pointing to a round table in the corner with worn banquette seating around it. They walked to the seats, alcohol in hand, and Jeremy shrugged off his backpack, placing it on the ground beside him.

Auntie Susan started, holding court like she was suddenly CEO of the entire mess. 'We're in a pickle here, Jeremy, and you're the only person who can help us out of it.'

Jeremy took a sip of rum and Coke which, judging from his reaction, was stronger than he'd expected. 'I know some of Misty's situation,' he said. 'The trouble with Atrax and Lady's Bar, but what does that have to do with you?'

Auntie Susan glanced at Joe, who quickly realised what this look meant. While Lady Lady had confided in Jessica about the bribery and the illegal attempts to keep Lady's Bar open, she hadn't told the full story. She must never have brought Auntie Susan's name into it, as the redhead herself would have demanded. There were secrets on top of secrets.

'O K . . .' said Auntie Susan, perhaps unsure how much information to divulge to this man she'd never met. 'How about this?' she said. 'If I'm one hundred percent honest and forthcoming with you, will you show me the same respect? Given that, you know, I've just saved your life.'

Jeremy thought about it, looking from Auntie Susan to Joe. 'Sure,' he said, raising his shoulders. 'There's nothing left to lose at this point anyway.'

'Maybe not for you,' said Auntie Susan, 'but for *us*, there's a lot on the line.'

'Where's the best place to start?' asked Joe.

'I'll start,' said Auntie Susan, taking complete control of the conversation and signalling to Joe that it wasn't their place to be involved. Not yet at least.

Joe was annoyed, though that was a normal sensation when dealing with Auntie Susan and why they'd usually be here as Misty, but they accepted that the older queen had more power in this conversation. She had more resources than Joe, better contacts. Perhaps for the time being it was sensible to let her take the lead.

Auntie Susan flexed her fingers with a crunch of knuckles and her cheap plastic nails gleamed under the pub's overhead lighting. 'I don't usually discuss my business with strangers, as Misty well knows, but I want you to understand the stakes here,' she said to Jeremy. '*I'm* the one who's been stopping Atrax from taking over Lady's Bar.'

'You?' gasped Jeremy. 'How?'

'I'm what some might call "well-connected", and I have a

friend of a friend on the council. When Lady Lady heard that a redevelopment proposal had been submitted without her consultation, she came to me for help. I was able to arrange a financial solution to keep that proposal from going through the usual channels of consideration. It's an arrangement that's been working for quite a long time.'

Auntie Susan seemed proud to admit this, almost smug. She leaned forward on her elbows and glared at Jeremy. The sickly sweet tone evaporated, leaving a rough growl in its place.

'So you see, Jeremy, you pose a problem for me. For us. We know you have a recording of Ginger Baker and Stefan Weber, but you're having trouble using it to stop her. We'll come to that shortly, but what I need to know first is, does your little tape include anything that might expose my arrangement? Anything that could spell trouble for me, Misty, Lady's Bar or the Plough?'

'Jessica told you about the recording?' said Jeremy to Joe. 'She did.'

'Well?' asked Auntie Susan. 'How worried do we need to be about its contents?'

Jeremy rubbed his eyes with the tips of his fingers. To Joe he seemed beyond tired, like the month he'd spent hiding in Dartmoor had sapped all his energy. 'I don't think you need to be worried. There's nothing on the video about Lady's Bar specifically, or about this financial situation with your friend at the council.'

'Good,' said Auntie Susan, leaning back. 'That's good.'

'Though of course,' Jeremy continued, 'if word gets out about what Ginger's doing, about how many venues are involved, all of it might be looked into. Everything could be scrutinized.'

'How many venues is she targeting?' asked Auntie Susan. 'You said seven in total, right, Misty?'

Joe nodded. 'Lady's Bar and six others.'

'Then I'm not worried,' said Auntie Susan. 'Stopping Ginger Baker quietly would be for the best, but if it comes to it and her ridiculous scheme is brought into the light, there will be too much else for people to talk about. It would be a scandal, and whatever's happening behind the scenes at Lady's Bar will be lost in the noise.'

Joe wasn't sure they agreed but Auntie Susan seemed confident. And perhaps she was right. In the worst-case scenario that the whole situation was dug up, even the council would fight to keep this particular thread of the story from public scrutiny. It wasn't a good look for anybody.

'Do you have the recording with you?' asked Joe.

'I do,' said Jeremy. He was uncomfortable with this admission and Joe sensed he didn't want to share it after holding on to it for so long by himself.

'We're going to need to watch it,' they said. It was more a demand than a request.

Jeremy hesitated, taking a sip of his drink. Joe did the same, but the double was too much, too strong for so early in the day.

'No . . .' said the photographer. 'I'll find a way to get it out there by myself, thank you. I didn't go to all the trouble of getting it in the first place just to hand it over to two strangers.'

Joe glanced across to Auntie Susan, to check her reaction. She was not somebody you said no to easily.

'Really?' she said, her eyes like fire. 'The way I see it, Jeremy, you've been investigating this for months with the help of a very successful journalist, and where has it got you? *Nowhere.* Worse than nowhere. Ha! You've been in hiding for a month, and now the journalist's done a runner too.' A nasty red grin stretched across her face. 'Your mother's so worried she crossed the Atlantic with a bra full of flyers and hired an investigator, but what happened to him? Oh, that's right, stabbed in the pissing chest. Your last-ditch attempt to get out of the country was so easily spotted you might as well have not even tried.'

It was a vicious assessment and Jeremy slumped in his chair like a child getting roasted by a headteacher. Joe knew that Auntie Susan wasn't finished.

'If it wasn't for me and Misty, you'd be in the hands of the suits right now,' she seethed. 'You can't go home, you can't travel and you can't work. I don't imagine that photojournalism pays a fortune, so your savings will be dwindling. Do you have anything left at all? Is there anyone's life you haven't ruined? You've got nothing to your name but that recording and you've no way of using it without us.'

'Wow,' said Jeremy, possibly on the brink of tears. 'Harsh.'

'Am I wrong?' asked Auntie Susan. 'About any of it?'

Jeremy paused and then sheepishly said, 'No.'

'No indeed. Now, we're going to need to watch that video.'

Joe held back a snort. What was that German word? *Schadenfreude.* It was strangely entertaining to see Auntie Susan's wrath unleashed on someone other than Misty Divine for a change, even in these dark circumstances. They did feel sorry for Jeremy though. She'd rinsed him. This is why they'd let her take the lead to begin with – she had a power that couldn't be denied.

Reluctantly, Jeremy lifted up his backpack from the floor and placed it on the table. He unbuckled it, pulled open a drawstring and took out a laptop. Joe and Auntie Susan watched in silence as he set up the computer and an external hard drive so that the screen faced them. He clicked through some file directories and then said, 'There was no need to be so mean about it.'

'Boo hoo,' said Auntie Susan. 'Just play the tape.'

Joe could hardly wait to watch it now, to know exactly what evidence Jeremy had against Ginger Baker so they could start to plan their next steps.

His finger hovered over the 'play' button and he was chewing the inside of his cheek with his back teeth.

'What is it?' said Joe.

'Before we watch this,' Jeremy replied, 'I need to tell you, this isn't my first encounter with Ginger Baker.'

'What do you mean?' asked Joe.

'I started looking into her a couple of years ago when I came across a blog on some of her business interests. It was written by a student and didn't get much traction.'

Joe remembered seeing a blog about Ginger online while they'd been travelling with Plimberley. It must have been the same one.

'Go on . . .' said Auntie Susan.

The photographer wringed his fingers. 'Things have been difficult, as I'm sure you're aware, with the politics back home. The tide's turning against our community, as it is in lots of places these days. I got drawn into it, obsessed over it, watching videos and podcasts until late at night, learning about the money behind the politicians and the rich and powerful who shape the agenda. That's when I happened upon the blog about Ginger Baker.'

'Not quite the sweetie-pie she appeared to be on the *Sally Jessy Raphael Show*?' snarked Auntie Susan.

Jeremy smiled but it wasn't happy. 'Quite the opposite. The blog claimed she was using her churches and celebrity to build a public persona that was untouchable. Who would dare speak up against the rosy-cheeked, God-fearing homemaker? But she's generating enormous wealth by targeting marginalized communities. Healthcare, energy, prison labour . . . you name it, she'll do it for a fast buck, and it's funded by the hate she preaches. She uses her innocent façade to whip up the vulnerable, the poor, the insecure and she gives them someone to blame. Usually, it's people like us. I couldn't stop thinking about her. I thought if I could expose her hypocrisy, I could make a difference. Make people safer somehow.'

'What happened?' asked Joe.

He moistened his lips with a sip of rum and Joe could tell he was uncomfortable, upset even. 'I confronted her last year when she came to speak at my old university in Chicago. Alumni were invited to a talk by her, so I booked a ticket. In hindsight I was dumb and naïve. I thought I could challenge her about her business dealings and everyone would see her for the monster she truly is. I tried. When I got the mic during the Q&A, I asked her about a rural gay bar she'd bought and turned into a mini mart.'

'She's done this before?' Joe asked. 'What she's doing to the British venues, she's done it in the States?'

'Yes, but not to the extent she's doing it here. This deal with Atrax, it's more blatant than she's been in the past, like she's embracing her super-villain status.'

'What did she say when you confronted her?' asked Auntie Susan.

Jeremy let out a sad little chuckle. 'She called me a loony liberal. She laughed at me and so did most of the audience. I fired back. I asked her about the prisoners who make her Bibles for twenty-five cents an hour. Someone tried to grab the microphone from me and I embarrassed myself, ranting and shouting. It was my only opportunity to ask her face-to-face, and I lost control. Her security dragged me out of the room. They like us silent, you see, and underfoot. Ever since, I've been trying to find connections between her businesses and the politics she supports so that I can expose her.'

'That's why you came after her to London?' Auntie Susan clicked her fingernails against the table top.

'Yes,' admitted Jeremy. 'I read online she's funding a new megachurch here, bringing her homely style of worship to the UK, but I knew she'd have an ulterior motive. For Ginger, the churches are a cover, her way of generating fast cash and public respectability while she schmoozes the powerful for unethical investments. And it's all done at our expense.'

The air hung heavy.

'I was following Ginger Baker to her various appointments in London and she led me to Atrax, as you'll see in the video. That meeting is what turned me to Jessica's article.

We'd been scraping opposite sides of the same coin all along and we ended up here. You asked me when we sat down to be one hundred percent honest with you, as you have been with me, so now you know everything.'

'It's time we watched the tape,' said Auntie Susan.

CHAPTER 38

Jeremy clicked open a video file that had been filmed on a hidden camera, perhaps attached to a button or brooch on someone's jacket or shirt.

'This is the bar at the Ritz,' he said. 'I'd been taking photos of her visiting the building site and followed her from there. I had the camera in my lapel.'

The video showed Jeremy's perspective as he moved through the swanky bar. Servers in smart uniforms were busy serving exceedingly wealthy customers in glitzy surroundings. Joe and Auntie Susan watched intently as he sat at a table and was approached by a waiter who asked what he'd like to drink. As the waiter disappeared to fetch the order, Jeremy turned his body to the left, showing the occupants of the neighbouring table, and both faces were clearly in view. There was Ginger Baker, the plump middle-aged evangelical with an eighties-style red perm, a floral dress and excessively large shoulder pads. She was with Stefan Weber, the waspish CEO of Atrax in his perfectly knotted tie and wire-framed glasses.

'Here they are,' Jeremy narrated. 'They don't say anything interesting for a little while – there's some general catch-up.'

He clicked the fast-forward button on the screen and

scootched the video along to about three minutes in. Joe and Auntie Susan leaned even closer.

Ginger spoke, a southern American twang in her voice. 'Stefan,' she said, 'you know I'm not one for piling on the pressure, but I'm afraid we're at risk of entering a state of disagreement if more progress isn't made soon.'

'We're doing everything we can,' the CEO replied. 'We're very close now with the venues in Edinburgh and Brighton. Just some i's to dot and t's to cross.'

Ginger shook her head. 'It's not good enough, Stefan. It's not fast enough. Not for the money I'm paying you.'

On-screen, Stefan Weber removed his glasses and cleaned them on a crisp white napkin.

'Ginger, things don't move so quickly in the United Kingdom as they do in the States. There's more regulation, and we're encountering some local resistance.' He paused, placing the spectacles on to the bridge of his nose. 'The support your politics enjoys there is not so strong here. The population will need more . . . convincing. Perhaps if you would share with me your full motives, Atrax could come up with a new strategy.'

'That is not what I hired you for,' snapped Ginger. 'I have my own strategy. I told you I want those gays out of those venues and I've paid you to do it quickly and quietly.'

Stefan sighed, pressing ahead despite her protest. 'Miss Baker, I must be frank with you.' His voice was almost a whisper but Jeremy's recording had picked it up perfectly.

'Go on,' replied the pink-blushed nightmare.

'If you confide in me your endgame, I can target Atrax's approach with precision. We are doubting that your objective is purely financial – a handful of bars and pubs here is worth peanuts against your existing portfolio. Your goal in the UK is therefore also political?'

Her lips pursed into a tight cat's arse and Joe's stomach turned. 'You are paid a princely sum, Stefan, and you are paid to act for me, not question me.'

'Yes, of course.' His German accent was thickening, becoming denser with his frustration. 'What I'm trying to explain is that we can act more efficiently for you if we understand why here. Why now, in the United Kingdom?'

Ginger huffed and raised her eyebrows. 'Our movement is not limited to one country. The creek is rising and you're not a foolish man. Here we sit together in London, an American and a German on the right side of the fight, with power and resources. A man like you understands true change must happen on all fronts.'

Stefan nodded sagely and Joe wondered whether he actually understood Ginger's nonsense.

'When you boil the frog slowly,' she continued, 'submerged, it won't know it's dying until its fat belly bursts, and when it does, it's you and I who get to feast on its juicy guts.'

'It is a financial goal,' he stated, matter of fact.

'On *all* fronts, Stefan, we whip the political frenzy faster and hotter and we profit. Politics, money, they're one and the same now.'

'Why these venues specifically?' he asked.

'They are low-hanging fruit and they were supposed to be an easy win. Even the LGBT-whatevers don't go to them any more. They're failing businesses with a declining and degenerate clientele. We weaken our opponents' solidarity, their resistance against what's coming next, and we profit from those who support us in the process.'

'Divide and conquer,' said Stefan.

Ginger sipped her tea, then calmly said, 'I am a woman of significant means and Atrax isn't the only solutions provider I have at my disposal. I trusted you, Stefan. I need you to do what you promised me. I *want* those venues. And once we've got this first wave, I'll be coming after the rest.'

Auntie Susan placed her hand over her mouth.

Suddenly Ginger turned in her seat, facing Jeremy, looking almost directly into his hidden camera. It was as though she'd realised she'd been speaking too loudly. Through the screen Joe could see her bright red lipstick and too-pink blusher. She looked him up and down.

'Hang on . . .' she said, raising a finger to point, 'I know you.'

Jeremy stuttered. 'N-n-no . . . I don't think so.'

Jeremy's recording wobbled and shook as he got up out of his seat.

'Why do I know you?' Ginger shifted her body around, fully facing Jeremy now. 'Were you eavesdropping? You're stalking me! Chicago! That's where I saw you! Stefan – this is one of those loony activists.'

The camera shook as Jeremy started to back away. 'I think I'll just leave,' he said.

Ginger looked around, worried. She waved at someone off-screen and moments later two suits arrived. 'He's listening to us,' she said. 'I want him checked.'

'Gotta run,' said Jeremy.

The video bounced up and down as he hurried through

the bar to the exit, his fingers reaching up to switch off the camera as soon as he got outside the hotel.

Jeremy leaned forward and shut the laptop screen. 'And that's it. A month in hiding began right there.'

'Holy shit,' said Joe. 'So she's coming after everyone.'

'That's what she said,' said Auntie Susan, cooler than Joe had seen her for a long time. 'The question now is, what are we going to do about it?'

CHAPTER 39

'What about social media?' asked Joe. 'Lady's Bar has twenty thousand followers on Instagram and I've got about the same on my Misty account. If I posted the video on both our profiles, would that be enough?'

Auntie Susan shook her head like Joe was an idiot. 'Do you know how easy it is to get videos or entire accounts taken down? I could spend as little as £100 right now and have someone do it in an instant. Mass reporting, hacking. It's possible if you know how.'

'Really?' asked Joe, surprised, feeling uninformed on the subject.

'Really,' said Jeremy. 'It's not hard to take down a social account if you know what you're doing, and Atrax would certainly have the resources.'

'So we're . . . stuck?' asked Joe.

Jeremy nodded. 'It wouldn't be enough even if you managed to keep the account active. This is where Jessica and I have been struggling, why we haven't been able to take any action yet.'

Auntie Susan groaned loudly and placed her glass down on the table. 'It's not often I could just shit with rage, but I'm so furious. If that Ginger Baker was in London right now,

I'd have half a mind to show up on her doorstep and rip that curly wig right off her head.'

'But she is . . .' said Jeremy, looking between Joe and Auntie Susan. 'That's why I was leaving today. You didn't know?'

Auntie Susan stood up and slammed her hands on the table top, seemingly astonished by this revelation. 'Ginger Baker is in London?! Now?'

Joe didn't like where this might be heading . . .

'Yes,' Jeremy replied. 'She's a keynote speaker at a huge festival at Wembley Stadium tonight. It's like a concert for born-again Christians, called Preach Party.'

'Then we'll go!' said Auntie Susan, her red hair falling around her face. 'I'll go to this Preach Party and tell her to her orange face. I'll tell her to get the hell out of our scene!'

'You won't get anywhere near her,' said Jeremy. 'She'll be backstage in some fancy dressing room and there will be an army of security.'

'Oh, I'll get near her all right!' said Auntie Susan. Her eyes darted from side to side as she was already formulating a plan. 'I can get us in. I just need to make a few phone calls. You two stay here and Misty, text Mandy – she'll need to find another host for tonight.'

She got up and walked through the saloon doors back towards her office, padded bum wiggling, red wig bouncing.

Jeremy rocked forward, 'I don't know about this . . .'

Joe's thoughts suddenly turned to Miles, thinking about whether they should contact him, let him know that they'd found Jeremy, seen the video . . . They knew they wouldn't, or shouldn't. Miles wasn't interested, but it felt strange doing all this without him. The chase at St Pancras, sitting here with Jeremy and Auntie Susan, it all would have been easier with Miles at their side.

'You must be tired,' said Joe to Jeremy, trying to be normal after their very stressful conversation, 'after all your travelling and disappearing.'

He nodded. 'I am. This whole thing's been a nightmare and, to be honest, I really miss talking to my mom.' Tears sparkled in Jeremy's eyes.

'She never gave up on you, you know,' Joe replied. 'She hounded the police, hired Sylvester, put up posters all over London and gave out flyers everywhere. She's really been worried.'

'I knew she would be,' said Jeremy, 'but what else could I have done? The day after the Ritz, the suits, as you call them, were outside my flat. I saw their guns, Misty, and I ran. That's why I reached out to John and why Jessica said I should hide for a while. I didn't know it would end up like this.'

'You couldn't have known, nobody could. Now we're all working together though, and we have Auntie Susan in our corner, we might find a way to end this.'

Jeremy looked up and stared Joe right in the eyes. 'No offence,' he said, 'but how are two drag queens going to do what two journalists couldn't?'

'Don't underestimate us because we're drag queens,' said Joe, perhaps sensitive to the suggestion that drag queens were intellectually inferior to journalists, or less capable. Joe knew better. Joe knew there were drag performers all across the country who were smart, perceptive and highly tuned to societal and political issues. They rallied, joined forces in pride, protest and defiance. 'If anybody's going to stop this threat to the queer scene, it'll be the drags.'

Joe wandered through the Plough's grimy performance room while sending their message to Mandy. They wrote a concise explanation of what was happening and asked if she could find a replacement host for this evening. Perhaps Plimberley could do it for the extra cash, they suggested. Mandy agreed and Joe hovered alone for a moment by the edge of the Plough's dingy stage.

Is that a mouse dropping? It didn't matter.

All this, it felt enormous.

Jeremy was still at the table in the main room, slumped and defeated. Joe headed straight behind the bar.

'I need a drink,' they said. 'Another rum and Coke for you?'

The photographer looked up with puppy-dog eyes. 'Yes, please.'

Joe set about pouring, thinking they could pay Auntie Susan for them later if she insisted.

They placed the glasses down on the table and sat with Jeremy again, just as the queen herself burst through the saloon doors.

'OK, friends,' she said. 'I have good news.'

'What's that then?' asked Joe.

Auntie Susan noticed the beverages and gave Joe a raised eyebrow that wrinkled her painted forehead. 'Drinks? Misty Divine, Soho's most spectacular free-loader.'

'Come on,' said Joe, 'it's just a gin.'

'I'm kidding, dickhead, but only about the drinks. I do have news.'

'Tell us then,' said Jeremy.

Auntie Susan joined them at the table, her tummy bulging under the tight white Lycra. 'We have a way into Wembley. Only for two of us and it should be me and you, Misty.'

'How?' Joe asked. Then, worrying about facing such a big moment without Misty's confidence, 'I'll need to get into drag.'

'No,' said Auntie Susan, 'you won't. This is a civilian mission. No drag queens allowed.'

'Why?' asked Joe, already craving their Misty Divine superpowers.

'Because we're going to *Wembley Stadium*, to the megachurch event. And while there are many Christians who love a bit of drag, Ginger Baker's crowd are definitely not them. You show up in your little red dress and your big blonde wig, you're getting burned at the stake, my love.'

Jeremy interrupted. 'Don't you think I should go? I've been working on this for years and I know how Ginger operates.' He was clearly annoyed to be excluded.

'Absolutely not,' said Auntie Susan. 'You're staying here. They'd recognise you in a flash and you'd go the way of Sylvester Green. I've cancelled tonight's show here and told the staff not to come in. Open bar for you, young man, and an entire pub at your disposal.'

'So I just sit here drinking?'

'Well, that's up to you, Jeremy. You could dust off your Grindr. There's plenty of trade around here and think of all the notifications you'll have missed.' Auntie Susan chuckled to herself and Jeremy rolled his eyes.

'OK,' said Joe, looking at their phone. 'It says here the Preach Party's an annual event where the most famous, and some of the most extreme, preachers from all over the world perform a gigantic five-hour show. I don't like the sound of trying to infiltrate that.'

'How will you do it?' Jeremy asked. 'How will you even find Ginger when you get there?'

Auntie Susan did her smug, know-it-all face again. 'Ginger Baker is the headline act and she's hired an event space called the Wembley Suite for a pre-show reception. That's where we'll find her, *and* we'll be on the guest list.'

'How did you wangle that?' asked Joe.

'Nothing's impossible when you know the right people,' scoffed Auntie Susan. 'Isn't that why you keep coming to me with your ridiculous predicaments?'

'You'll have to be so careful,' warned Jeremy. 'Twice I've been in the same room as her, and it hasn't gone well either time.'

This didn't sound like a fun night out to Joe and they were starting to feel too worried, their Misty Divine determination retreating like a turtle's head into its shell.

'I don't know,' they said with caution. 'Do you think there's another way we should do this? Two queens trying to confront a megachurch leader in a venue full of her most loyal supporters? Everyone there hates us.'

Auntie Susan's face turned into a scowl. 'Do you have a better idea, Misty? This is our one shot. We know where she'll be down to the room.' She slugged back a mouthful of booze. 'And everyone there doesn't hate us! Some of them do, but that's the same everywhere. We walk past people who hate us in the street every day, but not everybody who went to see the Sex Pistols was a punk. Not all Iron Maiden fans are metalheads. People will be going to this Preach Party for all kinds of reasons: friendship, community, faith . . . There will be people going because for them it's just a fun night out. Don't tar thousands of perfectly decent Christians with the Ginger Baker brush.'

Joe agreed. Auntie Susan wasn't wrong, but their fear of the extremists was strong, especially those surrounding Ginger, in light of what they'd done to Sylvester.

'What's the plan?' they asked.

'Getting this drag off for starters,' replied Auntie Susan. 'I'm going to go and scrape the face off. You two stay here and listen out for three knocks on the door. We have a delivery coming.'

Joe scrolled, aimlessly looking through social media of other, happier drag performers who didn't have all this stress to deal with.

Joyful bastards.

Jeremy had lain down on one of the filthy pub banquettes, telling Joe he was knackered and needed a nap. Their stomach churned as they watched the photographer place his cheek against the filthy threadbare fabric.

They switched from social media to WhatsApp, where Miles' name and profile photo jumped from the screen. Joe really missed him.

I should tell him this, they thought, *about going to confront Ginger Baker.*

As Jeremy's breathing slipped into a regular sleep pattern, Joe spent forever writing out an update for Miles. They didn't want to worry him, not when he was already so concerned and angry. And Joe thought it was probably important to tell somebody where they were going and what they were doing. Just in case.

In case what?

In case we end up like Sylvester. Or worse.

They reread the message over and over, making sure it was as sensitively phrased as possible before pressing send.

Hey Miles, I hope you're ok at your mum and dad's. Just wanted to let you know that I miss you and I love you and I don't like us falling out. I also want to tell you I think this business with the stabbing and bribery is nearly over. We found out the identity of the Atrax client who's been trying to shut down the bar. It's a megachurch preacher called Ginger Baker. Auntie Susan and I are going to see her this evening at Wembley Stadium. Hopefully when this is all over you'll come home and we'll be able to move forward. You mean the world to me. Joe x

The message appeared in the chat with a little whoosh and Joe saw it was delivered and read immediately. An instant reply came back.

Be careful, Joe. I love you too. X

Joe felt excitement, definitely relief.

Miles still loves me, despite everything.

Perhaps their situation wasn't unsalvageable after all.

After about an hour of waiting, Joe was bored. Bored of waiting for Auntie Susan to de-drag, bored of listening to

Jeremy's snoring. They'd made themself another gin and tonic; perhaps not the best idea, but it was keeping the nerves at bay. It was also making Joe a little woozy and they realised that despite it now being well past lunchtime, they hadn't eaten anything all day. They stole a pack of Scampi Fries from behind the bar, wolfed them down and stashed the empty wrapper deep in the bin.

Joe's heart skipped a beat when there was a sharp knock on the door. Three knocks to be precise; the knocks Auntie Susan had asked them to listen out for.

Jeremy's eyes opened and he said in a sleepy voice, 'Guess that's the delivery we're expecting.'

Joe rushed to the door and twisted open the lock.

Why is it sticky? they wondered. It was like the knob had been smeared with jam and left to dry. With all her money and connections, Joe thought Auntie Susan could probably source the occasional cleaner.

They pulled the door open and a man barged in. Baseball Cap, Auntie Susan's courier-slash-driver-slash-dogsbody. Even now, in spite of their multiple interactions, Joe was still cautious of him. Last year, when investigating Lady Lady's murder, Baseball Cap had terrified Joe. Now they knew he wasn't as scary as he appeared. This time, he had armfuls of bags and boxes and walked straight past Joe towards the pool tables, where he started laying everything out.

'All right,' he said.

'Hello,' said Joe.

Jeremy sat half-upright on the banquette and looked across the room to see what was being delivered while Joe moved to stand opposite Baseball Cap, watching as he placed everything down. He lay two suit bags flat against the green felt.

'Here are your suits,' he said.

'Suits?'

'And shoes. You're a size nine, right?'

'Yes,' said Joe. 'How did you . . .?' They didn't need to finish the question – they knew how. Auntie Susan knew everything, down to Joe's shoe size apparently.

Baseball Cap placed down two pairs of plain black socks, one next to each pair of shoes. This was attention to detail. The socks Joe was currently wearing were pink and blue zebra print.

Auntie Susan's scary courier reached into his jacket's inside pocket and pulled out two lanyards, with shiny tags attached.

'You'll be needing these,' he said.

Joe took one and inspected it. The lanyard was purple fabric, printed with white lettering that said 'Preach Party' all along it. The tag was an ID badge and Joe immediately noticed their own face: a corporate photo from when they'd worked at the Empire Hotel, before they quit to go full-time at Lady's Bar.

'Where did you get this picture?' Joe asked.

'Your LinkedIn,' said Baseball Cap.

I need to delete that profile.

At the top of the badge, above the photo, in big gold letters, it read: *AAA: Access All Areas*. There was a Wembley Stadium logo, a Preach Party logo and a holographic sticker in the shape of a crucifix.

'How did you get these?'

Baseball Cap winked and Joe felt a flutter of something.

Oh my God, do I fancy Baseball Cap?!

Maybe a little . . .

Something to work out another day.

'I just do the deliveries,' he said. 'Best not to ask, if you know what I mean.'

'Aah you're here!' called a voice as the saloon doors creaked back open. 'Just in time.'

Joe looked on in actual shock at the sight of Auntie Susan out of drag. Without her trademark red hair and heels, she was shorter, obviously. Joe had seen her on television, in the news, in person, for twenty years, but never like this. She looked like . . . well, she looked like someone's uncle. The kind of uncle who'd eat hot pasties in a bookmakers while talking about women's legs. She was jowly, something her make-up had well disguised, and her head was freshly shaved. Her arms were covered in faded blue tattoos and perhaps the most surprising of all – she was wearing a football shirt. Joe didn't know which team it was, but it was striped: blue and red. She had transformed completely and unexpectedly. If it wasn't for the voice and bone structure, Joe would never have recognised her.

'You can close your mouth, Misty,' she said. 'What do you think drag is?'

'Sorry,' laughed Joe. 'I just . . . well I wasn't expecting such a difference.'

Auntie Susan ignored this and walked to the pool table, inspecting everything that Baseball Cap had laid out. She unzipped one of the garment bags, revealing a black suit, black tie and white shirt. Joe noticed the jacket lapel had a small gold cross pinned to it.

'For God's sake, pardon the pun,' Auntie Susan muttered in a gruff voice. 'We're going to look like the cast of *Book of Mormon*.'

Baseball Cap shuffled nervously. 'That's what you wanted, isn't it?'

'The practice is often much less fun than the theory, my dear.' Then, turning to Joe. 'OK, angel of mine, it's time to get into drag.'

'Drag?' said Joe, confused.

Auntie Susan pointed at the suits and said coolly, 'Two big poofs dressing up like missionaries to infiltrate a megachurch . . . If you ask me, that's as drag as it gets, just fewer sequins.'

In Auntie Susan's gaudy office the two drag queens began stripping off their civilian attire to get into the black suits.

Keanu the chihuahua snoozed peacefully in his velvet bed and Joe felt a pang of jealousy. Keanu knew nothing of the trials and tribulations they were going through. His life was quiet and easy. The only thing Keanu had to worry about was the danger of passive smoking from Auntie Susan's indoor Marlboro habit.

'Misty,' said Auntie Susan as she pulled on the black suit trousers. 'Can I ask you something?'

Her voice was different to usual, lower and more serious. There was less playfulness, less of the taunting tone Joe was so used to. *Perhaps she's different out of drag*, Joe wondered. *Maybe Auntie Susan's superpower is like Misty's.*

'Of course,' said Joe.

'Have you ever been to church?'

'No,' Joe replied honestly. 'My parents didn't and so they never took me. My boyfriend, Miles, he says he used to when he was a kid, but he doesn't go any more. What about you?'

'I used to go,' said Auntie Susan. 'My whole family did. Sunday school, First Communion, the whole nine yards. Church was more popular back then, I think.'

'Did you like it?' asked Joe, buttoning up their white missionary shirt.

'To begin with. I liked being with the other kids. They were friends at first and Sunday school was fun.' She smiled as she reminisced. 'We used to sit around a big table in the church hall while our parents were in the service. There were snacks and orange squash. I have nice memories of that bit.'

Joe fastened their very top button and turned to face her, sensing already that Auntie Susan's childhood church experience hadn't ended well. 'What happened?'

'Nothing terrible, not like the awful things you hear about in the news.' She plucked the black tie from the suit bag and looped it around her collar. 'But before even I knew I was different, the other kids had worked it out. How do they always know? There was some bullying, some name-calling, and then when I was old enough to move from Sunday school to the main church, I realised I wouldn't be welcome there forever. Some churches, most of them back then, weren't built for people like us, Misty.'

'When did you stop going?' Joe was intrigued. This was the very first time they'd heard about Auntie Susan's personal life and they were keen to learn more.

'When I was eighteen. My parents said as long as I was living under their roof I had to go. I hated it. I hated it but at the same time I respected it. It was community, history, and for the people who believed in it, it had enormous value. That's how it felt then.'

Joe thought of their own parents and how they'd attended pride marches and protests together. That was community too and Joe recognised how important the sense of fellowship had been. The main difference between Auntie Susan's experience and their own was that Joe's community had accepted them for who they were. They'd been one of the lucky ones.

Auntie Susan shook herself and straightened her fastened tie. 'I don't know why I'm telling you this. I never talk about it. That's probably enough.'

'But I want to know,' said Joe. 'What happened when you were eighteen? What changed?'

'A boy,' she smiled, and although she was smiling, Joe noticed her eyes had turned glassy. 'Always a goddamn boy, isn't it? Michael was his name. He took me to see a show on the West End – *Hello, Dolly!* starring Danny La Rue. I remember the costumes, the singing, the glamour . . . and I just knew. That's what I wanted. That's who I was.'

'Is that when you became Auntie Susan?'

'A version of her. I wasn't destined to be the next Danny La Rue apparently, but I've done my best. I had my fifteen minutes of fame.'

'And Michael?' asked Joe. 'Was he your boyfriend? Are you still in touch?'

'Michael . . .' There was a pause as Auntie Susan ran her hand across her shaved scalp. 'A conversation for another day, Misty.'

She snatched up the black jacket in a stark announcement that the conversation was over. Stuffing her arms through the sleeves, she marched to the door and pulled it open. 'I'll meet you in the bar.'

Joe walked in a few minutes later feeling like an idiot in the outfit and a tinge of remorse for pressing Auntie Susan about Michael. The suit was horrible to wear. Not that it was low quality; it had certainly been expensive. It was horrible because it wasn't Joe. It was too bland, too monotone, too masculine. The leather shoes and black socks sent non-binary alarm bells ringing through their brain. This simply wasn't how they would ever choose to express themself.

Auntie Susan was waiting by the front door to the pub, her purple lanyard already hanging around her neck. She too looked strange. Joe was so used to seeing her in her white dress and red hair that now, seeing her dressed like a grandad going to a funeral, it was as though they were both in fancy dress.

Baseball Cap had moved to the table with Jeremy, who was sitting upright after his banquette power nap.

'You look like the worst drag queens I've ever seen,' laughed the photographer.

'Like the *Men in Black*,' said Baseball Cap, 'just need the sunnies.'

Auntie Susan spun her head around. 'We'll have less of the "men", thank you. Misty's non-binary.' Baseball Cap looked chastened.

'Oh,' replied Joe, 'don't worry about that. It's no problem, honestly.'

Baseball Cap changed the subject, looking at his watch,

realising time was ticking on. 'So, do we need to go now? The reception starts at five, doesn't it?'

'It does indeed,' said Auntie Susan, 'but you're not going anywhere.'

'I thought I was driving you. I parked right outside. I drive you everywhere.'

'Exactly. That car is too easy to trace back to us. We'll take a cab. I need you to stay here and keep an eye on this one.' She pointed at Jeremy and he looked indignant.

'I don't need babysitting!' he protested, standing up to face her.

'Tell that to every joker who's been looking for you for the last month, your own mother included. You're a flight risk. You're not leaving this pub until I say.'

He sat back down with a thump and folded his arms like a child having a tantrum. 'A prisoner at the Plough.'

'Don't look so sad about it,' Auntie Susan continued, 'you can help yourselves to the bar. Order a couple of pizzas or something. Now, Elder Divine, are you ready to face off with the megachurch billionaire?'

Joe wasn't ready and they didn't know if they ever would be. The stadium, the hordes of Ginger Baker fans, the private reception. It was a petrifying prospect.

'Yes,' they announced, channelling some Misty bravado.

'Excellent.' Auntie Susan turned to face the others. 'Be good, boys, and if we're not back by nine, send out the sniffer dogs.'

'Oh God . . .' said Joe.

'Exactly.'

CHAPTER 40

It didn't take long to hail a black cab from a couple of streets away and before Joe knew it, the two undercover queens were clambering into the back seat in their matching suits. They told the cabbie they were heading to Wembley Stadium and he nodded, turning the car around quickly and driving in the right direction.

'This is all very strange, isn't it?' said Auntie Susan.

'Very.'

Joe looked down at their hands and saw they were trembling. Auntie Susan saw it too and she reached out and clasped Joe's shaking fingers.

'Look at me, Misty. Look right at me.'

Joe did as they were told. Without her spidery fake lashes, Auntie Susan's eyes were more piercing than ever.

She squeezed Joe's unsteady hands even tighter and said, 'If you carry on like this you're going to blow the whole thing. You have to remember that this isn't about you. We aren't doing this for *you*. If Lady's Bar goes under, that would be sad, yes. If we both get caught for the bribery, that would be a problem, yes. But there is more at stake than your bar. Stop feeling the nerves now and start feeling the *rage*. This woman, this Ginger Baker monster, she's one of many like her, but she's coming for us, for our entire community, for the sake of lining her own pockets. If you can focus on that, we'll have a much better chance of stopping her.'

'Understood,' Joe nodded. 'How will we approach her when we find her? Assuming we can even get to her at this party.'

Auntie Susan tapped her fingertips against the taxi's leather seats. 'If we do manage to get face to face, I think we need to threaten her. We're honest at first, tell her what we have, what it says, and then we call her bluff. Let's tell her we have a big newspaper ready to publish the video unless she stops what she's doing. She'll know as well as we do that most of the British public would stand against such a brazen attack on the community.'

'Do you think that will be enough? With her power, her money?'

'You have a better plan?'

Joe shook their head. They did not.

The taxi came to a stop outside a kebab shop on Empire Way and the smell of the rotating meat reminded Joe that the only thing they'd eaten today was a pilfered bag of Scampi Fries.

Maybe there will be canapés at the Ginger Baker reception, they thought, before dismissing how ridiculous it was to be hoping for food when they were heading into a showdown with the evangelical billionaire.

Auntie Susan paid the driver in cash and bailed out of the car on to the street. Joe still couldn't get over what she looked like in the black suit and shoes.

'Right,' she said, 'it's that way, about a ten-minute walk.'

'Then why didn't we get him to drop us off closer?' asked Joe. 'We haven't broken these shoes in.'

Auntie Susan hissed and put her hands on her hips – a stance that would definitely have had more gravitas in her usual attire. 'Misty, I've seen photos of you doing the London Pride Parade in eight-inch stilettos. I'm more than certain you can manage a ten-minute walk in a pair of flats.'

'Do you think we have time to pick up a kebab to eat on the way?' asked Joe. 'I'm starving.'

'Oh, piss off, Misty.'

Auntie Susan bolted into the traffic, crossing over to the pavement opposite, much to the distaste of an approaching double-decker bus that halted quickly and beeped its horn. Joe followed behind, waving and muttering a 'sorry' that the driver could not hear.

'Do you know the way?' Joe called to Auntie Susan.

'Yes, I know the way!' she snapped. 'I came this way for Taylor Swift.'

They turned down a street called Fulton Road and Auntie Susan was walking so fast Joe struggled to keep up. They could feel sweat in their armpits.

'I know what you're thinking,' said Auntie Susan.

Maybe she does.

'About the name of the road?' she continued. 'It wasn't deliberate, it's just the fastest way to get there.'

'It feels appropriate,' said Joe. 'Like she's with us.'

'It does.'

Lady Lady's birth name was Fulton, like the road. Sean Fulton.

'She'd have loved all this,' said Auntie Susan, racing ever forward.

'I'm not sure she would have,' Joe replied. 'The venues, the danger, the secrets and lies . . .'

'The Lady Lady I knew,' smiled Auntie Susan, 'the young one, before our falling-out, she'd have hated Ginger Baker but she'd have loved the dramatics. These stupid suits, two drag queens in disguise trying to take down a toxic tyrant with a Deirdre Barlow perm. She'd have cackled about that.'

Beads of perspiration had popped up on Joe's forehead and they wiped them away with the back of a hand. 'Can we slow down a minute? I'm going to be roasting by the time we get there otherwise.'

Auntie Susan obliged, dropping the pace slightly. 'It's funny, isn't it? How we knew the same person, but not really. When we were young, in the eighties, chasing through the London drag scene, different as it was then, Lady Lady was a superstar. Raring, hungry, unstoppable. That much never changed, but she was wilder then than in her later years. I remember a baby Lady Lady performing a number in a night-club on Rupert Street in a bikini, smearing her entire body in tomato ketchup.'

Joe laughed. 'I can't imagine it!' In the years Joe knew her, Lady Lady was all about the glamorous gowns and perfect purple hair. Ketchup would never have been part of the routine.

'Oh,' Auntie Susan chuckled, 'there's a lot you couldn't imagine.'

Both of their shoes clicked against the pavement as they continued onwards and Joe remembered their mentor: her wit, her talent, her dead twisted face on her dressing-room floor.

'Do you ever regret it?' they asked. 'The falling-out with her? Do you ever wish things had been different?'

Auntie Susan answered without hesitation. 'No. We had the best time together, truly. We came up together on the circuit and had our TV deals and big live shows, but nothing's forever, Misty. No one's forever.'

'I suppose not.'

Miles, Joe thought, *maybe he's not forever either.*

'When you've been doing this for as long as I have, you'll see. Christ, even just being alive as long as I have. People retire, people move or vanish. People die. One minute you're best friends and the next minute she's gone. And you have to get hard to it, Misty, because it comes round fast. If you filled your mind with regret about each and every person who's left your life, you'd never find a moment's peace.'

They didn't speak again as they continued to the point where Fulton Road met Olympic Way, the famous walkway that leads directly to the stadium's main entrance. As they turned the corner, Joe was taken aback by the scale of it. Of course they'd been there before, but the thought of the enormous venue being filled with Ginger Bakers was a lot to take in. Their heart thumped and they could feel anxiety rising.

'Here we go,' said Auntie Susan.

Olympic Way was busy with people, all of them walking in the same direction. Auntie Susan and Baseball Cap had been right with their choice of disguises. There were plenty of men in suits also heading to the venue, so they blended in.

Others were wearing T-shirts with 'Preach Party' emblazoned on the front and back. Joe noticed two women wearing very conservative skirts carrying placards that said 'We Love Ginger' and 'Jesus Saves'. Joe could only imagine what Jesus would have really thought of a woman like Ginger Baker, exploiting the poor, the sick, the incarcerated . . . all for her own personal gain.

They put their head down and watched their own feet. 'I hate this,' they said.

'Get over it,' replied Auntie Susan. 'We're going in there as two of them whether you like it or not.'

As they arrived at the two sweeping ramps that led to the entrance, the crowd became more compact. People hustled against one another, some talking excitedly about the event ahead, some singing, some already praying out loud. It was noisy, and there was excitement in the air. It had all the vibes of a pop concert. Joe imagined that if they were an enthusiastic Christian, and not there on a dangerous mission, this would be the best night of the year.

The lines moved quickly and before they knew it, Joe and Auntie Susan were a few metres from the event's security team, who stood with handheld metal detectors and X-ray machines for handbags.

Auntie Susan leaned over and whispered with hot breath into Joe's ear, 'Remember, we're invited guests from a church in east London. We belong here. Just talk the talk and we'll be fine.'

Joe played nervously with the lanyard hanging around their neck. 'These passes are real, right? We're not going to get in trouble?'

'Yes, they're real! And they cost me a pretty penny. Now buckle up.'

Seconds later they were at the entrance. 'Good afternoon,' said the security guard in the high-vis jacket. 'Tickets please.'

'We don't have tickets,' said Auntie Susan. 'We have passes.' She held out the badge with the holographic cross and Joe did the same. The security guard inspected them one at a time and Joe got the sweaty pits again. Drenched.

'You should have come to the east entrance with these,' said the guard.

'Oh dear,' replied Auntie Susan, 'we didn't realise.' She was doing a bit of a voice, all calm and soft, and it didn't much suit her.

Joe's stomach gurgled. Hunger, perhaps, but more likely stress.

'Not a problem,' said the security guard. 'It's just with a triple-A pass you'd have avoided the queue that way. We don't see many of those passes coming through this door! Guessing you're VIPs!'

Joe let out a steady breath of relief.

'We can still come in this way, right?' asked Auntie Susan.

'Of course!' beamed the security guard. He held up a grey plastic tub with a laminated sign depicting bags, mobile phones, laptops and tablets. 'Still have to do the checks, I'm afraid. Devices in the box, please.'

Joe and Auntie Susan hadn't brought anything apart from their phones, so they dropped them quickly into the box and the guard sent them whirring through the X-ray. Then he scanned them down with the handheld metal detector. Nothing beeped.

'In you go. Have a great time.'

Before they stepped through the entrance, Auntie Susan said, 'Can you point us in the direction of the Wembley Suite? The Ginger Baker reception?'

The guard nodded and pointed towards a lift on the far side of the entry hall. There were so many people it was almost impossible to see, but through gaps in the crowd Joe could make out two more security guards blocking the entrance to the lift.

'Show them your passes and they'll let you through.'

'Thank you,' replied Auntie Susan, but Joe said nothing.

They stepped into the stadium.

'We're on,' said Auntie Susan quietly. 'We're bloody-well on.'

They passed the elevator guards with greater ease and were informed which level they needed for the Wembley Suite. Once in the lift, Auntie Susan pushed the button and Joe said, 'Why don't they just have signs for it? So people can find it easily?'

'I think it's one of those spaces they don't want people to find. It's probably for royals and V V I Ps,' Auntie Susan replied. 'They don't want all and sundry walking in.'

'Like us,' said Joe. 'Do you really think we can do this?'

'I think we're already doing it.'

Arriving at the suite, they found even more security. Getting in to see Ginger Baker was a challenge indeed and Joe could feel a background panic kicking in. What if they got caught? What if the suits were here? What if, what if, what if . . .

Shut up, Joe, they willed themself. *Let* Misty *handle this.*

They flashed their badges at the door staff.

'We're from St Joseph's,' said Auntie Susan with confidence, thrusting her lanyard forward.

How does she do this? Joe wondered. Was it age? Experience? Would Joe one day breeze through life with the gall of Auntie Susan?

Would I want to?

The woman with the guest list studied each of their Access All Area passes and then, without even a second thought, swung open the Wembley Suite and simply said, 'Welcome.'

The suite was much bigger than Joe had expected, busier, and almost everybody there was in formal attire. A lot of ties and blazers, and more shoulder pads than a *Golden Girls* themed drag show.

'What now?' asked Joe.

'We work the room,' Auntie Susan replied. 'We blend in. Then when we see Ginger Baker we take our chance.'

In the background Joe could hear a live band playing traditional hymns but couldn't see where they were located through the crowd. Some guests were laughing, smiling, and some were in small groups talking more seriously. Most of them looked rich. There were flashy watches, diamond earrings and expensive dresses. If Joe didn't suspect they were all absolute rotters on account of them being invited by Ginger Baker, it would have felt like a nice party.

A waiter passed with a tray of unoriginal-looking canapés: goat's cheese and sun-dried tomato tarts.

'Thank God,' they said to Auntie Susan.

'Mind your language,' she replied.

'You're one to talk.'

Joe scooped three tarts into the palm of their hand and took a little napkin, scoffing them as fast as they could, trying to fill up their empty stomach.

Shouldn't have had those morning gins . . .

The suite was a long, wide room with a glass wall on one side that overlooked the main stadium. From there it was possible to see the Preach Party main stage and the banks of seats gradually filling up with excited worshippers. As Joe admired the view, the sound of metal chinking against glass sounded from the other end of the room, drawing everyone's attention. A man had stepped on to a small platform and was tapping a champagne flute with a knife. He was old. Really old, like his skin might just plop off his face into a puddle of dry flesh at any moment.

'May I have your attention please,' he said with a shaky voice into a microphone. The room fell silent as people stopped their conversations and turned to listen. 'Thank you. We are blessed indeed this evening, not only to be here at this year's Preach Party, but to be at the Pre-Preach Party Party, hosted by none other than this evening's headline speaker. I know that to all of you she will need no introduction, but I shall introduce her nevertheless.'

There was a chuckle that rippled through the listening audience, though Joe didn't find the old man to have been funny at all. He'd have flopped on comedy night at Lady's Bar.

Auntie Susan whispered into Joe's ear, 'Let's move to the front.' She'd spotted an open route to the left of the attentive guests and so she moved, ever so gently in her black suit, towards the stage. Joe followed behind as the ancient man continued speaking.

'We know her as one of the United States' most successful preachers,' he was saying. 'From humble beginnings, to launching multiple churches across the country, she not only spreads the word of our Lord and Saviour far and wide, but she fights for change. Working at local, national and international levels, she helps to ensure that our politicians and business leaders operate with Christian mindsets at the heart of their work.'

At this, the audience broke into a round of applause and a danger alarm went off in Joe's head. They remembered Auntie Susan's words from earlier, about how not all Christians were the extreme ones, the ones who hated LGBTQ+ people, but this celebration of Ginger Baker told Joe these particular guests might be just that. Auntie Susan excused herself quietly as she squeezed past a group of men in suits almost identical to theirs. They too were drinking champagne.

They were halfway down the long suite when the old man announced through gravelly phlegm, 'Please welcome to this stage, your evening's host, Ginger Baker!'

The attendees went wild. Clapping. Wailing. A woman by a plush-looking seating area fell to her knees and raised her hands to the sky.

We shouldn't be here, Joe thought.

They continued their journey through the room and Joe watched as Ginger Baker stepped up and took the microphone. In person, she looked just as she had in the photographs they'd seen online and in Jeremy's recording. She was short, plump, shoulders accentuated by large pads inside a mint-green jacket. Her hair was strawberry blonde and styled

in a big tight perm. Her cheeks were pink with a strong application of blusher and she wouldn't have looked out of place in
a 1980s American television advert for pasta sauce or laundry
detergent. She looked sweet for someone so monstrous.

The home-maker look is part of the appeal, Joe thought. *It's
a façade just like these black suits.*

Joe knew that behind Ginger's disguise was something
much less wholesome: a toxic money-grabber intent on
destroying their community. That made it even more repul-
sive. And yet all these people here, hundreds of them in this
room, thousands more in the stadium, they supported her.
They loved her.

We shouldn't be here.

'Well, hello, London!' shouted Ginger into the mic.
Again, the devoted crowd cheered as Auntie Susan edged
ever closer to the front with Joe close behind. They were now
just six or seven people from the stage, near enough for a
clear view. Auntie Susan stopped and Joe took a look around,
checking the edges of the stage for any sign of the Atrax suits.
If they were there, they were well-hidden. 'It's fabulous, just
fabulous to be here at Preach Party! My fifth consecutive
year! And what a party it's going to be.'

Auntie Susan turned to Joe and rolled her lashless eyes.

Ginger continued, 'This reception is truly special, and
near and dear to my heart. In here we celebrate our achieve-
ments before the main event begins, and out there, there
are thousands of worshippers who have travelled from
all around the world to hear the word of God from that
main stage. What a wonderful thing.' She smiled, revealing
pristine veneers.

Knowing some of Ginger's side businesses: the Bibles made by prisoners, fossil fuels smashed out of protected land, taking over queer venues and redeveloping them ... Joe didn't feel as though any of this was a 'wonderful thing'. Quite the opposite, in fact.

The grin dropped from Ginger's face and she was serious, intense. You could have heard a pin drop. 'In these dark times it is more important than ever that we, the leaders of our community, gather and unite to tackle the threats Christianity is facing. When once we ruled the world in Jesus' name, we are now a persecuted group. A group under attack by businesses, governments and international institutions.'

A bit rich, thought Joe, a feeling of anger rushing through their body. Ginger was a billionaire weaponizing her religion, attacking minorities, and claiming that she herself was being persecuted.

'When once we dominated western societies, we now find that other faiths, non-believers, and even the sexual and gender degenerates are prioritized and elevated above us. Our beliefs are dismissed, belittled and ridiculed in favour of so-called progressive values. We see this time and time again in employment, social benefits, community resource allocation and public discourse.'

Sexual and gender degenerates?! Did she really just say that?

Joe saw Auntie Susan's shoulders tense up in front of them. She was surely feeling the same rage as Joe.

'It's time we put a stop to it,' Ginger continued. 'I will fight, and I know you will fight, to put decent, God-fearing morals back at the centre of our public and private institutions. Tonight is a step towards that, one of many I have been making during my time in the UK. Our work at Preach Party is not to convince one another. If you've been invited to this room, I know you need no convincing. No, our work tonight is to go out there and convince *them*. To recruit them so they fight alongside us. Over 70,000 people have bought a ticket for tonight's event – that's almost the size of the British military. We can have an army, my friends, an army to fight with us for what we believe in. Together, we can erase and eradicate the filth that has infiltrated our society. That is my mission for today's event and beyond, and I hope it will be yours.'

She nodded her head to end her speech and there was rapturous applause. Joe was horrified. No, not horrified, furious. They felt the rage Auntie Susan had spoken about in the taxi. It rushed through their entire being. Even their painted toenails, hidden under plain black socks, were furious.

Erase and eradicate. The words echoed in their head. And hundreds of people, every person in this room was clapping for it.

Auntie Susan leaned in towards Joe and Joe noticed a shiny layer of sweat across her brow. Even the unrufflable Auntie Susan had been ruffled.

'What the fuck?' she whispered.

'This is bad,' Joe whispered back.

Joe had never seen her look nervous before, but here she was, out of drag and in a suit, and Auntie Susan was most definitely nervous.

'I don't think we should do this after all,' she said. 'It's not safe here. *"Eradicate!"* It's worse than I thought it would be.'

Joe looked up and saw Ginger Baker stepping down off

the stage into the front rows of the audience, shaking people's hands, thanking them for coming, flashing her veneers in a revolting smile.

'Let's just go,' said Auntie Susan. 'We'll find another way.'

But as Joe watched Ginger greeting her guests, their own worries about being in the Wembley Suite completely dissipated.

Auntie Susan might want to leave, but if Misty Divine was here, there's no way she'd walk out.

I need to channel this fury. What would Misty do?

The burning temper coursing through Joe's veins meant Misty's no-messing, stomping-in personality jumped to the surface. Joe imagined themself in Misty's favourite red dress and big blonde wig and said to Auntie Susan, 'I'm not going anywhere.'

They moved past her, taking the lead and heading deeper into the crowd towards Ginger, who was finishing up her meet and greet.

'Wait!' said Auntie Susan, but Joe was unstoppable. Misty Mode had been activated.

Joe was only one person away from Ginger when she completed her final handshake and began walking in the direction of an exit at the side of the stage.

I have to stop her, they thought. It was urgent. Necessary. The words *'gender degenerate'* played on repeat.

They pushed through the front row of guests and could feel Auntie Susan close behind.

'What are you doing?'

'What we agreed!'

Joe's sights were laser-focused on Ginger.

Now. Now.

'Miss Baker,' they called. 'Please wait a second.'

'Here we go . . .' muttered Auntie Susan.

Ginger spun on her heel, a stumpy dumpy thing that was probably very expensive. Up close, Joe could see her make-up was thick and heavy, and all the wrong colour – the blusher was too pink, the foundation too orange, her eyebrows over-plucked. If Ginger Baker needed to erase and eradicate anybody, it was her glam squad.

Finally they were face to face, as they'd planned to be all along, a few steps away from the rest of the audience. Auntie Susan had chickened out so now it was up to Joe.

The moment had arrived and Joe/Misty wasn't going to go down without a fight.

CHAPTER 41

'Miss Baker,' said Joe, trying to remain calm and fighting the urge to make a scene like Jeremy had done in Chicago. 'Thank you for your speech. It was very good to hear your position.'

'You're welcome,' said Ginger. A blast of her breath revealed traces of a recently sucked peppermint. 'I'm sorry I don't have time to talk. I must be heading to the main stage.'

She's not getting away as easy as that.

'If you'd please indulge me for a moment,' said Joe. 'We're from St Joseph's in east London,' echoing the lie Auntie Susan had told earlier.

Ginger pretended to have heard of the fake church and nodded slowly. 'Oh yes, St Joseph's. I'm sure you're doing wonderful work, but I'm on a tight schedule.'

Her insincerity, her *Dynasty* shoulder pads, everything about her made Joe's skin crawl. They took a step closer, so they could speak quietly without being overheard.

'We don't think *you're* doing wonderful work,' they said. 'In fact, we think you're doing the opposite.'

'Excuse me?' said Ginger, evidently not used to being challenged, especially on her own patch. For Ginger, this was supposed to be a room of die-hard supporters.

'You heard,' said Joe, keeping their voice low enough so the neighbouring guests wouldn't hear. 'We've found out some information about you, information the British public wouldn't like.'

Ginger pointed a glossy-nailed finger in Joe's face. 'Are you a journalist? You're a journalist, aren't you?'

'I'm not a journalist,' said Joe. 'I'm a concerned citizen.'

The preacher threw her head back and raised her voice, 'Get out of here. You get out of here right now.'

Auntie Susan stepped up next to Joe, saying nothing. Nothing at all! Where had she gone? All her bluff and bluster, vanished.

Joe carried on. 'Listen to me, Miss Baker. We know about your partnership with Atrax. We know you've hired them to close down LGBTQ+ venues across the UK and we're here to tell you that it will not stand. You might have got away with it at home, but you won't here.'

'You don't know anything at all,' Ginger snapped, looking around, probably for security. 'How did you get in here?'

We don't have much time, Joe realised.

'I have proof,' they said. 'A video of you and Stefan Weber, and documentation showing Atrax's involvement in multiple venue closures. We know what you're doing and if you don't stop, we're going to expose you.'

'Are you . . . blackmailing me? Because heed this, it will not end well for you.' Her southern American accent was deep and drawling. 'I'm calling security.'

'No,' said Joe. 'This isn't blackmail, it's a promise. I'm going to expose you and shut you down. I have a national newspaper ready to publish everything. I'm giving you until midday tomorrow to back off the venues, or I will bring your plan crashing down.'

'Security!' she called. 'Security!'

'Did you hear me?' asked Joe. 'By midday tomorrow those venues will be safe, or I'm going to expose how you're using legal loopholes and manipulations to attack a protected group in this country.'

She leaned forward, breathing minty-fresh breath right into Joe's face. 'You don't get to come in here and dictate how I run my business, *queerboy*. There isn't a newspaper in the world who would dare publish whatever you think you have. Do you understand that? But I will find out who you are, and I will destroy you.' Her features were taut and vicious between her plump Barbie cheeks. 'I will ruin you,' she shook. White flecks appeared in the corners of her mouth. 'I will ruin your family, your friends and everything you care about, and I couldn't give a goshdarn damn about your protections.'

She meant it. Every single word. Her hatred seeped out of her with every syllable.

The exit behind her opened and two men stepped out.

'Heads-up,' said Auntie Susan, elbowing Joe.

Ginger spotted the suits. 'Security!' she called to them. 'They shouldn't be here. These two shouldn't be in here!'

'Run!' shouted Auntie Susan. 'Now!'

They bolted. They sprinted in a drama for the ages: two drag queens disguised as missionaries running for their lives from an evil preacher. Her arms spread wide, Auntie Susan literally pushed people out of her way as they launched back through the Wembley Suite to get to the exit.

'Move!' she was shouting. 'Get out of my way!'

Some guests budged, some guests didn't. A glass of champagne fell and shattered on the floor. Joe glanced over their shoulder – the suits were close behind.

'Stop them!' screeched Ginger Baker.

People scattered, aware that a scene was unfolding in what was meant to have been a luxurious private party.

Auntie Susan was not afraid of getting hands-on. Joe looked on in horror as she pushed an elderly vicar who was blocking her path. The vicar landed on a waiter, who flipped his tray of canapés, sending scores of goat's cheese and sundried tomato tartlets flying across the floor.

'Hurry up!' she called to Joe.

'I'm right behind you.'

One of the Atrax suits was really close now. Too close. Joe felt him reach out a hand to grasp the back of their blazer. They dodged to the left, narrowly escaping his clutches, but their hip caught the edge of a tall cocktail table, tipping it over, along with at least six glasses. Orange juice, wine, water, a wet mess in broken glass that crashed and caused a woman in a floral skirt to scream and jump backwards.

Joe leapt with elegant Misty Divine legs over the spilled drinks and heard a thud and a thump behind them, the sound of a fall. They looked back and saw the closest suit on the floor, palms full of broken glass and blood. He scrambled to get back up.

'Faster!' Joe shouted to Auntie Susan, realising this was their chance to get ahead.

'I'm sixty bloody four!' she called back. 'This is as fast as it gets!'

Auntie Susan burst with both hands out of the suite

and they staggered into the corridors of the stadium. The passage outside was buzzing with people, packed with hundreds of Preach Party attendees all making their way to their seats.

'Lose the jackets,' said Joe as they tried to squeeze and squish their way through the crowds towards a staircase at the far end of the space. They each shrugged off their blazers and let them fall to the floor. Joe's hope was that the few seconds headstart they had, combined with the change in appearance, would give them a chance at getting away. 'Heads down.'

Auntie Susan led the way and, despite a few bumps and grinds into passing strangers, they were soon on the steps heading to the lower levels of the stadium.

On the ground floor, the exit level, the crowds were thinner. Joe guessed this was because attendees were already inside waiting for the show to start. They saw no sign of the suits. They'd lost them in the throngs.

'This way!' called Auntie Susan, pointing a finger towards the main entrance.

The extra space meant they could run a little faster and they charged forward, heading towards daylight. Joe's whole body was in panic mode, but they made it. Out past the security team, moving in the opposite direction to everybody else, on to the ramps down to Olympic Way.

Now they sprinted, easily and freely, though Joe had been right about the shoes. They were definitely rubbing blisters under their ankles. They were out of breath and felt like they needed to stop to gasp in oxygen. Auntie Susan turned left off Olympic Way on to a road called Humphry Repton Lane by one of the big venue car parks, and once on this side street, they both stopped running.

'Holy shit,' heaved Auntie Susan. 'I'm too old for this.' She bent down and put her hands on her knees, catching her breath. 'Are they behind us?' she asked.

'I don't think so,' said Joe. 'We lost them.'

'Good. Then we'll walk this next bit until we find a cab.'

Joe was too short-winded for talking as they power-walked back towards Empire Way, where the taxi had dropped them off earlier. As they recovered, Joe thought about everything that had just happened and the commotion replayed in their mind. The decrepit host with the phlegmy voice, Ginger's evil speech, the confrontation, the minty breath . . .

'You don't get to come in here and dictate how I run my business, queerboy . . . I will ruin you.'

That's what she'd said. She'd called them *queerboy*.

And what had happened to Auntie Susan? She'd gone from the bold and boisterous to a nervous wreck, leaving Joe to take the lead. Thank the Lord for Misty else they'd never have got through it.

As they reached Empire Way, Joe flagged down a cab, which pulled over and wound down the front window.

'Where to, lads?' the driver asked.

Lads.

'The Plough, please,' said Joe. 'Near Roman Road.'

'Hop in.'

'What do we do now?' asked Auntie Susan as the car pulled away from the kerb.

'We need to talk to the others,' said Joe, 'to Jeremy and Mandy.'

Auntie Susan nodded. She was shaken, definitely out of character.

'What happened to you in there?' Joe asked.

She looked out of the window. 'I . . . I don't know. Something about the language, the speech. All sorts of things came flooding . . . never mind. I'm sorry – I wasn't expecting . . . Anyway, you confronted her well. You did it better than I would have.'

'I channelled my inner-Misty,' said Joe.

'That you did,' Auntie Susan replied. 'That you did.'

CHAPTER 42

Joe paid the driver when they pulled up outside the Plough and Auntie Susan stopped in front of the grimy entrance. She looked embarrassed.

'Don't tell the others that I couldn't do it,' she said. 'It's not like me, and I can't explain it.'

'I won't tell them anything about that,' said Joe, trying to reassure her. 'Between us we did it. We got in, we approached her, confronted her and got away. We both played a part. We were a team.'

'Thank you,' she said.

They stepped into the pub and there was a sudden commotion from the banquette seating area. Jeremy and Baseball Cap were moving in a fluster. Jeremy was getting up off the floor and Baseball Cap was hurriedly fastening his trousers shut. An empty Jack Daniels bottle stood on the table. They both looked embarrassed. It was clear what had been going on.

Joe laughed. 'Wow! There's a twist I wasn't expecting!'

Auntie Susan clapped. 'And here I was, thinking it was a pub I was running, not a bathhouse.' She was back in character, back on form. The quiet, sheepish Auntie Susan Joe had been privy to was gone.

'Sorry,' said Baseball Cap, coyly covering his crotch with his hands.

'Yeah, sorry,' repeated Jeremy as he swayed slightly on his feet.

'Don't be sorry, boys!' shouted Auntie Susan as she marched through to the back room. 'Love is love!'

Joe hurried through the doors behind her, eager to take off what remained of the suit. Once out of earshot, they said to Auntie Susan, 'I don't think it was love, to be honest.'

The older queen threw back her shaved head and cackled. 'I think you might be right, Misty. Ha! It's certainly cheered me up though. Good for them.'

As they changed back into their regular clothes, Joe said, 'Should we call the others now? Mandy, maybe Jessica?'

Keanu the chihuahua was yapping and running circles around Auntie Susan's feet as she slipped back into her football shirt.

'No,' she replied. 'It's getting late and we've had a stressful time. We need to be calm, to think it all through with clear minds. We should sleep on it. We can plan our next move in the morning.'

'Ginger Baker isn't going to stop,' said Joe. 'She wasn't even a tiny bit afraid of our newspaper threat.'

'She wasn't.' Auntie Susan scooped up Keanu and gently stroked his little head. 'That's why we need to look at this with fresh eyes. Besides, Jeremy's drunk and horny, and Jessica's God-knows-where.'

Joe agreed. They needed all the help they could get and Jeremy definitely wasn't in the right frame of mind.

'The other thing,' said Auntie Susan, 'is that we've just listened to some of the most disgusting queerphobic bullshit I've heard in a long time, in a room full of people cheering for it. And whether it's sunk in for you yet or not, that stuff messes with our brains. We have to take a moment.'

Joe finished tying the laces of their trainers and stood up. 'I'll head home,' they said 'and we can talk in the morning then?'

'Don't be stupid, Misty. You aren't heading anywhere. You're staying here,' said Auntie Susan. 'There's a spare room in my flat upstairs. We'll all stay here tonight. Is your boyfriend still at his parents'?'

'Yes,' said Joe. 'I think so.'

'You might want to call him and tell him not to go home tonight. Not until this is over.'

Oh God, thought Joe. Telling Miles there was danger in their own home was something they'd much prefer not to do.

Auntie Susan dropped Keanu into his velvet bed and popped a small meaty treat into his snarling mouth. 'I'll go upstairs and fetch bedding for *Heartstopper: After Dark* in the other room,' nodding in the direction of the bar.

Joe laughed. 'OK. I'll message Miles.'

Alone in the gaudy office, Joe typed up another text, reading and re-reading it before pressing send, hoping not to cause a panic or more trouble between them.

Hi love. There have been some new developments that I'll tell you about later, but for now it's probably best to stay at your parents'. I'm staying at the Plough tonight.

Joe could see from the ticks turning blue that Miles read it right away, but didn't start typing a reply. It took a minute of staring at the screen before they realised there wasn't going to be one. Maybe it was easier that way.

Everyone gathered in the bar. Baseball Cap and Jeremy were drunk and now sitting apart from one another with chastened faces. Auntie Susan had piled the pool tables with duvets and pillows and sleeping bags.

'So,' Jeremy slurred, 'are you going to tell us how it went at Wembley?'

Between them, Auntie Susan and Joe recounted their adventure, leaving out Auntie Susan's blast of nerves. When they reached the moment that Ginger Baker had used the phrase *sexual and gender degenerates*', Baseball Cap muttered, 'Disgusting.'

They finished by describing the escape: the vicar, the fallen suit . . . even the tartlets got a mention.

'I knew it wouldn't work,' said Jeremy. 'No newspaper is going to take the risk of publishing against Atrax and Ginger Baker and she knows it. She's too powerful.'

'We had to try,' said Joe.

'There isn't anything else we can do?' asked Baseball Cap.

Auntie Susan huffed and slurped down a mouthful of something she'd poured at the bar. 'We aren't giving up, that's for sure, but we all need sleep and you two need to sober up and get whatever's going on here out of your systems so you can help us think right tomorrow.' She stood up and gestured at Joe. 'Come on, Misty. I'll show you to your room.'

Joe got up too, leaving the new-found lovers at the table. 'See you in the morning,' they said.

Auntie Susan waved a finger between Jeremy and Baseball

Cap. 'Just know, I don't care what you get up to in here, but keep the noise down. I need my beauty sleep.'

The bed in Auntie Susan's spare room was comfortable, and the room itself wasn't what Joe had expected. It was grey, everything in complementary shades: the bedspread, the walls, the carpet, the curtains. It was soothing, unlike its owner.

Was it really only this morning that I found Jeremy? That I solved Sylvester's mystery?

Lying in the softly lit bedroom, Joe thought through everything that had led them to this moment. As they reflected on the details, there was a shift in how they saw it all. A moment they hadn't thought much about came to mind. A few days ago, on Misty's first visit to Auntie Susan to ask for help, she had asked for something in return. She'd asked to be a judge at the grand finale of Lady Lady's Star Search. In all the subsequent chaos Joe had almost forgotten that the final of the talent contest was tomorrow, at Lady's Bar.

Lady Lady's Star Search.

Now, Joe thought, they might have a way to stop Ginger Baker once and for all.

CHAPTER 43

Friday

Joe could hardly sleep, thinking through all the details of their plan, making thorough notes and instructions on their phone. It must have been 3 a.m. by the time they finally drifted off, their brain frazzled with Ginger Baker rage and a deep desire to destroy her.

Upon waking at around 10 a.m. and before they even got out of bed, the first thing Joe did was write messages to Mandy, Jessica and Plimberley, sending them each an invitation for a Zoom meeting at 11 a.m. They told them attendance was non-negotiable.

They stepped out of the grey bedroom and knocked lightly on the bathroom door on Auntie Susan's landing. Hearing no response, Joe let themself in and jumped in the shower, helping themself to a generous dose of Auntie Susan's expensive body wash. It smelled of roses and almonds, delicious and revitalizing. Showered, and dressed in yesterday's clothes, they made their way downstairs to the bar.

The others were awake already, eating bowls of Coco Pops from a box on one of the tables near the banquettes.

Jeremy and Baseball Cap were also in last night's clothes

and Auntie Susan was wearing nothing but a red silk robe with a black lace trim. It looked like something she might have bought at Victoria's Secret in 1990, and the hyper-feminine style was at odds with her shaved head and tattoos in a gender-bending way that Joe found delightful.

'Good morning,' she said, her voice rough and scratchy.

'Morning,' said Joe. They tried not to stare at Jeremy and Baseball Cap, but they definitely took a good look, trying to figure out whether anything might have happened between them in the night. There was no indication either way, but they both looked hungover: pallid faces said they were fighting off yesterday's Jack Daniels.

'I need coffee. Is there coffee?' asked Joe.

Auntie Susan pointed to the bar, her silken sleeve rippling. 'We don't have one of those fancy machines, but there's a kettle and a jar of instant over there.'

The water was already hot and there was a cup waiting next to it. Joe spooned in a heap of granules and stirred them into the water until they vanished before joining the others at the tables.

'I've worked it out,' said Joe, sitting next to Baseball Cap, who was munching loudly through his bowl of cereal. 'I know how to expose Ginger Baker without the newspapers.'

Auntie Susan dropped her spoon into her bowl, her open mouth revealing half-chewed puffed rice. 'How?!'

'I've set up a Zoom call for eleven o'clock. Mandy, Jessica and Plimberley will be joining. Jeremy, we'll need your laptop.'

'Plimberley Walsh?!' said Auntie Susan, shocked at the suggestion. 'What would *she* have to do with any of it?'

'You'll see,' said Joe. 'It's going to take all of us. I realised last night that we've all handled a different piece of the puzzle and we each have something, skills or contacts the others don't. If we bring it all together and approach it as a team, we can end this.'

'Tell us how,' said Auntie Susan.

'Not yet,' said Joe. 'It's complicated so I'll explain it to everyone at the same time, but this is the only way. It's the only way we can expose her and stop her for good.'

'So it's going to be a team-up?' asked Baseball Cap, looking up from his breakfast.

'Yeah,' Joe replied.

'Like the Avengers?'

Joe laughed, 'Yes, I guess like the Avengers.'

Jeremy set up his laptop at the end of the table and he, Joe, Auntie Susan and Baseball Cap gathered around it, waiting for the others to join. One by one, they logged in and appeared on-screen. Mandy first, from the Lady's Bar office. Jessica popped up second, clearly in a bedroom, long white wires hanging from her ears.

'What's going on, Misty?' she said.

'I'll explain everything when we have Plimberley.'

'Our Plimberley?' Mandy asked.

'For God's sake,' muttered Auntie Susan. 'How many *Plimberleys* do you know?'

Seconds later, Plim joined. She'd connected via a phone with poor signal. Her face was pixelated but she'd added a jazzy Zoom background – a waterfall cascade of Party Ring biscuits.

'Good,' said Joe. 'Everybody's here.'

'Now tell us,' demanded Auntie Susan. 'What's the plan?'

'What plan?' asked Plimberley. 'What's the goss?'

Joe started the meeting by explaining to the guests on the screen what had happened last night – the infiltration of the Preach Party reception and the confrontation with Ginger Baker.

'She's evil,' hissed Mandy.

Everybody nodded.

'The trouble we've had until now,' Joe continued, 'is that we've been thinking too small. Jessica, you were trying to find one outlet to publish the story, but that wasn't possible. We thought about posting Jeremy's video on the Lady's Bar social media, but that wouldn't work either because we think Atrax could hack the account, or have it taken down. That said, I've thought of a way for us to get it out there, to make so much noise nobody could ignore it.'

Jessica unmuted herself. 'It's going to have to be really big, Misty. It'll have to be enormous if it's going to do anything at all.'

'It will be,' said Joe. 'Once I've explained everything, you'll understand, but I'll warn you now, we may have to involve the police. We might need them.'

There was a cacophony of rebellion to this – nearly all of them had done something illegal to try to get out of this situation. Jessica's house rental in her sick mother's name, Auntie Susan's Wembley access, Mandy and Misty's bribery . . .

'You can't!' shouted Auntie Susan.

'Ridiculous!' said Jessica.

'But the bribery?' asked Mandy.

'P L E A S E !' called Joe, silencing them all with one word. They felt like Misty again, in charge and in control. She was wigless, but back in the room. 'Listen to my plan and you'll understand. This is the only way to get our lives back. There are tasks for each of you, tasks only you can do. And without each of you completing these, the plan won't work. So, if we're really serious about stopping Ginger Baker and Atrax, if we're going to save the queer venues and protect our families, I need you all on board.'

There was a moment of silence before Auntie Susan spoke up. 'Go on, tell us your plan.'

Joe ran through the details, explaining each of their roles and what was required. There was some resistance to begin with, especially from Jessica, who still seemed to be clutching to the idea that this was her story, that she somehow owned it more than anyone else. Joe quickly knocked her back.

'It's time for you to let go, Jessica,' they said as kindly as possible. 'You'll still get the credit, just in a different way.'

Eventually, she nodded in agreement. Joe was feeling a buzz of excitement like they'd had a full can of Plimberley's Power Hour. This was dangerous and risky, but maybe they had something here, a way to defeat the monster.

Plimberley was the easiest to convince. In fact, she seemed ecstatic to have been asked to participate at all.

'I'm just happy to be here,' she said.

'And the bribery?' Mandy asked again. 'The situation with the council? Are you sure we won't get in trouble for that?'

Joe shook their head. 'I'm not, but my feeling is there will be so much focus on Ginger Baker and Atrax, and there are so many venues involved, our secret will fly under the radar. This is a way out, Mandy. Probably the only way.'

They went through it all a second time, to be sure

everyone understood their assignments. This time, there was no resistance. Everybody agreed that Joe's plan was one that could actually work.

Plimberley and Jessica logged off the call to get started on their assignments while Jeremy took the laptop to a quieter corner of the pub to speak with Mandy for a technical meeting that was a crucial element of Joe's plan.

'I suppose we'd better head to the office and get started,' said Auntie Susan to Joe.

'Yep,' said Joe. 'We need to get on it quickly.'

Baseball Cap looked crestfallen, disappointed. 'Wait,' he said, 'so my job is just driving?'

'There is quite a bit of driving to do,' said Joe.

'Oh,' he replied sadly. 'I feel like the most boring Avenger of them all.'

Auntie Susan plonked herself on her office chair, behind her marble desk. Her silk robe fell open, revealing a hairy pierced nipple with a tattoo of a star around it.

'Oops,' she said, pulling it closed, 'flashing my tit at you. How crude.'

Joe laughed. They liked this character she played, this layer of personality that Joe had recently peeked beneath. She was more than the fierce, flirty and frightening redhead. There was a more complicated person in there, with a difficult and complex past. Knowing this made the drag persona even more interesting and Joe wondered whether she was hiding in it or protecting herself with it. Either way, the glimpses they'd had into the real Auntie Susan made Joe feel closer to her and less afraid of her.

'Aside from Lady's Bar,' said Auntie Susan, 'which Mandy's dealing with, there are six other venues to contact. I'm sure I have the numbers for all the owners. Let's take three each and start calling.'

'We need to get through them pretty quickly if we're to have time to get into drag,' said Joe.

'This is going to take some explanation. I bet most of these places won't even know it's Atrax behind their problems, and they won't have heard anything at all about Ginger Baker's involvement.'

Joe knew that was true, but they needed all the venues on board if this was going to play out the way they wanted it to.

'We'll do our best,' they said.

Auntie Susan clicked open her computer and lit a cigarette simultaneously, taking a huge pull on it and exhaling. 'Nothing quite like the first cig of the day.'

Within moments the room was full of smoke and she'd airdropped contact details for three venue owners to Joe. They set about making their calls.

Just after Joe had finished their first call, to a bar in Manchester, the office door opened to reveal Jeremy standing on the other side.

'I've finished with Mandy,' he said.

'Brilliant,' said Joe. 'She has everything she needs?'

'She does,' replied the photographer.

'Then go straight to Lady's Bar to set up if that's OK.'

Jeremy nodded and closed the door, heading back to the bar where Baseball Cap was waiting for his first journey of the day.

*

It took an hour for Joe and Auntie Susan to get through the calls to the venue owners. There were indeed long explanations required, and angry and upset responses when they learned the truth about why and how they were under attack. But there was gratitude and solidarity as the other owners were glad to hear they weren't facing Ginger alone.

'Mine have all agreed,' said Joe, feeling a mixture of excitement and dread now. *We're actually doing this.*

'So have mine,' said Auntie Susan. 'Brighton were especially angry when I told them about Ginger. Fuming, in fact. The *"erase and eradicate"* was a step too far for them.'

'So everyone's in play,' said Joe.

'At this stage, what do they have to lose? Most of them are on the brink of closing down.'

'Not for long,' Joe replied.

The third bedroom of the Plough's upstairs flat was a dressing room. They stood together on the landing and Auntie Susan said, 'Are you sure about this?'

'I am,' Joe replied. There was no other option. 'It's either this, or I do the whole thing out of drag.'

They knew they couldn't carry out the plan as Joe, and they didn't want to. This was something Misty had started, and only Misty should finish it.

'OK then,' said Auntie Susan. 'Let's do it.'

She pushed down the handle and swung open a room that could have been a set from a drag horror film. *Sequin Saw,* thought Joe. The walls and furniture were all painted bright white and it was pristine. At the far end was a vanity table with an oval mirror and the left wall was an open wardrobe with dozens of white dresses hanging, perfectly spaced. To an untrained eye they would have all looked the same, but Joe noticed variations in the designs. Some were glittery, some had rhinestones, a couple had built-in belts and bat-winged collars. The same dress: mini, Lycra and long sleeves, but different every time. The right-hand wall was wigs, and like the dresses, they were similar but not the same. Up-dos, high ponies, perms, bouffants . . . all scorching double-decker red. Lined up beneath the wigs were her red shoes: sequin, leather, PVC, suede. This was the Auntie Susan command centre.

The criminal mastermind grinned as she watched Joe take it all in. 'You'll be Auntie Susan before you know it.'

'God help me,' said Joe.

'Hey! Don't be such an ungrateful bitch about it. It's not every day I let someone wear my drag.'

'We can really do this, can't we?' they asked her.

'*You* can,' said Auntie Susan. 'If anybody can, it's Misty Divine.'

After Joe shaved, Auntie Susan handed them a bunch of unused make-up brushes and went to shower. Joe sat at the vanity table and studied her products, all laid out neatly. It was funny to Joe how, despite doing the same job, every drag artist had their own unique set of preferences when it came to tools, technique and product. Joe had heard of all of Auntie Susan's make-up brands, but had never used them. Could they pull off a full Misty face with someone else's make-up? She was about to give it a good go. It was Auntie Susan drag, or no drag at all.

*

By 3 p.m. the transformation was complete. Joe had gone from their plain-looking non-binary self to Misty Divine. Well, a three decades younger Auntie Susan version of Misty Divine. She'd opted for the white glittery dress, crimson sequin heels and scarlet bouffant hair.

'This is weird . . .' she muttered to herself as she looked in the free-standing full-length mirror in the corner of the room.

Auntie Susan burst in: white rhinestoned dress, red leather shoes. No wig.

'Jeez Louise . . .' she said, looking Misty up and down. 'It's like seeing a ghost!'

'Must be strange,' said Misty.

'Strange?!' exclaimed Auntie Susan. 'It's like I've birthed my very own clone. As if I'd pushed you out into the world from between my muscular and hirsute legs. It's hilarious. Now, I need hair.'

She turned and faced the wig wall, then glanced back at Misty.

'What are you thinking?' Misty asked.

'I'm thinking I should do the same hair as you. Twinsies.'

'Twinsies?'

'Why not?' said the older queen. 'If we're really doing this, let's at least do it camp.'

She reached up and pulled down a slightly curled fluffy wig that was very similar to the one Misty was already wearing. She sat at the vanity and used pins and bandage to attach it firmly to her head.

And then, standing in the Plough, in matching outfits with matching hair, were two Auntie Susans.

CHAPTER 44

Misty sat on a stool by the bar, her phone on the counter beside her.

'Do you want a drink?' asked Auntie Susan. 'A little gin to take the edge off?'

'No, thank you,' said Misty. 'I need to stay clear-headed today.' And she did. There were so many moving parts, so many people involved in getting this right. She'd save her gin drinking for afterwards, for when she'd taken down Ginger Baker.

'I'm having a vodka,' said Auntie Susan. 'A big juicy one.'

Misty's phone rang and rattled against the bar. She grabbed it and looked at the screen: Jessica Gethyn's secret burner number.

'Jessica?' she said, picking up right away. 'Is everything OK?'

'All good,' replied the journalist. 'I've got everything you asked for and I'm compiling it now. Just calling to confirm that I'll be ready on my side by 7 p.m.'

'That's great news,' said Misty.

Jessica hesitated for a second. 'Do you . . . I mean, I think this could work, Misty. I think this might be enough.'

'I hope so.'

A few minutes later the phone rang again.

Jeremy.

She pressed the phone against her ear to the clatter of red dangly earrings.

'Misty,' he said, 'we're all set at Lady's Bar – everything's fixed and good to go. I'll send you the link now. Can you pass it to Auntie Susan for the venue contacts? I don't have her number.'

'No problem, send it over. Thanks, Jeremy.'

Her phone vibrated in her hand as his message arrived.

'What should I do next?' he asked. 'Should I wait here or come back to the Plough?'

'Wait there,' Misty replied. 'Mandy should have arranged the extra security by now, so it's probably the safest place for the time being.'

'Yes, the bar's crawling with them,' Jeremy said.

'That's good to hear. We'll be there soon.'

She ended the call and placed the phone back down. Everything was falling into place. Well, not really falling. She'd orchestrated it, carefully engineering all the disparate pieces into a Misty Divine Masterplan.

She sent Jeremy's link to Auntie Susan, who in turn spent a few minutes forwarding it on. Once she'd done that, she drained her big, juicy vodka. 'Darren should be back by now,' she said. She seemed concerned, worried, looking at her watch to check the time.

Misty was confused. 'Darren? Who's Darren?'

Auntie Susan bulged her eyes with an exaggerated rock of the head. 'You can't be serious! My assistant, *Darren*, who you've known for ages, who picked you up from St Pancras. He was in here last night getting saucy with your photographer friend. You had breakfast with him this morning!'

Baseball Cap, Misty realised. She laughed to herself.

'What's so funny about that?' demanded Auntie Susan.

'I've never had a full conversation with him until today. In my head he was just called Baseball Cap.'

'You're a rude wench, Misty.' She looked at her watch again and her brow scrunched to the centre of her face. 'He should have been back a while ago.'

'Could be traffic?' Misty suggested. 'It is Friday rush hour after all.'

'Hmmm . . .' Auntie Susan wasn't sure.

'Call him, just to see.'

Auntie Susan started a call to Darren, tapping the screen to put it on loudspeaker. It rang a few times before he picked up.

'Auntie!' he said. He sounded breathless and panicked. 'I think I'm being followed! I'm on my way back and I've gone round the houses trying to shake them. It's those bastards in the suits. They must have been watching Lady's Bar.'

'OK, stay calm,' she replied. 'Where are you now?'

Misty didn't like this one bit. Suits in cars weren't part of her plan and she couldn't afford to lose Darren now. She needed him.

'I'm in Spitalfields,' he said. 'I think they saw me drop off Jeremy. What do you want me to do? I can try to lose them on the way back to the Plough, or I can run them on a wild goose chase.'

'Hold on,' said Auntie Susan. She pressed the mute button. 'What do we do?' she asked Misty. 'If he follows the original plan and comes back to collect us, he's going to lead the suits right to our door.'

Misty scratched her wig. 'But if he doesn't come to get us, we'd have to take a taxi and then we're stuck in a car with someone who won't be willing to break the rules if we need them to.'

'We need him for this, don't we?' said Auntie Susan.

'We do,' Misty replied. 'We're going to have to take the risk.'

Auntie Susan unmuted the call. 'Darren, come back here to get us and we'll try to stick to the original plan. If you can get rid of the suits on the way, that would be ideal.'

'OK,' he said. 'Just in case I can't, wait outside the pub for when I get there. Jump in quick and we'll bolt it back to Lady's Bar.'

'We'll be ready,' said Misty.

'Shit! They're getting closer!' he shouted. 'Gotta go. I'll be there in about twenty minutes.'

There was a beep as the call disconnected.

'Oh dear,' said Auntie Susan. 'This is very troubling.'

Fifteen minutes later, the Plough was locked and the lights were off. A 'closed' sign hung on the front door. Misty Divine and Auntie Susan waited on the pub doorstep dressed like . . . what? Mother and daughter? A bad drag queen *Sweet Valley Twins* tribute? Auntie Susan was clenching and unclenching her fists, playing with her hair, scratching her thigh. It was anxious behaviour. She was worried about Darren.

Misty tried to break the mood, thinking of something to say. She looked up at the pub's sign with the missing 'o'.

'You should fix that sign,' she said.

'It's not priority number one,' Auntie Susan replied sarcastically, 'and the customers come anyway. They're not coming for the "o".'

'I suppose not . . .' said Misty, failing in her effort to distract Auntie Susan.

After a pause, the older queen said, 'Was that an attempt to take my mind off Darren being followed by Ginger Baker's dangerous Atrax crew?'

Misty felt silly now. What a stupid thing to have said. 'Yes,' she admitted.

'It didn't work.'

The Plough was in an odd place for a gay pub, Misty always thought. On a residential street in the heart of east London, there were no surrounding establishments, no nearby takeaways for drunken revellers to indulge themselves after closing time. The road was nice, peaceful, rows of family houses with cars on driveways and hanging baskets by front doors. It was quiet.

No sooner had Misty thought this, the quiet was ripped apart by the sound of screeching tyres.

'He's here,' said Auntie Susan.

Seconds later, her black BMW sped around the corner, skidding across the street, leaving rubbery tracks on the ground. It was an expertly performed manoeuvre and the vehicle stopped with its back door right in front of the drag queens. The front window was open.

'Get in!' called Darren.

Misty yanked open the door and flung herself inside,

scrambling across the back seat to make space for Auntie Susan, who followed her in and slammed it shut.

Misty looked out the back window and saw a second car speeding into the street.

Suits.

'Drive!' she shouted.

As Darren tried to set off again, the suits' blue car rammed into the back of the BMW with a metallic crunch that sent all three of them flying forwards. Auntie Susan hit her face against the headrest in front of her, leaving an imprint of her cheek and lipliner on the leather.

'Bastards!' she exclaimed. 'Nearly lost a lash.'

'Hold on tight,' said Darren. 'And seatbelts. Now!'

Misty and Auntie Susan complied, securing themselves into their seats. Darren hit the gas and the BMW lurched forward, accelerating far too fast for the tranquil housing estate.

They sped through road after road, taking sharp turns, passing a primary school at alarming speed. And then a sudden left, back on to Roman Road, the major highway that led to central London.

There was a gap in the traffic on the opposite side of the street and the suits performed a rapid increase, pulling up alongside them, at clear risk of hitting any oncoming traffic. The suit in the passenger seat raised his right hand.

Auntie Susan gasped, 'Is that a . . .?'

'Gun!' called Darren. 'Get down!'

As Misty lowered her head to her lap, she caught a glimpse of a bus heading towards the suits, aiming for a head-on collision. The bus driver beeped her horn and the suits fell back into the correct lane behind them. The double-decker zoomed on by with its horn blaring.

'Jesus Christ,' Auntie Susan was muttering. 'Bloody guns!'

'Darren,' said Misty, her heart racing, 'how long will it take us to get to Lady's Bar?'

'I don't know,' he said. 'With this traffic, and these guys behind us, I just don't know.'

She grappled her phone under her face. It was 6.22 p.m. Everything was happening at 7. They had to be there by then.

'Will it be seven?' she asked. 'We need it to be seven.'

'I'm doing my best!' Darren shouted. 'But in case you hadn't noticed, we're being chased by some nutters with a fucking gun!'

'Do that thing,' suggested Auntie Susan unhelpfully.

'What thing?!' said Darren. He was obviously stressed, his forehead dripping. He pulled off his baseball cap and threw it on the passenger seat. Misty hadn't seen him without it before and he had quite a nice head of hair.

'The thing they do in films!' insisted Auntie Susan. 'Where you swerve as if you're turning. To trick them.'

'There isn't room!'

They carried on, forwards, forwards, as fast as the traffic and the car would allow. Darren overtook a couple of slow-moving vehicles, but the suits followed easily. Misty glanced up and peered out the back window – they were still directly behind.

'Stay down, Misty!' said Darren, and she complied.

What do we do now?

Their break came with a spot of luck and a huge dollop of dangerous driving when they reached the big junction by Bethnal Green tube station. Misty peeked up and saw multiple lanes of moving traffic, all driving into the junction at once.

'Hold on to your wigs, ladies,' said Darren.

He leaned back in his seat, pushing hard against the steering wheel with straight arms, and the pedal must have hit the floor. Everything in the car lurched as he ploughed through a red light.

'*Shiiiiiit!*' Auntie Susan screamed, her face still on her knees.

Misty couldn't keep her head down any longer. She needed to see what was happening. She sat up, just as Darren drove them straight into the busy junction.

There was noise. A *lot* of noise as vehicles of all shapes and sizes skidded to a halt. Cars crashed into each other. Drivers were beeping furiously and loud, prolonged horns rang out. There was a bang, a thud at the rear of the BMW, as a white transit van hit the back of them. Misty's head cracked against the window as the car spun wildly. She felt sick. It was like being on one of those G-force fairground rides and the spin had her pressed against the door.

All three of them screamed.

The car came to a halt and there was silence. She looked up and saw they'd spun a full 360 degrees. They were still facing central London and now there was no moving traffic at all. People were getting out of their vehicles, some certainly injured, even bleeding. They looked in shock. Misty twisted to see out the rearview window, which was now cracked and shattered into a glistening spiderweb. She saw the suits' blue car still there sitting right behind them.

'Go! Go!' she shouted to Darren.

He shook himself, straightening himself out, and pressed the ignition.

Misty couldn't believe her eyes. The very moment she heard the BMW engine fire up, an enormous articulated lorry thundered its way into the junction, seemingly unaware of the chaos and carnage. She gasped and put her hand over her mouth, realising what was about to happen in the split-second before it did. The lorry wiped the blue car out completely, suits still inside. There was an explosion of glass and sparks as the lorry smashed the car to smithereens. And, as if it weighed nothing at all, the suits' vehicle was thrown to the side of the junction like an empty crisp packet.

Auntie Susan saw the wreckage and before it had even settled in place, she called to Darren. 'Move, Darren, move!'

CHAPTER 45

Darren steered them through the multiple car wrecks at Bethnal Green and on to the other side of the junction, heading towards town. Misty rubbed the side of her head, trying to get her fingers to the bottom of the wig. It didn't seem to be bleeding, but there would definitely be a bump and bruise.

'We have to get out,' said Darren.

'We can't!' Auntie Susan insisted.

'We have to, and quickly. Emergency services will already be on the way and that means police.'

'He's right,' said Misty, thinking of the injured people, the damaged vehicles. She knew the whole place would be crawling with blue lights in minutes. 'This car's ruined. We'll be pulled over in no time.'

'Then what do we do?'

Darren tapped his fingers on the steering wheel. 'You're not going to like it.'

'Why not?' asked Auntie Susan.

Misty thought she already knew what he was going to suggest and she definitely didn't like it. Not at all.

'We're going to have to take the tube,' Darren said. 'It's the quickest way. We dump this car up one of the side streets and double back to Bethnal Green station. We can be in Soho in fifteen minutes on the Central Line.'

'For God's sake . . .' said Auntie Susan. 'I'd like to put on the record, Misty Divine, that I shall be sending an invoice to Lady's Bar to pay for a new car.'

BMW successfully abandoned in front of a row of terraced houses, Misty, Darren and Auntie Susan made their way quickly back to the tube station, the queens' heels clacking beneath them.

'What are we going to do about the gun situation?' Auntie Susan asked.

'We have to hope they don't have more of them,' said Misty.

'If there's one, there's more,' said Darren, his voice serious.

She thought about Jessica Gethyn's original Atrax article. She'd written that Atrax were rumoured to provide private military to corporate clients. Is this what she was talking about? Using mercenaries to shut down drag bars? Surely not. A ridiculous idea, but one that seemed possible now.

She hated Ginger Baker more and more with every second that passed, but soon, if everything went to plan, Misty Divine would put a stop to her scheming for good.

They ducked down the station staircase and tapped into the Underground, racing through the winding tunnels to find the platform that would take them to Tottenham Court Road. A few people did a double-take at Auntie Susan and Misty's matching outfits, but most didn't even seem to notice.

She checked her watch. They should just about arrive for 7 p.m., provided there were no more guns, car crashes or high-speed pursuits to contend with.

They waited on the platform and the LED screen said the next train was in one minute.

'I feel all shaky,' said Auntie Susan. 'That chase in the car. It's got me all flustered.'

'It'll pass,' said Misty. She felt it too, but she didn't have time to soothe Auntie Susan. 'Remember what you said to me in the car on the way to Wembley yesterday? This isn't about you. It isn't about me. It's bigger than both of us. We can afford to be shaky when the whole thing's over.'

Auntie Susan nodded and a wild gust of wind blew her red hair all around her face as a train roared into the platform with howling brakes. They waited for passengers to get off before boarding, as was the unwritten but loudly spoken rule in London. At the end of the carriage there were three empty seats, so they made their way to them and sat down. A man sitting opposite used his phone to take a photo of them, his attention indiscreetly drawn by the twinsies outfits.

'If you take another picture of me,' growled Auntie Susan, leaning forward across the aisle, 'I will snap your neck.'

Misty's phone vibrated twice in the palm of her hand. Two short bursts that meant she'd received an email.

Jessica, she knew. *This will be Jessica.*

It was. She scanned the email and opened an attachment. Everything was there – everything she needed.

'Do you have it?' asked Auntie Susan, eyeing the phone.

'I do.'

It only took ten minutes to arrive at Tottenham Court Road tube station.

'We need to run,' said Misty as they reached the top of the escalators on to the street.

'In heels?!' protested Auntie Susan.

'Yes!'

'Which way?' asked Darren. 'Through Soho Square?'

'Let's go!'

Misty led the charge, legs outstretched, striding as fast as she could manage, heading west down Oxford Street. There were so many people: shoppers, tourists, Friday-night revellers. It was a case of dodging them all, overtaking, hopping off the pavement and on to the road whenever there was a break in traffic.

They turned left into Soho Street, towards the famous square. It was a lovely warm evening, so the square was filled with people picnicking, sitting on benches and on the park's small lawns. It was a famous gay hangout and Misty and Auntie Susan were very quickly spotted.

'That's Auntie Susan!' shouted a guy with a big rose tattoo on his neck.

'And Misty Divine!' pointed his friend.

'Run, Forest, run!' they called together, before laughing out loud.

Darren and the drag queens continued with no response. They were almost there and it was just minutes before 7 p.m.

Misty was fixated now on the moments that lay ahead, on her disgust for Ginger Baker and the way she'd spent years manipulating the legal and political system for her own selfish gain. She needed to get to Lady's Bar. She needed to take her down.

Her feet hurt. Her head hurt. But nothing would stop her.

They ran down Frith Street and this was a more difficult one to navigate, as the pavements were packed with drinkers.

'Excuse me!' Misty called ahead. 'Coming through! Move! Move!'

Some revellers weren't happy with the orders, giving disgruntled looks and irritated mutterings, but Misty didn't care. Getting to the club was her only priority.

They ran the short stretch of Old Compton Street to the Lady's Bar entrance and pushed their way past a group of latecomers arriving for the 7 p.m. show. Misty looked at her phone. 7.03 p.m. She could hear Auntie Susan puffing and panting behind her, and her own body was feeling the effects of the run: her scalp was sweating in Auntie Susan's wig and her chest was heaving.

There were four security staff on the door, more than usual. Mandy had done her bit. Two of them already knew Misty and stepped out of the way to let her through. She was half a foot in the door when she heard something.

'Hey!' called someone from across the street, from outside Lady Lady's favourite coffee shop.

Misty turned her head. *A suit!* It was one of the suits who had confronted her inside the bar just a few nights ago. There was a second one standing beside him.

'Stop there!' he yelled, stepping off the pavement and crossing the street towards them.

'Inside! Fast!' said Darren. They shoved their way in and the four security officers formed a solid human wall in front of the door behind them, blocking the suits from entry.

Darren and the queens descended the staircase to the auditorium as fast as they could. Misty worried briefly about the stairs and heels combo, about whether she might trip and fall and break her neck before any of her plan could swing into action. Thankfully she didn't.

At the bottom of the staircase by the tiny reception desk was Tess, the Lady's Bar head of security.

'Tess,' rushed Misty, 'the suits are outside and they're going to try to get in. Don't let them, no matter what.' Then, leaning forward so the arriving guests wouldn't hear, she whispered, 'They might be armed. Call DI Davies at Charing Cross Police Station. Tell him to get here urgently.'

Tess's mouth dropped wide open. 'What kind of "armed", Misty?' she asked.

Misty hesitated, not wanting to worry Tess, but also knowing she needed all the information if she was to protect the bar and its patrons. 'Firearms,' she said. 'We've seen them with guns tonight.'

Tess nodded gravely and pushed a button to release the auditorium entrance. Misty, Auntie Susan and Darren stepped through.

Misty's entire body was relieved to be back at Lady's Bar: the red velvet, the polished tables, the smart servers . . . and there, across the room, was Mandy, waving anxiously. Her choppy black bob and big eccentric glasses felt like home.

Plimberley appeared in a blur of silver sequins and 18 inches of human hair wig. A glamazon!

'I did it, Misty! What you wanted. Look who's here – I can't believe they all came!'

Misty looked around the room. The cabaret tables were packed with special guests, ready for the 7 p.m. finale of Lady

Lady's Star Search. Plimberley had indeed outdone herself, completing her part of the plan with absolute panache. The audience was filled with familiar faces: famous drag artists and comedians who had performed at Lady's Bar over the years, influencers Misty recognised from Instagram, TikTok and YouTube.

'I told them, Misty,' said Plimberley, excited and bursting with pride, 'like you wanted. I said that Lady's Bar was at risk of being shut down and that you needed help, and they've all turned out!'

Sure enough, Misty could see friends and colleagues in every row: The Australian, Caesar Theday, Amour, Faddy Crannock, Cherry Kiss . . . Queens who'd been on big TV shows were there alongside a squad of kings who, between them, had won all of the capital's most iconic drag competitions. It was a veritable who's who of the London scene.

'Good work, Plim,' said Misty. She squeezed Plimberley's arm and started making her way to the front.

'Good luck, Misty!' called Plim behind her.

As Misty headed to the stage, she noticed that Mandy had also hit the phones. Among the drag personalities were other London venue owners who hadn't yet, as far as Misty was aware, been targeted by Ginger Baker. It was a powerful crowd. Misty mouthed a 'thank you' to Mandy across the room, who did a double thumbs-up in return.

She saw Jeremy sitting on a stool at the bar and Darren moved across to join him, ordering something from Jan the barman. Auntie Susan followed Misty and took a seat at the judges' table near the front. She was still out of breath.

The two finalists of tonight's Star Search were standing

nervously to the side, in full competition regalia, no idea that this show would not be the one they were expecting.

Misty stepped up the three short stairs to mount the stage and there was a cheer from the audience. She smiled and held up her hands, still clasping her phone. In the centre of the room, and on either side of the stage, cameras had been set up on tall, sturdy tripods by Jeremy and Mandy.

This is it, she thought as the audience roared for her. *This is the end of Atrax and Ginger Baker.*

CHAPTER 46

Misty took a breath as the applause died down. 'Welcome to Lady's Bar!' This in turn caused some whooping from the audience. 'Jackson,' she said to the technician in the booth at the back, 'may I have the screen down please? And the cameras on.'

He pushed a button to bring down a large white projector panel that entirely covered the back wall of the stage. Red lights appeared on all three cameras.

I can do this, she told herself. *I can bloody well do this.*

'You might not recognise me this evening,' she said to the crowd. 'I am of course dressed as the legend, icon and star that is Auntie Susan. And we're thrilled to have the diva herself with us for this important night.'

Auntie Susan stood up and took a little bow, prompting a raucous clap. Everybody would recognise her because she was a huge name, but these days she wasn't often seen outside of her own pub.

'For anyone here who doesn't already know me, my name is Misty Divine, and I'm one of the co-owners of Lady's Bar.' The microphone trembled in her hand, so she squeezed it tight. 'Some of you have come for our regularly programmed show, the finale of Lady Lady's Star Search. And some of you are here because you were invited at the last minute today by

Plimberley Walsh or by my business partner, Mandy White, to help us with something very important. In fact, it's not just to help *us*, but to help a number of queer venues all across the UK – venues who have joined us via the power of these cameras and the Lady's Bar complimentary Wi-Fi. My presentation this evening is being livestreamed directly to audiences in those venues too.'

This was Jeremy's part of the plan. He'd worked with Mandy to set up a broadcast to the Atrax-targeted venues, and live on YouTube. The link he'd sent for Auntie Susan earlier had been forwarded to the other venues, and their owners had done the same as Mandy: invited their most influential performers and supporters to watch Misty's presentation unfold.

Misty imagined the six other threatened gay pubs and lesbian bars across the country, filled with regulars, waiting eagerly to hear what she had to say. It was a lot of pressure.

'For the last two years,' she said, with a nervous wobble in her voice, 'an attack has been taking place on our community. It's an attack nobody's been talking about, that no newspaper wants to print. The people responsible are dangerous and powerful and have, until now, prevented anybody from speaking out. There are layers of secrets and lies that have kept this conspiracy hidden, but today, we will expose the person behind it.'

People shuffled in their seats. This wasn't the comedy drag antics some of them had come for, but for others it was excellent drama.

'I'm going to be honest with you all. This venue, Lady's Bar, is in the firing line. The only way we can stop it – the only way we know how to – is to make so much noise that we cannot be ignored. We have to get the word out, as widely, loudly and proudly as we can. Make no mistake, our venues are being targeted politically by an extremely wealthy, homo-phobic, queerphobic bigot.'

The audience members were uncomfortable – this wasn't an easy topic for many folk in the room.

You're nearly there, she thought. *So nearly there.*

'I am going to ask you all for a favour. It's a favour I would never usually ask of anybody, but in a moment, I'm going to show a video. Please, get your phones out and get ready to film it. Broadcast it live on TikTok or Instagram or wherever you have the most followers. I know your platforms are precious, but so are our spaces. Let your followers know this is happening because of one terrible person and the wealthy company supporting her.'

There was movement in the room as people pulled out their phones. Not everybody did it, but from a quick glance around, Misty guessed 80% – hundreds of them. That would be enough. More than enough. If the same was happening in the other venues, she was about to expose Atrax and Ginger Baker to millions of people online, in the UK and around the world.

Jeremy and Jessica's concern about using social media had been Atrax's technological capabilities, that they could get the Misty Divine or Lady's Bar accounts taken down or hacked. But there was nothing they could do about this. If hundreds of people posted the video all at once, there would be nothing Atrax could do. Jeremy's video would be out there forever and for everybody to see.

She quickly opened her phone to see the presentation Jessica had prepared.

'Jackson,' she said. 'First slide please.'

A huge picture of Stefan Weber appeared on-screen, the one Jeremy had taken, the one Misty had managed to get from his friend, John Smith.

'This man,' Misty announced, 'is Stefan Weber. He runs a company called Atrax based in the City of London. Next slide, please.'

A collage of seven photographs appeared– pubs, bars and cafés, including Lady's Bar. Misty continued. 'Each of these LGBTQ+ spaces is at risk of closure for a variety of reasons. Rent increases, redevelopment projects, hostile takeovers . . . the list goes on. There is one thing these potential closures have in common. Slide 3, Jackson.'

The third slide showed dry-looking documents all side by side; they were too small to read the detail, but one word had been highlighted in red on each page.

'Atrax,' said Misty. There was a little gasp and grumble from the watching audience. 'The common denominator in all of these legal battles is Stefan Weber's company. *Atrax*. However, he is not acting alone. Atrax has been hired to do this, paid significantly to force these venues closed, and they aren't stopping there. These seven venues are the test. Their intention is to come after every queer space in the country.'

People in the crowd shook their heads, shocked at the reach Atrax had managed to achieve without anybody knowing.

'Slide 4,' Misty said to Jackson. A photograph of Ginger Baker appeared on-screen. Shoulder pads, pink cheeks, teeth as white as a crescent moon. 'Some of you will recognise this woman. Her name is Ginger Baker. She is an evangelist, a megachurch pastor, and reportedly a billionaire thanks to her wrangling of high-value government contracts from her political friends in the USA.'

A couple of audience members nodded and nudged each other like they'd seen Ginger on *The Montel Williams Show* in the nineties. Misty could see confusion on some faces, while others were simply enthralled by what was unfolding onstage at Lady's Bar tonight.

'You might be wondering what on earth Ginger Baker has to do with any of this, so let me enlighten you. We've discovered, with the help of two journalists, that Ginger Baker is one of Atrax's clients. In fact, Ginger Baker is the client who has paid Atrax to close down our safe spaces, using whatever methods they can. And here's the proof, the video I promised you. Jackson, hit it.'

You could have heard a pin drop in the auditorium as Ginger and Stefan appeared on-screen, sitting at their fancy table in the Ritz. Phones were raised high, capturing the moment, pushing it out to hundreds of thousands of followers on social media. The tension was high in Lady's Bar. The air was electric. Misty stepped to the side of the stage as the video played.

Their voices boomed through the cabaret club.

GINGER: 'On all *fronts*, Stefan, we whip the political frenzy faster and hotter and we profit. Politics, money, they're one and the same now.'

STEFAN: 'Why these venues specifically?'

GINGER: 'They are low-hanging fruit and they were supposed to be an easy win. Even the LGBT-whatevers don't go to them any more. They're failing businesses with a declining and degenerate clientele. We weaken our opponents' solidarity, their resistance against what's coming next, and we profit from those who support us in the process.'

A few people in the auditorium booed at this and Misty noticed one of the other venue owners in the audience wave his arms forward in disgust, leaning his face into the palms of his hands.

GINGER: 'I need you to do what you promised me. I want those venues. And once we've got this first wave, I'll be coming after the rest.'

The video stopped, leaving a still image of Stefan and Ginger on-screen, and there was uproar in Lady's Bar. People were talking to each other hurriedly, tapping on their phones and sending their videos.

I did it, Misty thought. *I've done it.*

She hoped there was a similar reaction happening elsewhere, in the other pubs and bars that Ginger had targeted. She glanced at the clock. 7.30 p.m. exactly. This was the precise time that Jessica's part of the plan would spring into action, silently from her laptop at a secret bed and breakfast location.

At this morning's Zoom meeting, Jessica had been tasked with scouring every record at her disposal to create a complete dossier of evidence: irrefutable evidence that Ginger Baker and Stefan Weber were waging war against the LGBTQ+ community. At 7.30 p.m., the file was to be sent to every journalist Jessica knew and every major news outlet in the country, along with a link to Misty's YouTube livestream.

A WhatsApp message popped up on Misty's phone. From Jessica.

It's done.

Misty's relief was short-lived. She stood onstage alone as a ruckus sounded out from the auditorium door. She could hear Tess shouting. And men's voices.

Everybody in the audience craned to look as the door burst open in a shower of splinters and broken wood.

The suits.

They'd kicked the door through!

The suits ran into the back area by the bar, and Misty could hardly believe what she was seeing. They had both come in with weapons raised.

Guns, actual guns in Lady's Bar!

Pandemonium erupted. Screaming. A table upturned, a glass smashed. Misty watched in horror as sequin-studded Plimberley started grabbing customers, pushing them into the corridor to the dressing rooms, away from the danger. Mandy was doing the same at the kitchen door. The bar staff had ducked down out of sight. People were seeking refuge wherever they could.

Customers and guests screamed in their seats. Some got down on the floor, hiding under their tables.

'Sit down!' shouted Suit 1 at a gay couple who had jumped up from their table. 'Nobody move!'

The initial vocal panic faded out as the remaining attendees covered their heads, put their faces in their hands and tried to stay low. Suit 2 stayed at the back of the room while Suit 1 stalked towards the stage. It was quiet, the sounds of crying and heavy breathing the only noise.

'Turn that off!' He pointed at the screen with the image of Ginger and Stefan still showing.

'It's too late,' said Misty into the microphone. 'Everybody's seen it. The game's up.'

She didn't know why, and couldn't explain it even to herself, but she didn't feel afraid. She felt angry, and she thrust her shoulders back in defiance.

Suit 1 pointed his weapon at her. Misty didn't know anything about guns. She couldn't hazard a guess as to its make or model, but it was black and chunky like the kind she'd seen Matthew Gray Gubler use on *Criminal Minds*.

'I said turn it off,' said the suit, stepping up on to the stage and glaring at her.

'Jackson,' said Misty, 'switch off the screen.'

The screen went dark.

'It won't make any difference,' she snapped. 'We've broadcast that video all across the country. Everyone in here has filmed it and sent it out.'

Suit 1 scanned the audience, trying to determine if what

she was saying was true. He paced towards her and she stepped backwards to the edge of the stage. He kept coming, closer and closer, fury all over his face. And that was when something unexpected happened, something that shocked Misty completely.

Auntie Susan stood up in the front row, unseen by the suit who had his back to her. She raised a long glossy leg and stepped up onto the stage. Her red heels sparkled.

She pounced.

A mess of rhinestones and red hair flew through the air and landed squarely on the suit's back. He staggered forward as she squeezed her legs around his chest and scraped at his face with sharp nails, riding his back like a cross-dressing cowboy.

Misty took a breath and glanced to the back of the room where a similar struggle was taking place: Jeremy and Darren had Suit 2 in a tight grip, one on each arm, pulling him outstretched. Darren was battering the suit's hand with his fist to force him to drop his gun.

Auntie Susan screamed like a wild animal, 'You don't ever bring a gun to a drag show, you stupid goddamn bastard!'

She was almost on his shoulders when Misty sprang into action herself, reaching forward and grabbing his hand with both of hers. She wrestled his wrist around, pointing the gun towards the back wall in case it went off accidentally.

The suit was twisting, flailing, trying unsuccessfully to throw off Auntie Susan, trying to pull back his weapon from Misty.

'Get it, Misty! Get it!' Auntie Susan shouted.

Misty buried her French tips into the skin of his hand,

digging so hard that her fingers hurt and she could feel blood beneath her nails. The suit screamed and, with a thud, the gun fell to the floor.

The scramble began. Before Misty knew it, she, Auntie Susan and the suit were all bent over, grappling for the weapon. A few people in the auditorium were shouting out, words Misty couldn't hear through her wig amidst the action.

It was Auntie Susan who won the scramble. She snatched up the gun and took two rapid steps backwards into the spotlight. Standing centre-stage, white rhinestones glistening like a Christmas angel, she pointed the weapon directly at the suit.

'Sit down,' she said, her face covered in hair, panting, out of breath.

'*You* don't know how to use that,' he replied, flinching as though about to try and tackle her.

'I said sit the fuck down!'

He lunged towards her.

She fired.

CHAPTER 47

Later, Misty would hardly be able to recall the following minutes. She remembered the gunshot though. Everybody did. It was so loud, so unexpected. And there was a smell in the air afterwards: metallic and unpleasant.

The shot had hit the wall directly behind the suit's head, just centimetres from striking him. He yelled and ducked and clutched his ear. The stage floor was showered with dust and rubble, and the suit sat down instantly, finally doing as he'd been told. Auntie Susan kept the gun aimed at him to make sure he stayed put.

The audience had screamed in unison when the shot was fired. This wasn't a countryside hunting retreat, this wasn't a country at war. In London, most people lived their lives without ever even seeing a gun, never mind hearing one or seeing one shot. And not in a cosy, gorgeous cabaret club. Everything about it was wrong.

Misty saw that Darren and Jeremy had successfully restrained the second suit and handed his weapon to Tess. There was a shocked silence. Nobody knew what to do next.

It couldn't have been ten seconds later that the entrance burst open a second time. This time, to Misty's relief, it was a rescue mission. A dozen armed Metropolitan Police officers ran into the club, telling everybody to put their hands where they could see them. Two sprinted up the central aisle to the stage, where Auntie Susan was still holding the suit's gun. They pointed scary-looking assault weapons at her.

'Drop it!' they ordered. 'Drop it now!'

Auntie Susan bent forward and placed the gun on the ground in front of her.

'It's not mine,' she said. 'It's his.'

At the back of the room, dressed in bulletproof vests, DI Davies and DS Hughes entered the auditorium and Misty had never felt so pleased to see them. But that was when she realised, with a churn in her stomach, that the livestream cameras were still rolling.

The grand finale of Lady Lady's Star Search did not go ahead. Audience members were quizzed as witnesses, asked for contact details and sent home, many of them shaking and scared. The suits were arrested and taken out of the building in handcuffs.

Auntie Susan had some questions to answer, as she was the only person in the building who had actually fired a weapon, and both she and Misty were taken to Charing Cross Police Station to explain the entire affair.

Misty was joined in her interview by her solicitor, the incredibly handsome and irrelevantly muscular Mr Colin McDermott.

'You know you're all over the news,' he said when he arrived and greeted her in the station waiting room.

'I am?' asked Misty.

'What did you think would happen?' His voice was so

soothing she almost melted like an orange Calippo on a hot summer's day. 'Two drag queens in identical outfits fighting off a gunman, livestreamed around the world? I'm afraid to say you're famous again, Misty Divine.'

'Oh no,' she groaned, remembering the aftermath of Lady Lady's murder and how she'd gone viral for catching the killer on live television.

'Before we go into this interview,' said Mr McDermott, 'is there anything you need to tell me?'

Misty thought through everything that had happened: Sylvester's notebook, breaking into his office, Jeremy's phone records, Alice Gethyn's knicker drawer, the Preach Party, the multi-car pile-up at Bethnal Green . . . Yet again, Misty Divine had been breaking the law all over town.

'No,' she said with innocent doe eyes. 'Nothing at all.'

Thankfully, none of that came up in the interview and Misty didn't mention it either, though she suspected sooner or later she would be called back in for the car crash. There was bound to be CCTV that connected the two red-headed drag queens to it. But for tonight, the focus was firmly fixed on her evening's exposé of Ginger Baker and Stefan Weber. The dossier Jessica had prepared proved the suits were employed by Atrax, and the video showed that Ginger was Atrax's client.

'If you wanted people to know about it,' said DS Hughes, 'you've certainly done that. It's on every news site and all over the socials.'

'Good,' said Misty. 'Hopefully it'll stop what she's been doing.'

DI Davies scratched his head. 'How did you get all this? This file with the evidence?' He had a printed copy of Jessica's dossier on the table in front of him.

'I have friends,' said Misty, thinking of Jeremy, Darren, Jessica and Plimberley. And, of course, Auntie Susan. 'The drags stick together.'

DI Davies hummed and there was static in the interview room air. Everybody knew Misty had been involved in serious mischief, but nobody wanted to discuss it.

She leaned forward with her elbows on the table. 'You've arrested the suits from the club, but what about Ginger Baker? What will you do about her?'

The detective sighed. 'There's not much we can do there, I'm afraid. At 3 p.m. this afternoon Ms Baker's private jet took off from City Airport with her on board. We're still waiting to find out where she went.'

It was almost midnight when Misty unlocked the doors to her little flat in Russell Square. It was dark and still, and she knew right away it was empty. *No Miles.* Had he heard about tonight's events? Did he know it was over? She had no idea. She was physically and mentally drained and thought Miles was best dealt with tomorrow.

She kicked off Auntie Susan's red shoes on to the hall carpet and headed straight to the bedroom to de-drag. Lashes first, always. She peeled them off and placed them in front of her on the dresser. Next hair, then make-up.

The costume came off quickly because the little white dress stretched easily over her head and didn't have the fuss of a zip up the back. Padded bra, hip pads and tights were whipped off and dumped on the floor by the wardrobe. Finally, stripping out of their underwear, Joe got into the shower and washed it all away.

They took a quick peek at the locked homescreen of their phone before getting into bed. There were notifications. Hundreds of them. Emails, phone calls, text messages, WhatsApp messages, Instagram posts . . . They would look at them tomorrow.

For now, the threat was over. Atrax had been stopped. Stefan Weber was in custody and Ginger Baker had been exposed. Joe hoped that meant Lady's Bar was finally safe.

Now, it was time for them to sleep.

CHAPTER 48

Saturday

Sleep came easily to begin with, but didn't stay that way. Joe's dreams were filled with memories of the suit pointing his gun at Misty's face, the bullet smashing the wall to dust, Plimberley's sequins shining as she rescued audience members from peril. All of it swam around in a scary red fog.

When they finally woke, it was just after 10 a.m., and their whole body ached. They rubbed their eyes as they walked unsteadily to the kitchen to retrieve the phone they'd left charging on the kitchen side.

They unlocked it and saw the most recent message was from Auntie Susan, sent ten minutes earlier.

> *Are you awake? Why haven't you responded? They want us on BBC News! I want my wig back.*

Plimberley had also just sent a message. A link to a Sky News video accompanied by superstar and gun emojis. Joe didn't want to watch it, but they knew they had to. They clicked the link and a familiar studio appeared on-screen, with two serious-looking presenters facing the camera. Behind them was a grainy screengrab that showed Auntie

Susan riding the suit's back, while Misty fought to snatch his gun. The male presenter spoke first.

'Last night in Soho in Central London, two drag queens prevented a tragedy from unfolding as they fought off a gunman onstage in the legendary cabaret club Lady's Bar. The incident came moments after the club's owner, a performer known as Misty Divine, presented substantial evidence to the club's audience linking American megachurch preacher, Ginger Baker, and a city firm, Atrax, to the closure of LGBTQ+ venues all across the United Kingdom.

'Communities throughout the country have been shocked by the revelations, with church leaders, local councils and government officials speaking out this morning about the protection of safe spaces for marginalized groups.'

Joe sat down at the kitchen table and continued watching as the female presenter took over, the on-screen image changing to show last year's viral moment: when Misty had stopped Lady Lady's killer by throwing a vase at her head. This all felt like a horrible dream and they dreaded to think what awaited on social media.

'Viewers may remember Misty Divine as the drag artist who caught the murderer of television and stage icon Lady Lady, after she was found poisoned in her dressing room last summer, in one of the most widely watched videos of the year.

'We are informed by a Metropolitan Police spokesperson this morning that three men have been arrested in connection with last night's events and that the whereabouts of Ginger Baker are currently unknown. Two of the men apprehended have also been charged with the stabbing of a private investigator in Soho last week. Whether the two crimes are connected is currently unconfirmed.'

Joe switched off the video and placed the phone face down on the table. They couldn't describe what they were feeling. It wasn't pride, or even relief. It might have been fear. Of course, the plan had been to make as much noise as possible, but now they'd actually done it, it felt different. Now they would have to sit in this empty apartment and deal with the consequences – the messages and comments and attention.

Maybe I should just switch it all off and disappear, they thought.

They set about making a pot of coffee, treating themself to two heaped spoonfuls from Miles' expensive roast. And just as they were pouring hot water into the French press, the front door to the flat rattled. A key in the lock.

Joe rushed to the living room and was so overjoyed to see Miles they could have cried.

'What are you doing here?' they asked. While they were delighted to see him, they also knew that Miles might well have come to collect the rest of his belongings, to move out, to leave Joe forever and ever and ever.

Miles stepped in and threw out his arms, embracing Joe in a strong, tight hug.

'I saw what happened. I just saw. It's everywhere! Are you OK?'

'I don't know,' said Joe. Perhaps caused by the relief of Miles' return, or by his hug, Joe burst into tears in their boy-friend's arms.

*

Once the hugging and crying were all done with, Joe poured them both a cup of coffee, and they sat together in the living room. The phone, filled with its drama and nonsense, was left behind in the kitchen.

'I don't know where to start,' said Joe. 'I'm sorry. I guess that's where.'

'Joe, I'm sorry too.' Miles seemed guilty and sad. 'I've been taking everything out on you, but I've had time to think and I don't really believe it's your fault. Not what happened to me, the poisoning. I'm just having a hard time dealing with it, so when you said you were investigating something new, my brain went into overdrive. I needed a break to get my head straight.'

'So . . . are you coming back?'

Miles leaned forward, his elbows pressing into his knees. 'We need to talk about that,' he said.

Joe felt gutted. Disappointed that it wasn't an immediate yes.

'OK,' they said, trying to stay as calm as possible. 'What do we need to talk about?'

'What happened yesterday, at Lady's Bar . . . and I'm not blaming you, please know I'm not blaming you. This business with Ginger Baker and the venues, it was right to expose her. I think you did the right thing, one hundred percent . . .'

'But?' said Joe. 'There's a but coming.'

Miles nodded. 'You could have been killed. Any of you: you, Auntie Susan, Mandy, Plim, the people in the audience for Christ's sake.'

'I know,' said Joe, embarrassed and feeling the dread deeply. 'It was dangerous, but there wasn't another option. I did the only thing I knew how to do.'

'And that's what we have to talk about,' said Miles, 'because I don't believe this was the only option. Look at what's happened over the last year: two poisonings in the club, you were arrested for murder, a stabbing, armed men at Lady's Bar, Auntie Susan *firing a gun* live on the internet . . . It's spiralling, Joe. It's out of control.'

Joe nodded. Miles was completely right and that's how it all felt this morning: out of control. That was the feeling they couldn't put their finger on, that everything had just got away from them.

'I'm sorry,' Joe said again.

'Stop telling me you're sorry, Joe! I'm not here for that and I don't need to hear it again.'

'Well, what then?'

Miles looked Joe in the eyes, something Joe had missed while he'd been away. 'I love you. I've loved you forever and I'll love you forevermore, but something has to change if this is going to work.'

'I know,' said Joe. 'I can stop. I can stop investigating things and being nosy or whatever.' But even as they said the words out loud they doubted they were true.

'I'm not asking for that!'

'But I can. I promise.'

'Don't do that,' said Miles, shaking his head. 'Don't make me a promise we both know you can't keep.' He smiled: a small one, a soft one, but a smile nevertheless. Joe wasn't sure what it meant. 'You are who you are. Joe Brown and Misty Divine are a pair of busybodies who've watched too much *Silent Witness*. The next time a Lady's Bar customer vanishes, or a drag king has his beard stolen backstage, I know you'll be itching to get involved, to solve another mystery. And the truth is, despite the very public dramatics, you're actually quite good at it.'

Joe was confused about where this was heading.

Miles continued.

'I don't want to change you, Joe. I just need you to be safe. I need *us* to be safe.'

'I don't understand,' Joe replied.

'I've found a couple of training courses. I don't think you'll stop doing this, but the condition of me coming home is that you learn how to do it properly, and safely. I want you to take some self-defence classes and I think you should train to be a real investigator, with rules and regulations to follow, so if this happens again, *when* this happens again, you don't end up all over the news with a gun in your face.'

Joe was taken aback. This was a million miles from what they'd expected.

'Really?' asked Joe.

'That's the deal,' said Miles. 'If you accept it, I'll come home.'

Epilogue

Two Weeks Later

Divya had reluctantly agreed to meet Misty at University College Hospital, where Sylvester was recovering from his injuries.

'Hello,' she said, her tone like ice, as they met by the lifts in the hospital lobby.

'Hello, Divya. Thank you for meeting me like this.'

'Come on then,' she said. 'He's waiting for you.'

They took the lift up to the third floor, where the detective had been afforded a private room in which to get better.

In the weeks since the livestreamed showdown at Lady's Bar, Stefan Weber and more than a dozen Atrax employees had been arrested for a whole host of fraud and financial abuses, not only relating to the queer venues. Atrax, it seemed, was done, blown out the water by Misty Divine. Thankfully, so far, the Lady's Bar bribery hadn't been spotted in the aftermath.

Today Misty had a television interview with Auntie Susan, one of many they'd done together since becoming internet sensations. She'd dressed appropriately, of course. A stunning lime-green jumpsuit, with an ombré rhinestoned pattern from the ankles to the shoulders. But before her interview, she needed to speak with Sylvester. She had something to ask him, a very important question.

'I suppose I should say thank you,' said Divya as they stepped out of the lift and into a sterile white corridor. 'I don't like your methods, but you did it. The men who hurt Sylvester . . .'

'They'll go to prison for a long time,' Misty replied.

Divya nodded and led the way to Sylvester's room, walking a step or two ahead. She stopped and knocked on a narrow white door.

'Come in,' called the investigator from inside.

They entered and Misty was shocked by how pale he was, how old and frail he looked. Her surprise must have been visible on her face as Sylvester joked, 'I'm not dead yet.'

Misty smiled. 'And I'm very glad.'

'Divya's filled me in,' he said, 'and of course I've been following the news. You did it, Misty! You found Jeremy, took down the big baddie, solved the case. Not bad for a drag queen.'

'Hey,' she winked, 'nobody messes with a drag queen.'

'Oh, I've worked in Soho for long enough to know that that's the truth. Sit, sit,' said Sylvester, signalling to a chair beside the bed. She did as she was told and perched on the edge of the seat. 'Divya tells me you want to ask me something.'

'Yes. I've decided I'd like to train as a real investigator. I've found a course that looks good and it suggests getting a mentor or an apprenticeship to learn the ropes. I was wondering, would you let me shadow you on a case?'

Sylvester shook his head. 'I'm finished, Misty. This isn't an old man's game and I think I've had enough. No more cases for me.'

'OK,' she said, trying to disguise the disappointment in her voice, 'I understand.'

There was an awkward lull before Divya spoke up. 'Sylvester, what about . . .?'

'No,' he said gruffly. 'Not that.'

Misty's nosy instincts kicked in. 'What? What about what?'

The old man sighed. 'Divya's talking about a case, one I've been trying to solve on and off for over thirty years . . . I never could get to the bottom of it.'

'The one that got away,' said Divya.

'Of course it's a cold case now,' he said, 'but it might be right in your wheelhouse.'

'What is it?' asked Misty, desperate to know.

Sylvester paused, unsure of whether he was really going to do this. Then he said, 'Tell me, Misty, did you ever hear of a pantomime performer known as Dame Dot?'

Acknowledgements

What a year! It's been a fabulous twelve months, from publishing the first Misty Divine Mystery, *Murder in the Dressing Room*, to finishing this second instalment, *Missing in Soho*. I'm grateful to everyone who has read these adventures, the booksellers who have sold them, and the podcasters, bloggers and vloggers who have reviewed and shared about them. It's so fun to write these stories and I'm delighted you have experienced the MDU!

One of the most joyful aspects of the journey so far has been meeting readers in person and online. I've been welcomed by book clubs, attended literary events and exchanged a million DMs. It has been lovely to get to know you all.

Similarly, I am grateful to have felt embraced by the writing community. It's been gorgeous to make friends with so many fellow authors, to share woes and worries together and celebrate each other's wins.

Always and forever, thank you, Ronan, for being the greatest and for reading many versions of this book along the way.

Thank you to my literary agent, Hayley Steed at Janklow & Nesbit, who has been a Misty Divine champion since day one.

I have such awe and respect for my editors, Grace Long

at Penguin Michael Joseph and Annie Odders at Berkley. A dream team!

And Patrick Bustin at PBJ Management, thank you for your constant support.

I've learned that writing, publishing and promoting a book is a huge team effort, with many more people involved than I could have ever imagined. It's a wonderful collaboration of skills and expertise, and the teams at Penguin Michael Joseph, Berkley, Janklow & Nesbit and Madeleine Milburn Literary Agency are truly incredible. I am honoured to work with them on this project.

My Yorkshire terrier, Rex, has slept on my lap throughout the writing of this entire book and deserves special acknowledgement here also.

There are many more people I could thank – friends, family and colleagues who have supported my writing. There are too many to name individually but I hope you know who you are and that I couldn't do it without you.

Finally, Misty Divine is a fierce queen and a questionable detective. Her world is camp and extreme and most definitely a fantasy. But while Misty faces her fictional trials and triumphs, the real-world LGBTQIA+ community is under genuine attack. So, a small plea from me: where you can, please support queer artists, businesses and non-profit organisations. Support, protect and stand up for the LGBTQIA+ people in your life, your community and beyond. And book your drag show tickets in advance.

Misty and pals will return soon with a third dramatic mystery and I hope you'll stick around for the ride!